TRENTON

LORD of LOSS

GRACE
BURROWES

Trenton: Lord of Loss is Published by Grace Burrowes Publishing
21 Summit Avenue
Hagerstown, MD 21740
www.graceburrowes.com

DEDICATION

This book is dedicated to all the lonely lords and ladies.

GRACE BURROWES

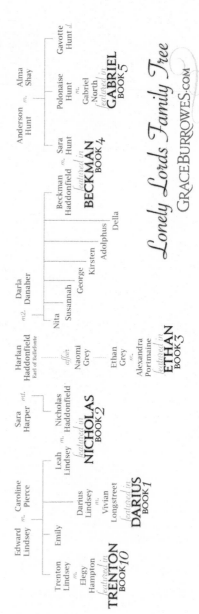

Lonely Lords Family Tree

GRACEBURROWES.com

Edward Lindsey *m.* Caroline Pierce

Trenton Lindsey *m.* Elegy Hampton — *featured in* **TRENTON** BOOK 10

Emily

Darius Lindsey *m.* Vivian Longstreet — *featured in* **DARIUS** BOOK 1

Leah Lindsey *m.* Nicholas Haddonfield — *featured in* **NICHOLAS** BOOK 2

Sara Harper *m.* Nicholas Haddonfield

Harlan Haddonfield Earl of Bellefonte

affair Naomi Grey

Ethan Grey *m.* Alexandra Portmaine — *featured in* **ETHAN** BOOK 3

m2. Darla Danaher

Nita

Susannah

George

Kirsten

Adolphus

Della

Beckman Haddonfield *m.* Sara Hunt — *featured in* **BECKMAN** BOOK 4

Anderson Hunt *m.* Alma Shay

Polonaise Hunt *m.* Gabriel North — *featured in* **GABRIEL** BOOK 5

Gavotte Hunt *d.*

CHAPTER ONE

"How long before the baby moves?" As Elegy Hampton, Viscountess Rammel, put that question into words, her world became mo re a wonderful place—also more frightening.

She poured her guest another cold glass of lemonade but left her own drink untouched. Something as prosaic as a glass of lemonade did not belong in the same moment with Ellie's question.

"A few weeks yet at least, closer to a few months probably," Mrs. Holmes replied. "You're not that far along, my dear, and every case is different."

I am with child. The drowsiness, the delicate appetite—even the lemonade tasting a bit off—the sense of Ellie's body being out of balance was not grief, but, rather, the very opposite of grief.

"Nine months seems like forever," Ellie said. "I suppose it could be worse." Horses took eleven months, poor things.

"Nine and a half months for most." Mrs. Holmes's

expression was beatific, a serene complement to snow-white hair and periwinkle-blue eyes. "That last half-month can seem as long as the first nine. Perhaps it's the Lord's way of ensuring mothers start off schooled to patience."

Oh, please, let's not bring Him into the discussion. Ellie and the Lord had not enjoyed cordial relations of late. Though having a baby…

She wanted to cry and laugh. *Oh, Dane. Thank you, damn you. Thank you.*

"Patience has never been one of my strong suits," Ellie allowed. Since her husband's death, the very air had acquired an unhappy weight, making movement, breath, thought, *everything* a greater effort and solitude a particular torment.

Yet now, Ellie was impatient to have the sunny, serene morning room to herself.

"You'll manage," Mrs. Holmes assured her. "But Miss Ellie? You'll forgive my bluntness if I suggest you occupy yourself with cheerful endeavors. Mourning must be given its due, but excessive fretting isn't good for the baby."

"Fretting?" Ellie had done nothing but fret since Dane's death.

"I will help you bring this baby into the world, and a certain directness of speech should characterize our dealings," Mrs. Holmes went on, though Dottie Holmes had never needed excuses for direct speech. "His lordship was a fine young man, and he should be mourned by his family, but you're young, you were a good wife, and you've much of your life ahead of you."

"I do mourn him," Ellie said, hoping it was true, though the words had the same off flavor as the too-sweet, too-tart lemonade.

"Of course you do." Mrs. Holmes patted Ellie's hand with fingers made cool by the chilled glass. "Nobody doubts you were devoted to him, and now you must devote yourself to the child. His lordship has been gone nearly two months, and when you are here at home, you might consider putting off your blacks, going for the occasional easy hack around the property, and enjoying the condolence calls when they start up in earnest."

How was she supposed to *enjoy* condolence calls, when the pleasure of even a glass of lemonade was in jeopardy? Ellie hadn't been able to venture to the stables for nearly a month after Dane's death, and she loved the very scent of the horse barn.

"You want me to ride when I'm carrying?"

"As long as your habits fit. Don't take stupid risks, Miss Ellie, and stay active. You'll carry better if you get fresh air, keep moving, and indulge yourself a bit."

Dane had excelled at getting fresh air, staying in constant motion, and indulging himself—more than a bit.

"I hate black," Ellie murmured, running her thumb down the side of her glass.

A lady ought not to hate anything, and the conduct of widows was supposed to put them only slightly lower than the angels.

Sad, angry angels.

"Black doesn't flatter much of anybody," Mrs. Holmes agreed, helping herself to a slice of lemon cake that, to Ellie, also had no appeal whatsoever. "Clearly, black for mourning was devised by men, who are much more at home in dark and forbidding colors. Have something to eat, dear, so I won't be self-conscious about seconds myself."

Thirds, at least.

"Of course." Ellie put a slice of cake on her plate. *I am having a baby. I am having a baby. I am having a...baby.* Women died in childbirth all the time. "I'm to take exercise and sneak into half-mourning, and what else?"

"Your digestion may act up from time to time." Mrs. Holmes nibbled her sweet complacently. "Your breasts might be sore. You've no doubt noticed a tendency to nap and heed nature's call more frequently. That's all normal. You'll be losing your waist soon, if you haven't noticed your dresses fitting more snugly already—your boots and slippers, too. Some lightheadedness isn't unusual, but it passes."

"I'll go barefoot," Ellie said, her hand going to her middle. Dane would have been horrified to hear her. In his way, he'd been a proper old thing—with her. "I went barefoot a great deal in summer as a child."

"And you'll have a child to love." Mrs. Holmes beamed confidently. "A reminder of his lordship and the happiness of your marriage."

Ellie already had a child to love, and what happiness she'd found in her marriage was of the tempered variety. Still, she hadn't been entirely miserable, and Dane should not have fallen from his horse at the age of twenty-eight. He was—*had been*—a bruising rider.

When sober. He'd claimed he rode even better when drunk—and he'd been wrong. Ellie regretted his death, but even before his passing, she'd reconciled herself to missing him and missing what their marriage might have been.

She was having a baby, and above all else, Ellie wanted solitude to savor this realization. "Another glass of lemonade, Mrs. Holmes?"

"Not for me, my dear, but drink as much as you please, particularly in this heat."

"I like summer." Ellie especially enjoyed feeling wet grass between her toes first thing in the morning and leaving her windows open to let in the bird song. "I like the lighter clothing, the long days, and the soft breezes. I like the sturdy young beasts finding their confidence in the mild weather. The nights are rife with the scent of the flowers and fields, and the mornings are lovely."

"You're an expectant mother," Mrs. Holmes replied around a mouthful of cake. "You should be in love with life."

When had Ellie ever been *in love* with anything, or anybody? She rose, in part to get away from that question, but also to suggest—politely, of course—that the call should come to an end. "I'm a widow, too. Like you."

"Some sixteen years now." Mrs. Holmes touched her throat, where a lock of sandy hair had been cross-woven in an onyx mourning brooch. "Widowhood gets easier with time, Miss Ellie."

"Does it?" Marriage certainly hadn't become any easier with time. Ellie went to a window overlooking a back terrace in riot with potted pansies. Mourning was difficult for several reasons, unrelenting loneliness only part of it. A steady flame of anger illuminated Ellie's days and nights, as did a rising tide of bewilderment. "Do the nights get easier?"

"Ah. This is difficult, because you are with child and young."

"A pair of blessings, supposedly," Ellie muttered, crossing her arms. One was supposed to keep such comments to oneself.

"The preachers would have us believe childbearing is a blessing, but the loneliness known to widows isn't often under discussion in the pulpits on Sunday morning."

Such *loneliness* was never under discussion on Sunday mornings. Ellie's pastor had, of course, called upon her following the funeral. He'd dropped back to monthly calls now, the same schedule he'd been on before Dane's death.

Ellie wasn't about to discuss her nights with old Vicar Hughes.

"How do you cope?" Ellie asked, dropping her forehead to the window glass. Why hadn't anybody opened the window when outside the day was so pleasant? "How do you reconcile yourself to years and decades of being alone? Dane and I weren't especially close, but he was a husband. He was *there*, however infrequently."

Though when he'd been home, Ellie had always felt some awkwardness, some sense that she wasn't passionate enough, desirable enough, or maybe not feminine enough to meet his expectations.

They hadn't talked about it. They'd talked about little, in fact.

The marriage bed had been mostly duty, but Dane had also dispensed a kind of casual, bluff affection when he'd been at Deerhaven, and Ellie missed his touch more than she could sometimes bear.

"You stay busy," Mrs. Holmes said, "and you use discretion."

Ellie whirled at that suggestion, but Mrs. Holmes was still placidly sipping her lemonade and nibbling her cake, the picture of grandmotherly complacency.

"You are scandalized," Mrs. Holmes said, "which does you credit, but, my dear, would his lordship have been celibate while he grieved your passing?"

That didn't deserve an answer, for nothing had come between Dane Eustace Hampton, Viscount Rammel, and his pleasures. Ellie paid the household bills and knew good and well that few of the fine snuff boxes, quizzing glasses, and rings Dane had purchased in five years of marriage were in her possession—or his.

Then too, Dane's nickname hadn't been Ram for nothing.

"How Dane would have consoled himself is of no moment. Gentlemen and ladies are held to different standards," Ellie said.

"Widows are a different breed of lady. We are considered safe by the menfolk, because we're experienced, discreet, grateful, and financially independent. You'll find the mature bachelors in the neighborhood singularly attentive to your grief."

Ellie was carrying a baby, and this conversation was not relevant to…anything. Though those attentive, mature bachelors might explain why Dottie Holmes enjoyed such unfailing good cheer.

"I'm breeding, Mrs. Holmes. What man would find that attractive?"

Mrs. Holmes gave an ungrandmotherly snort as she

buttered a cinnamon-dusted scone. "Most of them. They can't get you with child, can they?"

Cinnamon held inordinate appeal of a sudden, though the idea of bachelors leering at Ellie's bodice...*damn you, Dane.* "But my condition isn't common knowledge. I wasn't sure myself until you told me just now."

And if Ellie hadn't missed her courses—she *never* missed her courses—the notion still would not have occurred to her.

Mrs. Holmes added an extra dab of butter to her scone. "You attributed odd symptoms to grieving, which does take a toll, of course, but you are most definitely in anticipation of a blessed event. I'm merely suggesting these early days are an excellent time to find solace in the arms of a discreet gentleman or two."

Merciful Halifax. "Or *two?*"

"You need only be discreet." Mrs. Holmes popped a bite of scone into her mouth while Ellie digested this very odd advice.

"Think of it this way, Miss Ellie: By leaving you with a baby to love and care for, his lordship also left you with a way to find some comfort without suffering consequences. Decent of him, one could say."

"Shame on you, Dottie Holmes." But Ellie hadn't the knack of starchy propriety, and Mrs. Holmes was smiling as Ellie escorted her down the front terrace steps a few minutes later. "I do thank you for coming."

"I'll be back next month." Mrs. Holmes pulled on her driving gloves as briskly as any four-in-hand coachy. "You must send for me if you have any distressing symptoms."

"You'll keep this to yourself?"

A blue-eyed gaze flicked over Ellie's middle meaningfully. "Of course, though soon enough, the situation will be evident, my dear." She climbed into her pony cart, clucked to the shaggy beast in the traces, and tooled off down the drive.

Leaving Ellie's world forever changed.

"Is that the baby lady?" Eight-year-old Coriander came skipping down the steps, her eyes bright with interest—and her pinafore still clean, thank heavens.

Ellie held out a hand to her step-daughter. "She's the midwife. She's known me since I was your age. Were you eavesdropping?"

"Hiding," Andy replied, taking Ellie's hand and leading her back into the house. What did it say that the child must lead the adult indoors? For Ellie would have remained staring down that drive until nightfall.

As if she were expecting Dane to come cantering home, so she could tell him this happy news?

"You would have made me sit with my ankles crossed, back straight, and only one scone to console me," Andy accused—accurately.

The child had her father's blond good looks and his charm, which was fortunate. "I'd inflict such a dire fate on you and starch your pinafore until it crackled when you moved."

Andy sniffed at a bowl of roses wilting on the sideboard, though even from a distance, Ellie could tell the scent would no longer be pleasant.

"You're supposed to teach me manners, Mama."

"You're clearly in command of them, but, like me, you prefer theory to practice." Also going without her shoes. "Speaking of practicing, what are you doing out of the schoolroom, young lady? Luncheon hasn't even been served yet."

"Mrs. Drawbaugh sent me down to ask if we might picnic for supper. She says the weather is fine and time out of doors makes me behave better."

"She didn't say that." Minty and Andy had quietly decided time out of doors would do Ellie some good. The conspiracy of the schoolroom had grown only closer in recent weeks.

Andy grinned like the little girl she was. "I said it, and it's as true for me as it is for you, so please say yes. Mrs. Drawbaugh likes to be outside, too."

"Don't bat those eyes at me, Coriander Eustace Brown," Ellie remonstrated with mock severity. "The answer is yes, provided your schoolwork is done. If you dawdle on your exercises, Minty and I will enjoy nature without your company, while you have porridge in the nursery."

"Not porridge!" Andy lapsed into melodramatic gagging. "Never say it! Poisoned by porridge!"

Ellie cut her off with a gentle swat on the backside and a hug. "Upstairs, and get your work done. I'll expect a favorable report at supper."

"Yes, Mama." Andy paused just out of swatting and hugging range. "Why was the baby lady here?"

"She was paying a condolence call. People will start to do that, particularly when your papa has been gone three months."

"I'm not as sad now. Why offer condolences three months later and not when Papa died?"

Because no matter when they were offered, the condolences did nothing to make the departed any less dead. Waiting three months gave a widow some time to adjust to that reality.

"Blessed if I know, but you're stalling. Be off with you."

Andy scampered up the steps two at a time, leaving Ellie to wonder why she'd lied to the girl about the baby, when honesty was something Ellie and Andy both valued very much.

* * *

"Rest, eat regularly, mind the drinking, and don't forget to write."

Darius Lindsey sounded more like a stern papa than a younger brother as he delivered his parting admonitions. He hugged Trent once, then swung up on a piebald gelding and cantered off into the building heat of the summer morning.

Trenton Lindsey—more properly, Viscount Amherst— stood outside the Crossbridge stables, already missing his brother and mentally searching for ways to put off, of all things, a damned condolence call.

"If I wait until later in the day, it will be even hotter, and I'll be forced to swill tepid tea, while some puffy-eyed matron clutches her hanky and tries bravely to make small talk."

Arthur's gaze suggested commiseration, for he'd be denied his grassy paddock or breezy stall for the duration of that call.

Two weeks ago, Trent had been drifting from day to day in Town, a widower whom others would have said wasn't coping well more than a year after his wife's death. He'd spent his days and nights clutching the male version of the handkerchief, more commonly referred to as a brandy glass, though his difficulty hadn't been grief per se.

Darius had, to put it gently, *intervened* in his older brother's life.

"Darius is not a mile from our driveway, and I miss him already."

Arthur, ever a sympathetic fellow, swished his tail.

Trent needed the damned mounting block to climb into the saddle, which was a sad commentary on his condition.

"Though how much sadder is it that I've written to the children only once?" The guilt of that mixed with a sense of abandonment at Darius's parting to make the morning oppressive rather than pleasantly warm.

Arthur sniffed at Trent's boot, which fit a damned sight more loosely than it should.

Trent passed the beast a lump of sugar. "Do not wipe your nose on my boot, sir. Even guilt can be viewed as progress when a man has stopped feeling anything."

He arranged the curb and snaffle reins, pleased to note that his hands, after two weeks of regular meals and infrequent spirits, hardly shook at all.

In the interests of dawdling in the shade, Trent pointed the gelding toward the home wood, a great sprawling mess of trees, underbrush, bridle paths, and meandering streams. Small boys could spend entire summers in such a wood and never miss their beds. Of course, Trent was not a small boy.

Arthur's ears pricked forward in the sun-dappled depths of the wood, drawing Trent's thoughts away from shady hammocks and long, peaceful naps. He followed Arthur's gaze and heard splashing from the largest pond on his property. Trent urged the gelding a few feet off the path and swung down from the saddle.

How he'd clamber aboard an eighteen-hand mount without a step was a puzzle for another time.

The horse obligingly cocked a hip and settled in to doze in the shade while Trent passed noiselessly through the brush. Another splash, then a female voice singing a folk tune—something about "green grow the rushes"—carried across the summer air.

The woman had a sturdy contralto, suited to a sturdy tune, and she was sturdy as well. Trent was taken aback to find her standing in the shallows of the pond happy-as-she-pleased, wearing only a summer-length shift—and a *very damp* summer-length shift at that. Her long, dark hair rippled down her back as she trailed a line-and-pole fishing rod across the water and sang—to the fish?

A dairymaid playing truant on a pretty summer day, or a laundress or other menial. She had the defined arm muscles of a dairymaid and the earthy ease with her body that Trent associated with females unburdened by the designation "lady." While he stood mesmerized, she set the pole on the bank and, still standing in the water, began to plait her hair.

God above, she was a lovely sight. Trent resisted the urge—even urges had deserted him until recently—to tug off his boots, shed his clothes, and wade out to her side, there to do nothing in particular but be naked in the sunshine with her.

Sobriety could make a man daft, but not that daft. Rather than yield to his impulses, he stood among the trees and looked and gawked and looked some more, as if his eyes had been thirsty for this very image.

For anything that might make him *wake up.*

The lady was comfortable in the water, occasionally reaching down to splash herself. The shift became an erotic enhancement to bare flesh, outlining her figure, peaking her nipples, and creating a damp shadow at the juncture of her thighs. Her shape was thoroughly feminine—she had real breasts, real hips, not some caricature created by whalebone, buckram and clever stitching. When she lifted her arms to pin her braid on her head, the wet material shifted so one pink, tightly furled nipple slipped momentarily into view.

The image was purely, bracingly lovely. Trent mentally thanked the Widow Lady Rammel for causing him to be in that spot at that moment. He resolved to come fishing himself in the same pond and to vicariously join the dairymaid in her pleasures. The thought wasn't even sexual—he hadn't had *those* impulses for some time—but it was a sensual, happy thought.

And precious as a result.

He silently withdrew and walked Arthur some distance before using a handy stump to mount. Reluctant to leave the wood, he let the horse wander up one path and down the next until the hour approached noon.

"Come along," he said, turning Arthur to the east. "We have a widow to condole. No more of your prevarications."

All too soon, Trent was ushered into a pleasant family parlor done up all in cabbage roses; pale, gleaming oak; and sunshine. He steeled himself to endure not only the thoroughly feminine décor, but also fifteen minutes of social hell, tepid tea, and useless platitudes. When he turned to greet his hostess, however, the only thought in his head didn't bear verbalizing:

She's not a dairymaid.

CHAPTER TWO

Ellie's first thought was that Trenton Lindsey, Lord Amherst, had been to war. They'd been introduced at a local assembly several years before, and then he'd been an impressive specimen. Tall, fit, and possessed of dark, sparkling eyes to go with his dark, thick hair. He'd had an animal magnetism that Dane, for all his blond good looks, had lacked.

Now, Amherst was gaunt, his eyes shadowed, his clothing beautifully tailored but too loose and several seasons out of fashion.

"Lord Amherst." Ellie curtsied and held out her hand. "A great pleasure. It's too hot for tea, and the veranda will allow us some shade. May I offer you lemonade, hock, or sangaree?"

"Anything cold would be a pleasure."

Ellie attributed his surprised expression to her sortie out of first mourning attire. She was in lilac, one of her favorite colors and one abundantly represented in her summer wardrobe. Dane would not have been pleased with her departure from strict decorum.

Which was just too perishing bad.

"We are neighbors, are we not?" Ellie inquired as he offered his arm and escorted her to the back terrace. The gesture reminded her that Amherst had married several years back. Thus, he sported the kind of understated good manners husbands usually acquired—some husbands.

"Your land marches with mine this side of the trees," Amherst replied. "I don't recall your gardens being this extensive."

Had Dane even noticed the gardens?

"They used to be smaller, but I am not prone to idleness, and when the weather is fine, I like to be out of doors. Gardening provides the subterfuge of productivity and the pleasure of the flowers." Then too, even new widows were permitted to dig in their own gardens.

He tarried at the door to the shaded veranda to sniff at a potted pink rose. "Which is your favorite flower?"

Amherst snapped off the rose and offered it to her, the gesture so effortlessly congenial it took Ellie a moment to comprehend that the rose was for her.

"Forgive me," he said, his smile faltering the longer Ellie stared at the rose. "I do not socialize a great deal, and my small talk is rusty."

Ellie accepted the bloom, careful of the thorns. "Please allow your small talk to crumble into oblivion. I am heartily sick of sitting through every recipe in the shire for restorative tisanes, and everybody's favorite Bible passage for difficult times. At least a discussion of flowers is novel."

Her escort was quiet. Had she disconcerted him or even shocked him? Maybe mourning went on so terribly long because months were needed to get the knack of being a proper widow.

A proper, *discreet* widow?

"You'll not be planting lilies again," Amherst said.

Because they were standing in the doorway, Ellie caught his scent.

He smelled wonderful—masculine but sweet, spicy, alluring, clean, intriguing. She could have stood there all morning, trying to sort and classify the pleasures of his scent.

Carrying a child did this—made the faculties more acute, more delicate.

She picked up the thread of the conversation. "I won't be planting lilies, no. I've already put off blacks at home. Scandalous of me."

"Sensible of you. The departed are gone. They don't care what we wear."

"You don't think my late husband is peering down at me from some cloud? Commenting to St. Peter that I never was a very biddable wife?" That would be the least of Dane's complaints.

"You didn't force him onto that horse, Lady Rammel." Amherst's voice was so calm, so quiet, Ellie almost missed the keen insight of his observation.

She stayed right where she was, next to him in the shady doorway, while birds sang to each other in the nearby wood, and flowers turned their faces up to the welcoming sun.

"Say that again, my lord."

"Your husband's death was not your fault," Amherst said slowly, clearly. "By reputation in the clubs, Dane Hampton loved to ride to hounds, loved the drunken steeplechase, loved to cut a dash on his bloodstock. He died doing what he loved, and he was lucky. You are lucky, in fact, that he died while frolicking with his hounds. His demise wasn't your fault, and it wasn't a bad death."

Ellie wanted to make him say those same words all over again, but instead searched for a rejoinder.

And found none.

"Thank you." She'd focused so intently on his words that it came as something of a surprise to see her hand still tucked in the crook of his elbow. Life was brimful of surprises recently. "These calls ought to come with a manual of deportment, and what you've just said should be the first required words."

A smile threatened at the corners of his mouth. "I have no favorite Bible passage, and I'm fresh out of recipes for tisanes."

"I like the verse about the lilies of the field, about neither toiling nor spinning, but still meriting the Almighty's notice," Ellie said, making herself step back. She liked Lord Amherst, liked that he wasn't too self-conscious to stand near her, and that he didn't spout platitudes. "Because that passage mentions lilies of the field, the scent of which now makes me ill, I'll have to search out a new one."

"You haven't told me your favorite flower." Amherst followed her onto the veranda, and Ellie silently conceded the point: Flowers were alive, Bible verses were not. Two different sources of comfort, one dear to her, one expected by her neighbors.

All of her neighbors, save one.

"Lily of the valley," she decided. "For its scent. Roses, for sheer delicacy of appearance. Lilacs, for the confirmation they bring of spring, though they lack the stamina for bouquets. We"re given so many worthy flowers, it's hard to choose. Shall we be seated?"

He handed her into a chair at a wrought iron grouping at one end of the veranda, then took a seat beside her. Not across from her, but beside. How was it she'd had such a pleasant sort of neighbor all these years and had never become acquainted with him?

"Would you be willing to look over my gardens?" he asked, the chair scraping back as he arranged long legs before him. "I've allowed Crossbridge to suffer some neglect in recent months. I'm focused on the crops, the buildings, that sort of thing, but the estate once had lovely grounds."

"Surely you have a head gardener, my lord?" But she wanted

to do this. She wanted to make something pretty grow for her quiet, insightful neighbor and maybe make the acquaintance of his wife, if her ladyship were out from Town.

Friends being in shorter supply than she'd realized. When had she become so isolated—and why?

She also wanted to get off her own property and could slip over to Amherst's gardens without anybody knowing she'd been truant from her grieving post.

Anybody but Dane. Ellie wanted to aim her face at the sky and stick her tongue out.

"Crossbridge has staff," Lord Amherst said. "They have much to do simply holding back the march of time. The home wood encroaches on the pastures, for example, and my gardeners are busy clearing the fence rows, cleaning up several years of frost heave, and trimming the hedges. My flowers have been orphaned."

On the third finger of Ellie's left hand, a fat, shiny diamond caught a beam of summer sun. She took her rings off when she gardened.

"Dane left a daughter." Heat flooded up Ellie's neck, and she wondered if pregnancy also unhinged the jaw and the common sense. Amherst was a neighbor, true, and he'd likely know about Andy if he bothered to attend services, but he was a stranger.

A handkerchief appeared in her peripheral vision, snow white, monogrammed in purple, and edged with gold—also laden with his lovely scent. Ellie would not have suspected her slightly rumpled, out-of-fashion, overly lean neighbor of hidden regal tendencies, but his instincts were excellent.

"Perishing Halifax." She snatched the handkerchief and brought it to her eyes, though she hadn't cried for days. "Forgive me."

"You are not the one who left a daughter," Amherst replied evenly. "Perhaps the forgiveness is needed elsewhere." He didn't pat her hand, didn't move any closer, didn't murmur nonsense about time healing and God's infernal will. He lounged at his ease two feet away and let her have her tears.

"Andy is eight." Ellie blotted her eyes again. "Coriander. She's young enough to miss her papa sorely. Dane was decent to her."

Amherst still said nothing as Ellie defended Dane's memory. Dane *had* been decent to Andy, once Ellie had staged the first and only row of their married life and insisted the child be raised at Deerhaven.

"People will tell you the grief eases, Lady Rammel, and in some ways, it does. Life tugs you forward, and you add good memories to the store of losses. The losses don't cease hurting, though, not altogether."

Ellie stopped dabbing at her eyes. "Perhaps you'd better keep a Bible verse or two in your pocket, my lord. Your honesty is particularly bracing."

Also curiously welcome.

He inclined his head, not smiling. "My apologies. Grief is an old shoe that fits each foot differently, and I shouldn't prognosticate for others. Keep the handkerchief."

"My thanks." Ellie took a surreptitious sniff of his heavenly scent and signaled the footman tactfully waiting a distance away with the tray. "What shall you have, Lord Amherst? Cold tea, hot tea, sangaree, hock, or lemonade. Alas, no tisanes."

"Good company can be a tisane. I'll enjoy some lemonade." He didn't smile with his mouth so much as he did with dark eyes that crinkled at the corners. Dane would have liked Amherst, which was something of a comfort.

Ellie garnished his glass of lemonade with mint and lavender, which seemed to make it ever so much more palatable. When she'd poured for herself—*now*, lemonade appealed—she held up her glass in a toast.

"To consolation."

He politely raised his glass a few inches and sipped, his expression considering.

"You've a rebel in your kitchen. I've come across the mint with lemonade before, but not the lavender."

Ellie sampled her drink, finding it exactly to her taste, rather like Lord Amherst's brand of condolence call. "My own recipe. Not everybody likes it. Andy says I'm daft."

"An outspoken young lady. One wonders where she might have acquired such a trait."

"Are you teasing me?"

"On page forty-two of the manual, you will find that teasing is required." Amherst's tone was grave. "Right after ladylike sniffles and before a recitation of platitudes."

"Useless platitudes." Ellie couldn't help but smile, because teasing was indeed a consolation. "Were you sincere in requesting my help with your gardens, or was that a recommendation from the manual as well?"

He held the wet sprig of mint under his lordly nose, and Ellie realized he might tease her, but he wasn't a man given to simple banter. Dane had bantered easily and merrily. She'd found it charming—at first.

"The request was sincere. I'm short of staff, and the gardens are, of necessity, a low priority. I would not want to intrude on a time of grief, but I can use the help. Beyond a certain point, even the most well-designed garden can't be rescued, and my plots are approaching chaos."

The best-planned marriages could reach the same state of untenable disrepair all too easily. Ellie liked that his lordship would admit he needed help, though it threw into high relief that Dane had *not* needed her, except to produce an heir. In his lifetime, that priority had been untended to.

"Chaos sounds intriguing," Ellie said. "Weather permitting, expect me on hand tomorrow. What time suits?"

"It's cooler in the morning." Amherst removed the lavender sprig from his drink and placed it on the tray, when Dane would have either pitched it into the pansies or consumed his drink, garnish and all. "We'll tour the grounds, and you can give me your first impression. I'm usually off on my rounds by eight."

"That will suit."

Nothing in his tone suggested he was merely being polite by making this request, but Ellie still had a sense her neighbor was somehow dodging. She signaled the footman again. This time, he brought over a tray bearing a cold collation of meat, cheese, condiments, and sliced bread. "I thought you might enjoy some sustenance, my lord. May I fix you a sandwich?"

Amherst set his drink down and picked up the lavender. "I'll pass, but you should eat, my lady."

"You truly don't mind?" She did momentary battle with a craving for a bite of cheese—a sharp cheddar with dill would be splendid. "I'm famished, if you must know, but then, I lack the petite dimensions of a proper English beauty and probably always will." Swimming and fishing always put a sharpish edge on her appetite, even as they soothed her nerves.

An odd smile crossed Amherst's features. Even gaunt and dispensing sympathy, he was attractive, particularly when he smiled. Then too, there was his scent, his subtle humor, his gentlemanly manners. If all that weren't enough to endear him as a neighbor, he was also…kind.

Amherst twiddled the lavender, the scent rising on the breeze, while Ellie prattled on about flowers and consumed a real sandwich—not some stingy gesture with watercress and a pinchpenny dab of butter. All the while, as he made appropriate replies and sipped his drink. Ellie sensed that he drew pleasure simply from watching her eat.

Dane might have winked at her and joked about getting her a larger mount.

Eating for two was less guilt-inducing than eating for one. When Ellie rose to see her guest out, though, she stood too quickly and had to seize his arm while the sounds of the summer day faded behind an ominous roaring.

"Steady on, my lady."

He was stronger than he looked, bracing her against his body until the dizziness faded and Ellie's head was filled once again with the lovely scent of his person.

"Take your time," he murmured, making no move to step back. "Shall I call for a maid?"

"I'm fine." She'd been far from *fine* for at least two months, and possibly for much longer than that. "Though perhaps when you've gone, I might have a lie down."

He peered at her, and Ellie became aware—more aware— that he was quite tall, taller even than Dane, who'd been proud to top six feet. And wasn't that like a man, to be proud of something he'd had nothing to do with, no control over whatsoever?

"Let me see you into the house. Those naps can be a trap."

"I beg your pardon?" Ellie let him slowly promenade her down the veranda, his arm snugly around her waist, her hand in his. They were barehanded, because they'd been eating. His firm grip on her hand and waist reassured her more than she'd like to admit.

"The sleeping," Amherst went on. "Drifting from day to day is easy, and then you don't sleep at night, and the waking nightmares are as bad as the ones you'd have were you slumbering. Then you're so useless the next day, you're taking another nap and up all night yet again."

Ellie digested that and continued their measured progress toward the house.

"You've lost someone dear," she concluded, detecting a slight hesitation in his gait.

He withdrew the sprig of lavender from his pocket, but at some point, he'd fashioned it into a circle the diameter of a lady's finger. He presented the little garnish to her with a courtly flourish.

"Haven't we all lost somebody dear?"

* * *

"Trenton is doing better."

Darius Lindsey's hostess was one woman he didn't dare lie to. The dowager Lady Warne was a connection formed when Leah Lindsey—Darius and Trent's sister—had married Nicholas Haddonfield, Earl of Bellefonte. When Nick had joined the family, he'd brought his eight siblings and his grandmother along. With few exceptions they boasted commanding height, lightning intelligence, and a zest for living that made them individually and collectively overwhelming on first impression.

Lady Warne held out a plate of ginger biscuits, and Darius took two. She kept the plate before him, and he took two more.

"Define 'doing better,' my boy."

"He sleeps for more than an hour at a time, really sleeps," Darius began, searching for compromises between truth and fraternal loyalty. "He's stopped drinking, except for a glass or two of wine with dinner. He rides again. He's writing to family and not shut up at Crossbridge the way he was in Town."

Lady Warne ran an elegant finger around the rim of her glass. "For some of us, the best medicine is the land, the beasts, the out of doors. Not very aristocratic, but there it is, and quite English. Can you stay with him?"

No, Darius could not stay with his brother, and not only because Darius had promised to spend the summer in Oxfordshire helping Valentine Windham reclaim an estate from ruin.

"Hovering won't serve. Trent might have needed somebody to haul up short on his reins, but he's on his own now. Many a man has vowed to swear off gin, or gambling, or carousing, and two weeks later he's at it worse than ever. Trenton has a long way to go, physically, if nothing else."

Lady Warne's finger paused. "Amherst's health is poor?"

"He's a ghost." Darius could think of no more accurate word. "Five years ago, I would have put Trent up against any dragoon in the king's army. He could ride, shoot, handle a sword, or quote Shakespeare with the best of them. By comparison, he's feeble now. If the Crossbridge steward hadn't run off with the housekeeper, Trent might still be drifting around the town house, skinny as a wraith and twice as pale."

Run off, and taken a good sum of household money with them, so lax had Trent's supervision become.

"Five years ago, your brother hadn't capitulated to your father's choice regarding the succession."

Lady Warne had the elderly ability to ignore tender sentiments, and she was right: Paula—or her fat settlements—had been the Earl of Wilton's choice, and Trent, ever dutiful, had graciously recited the appropriate vows.

"Trent has been through a rough patch, but he's stubborn, when he has a reason to be."

"Unlike others." Lady Warne's smile was devilish. "Others are stubborn for the sheer fun of it."

"Is Emily proving stubborn?" Darius set his empty plate down, as if his little sister might be lurking behind the curtains, watching him eat a ridiculous number of fresh, warm ginger biscuits.

"She is sweet but sensible," Lady Warne said. "Particularly now that she's out from under your father's boot heel. If she doesn't present herself shortly, though, I will wonder if she hasn't perfected the art of the feminine dawdle."

"Wasted on a brother who wants only to take her for a ride in the park." And to make sure she was behaving herself.

"Let me fetch her." Lady Warne rose gracefully, leaving Darius to sip cold cider and wander the room. He'd been reasonably honest with Lady Warne, for she was old, and as sharp as the rest of her clan. Trent was sleeping, *some*. He was eating, *a little*. He was riding *short distances*, but only because a man without a land steward could either tramp all over his acres or ride a horse, and Trent wasn't up to the tramping.

Those glasses of wine at dinner—three or four of them— were consumed with desperate relish, too. Darius had *longed* to hover, longed to order the servants to empty every bottle of spirits, to put Trent on a schedule of riding and walking and a diet of good summer fare.

But barging into another man's life, destroying his dignity, and deciding his fate was the province of the Earl of Wilton, not his grown children. Darius had done what he could for Trent, then withdrawn to tend to other responsibilities.

He owed Trent the kind of faith Trent had shown him. Trent claimed Darius had saved his life by hauling him bodily down to Crossbridge, but in Darius's mind, that was simply the return of a favor owed.

* * *

Arthur, being six feet tall at the withers and gelded, stood biologically and physically above much of what made life trying. This made him an adequate conversationalist for Trent's return through the woods.

"And there I was," Trent muttered, "trying to make small talk with a widow, for the love of flowers." A papa of small children developed strange epithets. "A woman not three months past the loss of her spouse, and what do I do? Damned near put her in a faint, poor thing. She ought to burn my handkerchief and bury the ashes at a crossroads, mark me on this."

Arthur took a nibble of a passing branch.

"She's pretty," Trent went on, ducking to avoid the same branch. "Prettier the longer you look at her, and believe me, horse, I looked. Sat up and took notice." That had been the strangest sensation, like dreaming he was waking up. The longer Trent had listened to Elegy Hampton's voice and watched her hands and face, the more alert he'd become, but slowly, like shaking off a drug or a hard knock to the noggin.

He hadn't had the same peculiar sense when he'd seen her in her shift singing to the fishes. That had been a different pleasure altogether, though equally unexpected.

"And God help me, she'll be on the property tomorrow morning expecting me to converse civilly and offer hospitality."

A simple call between neighbors shouldn't overtax him. He knew the civilities, knew them in his bones, because excellent manners were the first arena in which he'd taken on besting his father. The first of many.

In the early afternoon heat, the lure of a nap pulled at him strongly, but in keeping with his determination not to scare his brother—Trent's label for what had been happening in his life before this forced remove to the countryside—Trent handed his gelding to a groom and ambled off on a slow walk instead.

Because, damn it all to hell and back, one quiet hack of a morning and a slow walk were about all he could manage.

His footsteps took him through the once-impressive gardens behind his manor house. The sun should have felt oppressive, but when he stopped to rest—to *think*—on a bench, the soft heat on his face bore the benevolence of an old friend's voice heard after long absence.

The gardens were in bad condition, neglected and overgrown past open rebellion. Some beds had succumbed to weeds. Others had been taken over by one of the hardier flowering species, and the whole business gave off an air of a cheerful botanical riot.

"Even my flowers…" Trent muttered, then caught himself. Talking to a horse was one thing, talking to oneself quite another.

"Thought you were dozing off," came a voice from behind a twelve-foot-high lilac bush.

"Show yourself, Catullus." Trent gave up the pleasure of the sun on his closed eyelids. "I do not pay you to skulk."

Cato emerged from the thicket of greenery, a sprig of mint dangling from the left corner of his mouth.

"Hiding from Cook, are you?" He seated himself beside his employer uninvited and leaned back to enjoy the sun right along with him.

"She tortured me with menus before breakfast and hinted mightily that a single gentleman ought to entertain when he's in the country of a summer."

"I entertain plenty," Cato replied, twirling the mint between his teeth. The oral gymnastics and the comment combined in a manner somehow lewd.

"You entertain the tavern maids." Trent's stable master was big, good-looking in a dark-haired Irish way, well muscled, and a thorough scamp with the women—and the ladies. His speech held a hint of a brogue when his emotions ran high or he was foaling out a mare, but his diction and word choice were otherwise refined.

Not quite Eton, but public school at least and maybe even university. The contradiction of a gentleman's education with a horse master's vocation hadn't struck Trent before.

Not much had struck Trent…before.

"Why aren't you laboring away in my stables?" Trent asked, settling lower on the bench.

"Work's done for now. You need to make a decision about your mares."

"What decision?"

"It's nigh June, your lordship." Cato's voice held a hint of irritation. "You wait any longer to breed them, and they'll be foaling in the worst of the heat and flies next year, with the best of the grass over and done. You can let 'em yeld this year, but a stable master likes to know these things, so he can put a few of the ladies in work. Then too, Greymoor's stud has a dance card to manage."

"Work a mare?" Trent snatched the sprig of mint from between Cato's lips and tossed it aside. He was irritated with himself more than Cato, because even following a conversation took effort when a man kept picturing a certain damply clad widow on a fishing expedition.

"A mare," Cato said with exaggerated patience. "A lady's mount, by any other name, perhaps even a mount for a sister, or sister-in-law, or daughter. You've seen the like, once or twice?"

"I have." Trent hunched forward and forced himself to apply his sluggish mind to the question on the floor: What would Lord Amherst like to do with the mares at his country estate, if anything?

Turn them loose in the home wood and spend the summer wandering after them.

"You weren't this stupid two years ago," Cato remarked when the silence lengthened.

Or perhaps the mares could trample the stable master.

"You are big enough and fast enough to make outrageous comments like that, Cato," Trent replied placidly, because Cato was goading him for some purpose known only to himself. "Don't think getting a rise out of me will provide a result you'll enjoy."

Cato shrugged broad shoulders and grinned a charming, robust fellow's grin. "Here in the wilds of Surrey, one finds one's entertainment where one can, *your lordship*." He rose with the easy grace of the strong and fit, though his observation went far beyond impertinent. "Let me know what you decide."

As Cato strode off, Trent's foot, independent of any decision by its owner, shot out and neatly tripped the stable master, who was laughing outright when he regained his balance.

Cato saluted with two callused fingers. "Better. Not your best effort, but a start."

Arthur would probably agree with that assessment.

Trent did, too.

CHAPTER THREE

The weather was glorious, his neighbor punctual, and Trent in a toweringly bad mood as a result. What—*what?*—had possessed him to invite this Lady Rammel onto his property, much less offer her a gardening project that could stretch for weeks? Even as he knew his anger was irrational—and he knew staying busy was a means of survival early in a bereavement— he resented the way she sat her horse, as if born on its back. He'd ridden like that, once upon time. Darius still rode like that. Cato road as if statues should be erected on his model alone.

And did Lady Rammel have to fill out her habit so... robustly? *He* used to take pride in the cut of his clothes and the elegance of his turn-out.

Did she have to damned smile at his useless stable master when Cato appeared from nowhere to help her off her horse?

"You're acquainted with my stable master?" Trent managed as Lady Rammel's mare was led away.

"He and Dane were thick as thieves in hunt season." She beamed as if this was famous good news. "They could natter on about cubbing and tail braiding and line breeding and heaven only knows what else for hours. I expect Mr. Spencer will miss Dane when the hunting starts up in the fall."

Mr. Spencer, being Catullus Sandringham Spencer, or Cato, to his many adoring familiars. Trent hated riding to hounds on general principles.

Also because his father thrived on blood sport.

"What have you done with Dane's horses?" Trent heard himself ask.

Could he have fashioned a more gauche question to put to a huntsman's bereaved widow?

Lady Rammel's smile dimmed. "Odd you should inquire. Dane's cousin is coming up at the end of the week to take them in hand. The stable lads are going through another round of mourning as we speak."

"His cousin?" Trent offered her his arm and searched the viscous morass of his memory for who that might be. Hampton had been titled, and somebody was no doubt dancing a jig on his grave in consequence.

"Drew," she said, with no inflection whatsoever. "Dane called him Dutiful Drew, and not only behind the poor man's back. Drew is the heir and takes his duties seriously."

"Is he putting your dower property to rights?"

"My dower…" Hers brows knit, then her smile reappeared. "I suppose, but I'm happy at Deerhaven. Papa owned Deerhaven outright and set it aside for me in the settlements, so here I'll stay."

"Lucky for me,"—the sentiment was genuine, though sentiments had also, until recently, gone into eclipse along with Trent's *urges*—"and for my flowers."

What *tripe*.

As the lady chattered on and they made several slow circuits of his gardens—he kept up with Lady Rammel easily—Trent began to enjoy his bad mood. Tripe? *Tripe?* How long had it been since he'd indulged in such a word, even in the privacy of his thoughts?

He cast his mental hounds, and other words came to mind, bold, articulate terms like *asinine, fatuous,* and *puerile,* words a man could toss out with some heat and substance behind them. He started to put all three in a sentence and searched for an appropriately colorful verb to hitch up to them when he realized his companion had fallen silent.

Some time ago.

Shite. "I beg your pardon, my lady."

"For?"

Trent kept his eyes forward. "My conversation has deserted me, which would be no great loss, except I've put yours to flight as well."

"I'm listening to the exchange between your wanton flowers."

Wanton was a fine old word. "What are they saying?"

"The irises are complaining their slippers are too tight," Lady Rammel informed him. "While the roses need a good hair combing but are planning to parade some splendid finery in a few weeks, nonetheless. The Holland bulbs are tired of dancing and ready for a supper break. The daffodils wish everybody else would hush so one could get some rest."

"Are all my flowers female?"

"Lilacs have woody stems, and they grow quite vigorously, so I think of them as masculine."

Woody…old words, vulgar ones, tripped through Trent's head, and it now became *imperative* that he keep his eyes front.

"May we sit a moment here?" Lady Rammel dropped his arm and settled on a shaded bench, the same one Trent had occupied with his stable master. "This had to have been your scent garden, and it's worth lingering over."

Trent settled in beside her, happy to note he hadn't needed the respite—not quite yet.

His companion was quiet, apparently content to inhale the effects of a scent garden growing riot on a summer morning.

Beside her, Trent's bad mood had eloped with his conversation, leaving him acutely sensitive to the pleasure of simply sitting beside a pretty woman in the morning air. She wore lavender well for a lady of her coloring, and she hadn't minced along beside him as if her full corset were torturing her bones.

He endured the most peculiar impulse to take her hand.

Lady Rammel closed her eyes and tipped her head back. "Andy wanted to come with me this morning. Her situation can be difficult."

"Difficult?" Trent sorted through the implications, while noting that Lady Rammel had long eyelashes. "She's an only child?"

"She's an illegitimate child," Lady Rammel replied, her tone mild, even weary. "One wants to protect her from unnecessary distress, but not overprotect."

The urge to take the woman's hand persisted. She had freckles over her knuckles, suggesting she didn't always wear gloves when she gardened. "You are wondering if I would censure you or the child, should you presume to allow her to accompany us through my gardens."

"Something like that." She opened her eyes and studied a tuft of silvery green lavender flourishing before some tall plants Trent didn't know the name of. "Would you censure me for bringing her?"

Of course not, but what was Lady Rammel really asking? A man who hadn't spent a long year clutching the brandy decanter would have puzzled out the subtleties easily.

"You wonder about the girl's welcome, because her father is no longer around to insist she be treated civilly?"

"Yes, though her father is no longer around to gainsay my decisions, either," Lady Rammel countered, the first hint of steel threading her tone.

Trent regarded the pretty lady beside him and permitted himself a flash of ire at idiot spouses who left children half-orphaned, particularly for something as foolish as a drunken steeplechase.

Though he'd left his own children more than half-orphaned for the dubious company of the brandy decanter, hadn't he?

"Miss Coriander is welcome at Crossbridge." Trent rose and offered Lady Rammel his hand. "I've a pony she might put to use, come to that. The poor beast hasn't been exercised to speak of in years."

"Miss Coriander will take up residence here if you let her know you've a pony going begging."

"God in heaven." Trent shot her a stricken look and stopped in midstride, his hand still wrapped around hers. "If you don't want her to ride, I will understand. My uncle took a bad fall, and my aunt—"

She stopped him with a shake of her head.

"Dane overfaced his horse, overindulged his thirst, and overestimated his skill in bad footing. Andy is a more prudent sort, for all she's only eight. I'm sure she'll take to your pony. In fact, even Dane would agree—*would have agreed*—it's time she met a few ponies."

"Then I must introduce you to Zephyr." Trent turned them toward the stables. "I adore her. She's the one female who isn't impressed with Cato's charms, unless it's feed time." He strolled with Lady Rammel along the walk, and when he realized he was still holding her hand, he decided to continue in that fashion rather than create awkwardness calling attention to his blunder.

Lady Rammel was friendly with the pony, who flirted back shamelessly, suggesting the little beast was partial to women, as some equines were. That necessitated introducing Lady Rammel to the pony's neighbors and confreres, including Arthur, who also flirted without any dignity whatsoever.

Lady Rammel scratched Arthur's big red nose. "He has such a kind eye. A gentleman, this one, and well named for royalty."

"He was named for a cloth doll my sister had when we

were quite young."

The only toy Trent could recall Leah owning, in fact.

Lady Rammel dropped her hand. "If you value your free time and your ears, you will not ask Andy about animals. She has a menagerie of zoological rag dolls, and they all go to high tea, picnics, story hour, and so forth."

The recitation sent a spike of homesickness through Trent, for his children, especially for little Lanie.

"An imaginative young lady," Trent said, as he strolled Lady Rammel right up to the house, though—had he been capable of rudeness—he might have called for her horse when they were in the stables. "May I offer you some sustenance now that you've spent half the morning tramping all over my domain?"

"You may." She beamed at him again, that smile he was starting to watch for. Had Dane Hampton, as he lay gasping his last in the mud beneath a gate, longed for one more glimpse of that smile?

For the first time since arriving at Crossbridge, Trent was smitten with spontaneous gratitude, rather than the manufactured variety. His stable master, cook and butler hadn't gone a-maying like his steward and his housekeeper, and he had sufficient staff that he could entertain a neighbor on an informal call.

He was alive; he could move about under his own power; and he had three lovely children. Any one of those was a substantial blessing, and he'd nearly allowed them all to slip from his grasp.

So he could clutch a brandy decanter?

"We'll have a reprise of breakfast," Trent said, taking a place beside Lady Rammel at a wicker grouping under a spreading oak. "Or for some of us, the first verse."

She eyed him up and down in a thoroughly uxorial fashion, sending a wash of heat over Trent's cheeks. "You haven't eaten yet?"

"One becomes involved in the day, and I'm adjusting to

country hours and country fare." To eating regularly, in any case.

"What's your favorite source of sustenance?" She settled in as if getting comfortable before interrogating him, though it wouldn't do at all for Trent to give his honest answer.

"I'm partial to sweets." Brandy was sweet. Sweetish.

She wrinkled her nose. "Not a thick, bloody beefsteak?"

Trent glanced around, making sure the footmen were not in evidence. "Just because you were married toRammel doesn't mean you had to adore his every choice and preference. Or *any* of his choices and preferences, for that matter."

Her ladyship found it necessary to rearrange the drape of her skirts. "Have you been reading the manual again, my lord?"

They'd start breakfast with a serving of honesty, because Rammel had not appreciated his wife, of that much Trent was certain.

"I loved my mother," Trent said. "She doted on us, preserved us from the worst of my father's temper, and wasn't above pitching a cricket ball to her sons when Papa was away. But she was stubborn, had a selfish streak, and could be close-minded. Even as I understood that she needed determination to survive her marriage, I could still acknowledge those traits weren't always healthy."

"How long has she been gone?"

"Years. She was ill for some time first."

"I wonder about that." Lady Rammel resumed smoothing her skirts. Had she been the one to sew all those rag dolls for Miss Coriander? "I wonder about whether a little time or a lot of time is better than death coming for you in an instant."

"And then,"—Trent reached over and stilled her hand—"you wonder better for whom."

"I don't miss the things I thought I would," she said, her gaze on Trent's bare hand. "I do miss things I thought of as… obligations."

Sex. She'd been a dutiful wife; Rammel had been a healthy

young husband, and she missed the sex. How Trent wished he'd lost a wife with whom he missed something so basic.

"You miss standing up with him in church?" Trent suggested as the footmen appeared with several trays.

She snorted. "Dane in church? He was a hatches and matches Christian, not overly fond of regular services. He did his part for the local living, and he tarried long enough in church to be shackled to me."

"He *told* you he felt shackled?" Rammel deserved to be trampled in the mud all over again if he'd taken that low shot.

To a man who'd been married for five years—*not* shackled, not even to poor Paula—Lady Rammel's smile looked forced. "Of course he didn't use those words. Shall I serve?"

"Please."

She was at home with the duties of a hostess, of a wife, and she had the knack of turning the conversation back to innocuous topics—his flowers, Miss Coriander's clever governess—while she fixed him a plate of scones and fresh strawberries to go with his gunpowder. For his part, Trent let himself enjoy the lilt of her contralto wending through his senses as her hands dealt with the tea service.

Unbidden, the sound of her singing, half-naked in the woods, stirred in his memory.

He wasn't particularly hungry, even with all their walking, but he ate to be polite. His guest, however daintily, ate to enjoy her food.

"Is there anything more pleasurable on the palate than perfectly ripe fruit?" She chewed a bite of strawberry, her eyes closed, then smiled as she swallowed. "I'm being tiresome to bring it up, but I can't help but feel as if I'm supposed to fade away, oppressed by grief, unable to eat."

"Some people grieve that way," Trent said, eyeing his buttered scone. Other people drank and drifted while they neglected themselves and their children.

"I am disappointed in Dane for dying," she replied,

munching another strawberry. "I am quite sorry for him, but the great black cloud of overwhelming loss has yet to engulf me for more than a few days or a few hours at a time."

Trent put his plate down because he knew exactly what his guest was asking and had asked it himself until the question had made him sick.

"Lady Rammel, if that great black cloud comes calling, I hereby admonish you to have a good cry, then run like hell, gorge yourself on strawberries and flowers and chocolates, wear bright colors, dance on the lawn, and sing at the top of your lungs."

Or fish in my pond, which he could also see her doing.

"I don't think Vicar would support your prescription," she said, her smile fading.

"Vicar wasn't married to the man," Trent said in exasperation. "How did Dane remark your first anniversary?"

"He was off shooting in Scotland." She picked up a large, perfectly ripe, red berry, but didn't eat it. "He wasn't about to miss the opening of grouse season two years in a row."

"What did he give you for Christmas last year?"

"He...something. Exactly what escapes my memory."

"What did he give Miss Andy?"

"A cloth horse doll," she said slowly. "That I made for her."

"Do you take my point?"

She put the strawberry down. "I don't like your point. If you're telling me I'm grieving in proportion to how I loved my husband, perhaps I should be offended."

"My apologies." Trent should have stuffed a scone in his maw, or remarked something inane about the weather, but instead he served up more honesty. "Though I risk giving offense, I'm suggesting you're grieving in proportion to how you were loved."

The emotions on her face were painful to see, anger and disbelief at his rudeness, then shock, more disbelief, and a dawning hurt.

Trent had hurt a woman, who'd done not one thing to deserve it—before breakfast was even off the table. "Forgive me. I should not have spoken thus."

"You know more about this grieving business than you should," she replied, her features composing themselves.

"Maybe more than anybody should. May I have another scone?"

He held out his plate, hoping desperately to distract her even if it meant he'd have to choke down the damned scone. When she left, he would find a brandy decanter. Yes, it was morning, and yes, he'd done better lately. But this…

She fixed him another scone, sliced it cleanly in half and slathered butter on both halves. "Jam, my lord?"

"No, thank you."

She passed him the plate, then turned her face away. By the funny little hitch of her shoulders, Trent knew, for the thousandth time, he'd inspired a woman to tears.

* * *

Until his cousin Dane's untimely death, the ladies had found Drew Hampton charming and occasionally worth a tumble or a waltz, though he was merely an heir presumptive, not an heir apparent. In the great whirling circus of titled society, he was barely worth a mention, particularly when Dane—handsome, robust, witty, and generous—had been unlikely to die for at least another two score years and had married a robust young lady well suited to childbearing.

Drew eyed the canopy of his vast bed and considered having winged pigs embroidered thereon.

"What has you smiling?"

His romping partner of the morning, Lady Somebody or Other, tiptoed her fingers across his naked chest, then headed south.

"The thought of a hearty meal following our exertions," he replied, trapping her wandering hand. "Shall I have a bath sent up for you?"

The buxom brunette—when relieved of her clothing, she answered cheerfully enough to Crumpet, Angel, or Darling—ceased her southerly peregrinations. "You're serious."

"I'm hungry. I've appeased your other appetites and mine, so now food is in order."

Women, apparently, didn't grasp that sequence of events as readily as men did.

"I should be grateful you didn't roll over and go to sleep." The brunette sat up and swung her feet off the bed, accepting the dressing gown Drew handed her. "You really need to work on your charm, sir."

"You found me charming enough twenty minutes ago." Drew set about dressing himself and glanced at the clock on the mantel—fifteen minutes ago, to be precise.

"You're honest. That has a certain backhanded charm," the brunette allowed, her smile reluctant. "You're wishing I'd take myself off, aren't you?"

"I appreciate directness in a lady, particularly in the bedroom." Drew offered a hint of a smile to soften the sentiment, though he truly was in want of sustenance.

She rose and started organizing the clothing she'd tossed over a chair earlier.

"As subtle as you are, one wonders how I was lucky enough to merit your attention." Her actions were abrupt, a minor display of pique Drew tolerated rather than provoke her further. He did need to work on his charm, or he would have needed to work on his charm, if he'd had any to start with.

She'd been a willing romp, so Drew let her get dressed in peace, obligingly doing up her stays and hooks. She was wise enough not to complain, and he'd send her flowers tomorrow, but their encounter was exactly as he'd intended it to be.

And likely far less than she'd hoped it could be.

All the more reason to observe the civilities and see the lady to her waiting town coach. He politely bowed over her hand and thanked her for her company, then took himself back to the comfortable confines of the Rammel town residence. He passed through the kitchen, letting the scullery maid know he'd take a tray in the library. In the hallway, he caught sight of himself in a mirror hung over a cherry-wood sideboard.

The fellow in the mirror was tired, not quite tidy, and going a bit hard around the eyes and mouth.

Less than three months after Dane's death, and he was behaving more like Dane, *looking* more like Dane—more arrogant, more self-absorbed, though Dane's blond, muscular appearance had been at variance with Drew's taller frame and dark coloring. Dane hadn't been a bad man, but neither had he been a good man. He'd been a viscount, a title, and no better than he had to be, as with most of the breed.

If dear Ellie were not carrying, Drew would soon become the next Viscount Rammel, and the thought brought no joy.

Dane, in typical viscount fashion, hadn't spared the coin when it came to his pleasures, leaving a stable of fine hunters to be dealt with. The thought gave Drew a pang, because it meant he'd be traveling down to Deerhaven the following day to see about the horses.

And that meant facing Ellie, who was his responsibility as well. Too bad there weren't broodmare sales for slightly used viscountesses.

He turned his back on the mirror, for that thought was callous even for him, even when not one living soul stood between him and his recently deceased cousin's title.

* * *

Men were so much easier to understand than women. If a man was upset with his fellows, he put up his fives, delivered a blistering set-down, called out his detractor, or ignored the whole business with cool, manly disdain.

Trent dug for his spare handkerchief, for women, unfathomable creatures, *cried.* For the entire five years of his marriage, Trent had been bewildered, resentful, and then downright despairing at his wife's tears. Nothing stemmed the flow of Paula's upset, not time, not solitude, and most assuredly not reason.

Reason, he'd learned early, was the surest way to provoke her further.

Lady Rammel blotted her eyes with the handkerchief he'd given her earlier in this burdensome morning, but when he reached out to pass over the reinforcements, she took his hand instead and used it to haul herself right over next to him on the wicker settee.

She bundled into his side, weeping against him in quiet torrents, the sound tearing at his composure as visions of brandy decanters danced in his head. His arms went around her even as he bent his head to try to decipher what she was saying.

"I'm s-sorry," she whispered.

"Don't be inane." Proximity to her was the price he paid for having been so ungallant with her grief, and the lady wasn't about to turn loose of him.

"Do you ever hate her?"

He'd bitterly resented Paula, for the middle two years of their marriage. "Who?"

"Your mother. The one who lingered and was stubborn."

That mother. "Nearly." He would worry about his unfilial admission later. "She inveigled promises from my brother and me, promises with lasting and hurtful consequences, and at certain times, if I didn't hate her, I came very close."

"And she was your mother." Lady Rammel nodded, apparently satisfied with his answer, and the gesture waved her silky dark hair against Trent's cheek. He resisted the urge to bury his nose in that feminine treasure, but allowed himself an inhalation of her fragrance.

"You've a different scent today from yesterday."

"I have my moods. Some of them inconvenient." She shifted as if to gather herself away from him, but Trent stopped her.

"Stay."

She heaved off another Sigh of Sighs and relented, turning her face into his shoulder. "Earlier, when I said I missed the obligations?"

Trent's fingers traced over the knuckles of the hand she rested against his chest. "I recall the comment."

"I miss paying his bills. I miss scolding him for getting mud all over my carpets and wearing his boots to table. I miss him coming in from the hunt field, bellowing for a toddy and his slippers. He wasn't company, exactly, but he was *there*."

The litany was pathetic in some ways, but at least she had a list, prosaic as it was. "That you miss him is good, a blessing."

She snorted, a ladylike explostulation of self-derision. "I missed him when he was alive. I didn't always like him, but I missed him."

For her, this was Progress. Trent laced his fingers with hers and offered her hand a consoling squeeze rather a platitude, Bible verse or tisane.

"I did not matter to my husband half so much as his favorite hunter," she said, with a tired sort of asperity, "but I comforted myself with the fiction that I did, that I might matter to him someday."

When she'd become the mother of Rammel's heir?

"You matter to Andy," Trent said, and that must have been the right thing to say, because along his side, her body gave up a remnant of defensive, resentful rigidity.

"I do. You're right about that, and it's important." She smiled at his much-abused handkerchief, and a tightness in Trent's chest eased.

That smile held something secret, female and sweet, a little maternal, but not without mischief. Trent's hand, the one that had been linked with hers, lifted as if to touch her smile, but common sense caught up with him, and he settled for returning his rambunctious appendage to his thigh.

Breakfast should not have concluded with his guest in tears, making awkward confessions as she wrinkled his handkerchief, but he made no move to shift away, and neither did she. In fact, as they lingered on the settee—lingered *cuddling* on the settee—Lady Rammel grew heavier and more relaxed against his side. Her eyes soon closed, and her breathing fell into a slow, steady rhythm.

The deuced woman had fallen asleep against him.

He tucked her more closely to his side, stole a whiff of her hair, and glanced at the clock—though he had no appointments, pressing or otherwise, on his calendar. Seven fragrant and peaceful minutes later, his companion stirred, but she didn't bolt upright, expressing ladylike horror at her behavior.

She…nuzzled at him. *Nuzzled.* Then gave a soft, sleepy sigh and drifted into stillness.

Arthur nuzzled Trent's pocket for treats. The house cat occasionally nuzzled Trent's chin to interrupt his reading or demand to be let out. A nuzzling female was novel and dangerous and stirred urges both protective and unruly.

Lady Rammel sat up slowly two minutes later, chagrin on her pretty features. "Perishing Halifax. I have lapsed mightily, haven't I? What must you think of me?"

"You have napped, a little." Trent tucked back a lock of her hair that had tried to snag itself on his lapel as he'd retrieved his arm. "Would a glass of lemonade appeal?"

"Yes, I believe it would, along with a nice big hole in the ground to conveniently swallow me up and rescue me from further apologies. A vow of secrecy would be appreciated as well."

"My daughter is a firm believer that after every bout of tears must come a restorative nap." Also a cuddle. Trent rather missed Lanie's cuddles. "Napping, in my daughter's case, is a constructive habit. Her way of leaving the scene of the drama."

"You've a daughter?"

"Just the one. I've sent my dependents to visit my sister, but my daughter can put the whole household into an uproar when she's peckish, or tired, or happy, or cranky." Trent shifted to a seat at a right angle to his guest, intending the distance to support her bid for composure.

Also his bid for composure.

The lady yawned with a sleepy sweetness. "Andy hates her given name. Her mother was a cook, and Andy thinks the name an insult. When the child is determined on her pique, we all hear about it at length."

She fell silent, smoothing the hanky slowly against her thighs for a moment before raising her head and peering over at Trent. "Having disgraced myself in your presence, my lord, may I make a further imposition?"

"Of course." He was a gentleman, after all, and she was a lady in distress.

"Nobody uses my name," she said, folding his handkerchief tidily in half over her knees. "Old retainers will call me Miss Ellie, but they're few and far between, and it isn't the same. We're neighbors. I would be pleased if you and yours would not stand on formality with me."

Trent had been happy to become Viscount Amherst upon his majority, because it was a step up from what his father typically called him. Now, he dreaded the day he'd be Wilton.

"I will happily use your name under appropriate circumstances," he replied slowly. "Except, my memory fails me. Your given name is Eleanor?"

She shook her head, stroking his hopelessly wrinkled handkerchief yet more. "Most people think it is, but my mother had a whimsical streak. My given name is Elegy, hence, Ellie."

"Shall I call you Elegy? The name seems a short removed from 'eulogy,' and I can't think that would be helpful."

"Ellie." She beamed at him, expectation in her gaze.

"Trenton," he replied, with a sense of yielding to fate—or

doom. "Trent to my family and friends." Though not to his wife. To Paula, he'd been unfailingly Amherst.

"I will call you Trent under appropriate circumstances and take my leave of you before I conjure more mortification, in addition to bawling like an orphaned calf and falling asleep like a tipsy dowager."

Trent drew her to her feet. "I've spent my share of time with the bovines and the dowagers, and I can't recall enjoying the experiences half so much as I've enjoyed this time with you."

"You are kind." She slipped her arm through his and let him escort her back to the stables. When they arrived, Trent was relieved to see Arthur had been saddled up, Lady Rammel's groom having been sent the short distance home rather than linger waiting for her at Crossbridge.

He rode along to Deerhaven with her, assisted her to dismount in her own stable yard, and about fainted dead away when she went up on her toes and kissed his cheek in parting. When she pulled away, she smiled up at him, a woman not given to vapors who had only needed a little comfort.

A neighborly kiss then, a widow's kiss. Nothing more.

He bowed and took his leave, letting Arthur amble back through the wood on a loose rein as Trent tried to put his finger on what had pleased him about the morning's exchange— because amid all the awkwardness and poor conversational gambits, they'd shared something gratifying, too. Lady Rammel—Ellie—was a toothsome woman with a lovely smile and a quick wit, true, but there was something more.

She'd *trusted* him. A woman did not cry, much less cat-nap, in the presence of a man she didn't trust. She'd let Trent *in,* to her emotions, her motivations, her thoughts. She should trust him, of course, because he was a gentleman, and yet, Trent found it flattering that she did.

Also disturbing as hell.

CHAPTER FOUR

"Isn't this a sight to restore a man's spirits?" Catullus Spencer flashed a toothy, charming grin. "Two lovely ladies to grace my morning. May I assist you down?"

Andy looked like she wanted to stick her tongue out at him, but instead ignored his proffered hand, hopped down from the dog cart, and scampered off a few paces. Ellie didn't make a fuss, because one remonstrated family in private, and Mr. Spencer was hardly unused to feminine moods or rejections.

"My lady." He bowed over her knuckles when he'd handed Ellie down, and while some might call it aping his betters, Ellie appreciated his attentions.

"My thanks, Mr. Spencer." His smile leaned to the flirtatious side of friendly. Ellie kept hers closer to polite. "Andy, if you can dredge up some manners, perhaps Mr. Spencer will let you meet Zephyr."

Andy studied her half-boots, which—small miracle!—still sported bows at the laces. "No, thank you, Mama. I'll go with you to the gardens."

"Miss Zephyr can wait," Mr. Spencer said agreeably, "while the weeds are growing apace, and his lordship will be anxious to greet you both. I believe he's on the back terrace."

"Come along, Coriander." Ellie held out a hand, which Andy took without even glancing at the barn where Zephyr, The Miracle Pony, waited. Last night, the child had chattered on for most of supper about meeting the pony. She'd also included the beast in her prayers—and now this.

"Are you nervous about meeting the viscount?" Ellie asked as they meandered around to the back of the house.

"My papa was a viscount. Soon Uncle Drew will have the title."

"Coriander Brown, you are not usually so oblique. What is going on in that pretty head of yours?"

"What's oblique?"

"Indirect. Hard to read. Subtle."

"I'm being polite," Andy said, glancing over her shoulder at the stables, where Mr. Spencer was leading their cart-horse around to the carriage house.

"Polite doesn't preclude friendly, Andy," Ellie chided. "Mr. Spencer might be a servant, but a stable master holds an important position, and he should be respected."

"Is Viscount Amherst important?" A nimble dodge, suggesting Ellie had made her point.

"His is still a courtesy title. Your papa was a viscount in truth because your grandpapa died before we married." Exactly one year before, and Ellie had been flattered that Dane hadn't wanted to wait one week longer for the wedding.

"So Viscount Amherst's papa is an earl, and he's still alive?"

"Right on both counts." This devolved into a discussion, not the first, of precedence, courtesy titles, and rank. By the time Ellie had led the child to the back terraces, Andy was arguing that churchmen shouldn't figure into an earthly hierarchy because God hadn't chimed in on the matter.

"But God handed down stone tablets when He wanted to," Andy insisted. "He makes bushes burn, and so forth, so it isn't that God can't speak up, it's that He doesn't view the matter as worth comment."

Ellie let the topic drop, because no illegitimate child wanted to dwell long on matters of succession and consequence.

"Ladies." Viscount Amherst rose to his considerable height from the same shaded table at which Ellie had eaten strawberries.

And cried.

And fallen asleep on the man's shoulder.

"This must be Miss Andy." Amherst bowed over Ellie's hand, then did the same for the child. "We've another pretty morning, but I thought we'd start with breakfast today, then wander it off in the gardens."

"I like breakfast," Andy volunteered.

"Just a nibble, Andy," Ellie warned. "You've had your porridge."

Amherst held Ellie's chair for her, then Andy's, something Ellie could not recall the girl's father ever doing for her.

Amherst took the chair next to Ellie. "Why, when we're young and spending our days racketing about at a dead gallop, are we to subsist on porridge, pudding and toast, but then, when we're old and gouty and sitting about all day, we're to stuff ourselves with steak and kidney pie, crème tarts, and port? What do you think, Miss Andy?"

"I think I like scones with butter and jam even if it's breakfast. Mama does, too."

"A woman of taste and refinement, your mama." He shared a look with Andy that Ellie didn't entirely understand. "My gardens are on her agenda, lucky me."

"You are lucky," Andy assured him earnestly. "Mama is a dab hand with the flowers, and her scent garden is the envy of the shire."

With every appearance of rapt attention, Amherst set

about buttering Andy a scone. "Why is that?"

While Ellie munched her fresh, flaky scone, his lordship and Andy discoursed vigorously on the appeal of spicy versus floral scents, about which Ellie would not have guessed either of them had knowledge or opinion. Amherst had the knack of appealing to the girl's quick sense of humor without shading into adult innuendo, and for the first time—the first time *ever*—Ellie could see that Andy had the potential for considerable feminine beauty.

"What of you, Lady Rammel?" Amherst sat back, chilled glass of lemonade garnished with strawberries in his hand. "Which is your favorite scent for indoors?"

"On my person or about a room?"

"A room. Let's say, a family parlor."

He looked as if he expected her to answer, as if her answer mattered, and not simply so a pair of adults could demonstrate the art of small talk for an attentive child. "Choosing a scent for a family parlor is a challenge."

"You put roses in our family parlor if they're in season," Andy reminded her.

"I do," Ellie said, pleased Andy would notice. "That's in part for their color and appearance. If I had one fragrance to grace my family parlor, it would likely be something brisk and friendly—balsam maybe, or mint. Lavender is a favorite, and rosemary is pleasant."

"She makes lists," Andy confided to their host. "Mama can go on like this, so don't ask her what her favorite dessert is, or who was the best monarch, or the worst, and so forth. Don't ask her who her favorite cat is, either."

"I appreciate the warning. I'd appreciate a jaunt through the gardens, too."

"I'm for that." Andy was on her feet, her chair scraping back loudly against the flagstones.

Amherst rose more slowly. "Now, Miss Andy, you've deprived me of the chance to hold your chair and show off my manners to your mama."

Andy grinned, unaware that her manners had just been corrected. "You can show off your pony for me when we're through with the gardens."

"She bargains like a female," Amherst observed, holding Ellie's chair then offering her his arm. While Andy gamboled ahead, his lordship tucked Ellie's hand over his arm. "I would have thought Cato might have introduced Miss Andy to Zephyr already."

"Andy is shy of some people. Where are you taking me, sir? I have a plan for how these gardens will be rescued."

"I'm taking you to the scent garden, or what remains of it. Miss Andy is delightful, and she'll be breaking hearts in very short order."

He didn't have to say that, but his observation pleased Ellie inordinately. "I don't know if she'll capture many hearts. Dane didn't leave her much of a settlement."

"Her dowry is her quick wit, her charm, and her integrity. My sister, Leah, snagged a formidable earl with less, and Nicholas wasn't looking to marry for love."

"Your sister had no dowry?" This did not comport with Ellie's idea of how an earl's daughter would be treated.

"My mother set funds aside for her, but my father pilfered them, for which transgression he now rusticates at Wilton Acres over in Hampshire."

"Good heavens. How unfortunate for your sister." But how lovely for Ellie that she'd be deemed worthy of such a confidence. To be reminded that the rest of the world had problems, in an odd way also made grief less powerful.

"Not well done of me," Amherst said, "airing the family linen like that. As for Miss Andy, she has you. You have time to see to her funds, and for now that will be enough."

"I'm not sure," Ellie said, while Andy sniffed at a rose. "Drew is coming down later today to look over the horses, and I'm concerned he might start throwing the title around to insist Andy be sent off somewhere."

"Drew's prospective title is unavailing." Amherst sounded very sure of his point. "Unless Dane left him some sort of guardianship, Drew can strut and paw and make noise, but all he has is a gentlemanly concern for the child, not a legal right."

Ellie was nearly certain Dane had left *her* some sort of legal authority in the will, but what did a will matter when a wealthy man sought relief from the courts?

"Drew can get legal authority over Andy, can't he?" she asked.

"Why would he?"

Ellie considered the question while Andy bent a tall rose cane down within sniffing range. "I'm not sure. I don't know the man well, and neither did Dane, which is odd, because they're both only children—that is, Dane *was* an only child and Drew his heir."

Amherst came to a halt, their arms still linked. "This concerns you? This visit from your cousin-in-law?"

"Yes. Maybe I hadn't admitted it to myself, but it does. Deerhaven is safe, Papa saw to that, but it never occurred to me Andy might not be."

Grief could make a woman stupid, could make her spend entire days staring out windows or wandering her house and seeing only draped mirrors and an empty chair in her late husband's estate office.

"Invite me over for dinner tonight," Amherst said slowly, as if the notion had only now occurred to him. "I'll pry Dane's agenda from him over the port."

"You'll pry…?" Ellie fell silent, knowing exactly what Amherst offered. She was in mourning, but the condolence calls had started, and Amherst was her closest neighbor.

"You're in the country," he pointed out, as if reading her mind. "A neighbor popping over to greet the prospective title holder is not a two-week house party."

The relief she felt at his suggestion made the decision for

her. "We dine at eight and do not dress."

"Thank God for that, and here we are, in the garden of not-quite-paradise."

"He has loads and loads of spices and flowers here, Mama." Andy was making her way nose-first from one plant to the next. "And loads of weeds."

Ellie's basket of tools had already been brought out from her dog cart, a sign of Mr. Spencer's attentiveness.

"If you send your head gardener by, my lord, I'll discuss the plan of attack with him, and we can devise a schedule to amuse the gods of weather."

"My gardener's name is Abel. He's on good terms with those weather gods. Ladies, my thanks. You've only to send to the house if you need anything. Miss Andy, a pleasure making your acquaintance, and if you need a break, you might consider introducing yourself to the pony in the corner stall with the low door."

Andy left off inventorying the garden long enough to bob a curtsy and flash a grin, and then Ellie was alone with her daughter and the riot-in-progress of Lord Amherst's scent garden. The state of the flowers nicely complemented the riot-in-progress that was her interior landscape as she watched Amherst striding back to the house.

He'd been in the sun, and unlike the fair, Nordic variety of Englishman—unlike Dane—Amherst tanned, making his dark eyes more luminous and giving his dark hair faint, red highlights.

And again, unlike Dane, Amherst was comfortable with a girl child. He was a papa, after all, a papa to a daughter and easy with it. How Ellie envied Amherst's wife—who must be off visiting his sister with the children—to have a man like that as her partner in life. Lady Amherst, Ellie concluded as she pulled on her gloves, must be so busy enjoying her marriage and raising her daughter, she had no time to see to the gardens here at Crossbridge.

* * *

Catullus Sandringham Spencer had experience with all kinds of women: wealthy, poor, exalted, humble, just out of the schoolroom and approaching their dotage. For the most part, females made sense to him. He flirted and flattered or sparred with them until he understood what they were about, then he gave them enough of what *they* wanted to get what *he* wanted. Bless their hearts, the ladies understood the game and enjoyed playing it with him—usually.

This type of female, however—small, of tender years and solemn eyes—flummoxed him. As Andy leaned over the half-door to stroke her hand down Zephyr's nose, Cato mentally sorted through his tools and tricks, discarding them one by one. Flattery, flummery, flirting, none of them would work.

In desperation, he seized upon his most rusty and unpredictable strategy: Unvarnished Truth.

"Don't go running off," he said quietly. The child whirled, spooking the pony to the back of her stall. "Ah, you see? You and Zephyr were having a fine, friendly visit, and now she's misplaced her composure."

Miss Coriander Brown, by contrast, had not misplaced her composure, though she was clearly scared and damned if she'd let it show.

He hunkered next to her. "Blasted saints, child. Do you think I'll sell you to the tinkers?"

She turned away and stretched out her hand to the pony. "Mama would fetch Lord Amherst if you did. You shouldn't use bad language."

And here he'd moderated his language in deference to her youth. "My apologies, but bad language is fun."

The girl regarded him through eyes very like her papa's, clearly unimpressed by Cato's honesty.

Time for some charm.

Cato fished in his pocket and came up with half a carrot. He broke it in two pieces and laid one flat on his palm, holding it out to the gray pony.

"You keep your hand level, and the pony will lip the treat from your hand without biting."

"I know how to feed treats." The child took the other half of the carrot without touching Cato's palm. She fed the greedy little beast easily then speared him with another look.

"I'll not bite you, either," Cato said, turning and squatting against the door of the stall. "You and I need to talk."

"You want to talk about what I saw."

Cato ran a hand through his hair, mentally reciting a quick Glory Be. "What you saw was…a mistake. A harmless mistake."

On everybody's part.

"You hit my papa." She said it with such a frown, Cato had the sense she was fishing, looking for verification, as if she couldn't fathom that anybody would strike her dear, departed papa.

"I slapped him once." He'd backhanded the man. "That was the end of it."

She stroked small fingers over the pony's velvety nose. "Papa died that morning. He was riding the horse you lent him."

"Bla—blessed saints." Cato rose, paced off and turned, because hearing the loss in the child's tone made him toweringly uncomfortable, as did the conclusion she'd so easily reached. Dane Hampton had been a self-indulgent, overgrown boy, and he hadn't been worth the girl's sorrow. Telling the child so would be pointless—and mean. Cato could be mean, though only to full-grown men, intransigent mules or others he considered his equal.

"You blame me because your papa took a bad fall?"

"He fell from the horse you put him on."

"I know that." Hadn't Cato told himself the same thing a thousand times? "Your papa asked to borrow that gelding, drank too much, and overfaced the horse in bad footing.

That's why he died."

"Papa always drank too much and never had a care for the footing."

Cato finished the syllogism for her. "Which leaves the horse I lent him. I grasp your reasoning, but your papa asked to borrow that horse, my personal mount, and if you'll recall, I ended up shooting the poor beast where it lay in the mud."

The girl turned, so the door to the stall was at her back. Her expression changed, becoming thoughtful rather than pugnacious. "You had to shoot Ghost?"

"Shattered a cannon bone." Cato looked away from those somber eyes. This was why he had no truck with children. They were too honest, and too...young.

"I'm sorry."

"Am I exonerated?"

She blinked at him, downy brows lowering.

"Let off, not guilty, no longer under suspicion?" Children were too simple, too, and too complicated.

"I won't tell what I saw. You lost your horse, and Papa said Ghost was the best hunter in the shire."

"And you lost your papa," Cato said softly.

Dane's daughter gave the pony one last, longing glance, then left without another word. As Cato watched her retreat, small, quick, quiet, and nimble, he wondered if the horse hadn't been the greater loss, and if the child didn't already know it.

* * *

"What in the hell happened to your stirrup leathers?" Cato's black Irish scowl was thunderous as he tossed the offending equipment onto Trent's estate desk.

Trent sat back and eyed his irate stable master. "I broke one last night coming back from Deerhaven. The paths were muddy, Arthur slipped, and we had a bad moment. Shall you sit?"

Cato's blue-eyed gaze snapped over Trent like lightning

dancing around a ship's rigging. "Are you insulting me, my lord?"

"Of course I am, Catullus." Trent rose, unwilling to adopt his father's posturing. Wilton never stood if he could remain enthroned around the help. "I endeavor always to annoy my senior staff. An estate, like a proper family, runs better when it's at war with itself."

Trent crossed the library to stick his head into the corridor—social constraints between master and servant having no purchase against the master's empty stomach—instructed the lounging footman and returned, closing the door behind him.

"My apologies," Cato bit out. "Your leathers did not break, my lord. They were cut. Both of them."

"I beg your pardon?" Trent picked up the leathers and took them to a window to peer at in better light. The leather was cleanly sliced through on one and cut down to a narrow strip of hide on the other. Not worn, not frayed, but cleanly cut. "You appear to have the right of it."

Cato crossed muscular arms as if bracing for an interrogation. "As dirty as the weather was last night, you're lucky you didn't break your neck, my lord."

"Arthur's a steady sort." On both leathers the damage had been done high up near the buckles and on the side of the leather lying against the saddle. Unless a groom had taken the stirrups off to clean the saddle, the sabotage would have been all but invisible.

Cato muttered in what sounded like Gaelic—something profane.

"Arthur is a horse," Cato said, as if the entire species had much to answer for. "The footing was nasty, and any mount can spook at a rabbit in the dark of night."

"You're spooked." Trent fell silent while a footman brought in a laden tray and set it on the low table before the hearth.

When the servant had departed, Trent gestured at his

stable master.

"Have a seat and eat something, or at least have a hot cup of tea. Because you and Cook didn't run off to Gretna Green, I am determined to show my appreciation to you both."

"*Cook* and I?" Cato's look of consternation was comical. "She's a veritable siren, if you don't mind a grumpy woman who enjoys wielding a knife with alarming skill."

Trent took a place on the sofa before the food. "She stood up to my father one too many times. Being in service to him would sour any female's humor."

"You've succeeded in distracting me," Cato said, sitting on the couch two feet away from his master. He sat gingerly, as if he expected to be caught by the butler humoring Trent's queer democratic start. Cato reached for a sandwich, then drew his hand back.

"Eat, Catullus. The occasion of my own hunger is so rare as to be cause for celebration." Trent helped himself to a sandwich, as much to put Cato at ease as because he was, indeed, hungry. When Cato followed suit, Trent poured them each a cup of tea. "Fix your own, and I'll do likewise. How did you discover my leathers had been tampered with?"

"I didn't." Cato munched slowly, some of the ire draining from his posture. "Peak showed me. He wipes down any gear that's been used, but especially if it's been out in the wet or left to sit in the sun."

Trent made a mental note to have a word with Peak—as soon as he figured out which stable hand answered to that name. "So my leathers were cut. Somebody found it amusing to try to put me on my arse in the mud."

"Dane Hampton died on his arse in the mud," Cato shot back. "That wasn't amusing in the least."

And Cato and Dane had been close, within the limits of their respective stations and the egalitarian spirit of the hunt field.

"The viscount was also drunk and attempting to jump a

damned gate any other man would have simply opened and ridden through. He wasn't on his own horse, either."

"How did you know that?"

Trent paused for a tactical sip of his tea. "Old gossip in the clubs, Cato, but hardly relevant to my stirrups."

Cato dusted his hands—his sandwich had been demolished—and rose to stare out the window at the gray, windy day. "He was on *my* horse, one of the best hunters I've trained."

"Ah." Then when Cato didn't say anything more, "My condolences."

Cato nodded without turning, but in the tension in his frame Trent saw confirmation that Cato had come under suspicion. As if an owner could tell a horse to sacrifice itself in the intentional murder of its rider?

Death by equine accomplice? "Was Dane's equipment in good order?"

"Absolutely. Peak could testify to that because he groomed for the meet that day, and Peak's word is good."

"You think somebody tried to cast suspicion back on you by tampering with my saddle," Trent suggested, taking Cato his tea.

Cato stared down at the steaming cup. "Somebody is trying to walk me to the gallows, and you're serving me tea? I am your stable master, my lord, need I remind you?" He took the cup and drank anyway.

"Best not to drink alone, and my mama swore by the ability of a nice hot cup of tea to ameliorate every woe."

"Daft," Cato muttered, finishing his tea in two swallows.

"More?"

"Go to hell, your lordship."

"Better." Trent set the empty cup aside. "Who are your enemies?"

"I'm Irish. Many find that offense enough."

"You're an Irish stable master who cleans up well enough,"

Trent countered. An Irish stable master who'd likely not been compensated for the loss of an excellent horse, too. "This makes you a coveted commodity in some corners."

Cato's shrug was a study in indifference. "I write to my mother once a month, and she reports all at home is quiet, or as quiet as home gets. The lads seem content. The neighbors put up with me because I'm decent with the hounds. A better question is, who wants to bring harm to you?"

Trent leaned back against his desk and considered the theory that Cato wasn't the target of the miscreant, but rather, harm to Trent himself was the intended result.

"Slicing the stirrup leathers would be a chancy way to bring a man down," Trent murmured. Though a fall from an eighteen-hand horse was not a short tumble. "Those leathers could have broken right at the mounting block or been switched to somebody else's saddle. If I'd kept Arthur to the walk, the damage would likely still be unnoticed."

Cato stalked over to the teapot and poured himself another cup. "Which suggests if you're the target, whoever is taking aim can't get inside your house, or hasn't yet."

Cato's concern for his employer, grouchy though it was, warmed Trent's heart, Would Wilton's stable master have made this great a fuss if the earl's well-being were threatened?

"Maybe the malefactor doesn't own a gun," Trent suggested. "My life is hardly of great value. I've my heir, a spare, and a healthy brother in the wings. The succession is secure, leaving me more or less expendable."

The notion would not have been at all disquieting only a few weeks ago. On the contrary, Trent might have viewed it as a consolation.

Perhaps he was daft—or had been.

Cato sat to stir sugar and cream into his tea. "You can't seriously regard yourself as expendable."

"Of course I do." Trent joined him on the couch and poured himself a second cup. It wasn't brandy, but on a cold, windy day, hot tea held some appeal. "We're all expendable, and Dane's example underscores the reality."

"He did not regard himself as expendable," Cato growled, stirring his tea…pugnaciously?

"He regarded your horse as expendable, and if the wheels are expendable, the cargo is at risk. Another sandwich?"

Cato took a second sandwich. "I've never met such a polite baby earl with such a poor grasp of his station."

"Being referred to as a baby earl will strain that politesse considerably, though speaking of earls, I'm jaunting over to Wilton on the first of the week."

"Papa summoning you to his side?"

"His steward is." Damn the man to darkest hell. "I have Wilton's power of attorney and must occasionally put in my appearance if the merchants are to be paid."

Cato tossed back his tea like so much gin and refilled his cup. One would think the man was thirsty for it—nigh parched, in fact.

"I didn't realize Wilton had handed over the reins. Decent of him, I suppose. I can't abide those old fools who leave their sons racketing about, waiting to inherit while Papa goes drooling and doddering off to the Lords each year."

Stout black tea made Cato loquacious.

"I didn't realize my stable master had an opinion on such a matter," Trent said evenly. Cato met his gaze only for an instant, before picking up a third sandwich. "Catullus, doesn't your employer feed you?"

"Below-stairs we get the coarse bread, the tough meat and the butter about to turn," Cato said. "Makes a man appreciate decent fare when it finds him. And your mama and mine would agree about the restorative power of a hot cup of tea."

While he stirred sugar into his tea, Trent added Cook to Peak's name on the list of employees he needed to have a word with. "You'll keep an eye on Lady Rammel for me when I'm off to Hampshire?"

Cato shot Trent a puzzled look. "Has she become prone to wandering?"

"She'll be working on the gardens, weather permitting, and likely bringing Miss Andy along with her."

"Miss Andy." Cato paused in his pillaging of the tea tray and sat back. "The child does not hold your stable master in affection."

Trent saluted with his tea cup. "A young lady of discernment. What of Lady Rammel? Does she share her daughter's disdain of you?"

Though why that inquiry was relevant, Trent did not know.

"Step-daughter," Cato said. "Her ladyship has no quarrel with me that I can detect. I'll look after them when they're on the grounds. How long will you be gone?"

"Less than a week. I do not enjoy my visits to the family seat, but needs must." He loathed the very sight of the place.

"Send your brother," Cato said, popping a tea cake with pink icing into his mouth. "Isn't that what younger sons are for?"

Trent set his cup down gently. "For a man whose expertise is horses, you are well informed regarding the doings of the Quality."

"Cut line, my lord." Cato delicately patted his lips with a serviette and rose. "The help always keep an eye on the Quality, and the Quality never even see the help. This is how civilization moves forward. What are we to do about your stirrup leathers?"

"Repair them."

"For the love of God…" Cato put his fists on his hips and glared at his employer. "Somebody tried to *kill* you, for all you know. Repair them… Bloody hell, Amherst, do you want to die?"

"We don't know if death was the object of the exercise." Trent rose and held out the plate of tea cakes. "For now, I'd say swear Peak to discretion and keep the saddle room locked."

"Amherst," Cato expostulated, "if tampering with the stirrups failed, then you must watch out for other avenues. Warn Cook, because poison is easy and the staff will always be blamed. Keep the footmen around you when you're far from the house. Stay the hell out of the woods, because poaching is considered tame sport by the locals, and don't let anybody know your plans in advance."

All very reasonable precautions. "You have a peculiar sense of how to go on when a mere prank is under discussion, but I'll heed your advice, to the extent practical."

Cato sighed mightily and before he quit the library, took two more tea cakes, having an apparent preference for pink icing. "At the very least let your family know what's afoot, and give serious thought to who could mean you harm."

"Sound advice." Trent walked with his stable master toward the door. "My thanks for your concern."

"Sleep with one eye open," Cato warned. "Better yet, don't sleep alone."

"Is that any way to address your betters, Catullus?"

"You're showing me to the *front door*, Amherst," Cato retorted, his tone long-suffering. "I'm not even considered an upper servant."

"This does appear to be the front door, and I'm tucking the last sandwich into your starving pocket," Trent said. "It's the least I can do when you denied yourself a lifetime of Cook's charms to tend my stables."

"Ever your humble servant." Cato bowed elaborately, accepted the linen-wrapped sandwich, and sauntered out the door.

Trent munched a tea cake of his own—one with lemon icing—and hoped that last part about being ever his *humble* servant had been the only lie to pass Cato's lips.

CHAPTER FIVE

The evening spent with Drew Hampton had yielded two results in addition to cut stirrup leathers. By virtue of delicate questioning over the port, Trent had learned that the Rammel heir was all but terrified of taking responsibility for young Miss Andy. A session of gentlemanly small talk was little price to pay for reassurances that the viscountess's authority over the child was safe.

The second, less sanguine result was an invitation to join Drew Hampton and the Earl of Greymoor, considered the local expert on horseflesh, in a review of the equine stock gracing the Deerhaven paddocks.

After more than two hours spent tromping around the wet fields and chilly barns, Greymoor and Hampton had volunteered Trent to explain the situation to the viscountess.

According to Hampton, that good lady had had the sense to remain indoors in a cozy private parlor. Trent tapped softly on the door, no doubt closed to keep in the heat of a fire on this dreary day. No response greeted him even after he tapped again, so he opened the door, expecting to find that her ladyship's whereabouts had changed without notice to the new viscount.

Lady Rammel was the sole occupant of the room. She sat in a rocking chair by the fire, a shawl around her shoulders, an afghan across her knees, while she slept, her chin dipped low. She was an endearing sight, all tucked up and warm, slightly rumpled by her slumbers.

Trent endured an impulse to kiss her awake. Not a naughty kiss, just a pressing of the lips to her cheek, or her forehead. A sweet kiss, a token.

And a stupid idea, if ever his brain had produced one.

He stepped back and drew the door closed, then rapped loudly from the corridor. He was rewarded with a sleepy summons, after which he paused an extra moment to give the lady a chance to compose herself. When he entered the room, he closed the door behind him, warmth being a greater priority between a widow and a widower than strict propriety.

"My lord." Lady Rammel smiled up at him, though when tousled and sleepy, she struck him as more of an Ellie than a Lady Rammel. "Please have a seat, for I'm loath to leave my comfy nest. Has Drew offered you tea?"

"He did." Trent lowered himself to the end of the sofa near the rocker. "Greymoor is with him, decimating your crème cakes as we speak."

"Cook will be pleased. You look like a man with something on his mind beside the pleasantries."

"I do?" That she could perceive as much was unnerving. "How is that?"

"You're...animated. You've sprung your mental horses. Did Drew say something to offend?"

"Amuse, maybe. He's not much of one for sport, is he?"

She straightened the shawl around her shoulders, a silky green paisley shot through with gold, the furthest thing from mourning colors. "He and Dane had some kind of cousinly agreement. What the one did well, the other eschewed, or appeared to."

"What does Drew do well?" Besides talk. The man could talk as incessantly as two little boys in anticipation of a visit from Father Christmas.

"He loves his books, and he's known as something of a collector of tea ware. I've been to his estate only once, but the place is packed with little gems of porcelain and silver, and his kitchen served the most exquisite fare."

The prospective viscount was also handsome, titled, and amiable—and sharing a roof at Deerhaven with the grieving widow. This was of no moment whatsoever, nor did it matter that the law offered no prohibition against marrying a cousin's widow.

"He'll find the title an imposition," Trent predicted.

"Dane certainly complained of it, but you didn't brave my company to listen to my biography of the Hampton cousins."

Brave her company, indeed.

"I did not." Trent sat forward and rested his forearms on his thighs, hands linked between his knees. "I'd like to put an idea before you, and I will apologize in advance if you aren't disposed to consider it."

Her ladyship waved a freckled hand. "Say on. I'm not easily offended."

"I want to purchase your broodmares, or most of them."

Her ladyship grimaced, though even that expression was attractive on her. "They are mine, aren't they? They're very pretty, and Dane enjoyed having them, but I honestly hadn't thought much about what comes next. I suppose they'll need a deal of hay and oats come winter."

"They're broodmares," Trent said, sitting back, because "no" hadn't been the first word from her mouth, and he scented the pleasurable business of a negotiation before him. "Dane was lax about ensuring they performed their intended function."

"I've wondered if he didn't have some kind of premonition." She traced a fold in the afghan on her knees. The colors were blue and green, the same shade of green as the shawl, putting Trent in mind of her gardens under a summer sky. "Dane died just as foaling season would have been getting under way, and what a nuisance that would have been, to contend with foaling in his absence."

Trent finished the thought. "You haven't been of a mind to breed the mares in the last few months, which is understandable."

Her brow knit, and she stopped fussing with her plumage. "Understandable? Why understandable?"

"Because you are in mourning? Putting a crop of foals on the ground eleven months hence is not a priority at the moment, is it?"

"Are they good horses?"

Bargaining was one thing and lying to a lady another. "Very good. Greymoor was impressed, and he turns down some of the mares people bring to put to his stud."

"This discussion doesn't make you uncomfortable?"

"No more than you. Little horses come from big horses, much the same as little people find their way into the world. It isn't complicated, on one level."

He batted away the *uncomplicated* image of a nearly naked Lady Rammel singing to his fishes.

Her ladyship smiled at her hands, the same secretive, female smile he'd seen once before. He wondered if she were breeding and then wondered where such a strange notion had come from. By force of will, he kept his gaze from straying to her middle.

The smile, alas, disappeared. "So we'll haggle over my mares. Unless I should keep them and breed them for myself?"

"Do you want to turn Deerhaven into a stud farm?"

She turned her head, rubbing her cheek over the shawl

draped over her shoulder. Lanie made the same gesture when tired or out of sorts if her favorite blanket was at hand.

"Really, my lord, who in his right mind would buy horses from a stud farm owned by a female? I like the mares, but I have neither the expertise nor the correct gender for such an undertaking."

"I do," Trent countered. "What I lack is a bottomless supply of ready coin."

"You are fearless," she marveled. "Coin and breeding in the same discussion. Why would you admit such a thing?"

"So you'll understand my motivation." Trent rose and propped an elbow on the mantel, ideas tumbling in his mind. "I'd have to buy them over time, making payments, or providing goods or services in kind."

Her ladyship sat up a little straighter in her rocker. "We haven't even agreed on a price. Is this how you fellows go at your business, all willy-nilly?"

"Some of us." Trent admired the lack of dust on her mantel—his own mantels were not nearly so pristine—and wondered whether he even had fishing poles at Crossbridge. "I've plenty of wealth, but I tied up a great deal of it in trusts for my children, in part to comply with my wife's wishes and in part to safeguard the children from my father's machinations in the event of my untimely demise. Then too, I'm a firm believer in investments that grow steadily, rather than riskier schemes."

"But you lack the kind of cash you think my mares are worth?"

"I lack a willingness to deplete my cash that greatly with a single, speculative purchase." He had the cash, easily, if he were to break his children's trusts, which was not a consideration.

"So you're prudent. One has concluded as much even based on our brief acquaintance. If the mares are as fine as you say, then wouldn't they make a sound investment?"

Was prudence truly a virtue? Her tone gave Trent leave to

doubt.

"To some extent, they are a sound investment, but if strangles or some other disease should sweep the shire, they're a flat loss. If they don't catch, if I lose them in foaling, if they throw foals that are too small, mean, over at the knee, cow-hocked—"

He'd made her smile, and that was lovely.

"Do hush, my lord. I'll be paying you to take them away before they eat me out of house and home."

"That's the idea, more or less."

She looked quite fetching in her shawl and blanket as she considered him. "You aren't joking, though I'm not about to pay you to relieve me of truly valuable horses."

"What if,"—Trent resumed his corner of the couch—"I provided the care, the feeding, the early training, and so forth, and you took a percentage of the profits?"

"What profits? Don't horses take nearly a year to carry their young?"

"Nearly, and then it's another two or three years before they can be sold as riding stock."

"Four years before I see any profit?"

"If such an arrangement with me has no appeal, you could sell them off now, but in any case you're better off breeding them before you do."

She did not appear offended at that blunt speech. "Because they're *brood*mares."

"And because Greymoor will lend you his stud to breed the lot of them at a very reasonable rate, rather than make you take the mares over to Oak Hall where he stands his stallion."

"Why would he be so reasonable? I've barely been introduced to the man."

"He'll be reasonable because he sees the quality of your ladies," Trent said. "His stud's reputation will be enhanced if the foals live up to their mamas' promise. Then too, summer is upon us, and it will soon be too late to breed anything. For

Greymoor, it would be a small windfall. He's reputed to be a decent sort. He'd do a good turn for a widowed neighbor."

Particularly if Trent nudged the earl stoutly in that direction.

"What would you do, if you were me?"

Interesting question—shrewd, actually.

"If I were a lady recently cast into widowhood, I'd be reluctant to embark on any substantial venture, particularly one that will take years to see a return—on the one hand."

"On the other hand?"

A gentleman would use a lot of pretty words to present the other hand. A gentleman would probably have left the door open, too, and to hell with staying warm when proprieties were at risk. A gentleman would not have mentioned breeding, Greymoor's stud, or profit, much less all in the same conversation, with a recently widowed lady.

Trent was apparently not that much of a gentleman.

"You're too damned smart to pretend you're content to crochet gloves and tat lace, Ellie Hampton. You are competent with horses, your estate runs like a top, and grieving doesn't preclude looking forward to a meaningful future. Your husband was letting those mares go to waste, and you can do better than he—much better. I think you should consider it, not for the money, not for the homage to your late husband's taste in horseflesh, but because you'd enjoy it."

Her hand went to her throat, as if a lump had formed there, while she digested this dose of plain speaking. "Gracious Halifax."

"My apologies. I did not mean to imply that *you* were going to waste, I simply…"

She waved a hand at him to shut him up, for clearly, he'd struck a tender nerve.

Or maybe he'd said the right thing to inspire her forward in any one of several positive directions. Inspiring the bereaved was a delicate, fraught art, as Trent well knew.

She studied a spot above his right shoulder. "I've always

liked horses, but Vicar warned me that mourning can be a time of folly, and I should not embark on any course impetuously."

Folly—an apt description for the last fifteen months or so of Trent's life.

"Heaven forfend you act impetuously with such a rackety fellow as I," Trent rejoined, but he wasn't teasing and his tone gave him away.

The lady's posture lost the last of its sweet, sleepy softness. "I am not inclined to set up a stud farm here, but I am loath to miss the chance to capitalize on those mares. Andy's future is less than assured, and ample funds for her dowry could address that situation."

Trent kept his tone diffident. "I suppose we could fashion some third alternative."

"Such as?"

She was being cautious or coy; either one, Trent had to approve of—they were, after all, negotiating.

"I don't know." He rose again and took up his spot leaning on the mantel. "Some combination of coin, services, breeding rights, shared profits…." He let the ideas hang in the air, just within her reach.

She shot him a dubious look. "You're suggesting a partnership."

"A partnership?" He mustered a disgruntled expression. "I suppose that's what it would be, if we both agreed. No offense, but I'd want the terms in writing."

"For both our sakes. You can't have a gentleman's agreement with such as I. What will your wife think of you taking on a lady partner in a business venture, because I would not want to be only a silent contributor."

Trent was preoccupied watching her ladyship's hands adjust the shawl and blanket. Competent, feminine, graceful… she had the sort of hands that—

"My *wife?* What would her opinion matter?"

"She is your *wife.*" Lady Rammel took a solid hold of the

rocker's arms. "Even Dane kept me informed of his major business activities and occasionally listened when I'd venture an opinion."

Trent was so taken aback by her question he nearly missed her use of the present tense: She *is* your wife.

"She can't venture an opinion," he managed.

"Why not?" The viscountess rose, shedding blankets and acquiring a hint of indignation. "Your decision materially affects her comfort and security, too, you know. Do you trust her to bear your children, but allow her no notice of your business associates?"

She lifted her hand as if to shake her finger at him, but that hand lost momentum, the color drained from her face, and Trent barely caught her before her knees buckled. For a single moment, she lay cradled against his chest, a fragrant, curvaceous and passive bundle of lithe female.

"I stood up too quickly," she murmured. "You can put me down, Amherst."

He settled her on the couch and sat next to her, one arm around her shoulders.

To his relief, she remained resting against him—fainting women were unnerving to any man. He could tell the moment she gathered her resolve to leave the sofa.

"Stay." He held her more snugly. "If you go rocketing about in mortification, you'll get lightheaded again."

"I simply rose too quickly," she replied, making as if to scoot away from him.

"Ellie,"—it seemed appropriate to use her name—"you'll have to tell Drew."

"Tell Drew?" She craned her head to glare at him. "They're not his horses."

"Not about the horses." He held her gaze, feeling nothing so much as compassion—for her, for what she was dealing with.

"Oh, blooming Halifax." She subsided against him,

defeated, caught out and, to Trent's mind, maybe even relieved.

"How far along are you, my dear?"

She sighed gustily. "Three months. We argued the night before Dane died and made up in one of our rare bouts of conjugal relations—I didn't just say that."

Oh yes, she had, and to *him*. "Of course not. Your children, like mine, will be found under a toadstool, left there by the fairies on a summer night."

"Winter night." She'd no doubt calculated her due date a thousand times already. "I haven't said anything because it's early days yet."

"And you weren't sure," Trent guessed, "it being your first. When and whom to tell are entirely your choice, my lady."

"Thank you."

She fell silent, though Trent had not one but three children and knew what to ask. "Are you nervous?"

"Terrified." She gave him more of her weight, and he smoothed her hair back the better to keep an eye on her profile.

"Greymoor's sending his countess over to visit with you. You must ask for her support. He claims she is formidable, and she's already presented him with his heir."

"Lady Greymoor? I've met her. She's a pretty little thing."

"And if she bore that great, strapping lout a child, you will fare easily."

"She is diminutive."

"While the earl is not." Not in his stores of charm, not in his equestrian expertise, not in any sense.

"Do you think Drew will be angry?"

"You can't concern yourself with that." Trent stroked his hand over her hair again, though her profile was plainly in view. "He had a life before Dane died. He'll have a life if you bear a son. Your first priority has to be bringing your child safely into the world."

"I know." She straightened a little, but only a little. "I must stop imposing on you like this. I'm becoming that pathetic widow who clings to and pets anybody she can get her hands on."

"You are not and you never will be. Shall I ring for tea?"

"A nice hot cup of tea?" She shifted away from him. "That couldn't hurt. I wonder where Andy got off to."

"She likely didn't want to disturb your cat-nap." Trent rose and went to the door to hail the footman—only to realize what he'd disclosed.

"You caught me napping?" Lady Rammel's—Ellie's—hand went to her hair. "I am to have no dignity, it seems. What would your lady wife think of me?" Her question was casual, even rhetorical, but it reminded Trent where their conversation had been before Ellie's spell of lightheadedness.

"You were haranguing me about my neglect of her. You need to understand something about my marital status."

Ellie's gaze skewered him, as if she anticipated one of those my-wife-doesn't-trouble-herself or my-wife-doesn't-understand-me soliloquies her husband had no doubt delivered to many other women.

"It isn't like that," Trent said, the accurate words for some reason hard to locate. "She's... Paula passed away more than a year ago. She's... dead."

* * *

"Why didn't you tell me Amherst was widowed?" Ellie chose her moment after the servants had withdrawn, firing off the question at Drew as he enjoyed a leisurely Sunday dinner with her.

"Why didn't I...?" He looked confused, resembling his late cousin not only in his robust physique and facial features, but also in his cautious, spare-me-from-testy-women expression. "Why didn't you know? I gather it's been some time, because he's no longer in mourning."

"He isn't at Crossbridge much at all, or he hasn't been since I married Dane," Ellie replied. "We were cordial, but barely acquainted. He and Dane had little in common. He seems recovered from his mourning, more or less."

He was steady and kind, and far too perceptive, in any case.

Drew picked up his wine glass and peered into its depths. "He *seems* like he enjoys your company, Elegy dearest." They were serving themselves, à la française, so Drew could speak freely.

As could Ellie. "What is that supposed to mean?" She twirled her wine glass, but spirits of any kind no longer appealed to her, just as the smell of tallow had become unbearable.

Drew took a meditative sip of his claret. "You're grieving. Finding comfort with a neighbor would be almost expected."

"Drew Hampton,"—Ellie's voice was stern—"you are half in your cups and you will apologize for your scandalous notions."

"Not scandalous." Drew patted her hand. "You're a widow now, Ellie, and your status has some benefits. Pass the decanter, would you?"

She set it near him much as she had often passed the decanter to her late husband. "You're not happy inheriting the title, are you?"

"I'm not happy with life." Drew poured himself more wine. "There you have it, the selfish, titled lord in the making. I'm a quick study."

"Is it the though of inheriting title making you miserable?"

"I'm not miserable, though I soon will be. Amherst and Greymoor spent much of their time warning me about predatory mamas, Prinny's greedy committees, and the unassailable imperative of setting up my nursery."

Rather than peevish, Drew sounded genuinely bewildered.

"Would you be relieved were the title to pass to someone else?"

"I'd have to die for that to happen, but yes, I probably would be relieved."

Amherst had told her she should be honest with Drew.

Good advice—much better advice than Dottie Holmes had handed out.

"You might get your wish."

"So you've been allowing yourself that comfort, have you?" Drew's smile was ironic. "That's fast work, Ellie my girl. I'll have to commend Amherst on his timing."

"*What?*"

"It's hardly news you and Dane weren't exactly setting the sheets on fire." Drew sipped his wine, gulped it, more like. "Even if you can't manage a bull calf, being the mother of what legally be Dane's only legitimate child will earn you something in the way of coin and respect."

Ellie rose in indignation. "You are not a very nice man when you over-imbibe, Drew Hampton. I am carrying Dane's child."

"Of course you are, love." Drew nodded his congratulations. Then he went still and peered up at her, all his nasty humor falling away. He grabbed her wrist when she would have stomped away.

"Of course you are." He repeated it as a statement, as if Dane had just clobbered him mentally with the truth. "Sit down, please." He set the decanter out of reach and rose to hold her chair. "Dane would be so pleased. How are you feeling?"

"Angry with you. Sometimes very angry with Dane."

"Most of us were, most of the time," Drew said, resuming his seat and covering her hand with his. "This changes things, Ellie." He sounded eager, not bitter.

"I might have a girl, Drew, and even if I have a boy, you'll be the uncle. You'll have to show the boy how to go on."

"I can do that. I think."

"Drew?"

"Hmm?"

Ellie withdrew her hand. "About Amherst. I haven't… He hasn't…"

"Of course not." He patted her wrist. "You're to be a mother." To Ellie's mind, that observation was a glaring non sequitur, but Drew wasn't finished. "We don't need to write to the solicitors just yet. You're feeling well?"

"Mostly." Ellie ducked her face, a blush rising. Why had nobody warned her? Pregnancy made one's personal business the happy topic of others' conversations, created peculiar relationships with cousins with whom one had been only cordially distant, and conjured pointless tears by the bucket. Worse, impending motherhood inspired one to kiss a handsome, kind, unsuspecting neighbor.

As if one were some strumpet on a corner in Seven Dials.

Drew chattered happily right through dessert, while Ellie passed on the trifle and recalled her earlier words. She *hadn't*, with Trenton Lindsey, hadn't...yet.

* * *

"Your lordship shouldn't be here."

Cook gave Trent the benefit of her opinion as she kneaded dough on a floured board. Like most of the women his father employed, she was buxom and comely in a sturdy, blond, English way. Her tenure at Wilton had been brief, because she was also outspoken and a shade more intelligent than the earl's usual underling. She hadn't been quite smart enough to keep her criticisms to herself, but she was clever as hell with desserts, and for that, Trent forgave her much.

She was trapped, up to the elbows in her floury dough, and thus unable to avoid the discussion Trent sought. "You shouldn't order me about when I've come to beg favors of a pretty lady."

She smacked at the dough with a closed fist. "You want your apple cake again so soon?"

"I will never turn down apple cake," Trent assured her, as the scullery maid decamped for the pantries. "If ever I fall into unconsciousness, you've only to wave a slice under my nose and I'll come right in a trice. The dessert menu wasn't on my immediate agenda, however."

Neither was flirting and flattering the help into doing their jobs, come to that.

"You're after some trifle then," Cook concluded heavily, as if her employer were a small boy who'd make himself sick on his sweets.

"I'm after some better fare for my staff," Trent said, his tone losing its teasing edge.

"Your people never go hungry," she shot back, smacking the dough over. "Never."

The footman blacking the andirons apparently needed to be elsewhere, too, which left Trent alone with the queen of his kitchen.

"The servants aren't hungry, though they're not satisfied, either. You're not at Wilton, Louise, and you needn't perpetuate my father's stingy ways."

"I beg your pardon?" She stopped her kneading, her disapproval of Trent all the more palpable for being silent. He couldn't tell if her ire was because he'd used her given name, or he'd dared speak ill of his father, whom she, for some reason, regarded as the apogee of all a titled head of household ought to be.

She ploughed her fist into the dough again. "His lordship the earl is not stingy. He practices economies, is all."

Wilton was a nipfarthing, penny-pinching, cheese-paring excuse for a peer.

"We needn't practice his economies here," Trent said, pleasantly of course, despite mention of Wilton. "Stop buying coarse flour for the servants' bread; stop setting the worst butter on their table; stop relegating them to viands only the hounds would enjoy. If you need me to establish their menus, I shall."

The bread dough took a sorry beating—as did Trent's patience—while he held his ground.

"Louise," he said quietly, "you may not like what I have to

say, but if you've some reason for putting poorer fare before the help, you've only to tell me. I'll listen and I won't turf you out for speaking up."

"You'll listen," she muttered, "and then you'll do as you lordly well please, like your papa. Don't blame me when you've no coin for your own."

Like his papa? Wilton would have let the woman go without a character when she'd presumed to criticize him for visiting his own kitchens.

"I would never blame another for my own woes, Louise, but does that mean you'll make me an apple cake tonight? I'm off to Wilton in the morning, and a piece or two in my saddlebags would see me nicely on my way to Hampshire."

Her expression became thoughtful, and the dough was allowed to lie on the board, thoroughly subdued. "You're for Wilton tomorrow?"

"I'm carrying letters from some of the other servants. Let me know if you'd like me to take a note or two for you."

"I will." She resumed abusing the dough, her expression shuttering.

"And Louise?"

"Cook, if you please."

"If I didn't say it before, I'm saying it now." Trent waited until she met his eyes. "You have my thanks, for staying here when I was not much in evidence. For not running off to a better post. For keeping my people fed when I wasn't paying enough attention."

She jerked her chin at the door. "Out of my kitchen with you. I've work to do."

"And an apple cake to make." Trent sauntered off, though he had the sense turning his back on Louise was not an entirely prudent course.

CHAPTER SIX

All the way to Wilton, through the shady bridle paths and farm lanes of Surrey, to the busier thoroughfares and cultivated fields, into the rich farmland of Hampshire, Trent considered a single, unexpected kiss.

Ellie—in his mind, she was Ellie now—had murmured some little platitude in response to his blurting out his widowed status. She'd gamely resumed their negotiation thereafter, not even fixing herself a cup of tea until they'd agreed to meet upon his return from Wilton and finalize details: She'd see to borrowing the stallion from Greymoor while Trent sent word to his solicitor to draft an agreement.

Then she'd walked him to the door of that cozy little parlor, leaned up, and kissed his cheek in parting.

And he, in a complete and irredeemable display of masculine miscalculation, had turned his head, to cadge another little whiff of her scent. Their mouths had brushed, caught, paused and then…

His mouth had come awake for the first time in years, startled into awareness by the unexpected softness of her lips on his. The rest of his body had followed at a roaring gallop, until he'd wrapped his arms around her, gathered her close, and reveled in a kiss so unneighborly, so unchaste, she'd been panting and dazed when he'd let her step back, likely horrified to the soles of her slippers.

Trent should have been horrified, too, and likely would be, when he had to see Ellie again, though first he hoped to talk himself out of wanting to kiss her exactly like that, over and over and over.

He'd been *starving* for such a kiss, going mad, shutting down, function by function, to cope with the ache of its loss from his life.

And he did ache, bodily, because Ellie had kissed awake his long-dormant lust, and now he could not argue or ignore it back to sleep. In hindsight, Trent could see all the instants she'd leaned on him or taken his arm, the times she'd been close enough to touch, the moments she'd allowed his body a little too near hers. His awareness had been stirring restlessly the whole while, threatening to come back to life, one sniff, one lean, one smile at a time.

Like a flaming spill touched to a well-oiled wick, a single kiss had him adjusting himself in his breeches two days later and completely unable to focus on the upcoming days at Wilton. Ellie's taste haunted him, for he'd driven his tongue into her mouth with no thought to teasing preliminaries, no pausing to silently ask permission. That kiss had been the most aggressive, glorious, *erotic* kiss he'd ever bestowed on a woman, and she'd been too stunned to do more than allow it.

He dismounted and jogged beside his horse in an effort to exercise off his lust, though he was soon winded and back in the saddle. He'd gained another mile in the direction of Wilton Acres, and no distance at all from his memories of Ellie Hampton and the desire they inspired.

* * *

"Amherst." Gerald, the Earl of Wilton, nodded coolly at his firstborn over a glass of excellent brandy. The future earl might have been a passably good-looking man had he not inherited both vulgar height and dark coloring from his blighted mother. Then too, Amherst had acquired a yeoman's complexion since last Wilton had seen him.

"Wilton." Amherst, ever inclined to the courtesies, bowed slightly and marched into the library as if he already owned the damned place. "You look well."

"For a prisoner?" Wilton gave the word a touch of ironic emphasis, though the situation was enough to make a peer of the realm into a Bedlamite. "Oh, I thrive here, Amherst, unable to vote my seat, unable to socialize with my peers save for the gouty baron or two in the immediate surrounds, hoarding up my allowance like a schoolboy. You cannot imagine all the ways I thrive."

"While you," Amherst replied evenly, "cannot imagine all the ways your children did not thrive, deprived of their rightful funds by your venery. Think on that, when you can't afford another couple of hounds."

The damned man was bluffing, though Wilton gave him credit for bluffing convincingly.

"You're here to pay the trades? I cannot think scolding your father sufficient reason to lure you from your busy life." Though from what the London staff had reported, napping and swilling brandy figured prominently on Amherst's agenda.

"I'm here to tend to the finances and to see you." Amherst poured himself a drink, which was a small victory. The civilities between father and son were such that the prisoner had not offered his warden a drink, though apparently one was needed.

"You'll see me depart for some grouse hunting," Wilton replied. "The season grows near, and journeying north takes time." Particularly when a man intended to tarry among the demi-reps in London for a few weeks first.

"Enjoy yourself." Amherst sipped with an appearance of calm, though the vein near his left temple throbbed. His mother had been given away by the same sign any number of times. "Know that Emily will be denied her come out if you go. Five years ago, you stole every penny of Leah's trust and all but cut Darius off. For five years, you will rusticate, or anyone you care about will suffer."

"You would not dare." Amherst had his mother's stubbornness, but none of her vitriol. Goading him was uphill work. "You would not dare to hurt Emily merely because I'm inclined to go shooting as I have every year for the past thirty."

Amherst studied his drink, while Wilton considered tossing his brandy at his son.

"You certainly dared to hurt Emily's siblings."

"Go to hell," Wilton spat and stalked toward the door. Before he could quit the room, he heard his firstborn son and heir murmur, "You first, Papa."

* * *

"It's the sweet time," Mrs. Haines told Trent when he and her two sons had come back to the farmhouse for a mug of ale. "Hay is off, shearing's done, the garden is producing well, and the crop is in the ground. The stock grows fat on summer grass, and the people can pause and rest up before harvest."

"Or grow fat on their mother's cooking?" Trent suggested, finding a perch on a sturdy porch rail.

Mrs. Haines' smile was the mirror of her sons' generally genial expressions. Hiram and Nathaniel shared their mother's blond hair, blue eyes, and sturdy proportions too.

"You're welcome to stay for the noon meal, my lord, though I'm guessing Imogenie Henly is pacing her parlor waiting for you to call on her papa," she offered.

"Her papa ought to be keeping his fowling piece handy," Hiram, the older son, muttered. "That girl will get some poor lad to the altar by first frost, but it won't be me."

His younger brother Nate held his mug over the porch

railing and let the last few drops of ale fall on the pansies below. "Won't be me either. I'll be too busy getting after the wood, tidying up the stone walls, clearing the brush from the bridle paths, or his lordship will know why."

"Those are suggestions," Trent said, downing the last of his drink. "Those tasks can all wait until after harvest, if need be."

Mrs. Haines collected three empty mugs. "That work had best not wait. Come November, the days are short, the nights are cold, and these two get cozy with their pints."

"As long as we're not cozy with Imogenie," Hiram retorted. "We'll get the work done, Mother."

"I know you will," Trent interjected, bowing his leave to Mrs. Haines. Both men accompanied him to the shady paddock where Arthur was munching grass. Nate took Arthur's bridle off a fence post and went to fetch the horse.

Hiram hung back, pushing dirt around with the toe of his big, dusty boot. "About Imogenie?"

"This isn't the Dark Ages," Trent replied. "You don't need the lord of the manor's permission to walk out with a pretty girl, Hi."

Hiram snorted. "I'm the last fellow she'd glance at. She's been spending time at the manor, my lord."

"At the manor?" Hiram's implication sank in, turning a pretty summer day sour. "Wilton's enjoying her favors?"

"Aye, if that man enjoys anything. The damned idiot female is trolling to become his countess, though her pa's a mere tenant, albeit a prosperous one. Wilton would no more marry her than he'd marry Henly's prize bitch."

"So why say something to me?" And yet, cleaning up after a father's messes was an oldest son's obligation. "I can't stop either one of them from their dalliance."

"Have a word with Henly's missus," Hiram suggested, "or send Imogenie to work at your London house."

Out in the paddock, Arthur, a good, dutiful beast, shuffled

toward Nate, having apparently napped and grazed enough for the present.

"If Imogenie thinks she'll be Wilton's next countess, she'll hardly take to service, Hiram. The best she could hope for in Town is to catch some tradesman's eye."

"Better that than dropping your pa's bastard on your doorstep."

"He's not that stupid." Wilton was that arrogant, however, and like a bully made to stand in the corner, he'd use any means to chafe against his banishment to the countryside.

Nate slipped the bridle over Arthur's head, then fed the horse a bite of carrot.

"For Imogenie's parents' sake, I hope you're right," Hiram said, taking out a plain linen handkerchief and mopping his forehead. "Ma says more than one man has thought himself smarter than God and learned differently."

On that note, Trent took himself to the Henly holding, where Mrs. Henly set out a mid-day meal fit for six kings. Young Imogenie was helpful to her mother, bringing plates and dishes to the table and refilling drinks, but the damned woman found ways to lean into Trent, to press against his arm, and brush her fingers over his.

She cast him portentous looks, simpered at his every comment, and flaunted her bosom all without drawing the notice of either parent.

A baggage. A thoroughgoing, scheming baggage who thought she was up to Wilton's weight, and likely believed herself possessed of Town airs. She was pretty, in a young, vivacious way that would fade all too quickly, particularly if she displeased Wilton.

"Perhaps Miss Henly would be willing to show me the orchard?" Trent suggested when the meal was done.

Her mother twittered, her father beamed—though, of course, the orchard was in plain view of the house and full of nothing but tiny, hard, green apples—and Imogenie fetched a shawl. When she came back to the table, she sported a lower décolletage under her shawl than she had previously.

"Your father is one of the hardest-working men I know," Trent observed as they strolled along. She was small, as Paula had been small, and Trent had to slow his steps to fit hers. "You must be very proud of your family."

"All he does is work," Imogenie replied, tossing her head. "Ma and the boys are no better."

"But look how well your property shows. Your mama grows not only vegetables, but all of those lovely flowers and herbs. Her cooking and her table impress as a result."

"Which means nobody ever has any rest," Imogenie spat. "These people know nothing but work and church and more work. It won't always be this way, though."

Trent gave up on subtlety because they'd walked far enough from the house to not be overheard.

"Miss Henly, if you think association with my father will change your circumstances for the better, you are sadly mistaken."

She met Trent's gaze with a depressing boldness. "That's not what *he* says. *He* says a woman with my looks can go somewhere. *He* says a clever woman can always find ways to better her lot. You don't know what Gerald's really like. Nobody does."

Gerald? God help her.

While bees droned lazily amid the branches overhead, Trent searched his manners and his honor for words that would avert looming disaster. Imogenie was young and believed herself in love, and worse, believed herself loved in return.

An orchard was a peaceful place in summer. Trent tried to gather some of that peace by studying the dappled shadows on the ground.

"Wilton tells you his wife didn't understand him, and that you're very special. He tells you he's been waiting years for a woman like you, and he can't believe his good fortune that you've noticed him. While he offers this flattery, he looks sincere and even bashful."

Trent suspected Wilton *practiced* looking sincere and bashful, for it was too great a mischaracterization to achieve casually.

"He wishes you'd been his countess," Trent went on, "and then he sighs and makes you feel such naughty, wonderful things, you want to give him everything a woman can give a man she cares for."

From her stunned expression, Trent concluded he'd repeated his father's litany almost point by point.

The dratted woman rallied in the blink of an eye. "You ridicule something you don't understand. His own children don't even love him. You're jealous of the attention he shows me."

The earl's hook was set, and yet Trent made one more try. "Miss Henly—Imogenie—Wilton is rusticating here for the first time in your memory because he stole from his children and worse. He may love you. I hope he does love you, but it's far more likely he's amusing himself with you and will cast you aside when the game has palled."

When she had a bastard in her belly and her life had been ruined before she turned twenty. Wilton thrived on ruination, the way a cancer grew until it destroyed the host that gave it life.

"You're an unnatural son," she declared, tugging her shawl tightly around herself. "To lie about your own father that way. He told me your sister ran off, brought shame and disgrace to the family, and your brother abetted her. Why should he keep such as those in funds?"

Wilton had driven Leah off, cast her onto her brothers' charity the way another man would fling away an empty gin bottle.

"Wilton spent money that wasn't his. He spent my mother's portion, reserved by contract in trust for her children—

contracts Wilton signed."

Imogenie turned her back. "I won't listen to this. The earl is a good man, and your mother never understood him."

The countess had understood Wilton too well, though too late. "Maybe she didn't, but your mother taught you not to allow a man, *any man*, favors until he's married you, or at least announced your engagement. That's sound advice, Miss Henly, and if you can't follow it for your own sake, then follow it for the sake of the children Wilton would get on you."

He stalked off—rude of him—knowing Imogenie glared daggers at his back. Without doubt, in a year's time, he'd be writing a bank draft to the girl's father and hoping she had relatives in the north to take her in for her confinement. According to Trent's late mother, the task of providing settlements for Wilton's bastards had fallen to her at least twice.

Wilton would leave the help at the manor alone as long as Miss Henly held his attention, which qualified as a pale silver lining—very pale.

Trent tried again with Henly when taking leave of his tenant on the farm's front porch. "You should consider curtailing Miss Henly's visits to the manor house, Henly."

Henly settled onto the porch swing, his expression disgruntled. "You'd begrudge my Genie a cup of tea with old Nancy Brookes? I didn't take you for that sort, Amherst."

Surely when Lanie was of age, Trent would not be so gullible a papa as Mr. Henly?

"I would not begrudge the ladies their tea and gossip, but my father has a wandering eye. He's bored, and Miss Henly is both pretty and of age." Trent backed up that blunt pronouncement with a very direct look, which had Mr. Henly chewing his pipe stem.

"I could send Missus with her."

"Every time. You absolutely cannot trust Wilton's honor, Henly. Cannot."

"Sorry thing to say about your own pa." Henly set the porch swing to rocking gently. "I've known the man since I was a lad and he was a spoiled young buck. Played hell with the ladies then, too. I'll watch the girl and so will Missus."

"Hiram Haines wouldn't mind walking with Imogenie of an evening," Trent suggested, though this gambit was pointless when Imogenie had her sights set on Wilton himself.

"Hiram's a good man. Works hard and plays a wicked game of darts. Not as wicked as his mother, though."

"Until next quarter then." Trent swung up on Arthur. "You'll have Mr. Benton send word to Crossbridge if you need anything."

"Will do." Henly saluted with his pipe. "Safe journey, milord."

Six more farms and Trent was ready to call it a long, hot, summer day. Aaron Benton, the land steward, met him on the Wilton Acres back terrace where they shared a pitcher of cold, fruity sangaree as the last of the light faded. They talked for two hours, sorting through this problem and that plan, until Trent was convinced he could leave the estate in Benton's hands for another quarter.

"I've warned Imogenie Henly's father the earl is importuning her," Trent said as they rose and walked through the darkness back toward the house.

"Fat lot of good that will do. She has her father wrapped around her finger, and she's a very determined young lady. Was that discussion why you didn't want me making calls with you?"

"In part." Also because tenants might speak more freely to the landlord if the steward weren't on hand. "You aren't smitten with Imogenie, too?"

Benton was blond, rangy, and had a ready smile and a store of charm. His family was well situated enough that he could have his choice of brides, and life here at Wilton had to be lonely for him.

"I am most assuredly not smitten with the buxom and naïve Miss Henley, Amherst. I've sisters, and I know how quickly a woman's dreams can lead her into folly."

Not only a woman's. "Speaking of folly, you'll tell me the moment Wilton attempts to leave the premises?"

Having this discussion in the dark with only the crickets to overhear it was easier on Trent's pride than the full light of day would have been, and Benton seemed to grasp this.

"Wilton can't get far," Benton replied. "The lads won't drive him, and we've put all the ammunition he might use where he won't find it. Short of holding us at gunpoint or trying to sneak off on horseback with a groom trailing him, there's little he can do."

An owl hooted off in the home wood, a warning to small, scurrying things to find cover.

"Who calls on Wilton?" Trent asked, because Wilton was nothing if not adept at charming the unsuspecting into doing his bidding.

"Tidewell Benning, occasionally. Baron Trevisham very infrequently."

Tidewell, as Paula's older brother, could claim a family connection, and yet, Paula hadn't cared for Tidewell, and Trent wasn't entirely comfortable to think of Tidewell and Wilton socializing. Baron Trevisham, on the other hand, Paula's father, Trent had genuinely liked.

"What about Thomas Benning?" For Paula had been less critical of the middle sibling.

"Tidewell comes alone, always bearing his parents' good wishes. I didn't see any harm in his calls."

Neither did Trent, exactly. "Don't let your guard down. Wilton has a little coin, and he can get Imogenie to buy him shot."

Benton's teeth gleamed in the darkness. "You're daft, and awake much past your bedtime. My regards to your family. I doubt I'll be up early enough to see you off."

"My continued thanks for all your hard work," Trent told him as they reached the house. "I'll see you in October."

"Sweet dreams, Amherst." Benton saluted with two fingers and disappeared up the stairs, because by agreement, he served not only as land steward but also as the house steward, and the earl's informal jailer. Nicholas Haddonfield had found Benton, said he was trustworthy, and left the details to Trent and Darius.

What a relief it had been for Trent, to stash Wilton into Benton's keeping, and get back to his brooding and drinking.

Trent's ride back to Crossbridge was a more thoughtful journey than the trip to Wilton had been. The situation with Elegy Hampton had become delicate, and in some regards, Trent dreaded seeing her again.

And in others, couldn't wait.

* * *

Ellie Hampton's late husband had kissed her a time or two, though Dane had limited himself to husbandly pecks on the cheek.

The difficulty was not that Ellie had been kissed.

The difficulty, Ellie admitted as she watched Trent Lindsey's big red gelding trotting up the drive, was that she had kissed Lord Amherst *back*, shamelessly, even passionately.

Far more passionately than she'd ever kissed her husband. Before Ellie could organize herself mentally for her guest's appearance, he was bowing over her hand and looking larger than he had a week or so past.

Also painfully kissable.

"Your travels to Hampshire were uneventful?" Ellie tossed out the question, hoping she sounded more composed than she felt.

"The usual business. Tenant calls, meeting with the steward. The Crossbridge gardens have come along nicely, though, which suggests I should absent myself further."

A silence fell. Ellie stared at his lordship's mouth, then

realized he'd *caught* her staring at his mouth. *Perishing Halifax.*

And then, they both spoke at once.

"My lady, I do apologize…"

And, at the same time, "I've never been kissed like that before."

A pause, and then they did it again.

"You haven't?"

And, "Not even by my husband."

Amherst went quiet, looking more than a bit wary.

"Shall we repair to the veranda, my lord?"

He offered his arm, and they progressed out of doors in the safety of silence. When Amherst had Ellie seated in the shade, he lowered himself beside her, which Ellie took as an encouraging sign.

Of…what, she wasn't exactly certain, but encouraging, nonetheless.

"Kissing you like that was badly done of me," Amherst said, sounding lamentably sincere in his contrition. "You're in mourning and in a delicate condition and the last woman who should have unwanted advances pressed upon her."

His kiss had been many things—badly done wasn't one of them. Neither was unwanted.

"My condition isn't that delicate," Ellie murmured, face flaming.

He glanced over at her, maybe at the truculence in her tone, and the first hint of humor came into his eyes.

"And it was only a kiss," Ellie added mulishly.

"Been telling yourself that, too, have you?"

"A nice kiss," she insisted. The humor—and relief—was more evident in Amherst's gaze now, and Ellie smiled, as well. "A very nice kiss."

"Like you've never had before. Then I did not offend?"

"You… did not offend. You… utterly flummoxed."

"I can admit to being flummoxed myself. We're to be business partners, one hopes, and such flummoxing is not well advised."

"When is it ever?" Ellie rose, bringing Amherst to his feet as well.

He winged his arm and led her down a shady path of white crushed shells, along beds of irises past their peak, and lily of the valley still making a good show.

"You're lonely," Amherst said, offering an excuse, not an accusation, the way he'd offered her a thorny pink rose not long ago. "You can't castigate yourself for that. You should castigate *me*, for knowing better and not behaving better."

Ellie considered the generosity and sense behind his comment, and rejected both. She'd been lonely every night of her married life.

"The way I kissed you might have been the same if Dane were alive. I was lonely then, too. Except, then I wouldn't have kissed you at all."

"Now you know you were lonely," he said, very gently. "The guilt and the knowing and the loneliness are trying. You should slap me, and that will tidy matters up all around."

"I'd rather kiss you again."

"Probably not well advised."

Probably? "Business partners and all that?" Ellie suggested, feeling more disappointment than relief.

"That. Then too, I've done my duty to the title, my lady. I'm not looking for entanglements, and you are…vulnerable."

Drat the man. Why couldn't he have been searching for a different word? A less honest word? Not that she was searching for entanglements, either.

"You kissed like a man who might be entangled," Ellie observed, pride be damned.

"Lady Rammel,"—he glanced around—"Ellie, just because I might be entangled doesn't mean you should be the one doing the entangling."

She had the thoroughly disagreeable thought he might be involved elsewhere—though his kiss had suggested he was overdue for some entangling.

"So, you were merely responding to the siren call of your breeding organs?" Ellie knew she should let the topic drop into obscurity *forever.* "Are you like Lord Greymoor's stallion Excalibur, then, to strut and paw before any female in season?"

And why was she abruptly more angry than embarrassed?

"I am not like Excalibur."

They crunched along the walkway, a pair of squirrels chittering and leaping about in the branches overhead, while naughty, naughty thoughts, about swords and entanglements, ran through Ellie's mind.

Amherst tucked a hand over her knuckles as if he were afraid she might flee—or make good on the previous slapping offer.

"Most honest men will tell you their thoughts closely parallel what passes for that stud's, my lady. How a fellow acts on those impulses is what separates him from the beasts."

More silence, thoughtful on her part, unfathomable on his. This was also different from Dane, whose thoughts were—*had been*—easy to read and generally lacking in variety.

Are these boots too worn?

Perhaps I'll pop 'round Tatt's and look at that pair of chestnuts.

Shall we give it go tonight, old girl? It's Saturday—no hunting tomorrow.

"What do you do with the loneliness?" Ellie asked. "With thoughts of a future reeking with sympathy, dull colors, and condolences? I am new to this business of being a widow, and I can't say I like it so far."

He maintained his silence, and the summer morning seemed to grow quieter around them.

Ellie hadn't been quite honest—she hated being a widow, and that was troublesome, but she'd also come to nearly hate being a wife. She studied the line of Trenton's Lindsey's broad shoulders, and kept that thought to herself.

CHAPTER SEVEN

"Lord Amherst," Ellie said, frowning in puzzlement a fraught moment later, "am I the one to offer apologies now?"

He blew out a breath, dropped her arm, and paced off a few feet, then shot her a look over his shoulder, part humor, part exasperation.

"Do you know you even *smell* kissable?" He turned his back on her again, his posture denoting irritation.

Or a need for a moment of bodily privacy?

"I can accuse you of the same transgression, my lord."

"We have a contretemps," he said, as if laying out the first part of a syllogism. "We're mutually attracted, lonely, and adult enough to realize it. If we don't change the topic soon, I shall kiss you again, and that can lead only to folly."

"Were we not considering a joint business enterprise," Ellie said slowly, "would it be permissible folly?" God in heaven, where was her dignity, that she would press him thus? And what was wrong with her, that she wouldn't quietly accept what her marriage had very strongly suggested: Most men would rather carouse on horseback in the rain and mud than spend time with her.

"If we were not contemplating a business venture, this folly might be slightly less impermissible," he said. "Though it's... May we sit?" He didn't wait for an answer but took her by the hand and led her to a secluded bench.

He kept her hand in his as he began speaking.

"I can dally with you, Ellie Hampton," he said, risking a glance at her. "I would like... I would *love* to dally with you, but I'm not the dallying kind, and I'd muck it up."

Must he look so dear as he said this?

With her free hand, Ellie swept his dark hair back over his ear. "How does one muck it up?"

He focused on the ground for a moment before he spoke, and Ellie had the sense a simple touch had distracted him. Out in the mare's paddock, the stallion trumpeted lusty intentions to the summer morning.

"People can hurt each other without meaning to," Amherst said. "They grow attached, and then disappoint each other, and that's why men keep mistresses."

A mare squealed, and the sound of hooves pounding across dry ground reverberated through the air.

"A man keeps a mistress to disappoint her?"

"To *not* become attached, to undertake folly in a manner that ensures nobody risks anything of value."

"Bearing Dane's child," Ellie said, brushing her hand through his hair again, "I am risking my life. You think the ladies of easy virtue don't know they're courting the same risk when they accept coin from their protectors?"

Amherst sat back, blinking. "Nothing that comes out of my mouth this morning is coming out right. I don't want to hurt you, and I'm not capable of protecting you from me while I'm dallying with you."

Dearer still—also exasperating. "You make this

complicated, Amherst. What if I protect me, and you protect you? Would that work?"

"You are determined to make a man feel desired." Amherst scrubbed a hand over his face and gave her a peevish-but-considering look.

"You are desired," Ellie assured him, surprised at her own boldness. "You must know that. The question here is, do you desire me? Or was that kiss a mere conflagration of unchecked instinct? I can accept it if it was, if you were caught unawares, and a little lonely yourself. I can be your business partner, Trenton, because raising horses is a good idea, and I know when Excalibur leaves that paddock, he'll be tired, but he won't be missing anybody in particular. I was married to Dane Hampton, for pity's sake, better known as the Ram himself, and if anybody understands about wayward male—"

Amherst shut her up with another kiss, this one very different from the last.

His kiss was a greeting and a surrender. He put his mouth to Ellie's quickly, almost as if trying to elude his own notice, then he stilled and stayed for a moment in that initial posture.

Ellie sighed against his mouth and sank her hand into the warm, silky abundance of his hair while he brushed his lips softly over hers. His arms went around her, bringing her closer, and then his thumb caressed her jaw, and his fingers traced her ear.

"I like that," Ellie murmured against his mouth.

He smiled and kept on kissing her, seaming her lips with his tongue, slowly, lazily. Gone was the pawing stallion *and* the prosy gentleman. In their place was the healthy, grown man bent on indulging in a kiss that should have been stolen, but was shared with increasing enthusiasm.

Ellie let him show her how to linger and be soothed, how to enjoy and be enjoyed in a single kiss. When he eased back, the peppermint taste of him was on her tongue, his scent was in her nose, and the contour of his long, lean, male body imprinted on her imagination.

"Here is what I can offer," he said, his arm around her shoulders, right where Ellie needed it to be when she was feeling floaty and lightheaded—and not as a function of her condition. "I can flirt with you, kiss you, give you every assurance you're a beautiful and highly desirable woman, Ellie. Carrying a child can leave a woman in need of reassurances. I can provide those reassurances."

Who would have thought that earnestness was a fine quality in a man's kisses but not in his lectures?

"However?"

He kissed her cheek and spoke very near her ear. "However, you have to promise me you'll not rush into this. I can be your distraction, your temporary toy, but you don't need to bed me, and I'm telling you, you should not."

Bed him. The very words made Ellie's body thrum. "This great caution is in aid of what? Is there a manual for this, too?"

"There is, and I've read it and you haven't, so attend me, and behave yourself." His admonition was underscored with a tightening of his arm around her shoulders.

And yet his voice was gentle. "I'll not let you rush into a situation like this, not so soon after your spouse has died, and not with me. I can protect you that much, and in a few weeks, when you're less fascinated with exerting your charms over my hapless self, you can step back, no harm done, a few pleasant memories stored up."

What he said made sense, but Ellie still felt a rejection in his words. A frustration, at the least.

"You are stubborn, my lord. But you kiss…"

"None of that. Those are my terms, and we'll not sign any business papers for at least the rest of the summer."

"We're to have a gentlemen's agreement?"

"We're to leave our options open. Your options open."

Ellie nuzzled his hand where it lay on her shoulder. Even his hands smelled good, so good it was difficult to consider his reasoning. They were to flirt but not gallop headlong for the breeding shed, which was resoundingly prudent. They were to start on their business venture but not make any irrevocable commitments or outlays of coin.

"We'll approach this your way," she said. "I know what you're thinking, Trenton Lindsey. You're thinking in a few weeks I'll lose my waistline, and dignity will prevent me from the worst mischief with you."

His eyebrows went up, and Ellie had the satisfaction of knowing she'd guessed his thoughts.

"The birth of her child should be a mother's focus," he said, like a man who knows he's on tricky ground—still.

"I've agreed to your terms." Ellie rose, and he was immediately beside her. "I haven't much choice, and they make sense." She had been married, and thus she knew that once a difficult topic had been aired, a man needed time to regain his balance. "Now, in your draft documents, you included a clause about exceeding loss projections, and it struck me as Draconian…"

She led him through the shaded gardens, into the sunshine, and back to the bench where they'd kissed, and when dear Trenton was knee-deep in an explanation of liquidated damages, she went up on her toes and kissed him again. A soft, sweet, kiss intended to distract him thoroughly from contract clauses of any variety.

So distracting, apparently, that she could take his hand and put it low on her abdomen. Trenton believed in issuing helpful warnings, and Ellie meant to put him on notice: She might be losing her waistline already, but she wasn't about to let that inspire any excesses of…dignity.

* * *

Arthur patiently listened to all of Trent's reasons for why a dalliance with Ellie Hampton was a wonderful, bad idea, an idea that had been adroitly disarmed aborning, Trent hoped. The woods were cool, and as Trent rode past the pond, he reflected that a protracted dip in the colder end might aid a man in marshaling his best intentions.

He was so lost in thought he didn't notice voices coming from his stable until he handed Arthur's reins to a slender, dark-haired lad who introduced himself as Peak.

"I have company?"

"Very large," Peak replied in an odd, husky brogue. "Blond, friendly, dotes on his mare. I've seen him at the hunt meets with Greymoor."

Trent resurrected a few curses a man with three children didn't make much use of, even though foul language was bad form before the help.

"The world's biggest broody hen has come to check on a chick. Spoil dear Buttercup rotten. Bellefonte takes the care of all in his ambit seriously, most especially that mare."

Peak scratched Arthur's withers, provoking a sigh from the gelding. "His lordship's going a round with Cato over docking tails. They'll be at it all day."

"You can escape the line of fire by walking Arthur out." Trent did not run up his stirrups. "In the shade of the woods might suit."

Peak gave him a momentary, charming smile and swung onto Arthur's back without benefit of a mounting block. His feet didn't reach the stirrups, for he was a good foot shorter than Trent, and he had to cross the leathers over the gelding's neck, but Arthur obligingly toddled off toward the woods nonetheless.

"Amherst." Nick Haddonfield emerged from the stables, grinning broadly. "One of my two absolutely favorite brothers-by-marriage." He treated Trent to the kind of careful hug he probably gave his grandmother. "Leah sends her love, as do Ford, Michael, and probably Lanie, when she isn't bellowing about her nappy being wet."

"Darius unleashed you upon me," Trent said, ignoring a pang of guilt at the mention of his children. "He must not only spy himself, he must send reinforcements. Come along, because this spying business works both ways. How is my sister?"

They caught up on Leah, the various children, and Emily's summer thus far with Nick's grandmother, Lady Warne. When the civilities had been observed and a plate of sandwiches demolished, Nick yawned indelicately.

"Beg pardon. Woke up too early."

Trent rose, happy to dodge the real inquisition for another hour. "I'll show you to a room. You've yet to tell me how long you can stay." He paused at the library door to give instructions to a footman, then led Nick up to the next floor.

"I apologize for not sending you a note." Nick trailed along beside him, no doubt inspecting the state of the plaster (dusty), the carpets (in need of beating), and the windows (in need of a good scrubbing with vinegar). "My peregrinations are sometimes hard to predict. You're an afterthought to a visit to my brother Ethan at Tydings."

"Three miles northeast or so?"

"Roughly. Pretty place, and he's held it for some seven years, but I'd yet to visit. If you've a suitable bed, I could use a room tonight."

Trent's brother-in-law was the largest man he'd ever beheld, and all of it muscle or charm, depending on Nick's mood.

"I don't have state chambers, but come along, we've at least one formal guest room from bygone days that sports accommodations worthy of you."

"I knew I married well. Having imposed on your hospitality, when will you reciprocate and come see us at Belle Maison?"

Well, of course. Thumbscrews, applied to Trent's paternal conscience with every appearance of bonhomie. Nicholas was family, after all.

"Aren't you observing mourning for the late earl?" Trent asked as he opened the door to a large guest room. "Sending the children to their aunt for a summer visit is one thing. It's another to impose myself on you."

"Papa considerately forbade deep mourning except in public, and that for only six months." Nick followed him into the room, his gaze traveling up to the twelve-foot ceiling. "This will do, Amherst, and nicely."

"So I'm to call you Bellefonte?" Trent opened the French doors to the balcony because the room was a trifle musty.

"You're welcome to try, though I might have to take exception and toss you down into those roses."

Trent peered over the railing. "Or whatever they are. My neighbor is taking the gardens in hand as a sort of charity project, but progress is slow."

"What of your housekeeper?" Nick asked, resting his elbows on the railing beside Trent. "Has she taken a holiday from dusting and cleaning your windows?"

"Darius didn't tattle? My housekeeper ran off with my steward nigh six months ago, and had my stable master not alerted Dare to the situation, I'd still be sitting on my pickled and indifferent fundament in London."

Or he'd be…damned near dead. He deserved thumbscrews, at least.

Nick's gaze stayed on the gardens, which were plot by plot coming under control.

"Say something, Nicholas. This is a sneak attack, and you wouldn't stoop to such tactics were you not concerned." Which was the primary reason Trent bestirred himself to graciousness.

"Leah was concerned."

Trent lowered himself onto the balcony's chaise. "For that I am truly sorry. I suppose my children have expressed concern as well?"

"Not overtly." Nick turned and braced his elbows on the railing, six and a half feet of doting brother-in-law at his handsome ease. "Whatever difficulties you're having, you've managed to shield the little ones from most of them."

"I was wallowing," Trent said tiredly. Nicholas was too damned large and fit for Trent to toss into the gardens, and he was a good confidante.

"In?"

"Grief?" Not quite the right word. "Relief, anger, I don't know what. Sadness, maybe, an aching, endless bodily fatigue and a mental fog as thick as any London has produced."

"I am almost certain Leah is carrying," Nick said slowly. "I'm realizing now, as I hadn't previously, that childbirth is a dangerous undertaking. I could lose the wife I love more than life itself. You went through three pregnancies, and then you did lose your wife. This… terrifies me."

The quiet admission said a great deal—about Nick's courage, more than anything.

"Those who've lost a spouse can frighten those who haven't," Trent said, though it was insightful of Nick to present the topic this way. "Men I thought were my friends suddenly looked at me as if I might purloin their wives or daughters. Women I thought were my friends started pairing me with strangers or trying to get into my bed."

Nick's blond eyebrows rose. "Was that a silver lining of some sort?"

Trent gave the thorny roses beneath the balcony further consideration.

"Suppose not." Nick straightened, frankly studying Trent. "You've lost some of that peaked, city-boy look you had at the wedding."

"I've yet to replace my steward, so I'm playing steward, but I need to inquire into who's ordering my housemaids about. I thought Cook might have taken a hand, but apparently not."

"You want a fat housekeeper," Nick stated briskly. "A jolly, fat housekeeper who likes pets and children. A cranky housekeeper is worse than a wrinkle in the underlinen. And I suggest you let that cheeky nursery maid of Michael's go, too."

"Hull?"

"Big…" Nick humped his hands over his chest. "Saucy mouth? She pinches the children, and not like your granny pinched you, and she tipples."

"Write a character and give her some severance," Trent said, feeling another stab of guilt. "How about if I give you a minute to settle in here and then I show you some of the grounds?"

"Give me an hour." Nick began to undo his sleeve buttons. "I'd like to pen a few notes, rest my eyes, and get my bearings."

"In an hour then, and for all that you're here on inspection, I am glad to welcome you, Nicholas."

Trent made his way to the kitchen, wondering what was wrong with him, that he hadn't noticed the effects of the housekeeper's absence until Nick was underfoot. Trent's meals showed up on time, his sheets were changed, his laundry and ironing done, but the house itself—

Could be set to rights.

He spied his cook, cleaver in hand, cutting a chicken carcass into parts. "Greetings, Louise."

"Your lordship." *Thwack!* Off came a wing.

"I come bearing correspondence for you from Nancy at Wilton."

Thwack! The other wing, then she paused and set her cleaver aside.

"A moment, please." She turned her back to wash her hands then dry them on her apron. "I trust all are well at Wilton?"

Trent passed her the letter. "As well as can be expected when the earl conducts himself like a spoiled eight-year-old."

"You show him no respect." Louise frowned at the letter as she recited her litany. "He's an earl, a peer of the realm, and above the common touch."

"We've another earl visiting our humble abode," Trent said, unwilling to be scolded by his help. "Bellefonte has come to call, and we'll need a meal for a hearty appetite."

Louise fingered the epistle from old Nancy, the former

housekeeper at Wilton Acres. "Bellefonte's that big git? Shoulders like this?" She braced her hands a yard apart.

"Language, Louise. My dear brother-in-law is an earl, not a git, and due respect on that basis alone, in your opinion. He's been traveling and likely has a hunger in proportion to the rest of him."

"Beef then, and pork, at least. Formal?" She sounded so damned hopeful.

"*Not* formal. We'll eat on the terrace, and Louise?"

"That's Cook to you, my lord." She was already bustling off, apparently taken with the challenge of the evening meal.

"Who's been seeing to the housemaids?"

Louise shrugged as she tore the chicken wings apart with her bare hands. "They see to themselves. If they get to squabbling, Upton will stick his nose into it, but he's not good at it. Lets 'em get away with too much."

"Do you approve of any living male, Louise?"

"Alfred the Great," she replied, eyeing the pantry mouser sunning itself in a window sill. "Wilton."

"Equally useless, the pair of them."

Trent exerted his lordly prerogative and left before Louise could get another word in. He found Nick an hour later on the back terrace, scribbling away at a letter to some sibling or cousin.

Nick tossed his pen down. "Did I see Greymoor's stud disporting among your neighbor's mares?"

"Is there anything that escapes your notice, Nicholas?"

Nick wiggled his eyebrows. "Little of that nature. I am missing your sister terribly, too, so Excalibur pursuing his intended purpose would not escape my notice. He's an elegant beast, if on the small side. And loud."

"If one is breeding mounts for ladies, a smallish stud serves better," Trent pointed out. "Now that you've brought up the topic of horses, let me apprise you of a project I'm considering."

He went on to describe the potential for a breeding operation undertaken with his neighbor, who was in a position to supply the mares, while Trent had the labor, land, know-how and connections.

While they talked they wandered down the stable aisles, along paddock fences, through the gardens, and into the woods. When they came to the pond, Trent settled on a boulder and considered his sister's husband.

"How's the earldom coming along?" Because interrogation could be a game played by two, and Nicholas, for all his genial charm, looked tired.

"Earling is trickier than I thought it would be," Nick said, scooping up a handful of pebbles. "Papa had some unfinished business, and those chickens are coming home to roost now, on my watch. I find myself thinking, I'll have to bring this up with Papa, or let him know what I think about that, and then…"

"No Papa," Trent said softly. "Aggravating, and it keeps happening long after you think it wouldn't."

"You still miss your wife. How long has it been?"

"Close to a year and a half. I used to know how many days and months, exactly, without even trying to keep track." When had that changed?

"So you're making progress. My friend Axel Belmont is a widower, and he says you're making progress when you can admit the things you don't miss about a departed spouse."

"Then I started making progress fairly early." A pair of red squirrels went skittering overhead, nimbly jumping from the limbs of a stately chestnut to the neighboring oak. For some reason, this put him in mind of kissing Ellie. "The wife my father chose for me was not a restful woman, and I am not one who appreciates dramatics."

Nick tossed a pebble into the center of the pond, rings rippling out to form a target on the water's surface.

"I do not know why the Lord in His mercy gave me your

sister as my spouse, for I could not have chosen a better mate had I been intent on the goal," Nick said. "But what do you do for companionship?"

Trent watched the squirrels go dancing around the tree trunk, then dash from branch to branch as easily as if they'd been on solid ground. Amid a chittering scold from the one little beast, the other caught up and commenced fornicating right there in the trees.

"Drink, I suppose, though that wasn't going so well." A spectacular understatement.

"Seldom solves the real problems in this life. We've some friendly maids out at Belle Maison. You might consider a visit."

"And dip my wick?" The idea held no appeal, and that was... vaguely disquieting. "What about to retrieve my children?"

"I was wondering if you'd ask." Nick tossed two pebbles into pond this time, so overlapping target patterns formed. "If you need more time, Amherst, we're happy to keep them. I have Ethan's pair, too, and with four little boys underfoot, the summer promises to be riotous good fun."

Riotous and good fun were contradictions to Trent's way of thinking. "You like all that commotion?"

Nick tossed another pair of pebbles. "Belle Maison is huge. Large enough that a family of twelve can rattle around in the family wing without bumping into each other. And yes, I like having friends and family on hand, and I think Leah does, too."

"Where you can manage us."

"Look after you." Nick threw an entire shower of pebbles into the pond. "Though I wouldn't have to if you'd recruit a good woman for the task."

Trent rose, needing to get away from such a topic. "Not you, too, Nicholas."

"It isn't good for a man to be alone," Nick quoted. "Nor any damned fun, just ask Excalibur."

"I am not a randy stud colt," Trent shot back. "Having fun

can have serious consequences." Why was he having to explain this more than once in a day?

Nick rose and dusted his hands together. "Do you mean to tell me you've been a choir boy, Trenton? No wonder the decanter has had so much of your attention. Heed me, for I know of what I speak: You find a woman who knows the rules, and you pleasure her witless and yourself as well. Does a man a power of good and leaves the lady in better spirits, too."

"You make it sound so simple." Trent jammed his hands in his pockets and started back toward the bridle path.

"Trenton," Nick said patiently, "it *is* simple: your pizzle, her quim, you both enjoy each other until you can't move. Nothing simpler. You have three children, for pity's sake, need I draw you diagrams?"

"With my own wife, it was not simple." He should have left matters there, changed the subject to something harmless and genial, and deflected any further attempts on Nick's part to pry.

Though that approach to difficult topics had left him skinny, tired, befuddled and emotionally...rancid.

As Nick fell in step beside him, Trent's mouth kept uttering words. Calm, awful words.

"Imagine that you ride on home to Belle Maison, and you find your Leah, whom you love, shut in her chambers and unwilling to come out. You consider maybe it's the female complaint and tend to a few hours' correspondence, visit the nursery, the kitchen—she has neglected to provide the cook menus—your steward, but she still doesn't show up at dinner."

Nick walked along beside him for a few silent moments. "Leah wouldn't do that."

"You hope not, but suppose she did, and this went on for three days, until her maid tells you in all that time, she hasn't left her bed, except to use the chamber pot."

"I'd assume she was ill," Nick said, his gait slowing. "I'd hope she was ill."

"But she's not." Trent walked ahead a few steps of his guest. "She's physically, in every sense, sound, but in her bed, weeping and weeping, and she doesn't want you to touch her, or talk to her, or even be in the same room. She shrieks like you've taken a knife to her if you even sit on the bed or open a window shade."

"I'd call for the physicians. Reluctantly."

"They can tell you nothing." The brave few had suggested a repairing lease for her ladyship at one of those walled rural estates in the North, and Trent—God help him—had been tempted. "They suggest you bleed her, because she melancholic humors plague her."

Nick kicked at a rock and sent it sailing a good dozen yards. "It wasn't her menses?"

"Wilton chose her for me." The rock came to rest against a half-rotten stump, from which toadstools sprouted. "I am confident dear Papa knew exactly what he was about."

"Why would he choose such a weak vessel for his own heir?"

"I have not the first clue, but I will retrieve my children from you once I've set the house to rights here." This decision had come upon Trent somewhere between the pond and the present moment, and it felt…right.

Nick's arm settled on Trent's shoulders, a heavy, comforting presence. "You did the best you could, Trenton. Even the Almighty can ask no more."

"I nearly hated my late wife at times."

"For dying? You loved her, too." Nicholas was such a good-hearted soul, and in some ways, an innocent.

"Not for dying. I can only hope I loved her. I cared for her, and she had positive qualities."

"I'm sure she did," Nick allowed, but he was unable to hide his puzzlement at Trent's disclosures. "I spent most of the spring fretting over your sister, and then your baby brother, and it was you I should have been fretting about all along, wasn't it?"

"Most assuredly not. I'm fine, and Leah and Dare needed your assistance. I was just…floundering, for a time." Trent started moving again, shifting out from under Nicholas's arm.

"God knows I floundered for a time. Floundering is something of a Haddonfield family tradition, I fear. Your sister got me unfloundered, though. Brave woman."

Trent smiled over at him. "You got yourself unfloundered."

"You will, too."

Trent thought of Ellie Hampton's unnerving determination to dally with him. A man could find more than one way to flounder, and the most dangerous options in that regard apparently did not involve the brandy decanter after all.

CHAPTER EIGHT

Trent saw Nick off the next morning in the gray mists of dawn, knowing the early start was intended to get the earl home to Belle Maison—and to his countess—before dark. As Nick's mare cantered down the lane, Cato sidled out of the barn and stood beside Trent for a moment in silence.

"You want we should saddle up Arthur?"

"Am I that obvious?"

"Bellefonte's an in-law. You're happy for the company but then happy to see him go, and as besotted as he is, I'm happy to see him go, too."

"Happy." Nick's mare disappeared around the bend at the foot of the drive at a near gallop. "Probably an overstatement, but yes, saddle up my steed, and we'll take advantage of the cooler air."

While Cato groomed and saddled Trent's gelding, Trent walked through the wet summer grass to a pergola standing between the stables and the scent garden. He'd ride his horse this morning, because Arthur was in want of the conditioning, but then, by God, he'd lock himself in the library with a full decanter.

Last night had been a familiar hell of nightmares, brooding, regretting, and punching his pillow—a truly bad night.

For a few weeks he'd managed to fool himself, managed to hope the past was finally fading. Then the discussion with Nick, and Nick's incessant references to his domestic happiness over a long meal and longer visit over the port, had forced the ugly truth back into the light.

Trenton's past would never fade. Paula would haunt him for the rest of his days, and life purely stank.

So secure was he in this conclusion that he decided to forgo his ride and head directly to the library—not to the breakfast parlor, not to his bedroom to change into proper attire for the house, not for a walk. He left the pergola to tell Cato to put the horse back in his stall when Peak lead a rangy, nervous young gelding out of the barn.

"I'll be taking himself out with you," Peak informed his employer. "Nero wants for company when he's hacking out, and Arthur's the steady sort. He'll give the wee lad some confidence."

Trent eyed the horse, though he barely recalled purchasing the animal. "The wee lad looks like he has confidence aplenty. You can't take him for a gallop on your own, Peak?"

Peak ran a hand down the horse's neck, and that single caress seemed to calm the beast. "Galloping about alone on a green horse over wet grass when company's available would be plain dicked. You wouldn't want me to risk your horse like that, my lord."

True enough, so Trent dodged the reproach in Peak's eyes and resigned himself to riding out with a groom. At least Peak was quiet, concentrating on riding the gelding and leaving Trent to his roiling, miserable thoughts.

"Let's open 'em up a bit," Peak said when the horses were

warmed up. "The bridle path follows the stream, and Nero won't get overeager when old Artie's leading the way."

As if Arthur were showing off for the younger beast, when Trent gave him his head, he set a fast clip down the path. They met logs and ditches to hop when they ran out of stream, and when Trent glanced back, Peak was up in his irons, grinning like a lunatic, enjoying every stride.

So Trent swerved into a farm lane where Peak could pull even, and they let the horses race, neck and neck, for a good half-mile. When Peak's mount dropped back, sides heaving, Trent pulled Arthur up first to the trot, then the walk.

"Old Artie's getting his wind back," Peak observed.

So, apparently, was old Artie's owner. Trent whacked the gelding on a muscular shoulder. "He's a good lad and more athletic than he looks."

"It's been too blessed hot to really let Nero loose. He was a proper gent, considering his youth and inexperience."

Arthur went into a half-hearted curvet. "Nero half ran off with you, Peak. If you weren't such a decent rider, he'd have left you in the stream."

"He half *didn't* run off, too. In a young fellow trying to figure himself out, that means a lot."

Horseman's logic, another contradiction in terms. "You and Cato. If it has a mane and a tail, it can do no wrong."

"One of Mr. Spencer's few redeeming qualities. A good one to have."

Peak rode like a Cossack. He wasn't overly tall, but he was lanky, lithe, and stronger than he looked. His clothing was the typical scruffy attire of a stable boy, but his features were so refined as to be almost elegant. He had a spark of intelligence in his eyes that somehow set him apart, too.

"Cato says you're the one who prompted him to write to me," Trent said. "My thanks."

Peak's expression shuttered. "Mr. Spencer would have got around to it, by and by, but I could not have kept body and soul together on what the witch in the kitchen doled out for meals."

"I hope the fare has improved somewhat."

"Somewhat."

They walked their horses the remaining mile back to the stables in silence, with Trent resigning himself to stopping by the kitchen before he kept his date with the decanter.

Louise was murdering some cut of pork when Trent strode into the kitchen, and though he still felt mean and unhappy, the ride had left him physically more relaxed. A good scrap with Louise held some appeal and would make a nice addition to a miserable morning.

Trent didn't wait until she put her cleaver down. "Greetings, Louise."

"Greetings, your lordship." She set the cleaver aside after a particularly hearty whack. "That's Cook to you."

"So you tell me, but rather than spout instructions to your employer, how about you listen for a change?"

His foul mood must have communicated itself to her, because she wiped her hands on a bloody apron and faced her employer—no turning her back, no more lecturing him, and certainly no more singing the dubious praises of the Earl of Wilton.

"I'm listening."

"A novel and welcome change. I've decided your wisdom should prevail, Louise."

"My wisdom?"

"We must practice economies where we can, and to ensure that the kitchen is run as economically as the rest of my estate, we will prepare one menu for the entire household."

Louise's blond eyebrows knit. "I already make a menu for you and any guests you might have."

"But the rest of the household, the two dozen or so maids, footmen, gardeners, stable lads, and so forth, you have to puzzle out what to feed them, too, don't you?"

Louise turned back to her task, casually tearing apart gristle and meat from bone. "Not much of a puzzle. They eat what I fix 'em."

For half an instant, Trent understood why his father had turned her off without a character. "Now I will, too."

"You will…" Louise's mouth worked, and her eyebrows went down, then up, then back down. She glared, she glowered, and she fisted her hands then unclenched them.

"I'll not put brown bread on my lord's table," she said, the way a man might have told Trent to choose his seconds.

"Then we'll all enjoy white bread, won't we?"

"But you're the lord," Louise hissed. "You'd have the tweenie dining on truffles and sipping wine."

"Perish the thought. I'd have me, rather, dining on coarse bread and niggardly cheese parings in my eggs, while I wash it all down with flat ale."

"Ale?" Louise's expression became thunderous. "You told me to serve the household more white flour, I did. You told me to use the fresher butter, I did. Now you're telling me to put pigswill before the master of this house, and I won't do it."

"Suppose you'd best puzzle out the alternative, Louise, because if you can't"—Trent heard his own tone of voice and didn't back down—"maybe another post might suit you better."

"Stubborn as your father, you are." She grabbed the cleaver and started chopping again. "You want to go to the poor house feeding the mob here, then you'll go, and you'll be so fat you won't fit through the door, mark me, your lordship."

"As long as we understand each other."

Trent left, the pleasure of the confrontation eluding him.

God help him, he'd sounded like a man whose every whim and fancy ought to be imposed on all and sundry. He'd sounded like…his father. *Exactly* like him, and if that wasn't reason to drink his breakfast *and* his lunch, nothing was.

* * *

Fancy finishing schools for the daughters of the peerage taught many important skills: how to seat a dinner party of thirty in strict adherence to order of precedence, how to gracefully manage a Haydn sonata when one's nose itched, how to accept or reject a proposal of marriage, and which response was called for under what circumstances.

To Ellie's unending frustration, her instructors had neglected to provide the first clue about what an increasing woman wears when she's going gardening with seduction in mind.

"Eve had it aright," Ellie muttered. "A few well-placed fig leaves, a nice sunny day, some temptation…"

She'd been up the live long night, replaying her conversation with Lord Amherst—Trenton—in her head. Had she propositioned him? Had he allowed as how he might humor her?

Was that flattering or insulting, or just plain intriguing?

She settled for a comfortable old walking dress, one with a raised waistline, whose blue hues had faded to the shade of violets. The color was close enough to lavender for the proprieties of informal mourning, while the fit was loose enough to be comfortable but presentable—for grubbing in the dirt.

She wore jumps instead of stays—the day would be warm—and found an old straw hat and a pair of worn half-boots. She took her time crossing through the woods, forgoing a stop at the pond to soak her feet.

Gardening was a pleasure, a chance for a lady to be informal and still not call it idling. In her own gardens, Ellie had often gone barefoot, letting the cool grass tickle her toes and refresh her senses.

And surely, amid the weeds and flowers and warm breezes, she could think of something seductive to say should Lord Amherst happen by while she worked.

* * *

A man bent on indulging his thirst could be forgiven for doing so while still windblown and sweaty from his morning ride, but Trent's feet took him past the library and on up to his rooms. If his drunk proved to be a long one, he might as well start it out in clean clothes.

He stripped to the waist, washed, and found a clean shirt and waistcoat, but he'd be damned if he'd bother with a cravat. Turning back his cuffs in anticipation of the heat, he then dragged a brush through his hair and decided the room should be well aired if his footmen had to pour him into bed later in the day.

When he opened the French doors, all he noticed at first was a woman in a straw hat, kneeling on an old blanket among the flowers in his back gardens. She looked comfortable, pulling weeds, tossing them into a bucket, her gloves dirty at the fingers. She *sounded* comfortable, too, singing a quiet tune in a major key, meandering between syllables and humming.

Trent's nymph of the pond had removed to his garden.

For a long time, he remained propped in the doorway, watching, listening, and letting the peace of the scene make inroads on his foul mood.

If he slept beside a woman like that of a night…

After a few more verses of humming, Ellie picked up her blanket and moved to the other side of the plot. From his place in the shadows, he could see her in profile, see the curve of her back and hip, see the soft play of her breasts beneath her old dress. Her hair was giving in to the growing humidity and escaping its pins.

Trent's hand brushed over the front of his falls, responding to an unlooked-for gathering of desire. Not entirely sexual desire, either. Want curled low in his belly, a sensation he might have pushed aside as ungentlemanly, except he'd had a lousy damned night. Another lousy damned night, courtesy of a woman he couldn't even decently resent because she was dead.

He pulled a comfortable chair as close to the French doors as he could while still keeping in shadow, fished out his handkerchief, opened his falls, and settled back. Watching Ellie garden, he stroked himself absently, prepared to be unable to finish—he'd often been unable to finish when he sought to pleasure himself, at least since becoming a married man.

By increments, his arousal intensified, building slowly, like the heat of a summer morning, until he knew he would finish and could, for the first time in *years*, simply enjoy pleasuring himself. When Ellie tipped her head back, knocked aside her hat, and took a long drink from a canteen, he let himself go.

Watching the lovely curve of her neck and the way her breasts lifted as she arched her back, he came and came and came.

When he awoke, he was still sitting in that chair, his handkerchief wadded in his hand, though he'd apparently had the presence of mind to button his falls before he'd dozed off. His body felt more relaxed than it had in months, and his mind...

His mind was not dull, not befuddled by a gray fog. His mind was simply... quiet.

He didn't recall putting his clothes to rights. He recalled Ellie, tipping her head back and drinking.

When he went to find her, he walked right past the library door—and the decanters therein—without pausing.

* * *

"You're without an assistant today?"

Ellie startled, so deeply had she been contemplating names for her baby while she brought order to the daisies getting ready to bloom.

"My lord."

Lord Amherst's hand was extended down to assist her to her feet.

His bare hand.

Ellie drew off her gloves and let him pull her upright—he

accomplished this easily—then let him steady her with a light grasp on her elbow while she assayed her balance.

"All right?"

"Give me a moment. I was growing roots and didn't realize it."

He smiled, as if she'd said something privately amusing, and tucked her hand over his arm. "You're a pretty sight growing in my garden. You've made progress."

"Your people are doing most of it."

Amherst was not only without gloves, he wore no cravat, no jacket, and was still in his riding boots, an altogether fetching state of male dishabille.

"You've taken Arthur out already?"

"I did. If you'd like the occasional horseback escort, you've only to ask."

"I'll take you up on that soon. My habits are already about as snug as I can tolerate without having the seams let out." She could tell him this without blushing—much.

"I thought the first baby took longer to show."

"Longer than what? If it's one's first, one hardly knows what to look for, does one?" She liked how direct he was. She also liked seeing his throat and that small patch of male skin between throat and chest.

What would he taste of there?

He'd led her onto a shaded path, one that wound away from the house, gradually joining the wood, and Ellie was all too happy to go where he led. She'd been in the sun longer than she'd intended. Either that, or dealing with Amherst had become a more dizzying proposition.

Proposition—oh, Halifax.

"You've consulted a midwife?"

"I have. Fortunately, I am not at the mercy of Mrs. Grimm, but may rely on an acquaintance of long standing. Mrs. Holmes assures me matters are progressing normally."

Dane had never perfected the art of escorting a lady. If

a man, particularly a man taller than his companion, did not match his steps to the lady's, the result of linking arms was a great deal of bumping forearms, almost to the point that the lady's progress was hampered rather than helped by the gentleman.

Amherst had the knack of it.

"You would know if matters weren't as they should be," Amherst said, his hand settling over her knuckles. "My late wife carried the Wilton heir and spare, and thus her health was closely monitored. The accoucheur made it a point to keep me informed of every detail."

"I can't imagine any man would enjoy that. Childbearing isn't a tidy or delicate business."

"Like most of life." His expression became introspective, and when he might have made his excuses and sauntered away, Ellie dropped his arm.

"Life is untidy," she said, taking a seat on a sun-dappled stone bench. "That is part of both its charm and its aggravation." Amherst's informal attire was reflective of some change in his outlook, a change she couldn't quite parse. She took her floppy straw hat off, and not only because they were in partial shade. "You're in a mood this morning, my lord."

"At sixes and sevens. My brother-in-law dropped by on his way home to Kent, and he is blissfully happy with his marriage."

"Blissfully? That would put me in a mood, too." Her answer seemed to surprise him, then please him as he sat beside her without her having to ask it.

"Why would another's conjugal bliss put you in a mood, my lady?" Lord Amherst wasn't asking idly. He invited closer acquaintance, a degree of intimacy beyond letting out the seams of her habit.

"My parents loved each other," Ellie said. "Really loved each other, and in this regard, I think a baron has options an earl's heir lacks. Mama and Papa touched frequently, in little ways. They never took separate bedrooms unless one or the other was ill. They were not fashionably estranged during the social Season. They never traveled separately from one another if it could be helped."

The memories were painful now in a way they hadn't been when Dane was alive, for hope of that sort of relationship in Ellie's marriage had died with him.

"A devoted couple," his lordship observed. "They do exist outside of fairy tales."

"Yes, devoted. A little in love until the day my mother died and even thereafter. My father was relieved to see me wed, because it left him free to join my mother and to stop being distracted by life on my account."

Amherst ranged an arm along the back of the bench, the shift in his posture bringing the lovely, spicy scent of him to Ellie's nose.

"So, blissful couples make you miss your parents?"

"They do, but more than that, they make me angry with myself, for what my marriage was with Dane." She set her hat down beside her, lest she knot the ribbons beyond recall.

His lordship might have shifted away. He might have risen and changed the topic. He stayed right beside her. "Your marriage was not blissful?"

She closed her eyes and tilted her face up to the breeze. "We were to appearances content, but it wasn't…"

"Honest," Amherst supplied, easily, as if he'd had time to ponder the matter. "The aggravation of my sister's marriage isn't that Nick is blissful with Leah. It's that he can be honest about the state of his marriage, whatever it is."

Ellie opened her eyes, the better to regard her companion. Had his lordship ever spoken thus with his late wife? She suspected not, which meant the lady deserved some pity.

"Maintaining appearances comes at a cost, to the integrity," she said. "I want to be vigilant, to make sure I don't believe my own lies, especially when that would be easier and more respectful of my departed spouse."

Who had not been very respectful of Ellie.

His lordship was silent, maybe agreeing, maybe losing interest in the conversation, and Ellie wondered how she would coax more kisses out of him when she talked only of lies and appearances and melancholy truths.

He leaned back, all relaxed male in his prime.

"My wife was not happy with me. I knew it, she knew it. I was not her choice. I don't think marriage was her choice, not to anybody."

"I am sorry," Ellie murmured, lacing her fingers with his.

He squeezed her hand, gently, and she let her head rest on his shoulder. This wasn't what she'd expected when she'd come gardening this morning, not these sad confidences, but she'd shared hers with no one else and suspected Amherst hadn't, either.

He lifted his arm, bringing it around her shoulders and keeping it there, until she dozed off, thinking that she'd kissed Dane many times, but what a pity that she'd never napped with him like this on a lovely summer morning.

* * *

When Ellie stirred beside him, Trent dipped his head and kissed her cheek. She came awake wearing a soft, radiant smile that made his breath hitch and his male parts come awake—come awake again, *already*—as well.

"You'll blame me for a fresh dusting of freckles if you don't put on your hat, my lady."

He reached her around to pass the hat to her, just as a loud report sounded from the dense woods behind them, followed by a solid *thunk!*

"Down!" Trent dragged Ellie off the bench, keeping his body between her and the undergrowth. The bench was stone and flanked by overgrown planters on both sides, providing cover in all but the direction of the house.

"Are you all right?" He kept his body half over hers,

needing to protect her with his sheer mass if nothing else.

"I'm fine. You're heavy. Was that a gunshot?"

"At close range." He lifted away an inch. "We'll run for the pergola, if you can?"

"I'll contrive. I might faint once we get there."

"Take my hand." Trent shifted up and got his feet under him but did not rise. "Somebody is discharging firearms on private property. If I fall or am hit, keep moving, Ellie. And we're making a mad dash, none of this dignified promenading."

"Right." Ellie crouched beside him and gathered her skirts in one hand.

He had her on her feet and skimming along beside him in the next instant. He was nearly dragging her, keeping her upright and moving across the grass as Cato and Peak emerged from the stables.

Peak started for them at a brisk trot, Cato on his heels.

"We heard a shot," Peak said. "Nobody would poach in those woods with you in residence, my lord. Is the lady unhurt?"

"I'm fine," Ellie panted. "Winded."

"Did you see who fired?" This from a mightily scowling Cato.

"We did not," Trent said. "The ball hit a tree trunk not far from where we were sitting."

"Jesus, Mary and Joseph," Cato hissed, his brogue in evidence. "Peak, get the lads together and we'll—"

"Peak, get back here," Trent snapped. "A herd of stable boys beating the bushes will only obliterate what sign there is. My first priority is Lady Rammel, who must be safely escorted home. The dog cart should do."

"I can walk," Ellie protested.

Preserve me from independent females.

"Through the woods, from whence a shot was just fired at the two of us?"

He'd nearly bellowed at her, and the confounded woman

looked pleased. She tucked a lock of loose hair back over his ear, calm as she could be—though in the middle of a summer morning, her fingers were cold.

"No need for dramatics, my lord. Not over a poacher or boys out playing war."

"With real bullets!" Trent all but roared.

Three pairs of eyes found somewhere else to look in the ensuing silence, but God Almighty, this was a time for bellowing some sense into the woman. "I beg your pardon for raising my voice."

"I'll get the dog cart." Peak jogged away toward the carriage house.

"Cato, you'll see Lady Rammel home," Trent said. "I don't mean you wave her on her way in the drive. You will see her into the hands of her staff, in her own house, and you will not leave her until you are satisfied she is safe, and she assures you of same."

Ellie looked like she might argue; Trent's expression must have changed her mind.

"We have our orders, Mr. Spencer."

"You,"—Cato addressed his employer—"will show me where this accident occurred when I return, and you will not go poking about in those woods by yourself."

When he would have torn a strip off his presuming stable master, Trent felt Ellie's hand on his arm.

"Yes, Amherst. Please? It can't hurt to wait a bit before you explore the scene, can it?"

Of course it could hurt—anybody with any sense would need only a few moments to destroy any evidence of their passing or to pry the spent bullet from the tree.

Trent wanted to stomp off that instant. His intentions were a palpable, angry thing writhing in his vitals, but Ellie held his gaze, her lovely eyes boring steadily into his, her hand patiently resting on his arm.

"I will pen a note for the magistrate," Trent said. "I'll load my pistols and await Cato's return."

"Thank you." Ellie looked like she wanted to say more, to kiss him, to at least whisper at him to be careful.

Paula had never once looked at him like that.

Ellie's concern steadied him and steadied his resolve, too. "I will see you safely to the stables, my lady, and ask that you say nothing of this to your staff."

Cato fell in on Trent's other side and sucked in a breath.

"You disapprove, Catullus?"

"I hadn't thought of it, is all. I'll see if any of Rammel's fowling pieces are missing while I'm at Deerhaven."

"This sounds serious," Ellie said from her place between them.

"It is," Cato replied for them both, which was convenient, because Trent's teeth

were clenched. "Blessed, blasted serious."

When Ellie had been handed up beside Cato into the dog cart, Trent brushed a kiss to her cheek, oblivious to the help trying to ignore such a display.

"Don't come through the woods alone, my lady. I'll call on you later and let you know what we find."

"Don't take stupid chances." She kissed *his* cheek, and Cato signaled the horse to move off.

Trent watched them go, not turning until the vehicle had rolled smartly through the gates at the foot of the drive.

"Best not watch her like that where all can see, my lord," Peak said.

Oh, famous. Now the stable lads were dispensing unsolicited advice. Trent kicked a pebble hard enough to send it skittering into a weedy bed of hollyhocks.

"Lady Rammel was damned near killed on my land, Peak. It's all I can do not to bundle her up to the house and lock her in a tower until hell freezes over."

"*You* were damned near killed on your own land."

The dog cart clattered around the bend, and Trent

wanted to run after it, to keep it in sight the entire distance to Deerhaven. "Nonsense."

"Wait until Lord Heathgate gets here," Peak said, whacking a dusty cap against his thigh. "You'll see what manner of nonsense you're dealing with. Old Delphey Soames is often in your woods with his fowling piece, and he takes a nip or two betimes. He might have an explanation."

That was more sentences at one go than the young fellow strung together in most entire days. "Soames is poaching? Openly poaching?"

"Nobody need poach. Heathgate opens up Willowdale on certain days for the locals to thin the herds and flocks, as he puts it. Greymoor does the same thing. My guess is several of the other gentry do as well. It isn't like we've wolves to tend to it anymore, and Delphey likes to keep clear of his missus when she gets to drinking, which is to say, after sunrise."

An entire drama unfolded in Trent's woods, if Peak were to be believed. "Soames is routinely strolling about on my land?"

"You were never here." Peak swiped a hand through unkempt dark hair that reached nearly to the lad's shoulders, then tugged his cap back on with an air of pugnacity at variance with his delicate features. "Even when you popped out to check on things, you weren't here."

"Insubordinate, young man. You're taking on too many of Cato's characteristics."

Peak strode off toward the stables. "Not insubordinate. Honest. A man needs honest help, especially when he's not about."

Trent let him go, too angry and overwrought to do otherwise.

The intensity of the emotions was unfamiliar and inconvenient, though not entirely unwelcome. Because he'd given his word to Ellie, Trent did go to the house, dash off a note to the magistrate, then clean and load his favorite pistols. The decanter beckoned, but he hardly wanted the king's man to find him drinking his temper into submission, so he started on notes to Darius and Nick as well.

CHAPTER NINE

At Lord Heathgate's instruction, Trent and Cato took seats on the bench beside Ellie's old straw hat. In the pretty sunshine, the hat was disquietingly innocent, given what might have happened.

"Gentlemen," Heathgate called from the undergrowth several moments later, "you may join me, but please remain on my left as you approach."

The marquess was a tall, broad-shouldered man, his age somewhere north of thirty, his hair sable, his eyes a gimlet blue that likely scared confessions out of felons and small children alike. Trent didn't know him well, though Heathgate was reportedly besotted with his marchioness and a genial host when she inspired him to it.

"Tracks," Heathgate said, hunkering in the undergrowth and pointing off to the right, "which, of course, come up from the stream, where we'll no doubt lose them. A medium-sized fellow, or perhaps a smallish man with largish feet, but he chose this spot and knelt here,"——he sighted down the stock of his riding crop—"and aimed carefully. You must have tarried on that bench."

"We did, maybe fifteen minutes."

Heathgate rose and turned his scrutiny on Trent. "My guess is that you, Amherst, were the target, but as close as you were sitting to the lady, that is only a guess."

"Poachers?" Cato asked.

Heathgate swung his riding crop at some honeysuckle, sending leaves, blossoms, and fragrance cartwheeling through the summer air.

"Poaching isn't likely. For one thing, nobody needs to poach hereabouts, because none of the landowners are stingy with their game, and second, if you're intent on poaching, you don't do it within sight of a working stable where people are always on hand."

"So we're back to motive," Trent said. Cato bit off oaths in Gaelic. "Did you tell him about the stirrups? The ones that were cut, on both sides of your personal saddle?"

"Come along." Heathgate waved them away from the bench. "There's apparently more to the tale than Amherst has had time to relate, and this heat makes a man thirsty."

When they reached the house, Trent canvassed his companions, and the choice of drink was lemonade, which came as a peculiar relief. In the course of the last few hours, Trent's previous determination to drain the brandy decanter had become...distasteful, unseemly even.

Had he been half-drunk when that gun had gone off, could he have shepherded Ellie to safety? Would his children have become orphans on this pretty, sunny day because their papa had stumbled in the grass?

When Trent, Cato and the marquess were seated on the back terrace around a tray of sandwiches and a tall pitcher of cold lemonade, Heathgate picked up a sandwich and aimed his gaze at Trent. If the man thought it odd that Cato joined them, he had the good manners to say nothing to his host.

"Tell me about the stirrups."

Heathgate listened, blue eyes narrowing as his lordship put away food and downed lemonade at a great rate.

"Our man Peak seems to be quite the busy fellow," Heathgate said. "He was first to reach you and Lady Rammel today, and he noticed the stirrups."

"He's the one who sent for me," Trent said, the realization dawning only as he spoke. "Indirectly."

"I wrote the letter," Cato said. "Peak merely grumbled about the food until I was more annoyed with his complaining than I was with Cook's fare."

"That isn't how you described it to me earlier, Catullus," Trent said softly.

Cato leaned back, as if entreating the oak limbs above them for patience with his betters.

"You can't suspect Peak of shooting at you when he was in the stables with me. He's your best lad, and if he wanted to end your life—for motives we have not yet concocted—he could have put out your lights this morning when you both rode in on thoroughly lathered mounts."

"What Cato says is true," Trent said, with no small relief. "I like Peak. Moreover, the horses like Peak, and at the inquest regarding Rammel's death, Heathgate, you yourself found the man's testimony sufficiently credible that Cato was exonerated of any wrongdoing."

Heathgate studied a sandwich of chicken with herbed butter and cheddar on white bread—Cook had apparently noted the rank of Trent's guest.

"The only wrongdoing I found was by Rammel, who was too drunk, stupid and arrogant to pull his horse off a gate he never should have attempted. I asked Greymoor if he would have taken such a jump, and his response was not unless it was life or death, never when in his cups, and never on a borrowed mount, meaning no insult to your late horse,

Spencer. My younger brother's judgment in matters equestrian is nigh flawless."

Cato rose without having touched the food. "A nasty damned pattern emerges here."

Heathgate flicked a cool, appraising gaze over the stable master.

"You think somebody wants to make you look like a killer, Mr. Spencer? As you stated, the estimable Peak was in the stables with you, and both Amherst and Lady Rammel saw you and Peak approach the scene from the stables. Rather than circle uselessly around what little we know, I suggest somebody track down Delphey Soames. He considers himself the informal gamekeeper hereabouts and would know if we've had any strangers prowling our woods."

"Good idea," Trent said, wanting Heathgate gone, for Cato would not eat as long as the magistrate was about. "Cato has a point as well. His letter to my brother, Darius, was the reason I repaired here for the summer, and Cato could be perceived as luring me to my demise. Moreover, Cato has access to my saddlery and to firearms."

Cato let loose with another Gaelic oath, or perhaps it was a prayer, him likely being Papist. "Are you accusing me, Amherst?"

Heathgate's dark eyebrow swooped up at the familiarity, but he merely waited for Trent's reply.

"I am not," Trent said evenly. "Not in any regard, Cato. You have no motive for seeking my death, just as you would have had no motive for killing Rammel, but if we're listing my enemies in a search for motive, we should be listing yours as well."

"Good point," Heathgate said. "Sit down, Spencer, and eat something lest I spoil my luncheon entirely and earn a scolding from my marchioness. I'll need to know exactly who works in the stables, who has access to guns, and where those people were earlier today."

While all Trent needed to know was that Ellie was safe and settled, and not suffering as a result of the day's events. The worry—the anxiety—was roiling in his gut, a burden and a bother that would not go away.

"I wasn't aware Lady Rammel was a gardener," Heathgate said nearly an hour later as they walked toward the stables. "Has she taken your roses in hand yet?"

"You'd have to ask her." She'd made short work of the daisies, though, of that Trent was certain.

Heathgate stopped near the pergola, halfway between the house and the stables. "I intend to question the lady, you know."

"About?"

"This incident and whatever other factors I deem relevant."

That Heathgate could be delicate was something of a surprise, though the man was rumored to dote on his marchioness and children.

"It isn't my child," Trent said, because a man who doted on his marchioness was probably in that lady's confidence, too. "If that's what you're asking. I didn't know Rammel had died until I removed here, and the vicar started yapping about neighborly obligation and condolence calls."

"You made yours early."

"A little. Yours is overdue."

"Suppose it is." Heathgate resumed walking. "I don't deal well with all that funerary tripe. Never have. My marchioness is a blessing in this regard."

"One hears you and she are devoted."

"Go ahead and say it." Heathgate's smile was fleeting, self-deprecating, and charming. "Despite all reputation to the contrary, or my just deserts, my wife and I are smitten with each other."

"I was thinking more that you might castigate me for making advances to a new widow," Trent said slowly. Though in truth, the widow had made an advance or two toward

Trent—a delightful realization.

Heathgate's smile became mocking. "As if my own brother didn't marry his countess when she was less than six months into mourning her first spouse?"

"I wasn't aware of that." Trent hadn't been aware of *any* of the neighborhood gossip, though he'd no doubt Ellie could catch him up.

Fifty yards away at the stables, Cato stood at the end of the shed row, his hand on Peak's shoulder, his attitude toward the smaller man suggesting fraternal concern.

"What do we know of your Mr. Spencer, Amherst?" Heathgate asked softly.

"Not enough. The horses like him, too, and I haven't had any complaints. If anything, he's shown unusual loyalty."

"You pay fair wages, and Crossbridge is comfortable. In what regard has he shown this loyalty?"

Trent gave up trying to elude Heathgate's inquisition. "After my wife died, I was occupied with ensuring Wilton didn't get his hands on her settlement trusts and in seeing to my sister's welfare as best I could. My brother was also in some difficulties, so he became a frequent guest under my roof. I was kept busy with those concerns, until Bellefonte began courting Leah."

As fictions went, Trent's recitation was masterly.

Heathgate's expression suggested he knew it. "And now?"

"It's no secret I was going to pieces," Trent said, his gaze on the shady green canopy of the overgrown home wood. "I sent my children to my sister and Bellefonte, essentially for safekeeping, and let most of my staff in Town go."

And yet, Trent hadn't been grieving, precisely. Not for Paula, at any rate.

"If my marchioness were taken from me, I'm not sure how I'd go on."

"But you would," Trent assured him. "For your children, your wife's memory, your brother, king and country, you'd find some damned reason to soldier on."

For an interminable silent moment, Heathgate considered the pink roses climbing up the side of the pergola. "You haven't found those reasons to soldier on?"

The question of the year. "I'll see my children raised. I owe them and my brother that much."

"Assuming your very own stable master isn't plotting your demise."

Trent sent the marquess a look intended to inspire overly inquisitive magistrates onto their horses and back to their besotted wives post-haste.

Heathgate merely resumed admiring the roses.

"Cato Spencer wouldn't let Crossbridge, my only holding, go to ruin in my absence. He wrote to me, not once, but several times, when my housekeeper and steward ran off with the household money. When that didn't get my attention, he tracked Darius down by letter and put the unvarnished truth before the one person able to command my notice."

Heathgate touched a delicate pink petal. "Why would a mere stable master go to such heroic lengths?"

Damnably valid question. "I want to think for all Cato's womanizing and jolly-good-fellow-at-the-meet, he's a decent man and capable of compassion."

"He's also,"—Heathgate pitched his voice to not carry— "quite possibly in line for an earldom."

"I beg your pardon?"

"An Irish earldom," Heathgate clarified, bending to sniff at a thorny little rose. Heathgate bred roses. Where had Trent heard that?

The marquess snapped off a bloom and affixed it to his lapel. "My brother trades horses all over creation, and the Irish do love their ponies. Greymoor has heard rumors that the Earl of Glasclare's son trifled with one too many decent women, and one of them claimed to be carrying his babe. The young man denied the accusation and took off rather than wed himself to a scheming female. He's gone to ground in Surrey and vowed he won't go home until the woman in question recants."

"Good God. I thought my life was complicated."

"Challenging, certainly." Heathgate's understatement conveyed compassion rather than judgment.

Which was interesting—also fortifying.

"If Cato is Glasclare's heir," Trent said, "then he'd have sympathy for another earl's son who was in difficulties. He did claim Peak was the one to inspire him to put pen to paper." Were he an earl's son, Cato would also have had a proper education, access to good horseflesh, and enough coin to bolt for England when Ireland's charms paled.

Heathgate pulled his riding gloves from a pocket, an encouraging sign of impending departure. "How bad off were you?"

A falsely encouraging sign. Trent said nothing while he considered his plans upon arising that very morning.

"I see." Heathgate courteously kept his gaze on the stables, where Cato had patted Peak's arm then moved off in the direction of Heathgate's horse.

"You'll stop to see Lady Rammel next?" Trent asked.

"I will not," Heathgate replied, resuming their progress toward the stables. "I'm off in search of Mr. Soames, who can likely be found at our local watering hole, and then I'm for home. You may tell the lady to expect me in the morning, if it suits her."

"When may I tell her this?"

"You're on your way over there, to return the lady's hat to her, of course, for ladies do become attached to their bonnets and such. You will also make a visit to see for yourself that she's in good health. You, moreover, are better suited than any other to assure she will continue in that condition, at least as long as you draw breath."

"I am merely her closest neighbor and a cordial friend."

"Right," Heathgate tossed over his shoulder. "How long were you sitting in close proximity to your *neighbor* on that bench?"

Cordial neighbor. "Minutes. Well, a quarter hour, perhaps."

"Though a lady's reputation will always be safe with me, Amherst, I have to ask myself why she was sitting practically in your lap and why, if she's mindful of her complexion, her hat was off on a bright summer morning for the duration of that quarter hour?"

Trent opened his mouth, then closed it. Heathgate was besotted with his marchioness; he was not stupid.

* * *

"Her ladyship will see you in the family parlor."

Ellie's housekeeper beamed at Trent genially and took his gloves and hat. He ran his hand through the hat creases in his hair and followed the woman up to the first floor.

"Viscount Amherst come to call."

"Amherst." Ellie was ensconced on a pale green sofa awash in cabbage rose pillows, her smile as welcoming as if she hadn't seen Trent for a week. "May I have the kitchen bring us something?"

"Cider, lemonade, or meadow tea would do."

"Mrs. Wright, you'll see to it?" Ellie's smile shifted to include the housekeeper. "And maybe some sustenance. Have Annie bring it to the balcony of my sitting room."

"Very good, my lady." Mrs. Wright, a portly old dear with a lined face, was gone on a swish of gray skirts.

Ellie looked fine, but then, she was probably adept at *looking* fine. "How are you, my lady?"

"Getting a stiff neck." Ellie came to her feet. "Let me show you to my sitting room, where we'll be able to talk undisturbed."

Trent offered his arm, mostly to quell a compulsion to touch her, to touch her anywhere at all.

"Is that why I'm to have the privilege of your sanctum

sanctorum?"

"My holy of holies," Ellie said dryly, "has a breeze and a pleasant view, a shaded balcony, and privacy. Did the magistrate make an appearance?"

Heaven help him, he *needed* to kiss her. "We'll get to that."

Trent let her usher him upstairs to a pretty, comfortable room with its own fireplace and an embarrassment of cut flowers. As soon as she'd closed the door behind them, he enveloped her in a fierce embrace and a fiercer kiss.

She kissed him back, but gently, running her hand over his hair in slow, soothing motions, then brushing her fingers over his cheeks and jaw and ears.

"If I ever," he breathed against her neck, "*ever* find out who fired that gun, he will pay, dearly, at length, and painfully."

"It might have been an accident. Mr. Soames is not known for his sobriety, or so I'm told. You can't torture the man for an accident."

"Accident," Trent said, lifting his head. "I can think of no more vile word for a life lost due to negligence or careless malice. Somebody knelt in the underbrush, Ellie, and took aim at us. Heathgate is satisfied this was intentional mischief."

"You still don't know the intention was murder." Ellie slipped her arm through his. "Somebody might have wanted to frighten us, or warn, or who knows."

"You are good." Trent hauled her into another hug. "Innocent, sweet, dear, and utterly wrong. Somebody meant one or both of us harm, Ellie. Promise me you won't be alone in those woods again."

"I promise."

She replied easily, sincerely, didn't haggle, didn't make him beg, didn't argue or subject the entire household to hysterics. He loved her a little for that and felt a measure of calm at her assurances.

"If you prefer, I also won't go anywhere without a groom or a footman, even on my own land."

"I prefer," Trent said, his breath coming more easily. "I'd prefer even more if you'd stay shut up in your house, or better still, in mine, where I can post sentries at every window, bar the castle door, flood the moat, drop the portcullis, and plant archers on the rooftop."

Ellie tugged him out to the balcony. "Feeling medieval?"

"Feeling scared, Ellie." Trent was angry as hell, exhausted from a sleepless night and a long day, but also frightened—for her—and resentful of the entire mess. "I've racked my brain for who could mean me ill, and I cannot come up with a soul. Your case is easier to fathom because you carry a potential heir, and Drew or Drew's heir might mean you harm."

"Except Drew has no heir," Ellie pointed out, "and Drew doesn't mean me harm. I don't think he wants the title and the bother that goes with it. Sit with me?"

She'd made her balcony into a pleasant bower indeed, with pots of fragrant pink and white roses along the railing and a hanging swing the width of a love seat.

Trent lowered himself beside her, the chains and the swing creaking at his weight. "You have a talent for making things comfy."

She ran her finger down a velvety pink petal nearly the same shade as her lips. "I like my comforts. I was alone a great deal when Dane was alive, except for Andy and the servants, of course, and I wanted my prison to be at least welcoming."

"Prison?" Trent's marriage had felt like prison. He could admit that now...here and now.

"Dane kept more to the family seat, closer to Town, though I usually knew where he was. He used the town house in London, the Hampton family seat, a hunting box in the North, and so forth. My job was to stay out of his way except on those occasions when he'd feel the need for a repairing lease. Then I was to cosset and fuss and be glad to see him."

Reminding Trent that resentment might not be an exclusively male sentiment. "Were you glad to see him?"

"His visits were a break from my routine, some assurance I wasn't entirely extraneous to his plans."

"Did you ever wish him dead?" Trent watched her expressions. He also took her hand in his. "I ask because I suspect Heathgate might inquire."

"Heathgate?"

"He's serving as magistrate, and he's… shrewd. He likely knows you're expecting, and he's already surmised we might be more than neighbors."

"How did he surmise that?"

Trent explained the basis for Heathgate's conjectures.

"He presumes a great deal. His presumption is particularly irksome when I consider that, except for a few kisses, you and I aren't more than neighbors."

She withdrew her hand, else Trent might have missed the hint of pique in her tone. Did mere neighbors endure a compunction to touch each other, to kiss each other?

The serving maid, Annie, brought a large tray, curtseyed, withdrew. Ellie waited for a moment as if collecting her thoughts then closed the door between the sitting room and the corridor and returned to the balcony.

"Ellie, we ought to leave the door open."

"I am a widow," she said in a low, fierce tone. "I'm in my home with a widower to whom all would agree no hint of scandal clings. Cease carping, Trenton, lest I turn you over my knee."

"Interesting proposition." One that would have horrified Paula into a week-long fit of the vapors. He sipped his lemonade, letting it cool his throat, while the sight of Ellie, safe, tidy, and at peace, cooled his temper. He wrapped an arm around her when she took the place beside him on the swing.

She obligingly set her drink beside his and cuddled up. "I feel a nap coming on," she declared. "This occurrence has become frequent, but I'd like not to waken to a gunshot this time."

"Oh, no you don't." Trent shifted off the swing and scooped her up against his chest. "You can nap in a bed, like the rest of civilized society." He wasn't about to let her torment him with her soft, sleepy warmth against his side, not again, not today, maybe not ever. He carried her through the door connected with her bedroom then stopped abruptly.

"Trenton?"

"Is that a bed or a fairy tale with pillows?"

Ellie slept on an enormous four-poster, the covers and shams all in white, the pillows in lavender, pink and gold.

"I like my comforts." She tucked her nose against his neck. "And, no, Dane couldn't bring himself to exercise his conjugal rights in that bed, said it gave him nightmares to contemplate it."

"It's...different," Trent said, setting her down on the mattress. "You'll sleep more agreeably here than on a swing."

"Open the doors to the balcony," Ellie suggested, sitting up to pull off her slippers. "I didn't plan to nod off at the sight of you."

"Nod off whenever you need to." Trent opened the bedroom's doors to the balcony then jammed his hands in his pockets lest he start taking down her hair.

"Come cuddle with me." Ellie held out a hand, and Trent took in the invitation, and the fact that she'd bathed and changed since their morning adventure, whereas he...

"That isn't a good idea, Ellie." He kept his hands in his pockets, but his benighted cock was making plans for that fairy tale bed.

"Cuddling isn't a bad idea," she corrected him, taking pins from her hair until a thick glossy braid dropped over her shoulder. "You look exhausted, and I never sleep for long."

"I'm not fresh from my bath." He went to the doors and turned his back on her, deliberately removing the sight of her from his gaze. "I'm not in a settled frame of mind, it's broad daylight..."

"Next you'll be telling me you're a tender-hearted virgin."

From the corner of Trent's eye, he saw Ellie yawn and stretch like a lioness in anticipation of a good hunt.

"You're fresh enough, Trent, and a nap will settle your busy mind, and broad daylight matters naught to me. I want to be near you—need to. *Come to bed.*"

Three words, three words his late wife had never said, and particularly not in such simple, straightforward welcome. To heed Ellie's summons would be ungentlemanly, and to refuse her...

Worse than ungentlemanly, also impossible.

He tugged off his boots, cravat, waistcoat and shirt, while Ellie curled on her side, watching him with sleepy appreciation.

"You are one of those fellows who will be strong when he's seen his three score and ten. The young girls will flirt with you and be half-serious about it."

"Perish the thought." Trent surveyed the bed and its contents and prayed for strength.

"I can get rid of this." Ellie sat up and drew her old-fashioned, high-waisted dress over her head before Trent could formulate a protest. "Cooler that way."

She tossed the dress to the nearest chair and was back on her side, eyes closed, mouth slightly parted, looking like some princess of old on her magical bed.

Trent crawled across the bed to lie beside her on his back. The woman wore neither stays nor jumps, as if she'd planned to perpetrate her ambush-by-nap.

"Mm." She kissed his biceps without opening her eyes, then subsided, apparently intent on her nap and nothing more.

And yet, Trent was still quite, quite ambushed, God help him. He was in bed with a female whom his body told him he had to have. *Had to*, and she was falling asleep beside him. Such a contretemps made for the sweetest, most frustrating twist to his day. He closed his eyes, and while he busily lectured his parts into submission, sleep took him captive.

When he awoke, Ellie was spooned around his back, a novel sensation though welcome.

"You napped. I told you we would." Her lips on his nape punctuated her point. "You're exhausted, the day has been eventful, and now you feel better for having a rest. What is this?"

She traced a scar over one shoulder blade—with her tongue.

"Scar," Trent managed. "Fell off my pony."

"And this?" She used her finger this time, thank a merciful Deity.

"Another fall."

"You must have had a fractious pony," she said, hugging him from behind.

He'd had a succession of demon ponies. "Elegy Hampton, what have you done with your shift?"

"It's cooler this way." She pressed her breasts against his back to kiss his nape then eased away. "A lady has to be resourceful when she's bent on seduction, and you strike me as a man much in need of seducing."

"Ellie…" He wanted to turn and face her, but she was *naked, warm, and in bed with him*, so he kept his eyes on the flowers on her balcony. Flowers the same color pink as a—

"My lady—*Ellie*—this is not a good idea."

CHAPTER TEN

"You're growing repetitive." Ellie crawled up over Trent's shoulder and took his earlobe in her teeth, causing sensation to reverberate through all manner of interesting and naughty parts of his body. "Impending motherhood is making me very forthright, I think. Shall we get under the covers? Is it the sight of me you'd rather avoid?"

"How can you think that?" He rolled over to face her without having willed it, and God in heaven, she was lovely. Her hair was a soft, fuzzy braid curling down over one bare shoulder, her neck and throat a long, lovely study of graceful curves and female bones, and her breasts, ye gods…

He rolled away again.

"I can't think when I see you unclothed, except to consider how I might take advantage of you."

For months, for months, he'd regarded the absence of lustful inclinations as a relief.

Ellie's hand trailed along his waist to smooth over his bare ribs. "I have often wondered if men and women aren't more similar than men would like to admit. Are you shy?"

"God yes, I'm shy." Trent glared at her over his shoulder then whipped his head back around. His cock was not shy. His cock clamored to be out of his breeches, to enjoy what the lady was so damned determined to offer.

"Shyness is endearing." Ellie said, her hand trailing higher. "Are you sensitive here?" She feathered her fingertips over his nipple. "I swear, Trenton, I think I can almost hear with my breasts, they are so sensitive these days."

A tortured chuckle escaped him at her observation, followed swiftly by an indrawn breath as she climbed over him, pushed him to his back and straddled him.

"Look at me, Trenton, *please.*"

He surrendered to his fate gracefully, and when Ellie remained silent, he let himself appreciate the magnificent view.

He drew his fingers slowly along her jaw. "You are lovelier than a mortal man could convey in three languages and six lifetimes." Her gaze was anxious, so instead of lingering on her features, he took in the full, round perfection of her breasts, the slight convexity near her waist, the soft patch of dark curls over her mons, the lean strength of her thighs and the feminine delicacy of her features.

In five years of marriage, he'd never once seen his wife unclothed. He'd regret that. When he was strong enough, when he was alone enough, he'd find the strength to face and withstand that regret.

"Come here." He held out his arms, and when she folded down against his chest, he gathered her to him. "You should not share such a treasure with me, Ellie. I am not worthy."

"You are," she countered, nose against his throat. "You look at me."

"Dane didn't?" He traced the bones of her back, shoulder blades, spine, the crests of her hips, her tailbone.

She tucked closer. "Never once. He was one to dispatch

with matters after dark, candles out, under the covers, and off we go."

The viscountess had regrets, too. "Shame on him. What a fool the poor man was. You are worth savoring in the broad daylight, Ellie Hampton."

He felt the doubt in her, even as he knew exactly how that self-doubt corroded one's entire life, and like a stubborn, miserable taproot, it grew right down into the soul. He wouldn't join his body with hers, wouldn't couple with her, wouldn't swive her.

He would *make love* with Dane Hampton's widow, and thank God he'd pleasured himself earlier in the day. Otherwise, he'd have already spent in his breeches.

"Up you go." He patted her bottom. "I need to divest myself of my remaining clothes."

She smiled Eve's smile and hopped off of him so quickly he had to smile back.

He paused with his hand on his falls. Her experience had all been lights out, under the covers. "Maybe you shouldn't look."

"Maybe you shouldn't try to stop me."

He stood beside the bed, hands at his sides, and let her unfasten his breeches. Her fingers were nimble, and she soon had him standing naked as God made him, his cock arrowing up shamelessly along his belly.

"Holy Halifax." Ellie reached for his cock, and Trent arched away.

"Gently," he cautioned, drinking in the unabashed eagerness in her eyes. "Slowly, like you would a two-week-old kitten."

He recalled the way his wife had grabbed at him and practically shoved him into her body after Michael had been born.

The whisper-soft caress of Ellie's finger up his rigid length distracted him from that memory. While he tried to recall

Caesar's Gallic letters in the original Latin, she repeated the caress, then went on to slip her fingers over his stones and then the length of his cock again.

"Am I doing this right?" She brushed her thumb over *that spot* at the tip, and Trent's self-restraint strained its short, frayed leash.

"I'll spend, Ellie," he managed. "If you do that one more time…"

"Dane did." She sat back, regarding him from a too-short distance. "At least half the time he'd lose control before he even managed… I should not be saying such things, but I know it bothered him."

Rammel's lack of control had clearly bothered her, too, feeding her feminine self-doubt.

Trent put a finger over her lips. "Leave the poor man a little dignity."

She peered up at him. "Why? Dane is gone and he wouldn't let me even see him, much less touch him—Dane, the supposed great Ram—and here you are, and you're…glorious."

"I'm aroused." Trent climbed on the bed, wondering at a swaggering lordling who hadn't had a clue how to appreciate his own wife. "You mustn't malign a man who can't defend himself. Maybe you were too much inspiration for him."

But holy God, had Trent's wife even *wanted* to look at him, much less enjoy looking at him, how different might their marriage have been?

Ellie scooted across the bed. "In complete darkness, I was too much inspiration for him?"

"He's not here. We are. Now, how can I pleasure you?"

"How can you…?"

She didn't understand the question, and Trent was abruptly finished defending dear old Dane's memory.

"Are you still comfortable on your back? Or would you prefer to be on top?"

"I didn't know I could be on top." Ellie's gaze lit on his

cock, and Trent's went to her breasts in retaliation.

Bad idea. Beautiful, lovely, succulent, lush, *bad* idea. His hand, at complete variance with the inclinations of his brain, reached out so his fingers could brush against the full underside of one breast. Ellie closed her eyes and tilted her face up, as if he were beaming sunshine onto her soul.

"You like that?"

"I don't know." She opened her eyes, her smile mysterious. "Do it some more and I'll decide later."

"Come here, wench." Trent lay on his back and gently wrestled her over him. "Touch me however you please, and we can refine the details some other time. When you've frolicked enough, I'm available for your pleasure."

"What does that mean?" Ellie sat on him, her damp sex poised over him, her expression puzzled.

"When you're ready." Trent flexed his hips so she could feel him rampant beneath her. "Take me inside you, but I warn you, precipitous moves will be dealt with sternly."

She leaned forward and, to his relief, simply cuddled onto his chest.

He tucked his chin over her crown, wrapped his arm around her and waited.

And waited.

"Ellie?"

"Hmm?"

"Maybe a kiss to get us started?"

"I like kissing…you." She peered at him. "Then what?"

Women were notorious for posing difficult questions with no correct answers. This wasn't such a question. "Then whatever you want, however you want it."

* * *

For the first time in her life, Ellie Hampton was inebriated.

Trenton Lindsey gazed up at her as if she were some great work of art, one he'd come upon at the end of a long and arduous pilgrimage. His hands were *reverent* as they trailed along her arms and over her shoulders. His eyes glittered with what she was sure was a determination to possess.

But what on earth was he waiting for?

"Touch me, Ellie," he coaxed. "Kisses, touches, anything. I'll take anything you'll give me."

She ran her fingers over his hair, and he closed his eyes, so she did it again, loving the silky feel of each lock.

"Kiss," he whispered. "Please."

She bent forward, and her braid slid over her shoulder to land on his chest. On impulse, she trailed the end of it across his nipple as she brushed her lips over his. He groaned, a sound of pleasure and longing that she'd caused, and low in her belly, something started to *dance*.

She managed to kiss him again, even as she continued to torment him with her braid.

"I'll grow my hair long enough to braid," he threatened between kisses. "My revenge will be merciless."

She settled her lips over his, because any more of such talk and she'd beg him to show her what he meant. His arms anchored her to him and urged her lower as she joined her mouth to his.

"Give me your weight, Ellie. Please."

Gingerly, she lowered herself closer as his tongue teased at her lips.

"More of you, Elegy."

They touched. Her sex against the rigid length of his cock, and the contact ricocheted through Ellie like a hot, roaring wind.

"More, love. All of you," he whispered, his tongue asking for entry. "Move on me."

Move on him? Ah, that she could puzzle out. Slowly, she rocked her hips, caressing the length of him the way his tongue caressed her lips. He let out another one of those groans, but softer, more in his chest, and she did it again.

"Exquisite," he murmured. "Lovely. Kiss me."

Teasing him bodily was more than exquisite… But so was the sensation of his tongue teasing at her mouth. She took that tongue and drew on it, fleetingly, and he pushed his body up more snugly against hers. Something was building between them. She could not have said what or how to construct it— but Trenton knew.

Clearly, her marital experience had left gaps in her intimate vocabulary, and it was too late to hide that from the man in her bed.

"Trenton." She curled away from his kisses and stilled her hips. "I don't know what to do."

He relaxed beneath her, and his arms encircled her.

"Then just kiss me. Let me do the rest, and we'll take it slowly."

He didn't hop off the bed with a kiss to her forehead the way Dane so often had, but Ellie still felt defeated.

She nuzzled his chest and wanted to cry. "I'm sorry. I didn't realize there was so much more to it."

"Hush." Trent's voice was right near her ear. "You tell me what you want from me, or you take my hands and put them where you want them, Ellie. There's no apologizing for what happens in this bed."

She managed a nod.

He slipped a hand over one bare, full breast, and Ellie arched into his palm involuntarily. "You're not too sensitive to enjoy that?"

"Your touch feels good, Trenton." *Heavenly*, in fact. In all the years she'd been married, Dane had never—

"Up a little. Let's see what you like."

Trenton drove her to madness, caressing, kissing, suckling, and ever so gently kneading, then found her favorite touch was a slow, subtle caress of the soft, soft undersides of her breasts.

"I think we have to stop." Ellie panted, hanging over him. "This is…I didn't know I could feel this."

"Then we're getting somewhere." He teased her nipple with his tongue, while his hand plied the other breast and he didn't relent until Ellie clutched him to her and rocked herself along the length of his cock in a slow, needy rhythm.

"I am…overset," she rasped in his ear. "It wasn't like this… before."

"You're close." His hand slipped down her abdomen. "Let me bring you closer."

Had she been capable of coherent speech, she might have questioned his meaning, but he'd slid his thumb over a particular part of her that screamed in response to that one simple touch.

"Trenton—"

"You feel that." He did it again, and she pushed hard against his hand. "Take your time, Ellie. Find what you need."

The moment became a procession of moments. He touched her with patience and skill, until all she needed was *more*, from his hands, fingers, mouth, and body; until pleasure cascaded up from her center in a great deluge. Sounds came from her throat, soft, unladylike sounds of overwhelming gratification, and then, when he entered her in one smooth, deep lunge, she shook with the satisfaction of it. The luscious, thrusting heat of him turned her mad, fearless, and wanton in his arms.

The bodily tumult ebbed but didn't recede entirely, and at first Ellie could not have said why she was crying. Trent's hands stroked her back, then he drew something over them, a cover, a sheet, it didn't matter. She burrowed into the warmth of him, the strength and quiet comfort, and her feelings sorted themselves out.

"Damn him," she rasped against Trent's chest. "Damn that selfish, greedy, ignorant, stupid man. Damn him to Halifax."

"He's gone, love," Trent replied, "while you're alive, and so, thank God, am I."

* * *

Ellie fell asleep—of course—her weight a warm, cozy comfort on Trent's chest. He was glad for the respite, even as he felt himself slipping from her body. He retrieved his handkerchief by virtue of careful stretching and contained the damage as best he could without waking her. She stirred against him then subsided after rubbing her nose against his chest.

He treasured that small gesture of trust, and familiarity, too.

If he lived to be a hundred, he would not forget the pleasure of this terrible, wonderful day.

If he lived to be a thousand.

If he lived forever—

He'd pushed from his awareness, if he'd ever known, the profundity of the pleasure that could be sexual intimacy with a caring partner. With Paula, the whole business had become twisted, wearying and burdensome. He'd eventually been not unwilling to perform, but *unable*.

Three years…since he'd had sex. Far more years than that he'd gone without feeling the hot, wet glory of a woman's arousal, without hearing her breathing quicken with surprise and urgency, without feeling her seize around him in mindless abandon… While for Ellie, unbridled passion had apparently been entirely unknown territory.

He was her first, in a sense, and the joy of that, the newness and singularity of it, was a precious secret.

Who knew what had been amiss with Rammel? Too much liquor maybe, too jaded a sexual palate, or too guilty a conscience from swiving too many demi-reps or straying wives. What mattered was that Ellie Hampton had sought Trent out to set the matter to rights, and he hadn't failed her.

Affection for her bloomed as she raised her head and blinked sleepily.

"I'm awake." She closed her eyes and settled back against him. "What does one say in such circumstances?" She gently bit the tendon between his neck and shoulder. "I am more than a little mortified. You engender this state in me, apparently."

"You are magnificent, Elegy." He kissed the side of her neck. "One says, 'Thank you, Almighty God, and may I please be so blessed again in the immediate future?' At least one does if he's me."

She tilted her head back to look at him, then ducked her face again. "Noise."

"I beg your pardon?" Trent couldn't let out the laugh he felt, not when she was plastered to his chest and obviously feeling on her dignity.

"I've never made such noises." Ellie pushed up on a sigh and peered down at her breasts. "And these. Who knew what mischief one might undertake with such seemingly prosaic and maternal apparatus?"

Trent tucked her braid over her shoulder. "Ellie, this mischief is a good thing, this"—he caressed her breasts—"apparatus should be a source of mutual delight. I'd forgotten that. You were right to drag me into your bed."

She beamed at him. "I was right, and you were wrong."

"Would you like to be right again?" Trent used her braid to bring her within kissing range. "Maybe on your back with a little more company along the way?"

"Hmm?"

He rolled them, then nudged at her sex with his restored erection.

Her expression of surprise, replaced immediately by pure feminine speculation did make him laugh.

"I think you'd like to be right again." He gave her a shallow penetration. "What do you think?"

Ellie wrapped her legs around him, fastened her mouth to his, and let Trent show her the worthiness of a man who could admit when he'd been wrong.

* * *

Afternoon was stretching into evening when Trent handed his reins off to Peak. Ellie had dozed again, slipping into sleep while Trent was still inside her, reeling with the pleasure and glory of making love with her. She was artless and shy, generous and bold. Most of all, she was eager—for him, for what he could give her.

The eagerness wouldn't last, of course. Clearly, Dane hadn't known how to go on with his wife, but he'd been inept rather than mean, and once Ellie had her confidence restored, she'd no doubt relegate Trent to a fond place in her memories, while he…

He'd cope. A little *affaire de coeur* wasn't an excuse for excesses of sentiment or attachment. In time, he'd acquire the knack, probably, though he hoped never to resemble his parents for the velocity and viciousness of their affairs.

"Is Cato about?" Trent asked.

"Pitching the evening's hay," Peak replied. "Heathgate sent a message up to the house for you."

"Send Cato along when you can spare him, and please look after Arthur. He's had a long and trying day."

"Oh, right. Poor old Artie looks worn to a veritable nubbin. Is her ladyship bearing up?"

"Doing fine."

Peak patted Arthur's neck while the horse stood placidly, one hip cocked. "Breeding females. They have that secret look about 'em, like God whispered a private joke in their ear."

"Or assurances of a happy ending to some fairy tale. Cato will find me in the library."

"I'll let him know. Come along, your highness." Peak led Arthur away, muttering something about the Quality and their stubbornness.

As Trent walked up to the house, he debated ordering a bath, but he'd ridden home at a sedate walk, keeping to the lanes rather than the bridle paths, the better to think through his circumstances—and avoid the woods.

His interlude with Ellie had been unexpected, unspeakably sweet, and troubling.

He hadn't meant to actually bed her, but her instinct had been accurate: He'd needed, desperately, not only bedding, but *loving*. He'd craved without knowing it the tenderness and intimacy Ellie had brought him. He'd needed to feel the silky smoothness of a woman's skin under his hands, needed to feel her weight on him, her hair brushing his arms, belly and chest. Hear her sighs and whispers, taste the sweetness of her kisses.

And that bed... Ellie slept in a fancy, a confection. The bed was a bit of whimsy in a practical lady whose loveliness had been too easily overlooked by her late husband.

"There's a rumor." Cato's voice sounded just behind Trent on the path. "The rumor's that you've ordered Louise to abide by only one menu a day, and we're all to dine on truffles as a result."

"Are they in season? I don't particularly care for them, but one should have variety in the diet."

Trent had asked Cato to attend him, and yet, he mightily resented his stable master's presence. That's how badly he wanted to wallow in memories of the afternoon's pleasures.

Cato drew even with him. "Are you to eat peasant fare?"

"Louise had to be stubborn to survive at Wilton Acres, but the rumor has a basis in fact. She was not conscientious enough in implementing my direction regarding the household's victuals, so I made my intentions easier to understand."

"Getting crotchety in your dotage?"

No "my lord," no "Amherst," and Trent wasn't inclined to correct him. "I am unwilling for a female's eccentricities to make my entire household miserable."

Ever again.

"About damned time," Cato muttered.

Any other evening, Trent might have let the remark pass, but having spent time in Elegy Hampton's bed had put him more on his mettle. Interesting.

"What is that comment supposed to mean, Catullus?"

Cato held his silence until they were in the library, where a sealed missive awaited in the center of the blotter on Trent's desk.

"Let me order us a meal, then you will answer my question."

While Trent dispensed with cuff links, cravat, and riding jacket, Cato studied the spines of books written in Latin, French, English and German. Trays came up from the kitchen, along with a pitcher of cold lemonade and chilled white wine.

"Eat." Trent took a seat at a table by the window and gestured for Cato to do likewise. "Or make yourself useful and pour some of that wine. I suspect I'll need it when I've read Heathgate's missive."

Cato for once didn't argue, scold or fuss, but sat and sipped his wine. "Jaysus, Mary and Joseph. At the end of a long, hot, miserable day, that is ambrosial."

"German." Though Ellie Hampton's kisses were the definition of ambrosial. "The German wines have a sturdiness that holds up better to hearty fare or hot days. So what did your comment mean, Catullus? It's about damned time?"

"Nothing. You hear too well, and I would never think to judge my betters."

"For what I and this coy, mendacious jackanapes are about to receive…" Trent intoned, picking up his fork.

"And for nobody getting blasted to kingdom come today," Cato interjected.

"We are grateful, amen," Trent concluded. "You're stalling, Catullus, and I've always taken you for a brave man."

"Why would you make that mistake?" Cato started on a small mountain of mashed potatoes sporting a fat puddle of gravy.

"The ladies," Trent said, tucking into his own meal. "A man with a reputation for racketing from bed to bed the way you do has to have a certain amount of courage."

"Manly humors do not courage make. God in heaven, I have missed good food. To what do I owe the privilege?"

"I want for company and I will have an answer, your

lordship."

Cato's fork clattered to his plate. "I will forget I heard that," he said slowly, "if you'll allow me to."

Trent sliced off a piece of perfectly turned beef. "Will some angry papa come haring across the shire, blunderbuss in hand, demanding my stable master make things right with his daughter?"

"He will not."

"You hope." Trent resigned himself to prying, though the food was excellent, and he'd passed hungry halfway up the lane. "Catullus, what is afoot?"

"I am many naughty, disreputable things," Cato said, staring at a forkful of potatoes. "I take responsibility for my sins, though, and Megan McMahon was not among them. I was with a female who answered to Meggie's description, and Meggie no doubt saw us, but that lady was not Meggie."

Trent chewed thoughtfully. "You were with a married woman, then. You couldn't say anything without getting the lady in a deal of trouble, and Meggie probably knew it. Shrewd, but not shrewd enough."

"I wasn't *with* the lady, not in the sense you implied." Cato took another drink of wine, probably stalling, the better to choose his words. "She was merely lonely and in want of a friend. I obliged with my company only, because my affections were elsewhere engaged."

Trent pushed the decanter closer to his stable master. "This is what comes from crying wolf, or some such. You were hung for a ram and thus I find Glasclare's baby earl in my stables."

Cato looked miserable and did not top off his wine. "Glasclare himself."

"My condolences," Trent said softly. "When did your father die?"

"About six months past. My cousin Brian is maintaining appearances, says I'm off on a sea voyage and will no doubt be back before seven years is up and I'm disinherited."

"You poor bastard. You'll have to show up married unless you want Meggie's papa to meet you with a shotgun. Has it been so bad, being my stable master here?"

"Not bad at all." Cato's smile was oddly bashful. "Except for Cook's idea of what the help should subsist on, but you're putting that to rights."

"One hopes." Trent poured more wine for his…his guest. Who outranked him. "Now that your personal peccadilloes are thoroughly dissected, Catullus, you've yet to explain what you meant earlier, when you said it's about time I stopped letting a female's eccentricities make an entire household miserable."

The exact words would not leave Trent's tired mind.

"A thousand apologies, and please don't call me out, but your late wife was a flaming horror." Cato put his utensils down and crossed his arms over his chest. "The help at your town house talk. They talk more than they work, if you want the truth, and whenever I'd take a team into Town, to bring in a load of produce or firewood, all I heard was how lucky we were out here, free of Lady Amherst's hysterics and sulks."

"She was sensitive." Trent used a flaky, buttered roll on his extra gravy. "That's all that need be said." Lest he start drinking too much and too quickly, and ranting.

"Amherst." Cato's voice became carefully even. "That is not all that need be said, and you know it."

"Another roll?"

"Please."

What was the point of evading this difficult conversation? For whom was decorum to be observed in this library at the end of this day?

"What else would you say, Cato?"

"If you want to look for people who hold you in low esteem, people with a grudge against you, you need to include Lady Amherst's family."

Trent stopped chewing and reached for his wine glass. "How much do you know?"

"Enough." Cato ran a callused finger around the rim of his glass. "They have to hold you responsible for her death, and for the fact that your nursery was full to bursting in five years flat and she was bloody miserable for the duration. The help was full of tales of her fits and pouts. She wasn't a stoic woman, Amherst."

"One perceived this when wed to her. You have a point, nonetheless." A point that Trent, preoccupied with his neighbor's kisses, had missed entirely.

"She was an hysterical female. That temperament can be inherited, which means it isn't a rational set of grieving in-laws you're dealing with, but instead, a pack of—"

"Lunatics," Trent concluded quietly. "I don't know them well, particularly Paula's mother, but her father seemed steady enough."

"Where does her family bide?" Cato polished off the last of his buttered green beans.

"The seat is in Hampshire, not far from Wilton Acres. I can ask our steward at Wilton to look into it, make sure they're all present and accounted for." Though the notion of ill will from Trent's former in-laws made a good meal sit poorly.

"All of them?"

"Paula has—*had*—two brothers, both older than she—Tidewell and Thomas—still racketing around without benefit of marriage. Her father is the Baron Trevisham, though, so one of the brothers will wed eventually." Trent did not envy their wives.

"How did her ladyship's brothers take her death?"

"I don't know," Trent said, thinking back. "We held the funeral before they could have come up, given it was winter, and my own situation was such that I haven't kept more than perfunctory contact with them."

Which had somehow slid into perfunctory contact with his entire life, until Darius had taken him in hand.

"Her family doesn't visit the children?"

"The baron did, once, but Ford was the only one born then."

"You English." Cato reached for the basket of rolls. "You're too trusting. You need to keep an eye on these people, Amherst. Their grief or indignation or what have you might be the source of your difficulties."

"Butter?"

"Of course."

"And you Irish," Trent replied. "You've been dodging bullets in your bogs for so long only the wiliest among you is left to breed."

Cato lifted his glass a few inches in salute. "And the most charming."

"Daft." Trent lifted his wine in acknowledgement. "I'll say something about Paula's family to Heathgate when next I see him, but speaking of the marquess, he's sent an epistle, which will no doubt include the secrets of the universe."

"He knew who I was?"

"Does it matter?"

"Yes."

"He strongly suspected." Trent slit the seal on the note, read it, then passed it to Cato. "Delphey's nowhere to be found, and Mrs. Soames thinks he's been gone at least a week."

Cato set the letter aside. "Which means he could be your culprit, or he was paid by your culprit. In any case, Heathgate won't get any answers out of him."

"Heathgate's brother had connections among the Irish aristocracy, because they breed horses with particular success," Trent said, going after the rolls himself because he'd cleaned his plate but wasn't full. "He would not suspect who you are but for that connection."

"So both Heathgate and Greymoor know." Cato blew out a breath. "I do not want to travel further afield than I have already, and I am bloody homesick."

That a fit, muscular, handsome man would admit such a

thing was at once touching and uncomfortable.

Damn all family intrigues anyway.

"So go home. Tell the grasping little twit you'll provide for her child, but she'd best recant her accusations if she wants your coin. Send her here. I can use a housekeeper, and the child would likely be about Michael's age."

"You'd accept an Irish bastard in your nursery?"

"I'd accept a young woman willing to work for honest coin, and last time I checked, toddling children ate little." Trent slapped butter on his roll and wandered off to sit on a corner of the desk. "Do not scold me in my own library about dropping crumbs, either. You can't drift forever, Catullus, and you've a duty to your papa's title, too."

Much as Trent winced to hear the very words.

"I know." The way a man new to a title knew and resented his unfulfilled duty.

"Are you married, Catullus?"

"And if I were?"

"It would be none of my affair, other than to wish you felicitations."

"If I were. But I'm not. Not yet."

"There's time." Trent shoved off the desk and tamped the cork back into the wine bottle. "The right wife would spike Miss McMahon's guns. Still, we won't solve all the world's problems in one day."

"We won't." Cato finished his wine and headed for the door. "My thanks for the meal and for your discretion."

"Catullus?"

"Amherst?"

"Why did you send for me, in truth?" The question was not the product of any accusation, but rather of genuine curiosity and no little gratitude.

"I have seven sisters I haven't seen in two years," he began. "Little ones, nieces and nephews I've never held. I wasn't there for my father's funeral, and my mother misses me like only an

Irish mother can miss her firstborn prodigal son. But you... your brother and sister, your wife, your children, even your benighted excuse for a father, they can all count on you. I've watched, and you always, always rise to the occasion when called upon, or before, if you can perceive the need. I thought you could use somebody at your back for a change. I thought you might be able to use a...friend."

Spare me from honest Irishmen. "You were right, Catullus." Trent passed over the wine bottle, then extended his hand. "You were, and you are, right."

Cato looked at that hand, hesitated only moment, then shook it firmly.

CHAPTER ELEVEN

"I'm here to discuss with you certain aspects of my situation." Trent wished that, of all people, he didn't have to disclose his history to the dour, perceptive Marquess of Heathgate.

"Any particular aspects?"

"Who might wish me ill."

Heathgate regarded him with blue eyes so cool their impact eclipsed the warmth of a summer morning. Then the music of little feet thundered overhead, and those eyes softened.

"We're about to be invaded, Amherst. Prepare to repel boarders."

"Papa!" A little boy, perhaps five years old, followed by smaller siblings, a boy and girl each, charged into the study and clambered up onto their father's chair. The girl assumed pride of place in his lap. The two boys flanked her more or less on the arms of the chair.

The female child turned guileless blue eyes on Trent. "Papa has a guest."

The boys scrambled down and offered Trent respective bows, the elder, then the younger. Trent rose and offered them reciprocal courtesies, after which the children bounced back into their father's chair.

"We're sailing away on a treasure hunt," the oldest boy informed his father. "We shall be pirates, and Joyce will be our captive princess."

"Is there a sea monster?" the marquess inquired, "or is this to be a land-based mission?"

"Uncle Andrew makes the best monsters," Joyce said. "He isn't coming, so no sea monster. Will you be our dragon?"

"Alas, Lord Amherst and I must tarry here in our dungeon." Heathgate looked genuinely regretful. "What is this treasure?"

"Mama won't say," the younger boy reported. "But she was *baking* yesterday."

"We know what that means." The marquess shared a look with his children. "Well, good luck, mates. Recall the Crown must have its share of the booty."

"Is that you?"

"Heavens, no. I am merely the lowly papa, but your mother certainly should have royal honors, don't you think?"

"If we want her to make more cookies," Joyce agreed, hopping down with her father's assistance. "Come on, you two, and take me prisoner."

The invading forces disappeared as quickly as they'd arrived, leaving Trent to regard his host in a far kinder light.

"Heathgate, you are a fraud."

"I am a parent, as you are yourself, so my secret is safe. Don't suppose you'd like to play dragons and sea monsters for a bit?" The invitation was only partly in jest.

"I'm on holiday from monster duty. My three have been with their aunt and uncle at Belle Maison for much of the summer. They're due back next week."

"Is that wise?" Heathgate went to the French doors, which looked out over the gardens. The marchioness, two nurses and a footman progressed across the lawns with the small band of pirates.

"Hear me out," Trent said. "If you think it necessary, I'll send word to Nick and Leah to keep the children with them awhile longer."

"I'm listening." Heathgate turned his back on window and the pirate parade with every appearance of reluctance.

"You inquired the other day whether I had enemies, detractors, people with a reason, real or otherwise, to take a shot at me at close range."

Heathgate settled in behind an enormous mahogany desk. "At you or the lady in your company."

"I could think of no one who'd have cause to shoot at either me or Lady Rammel, except perhaps Drew Hampton, who might want to ensure he inherits his late cousin's title."

Heathgate reached for a silver inkwell topped by a rearing unicorn. Trent didn't know the man well enough to decide if his scowl was thoughtful, ill-humored or both.

"Lady Rammel might bear a girl child," Heathgate said, "in which case she's no threat, and if the child is a boy, it's far easier to kill a child of whom one is guardian than a grown woman obviously carrying your replacement. While I don't know Drew Hampton well, neither have I heard he's impulsive or prone to flights of irrationality."

"My wife was." Oh, to be a pirate on the high seas of Surrey, battling monsters for fresh ginger biscuits instead of walking this particular plank.

Heathgate set the unicorn down in the exact center of his blotter, the horn aimed at Trent like an admonitory finger.

"Explain yourself, Amherst."

"Paula was my father's choice. She wasn't stupid or mean, but she was prone to flights of many types. I did not know her well when we wed. In hindsight, I can see our meetings were few and carefully orchestrated to show the lady to her best advantage."

"That isn't unusual."

Heathgate's courtship of his marchioness was rumored to have progressed upon very peculiar lines. One day, Trent might ask Ellie what she knew of those particulars.

"I wasn't a callow lad, just down from school," Trent countered. "I should have been more cautious of any scheme that had my father's approval, but Paula had money, and Wilton has all but bankrupted the earldom."

"So you married well for the sake of your progeny." Heathgate steepled his fingers, while out in the garden, shouts and shrieks suggested somebody had been taken captive. "Or thought you did."

"Oh, the money was real." Trent rose and went to the window, but the children—the pirates—were nowhere to be seen, though a bed of pink roses was in riotous bloom beneath the window. "I'm comfortably fixed, my children comfortably fixed, and with Wilton buttoned up at the family seat, my siblings need not worry, either."

"A happy ending, then." Heathgate remained seated while Trent wondered what Ellie was doing at that moment. Did little Andy play pirates? Did she have anybody to play pirates with?

"Not a happy ending for Paula." Trent tried to focus on the flowers, which bore a resemblance to vine gracing his pergola. "Paula was unhappy for most of our marriage."

For every single day and night of their marriage, even on those occasions when she was overcome with hilarity out of all proportion to the moment, she hadn't been well.

"Some people are determined to be miserable," the marquess observed. "I was once among their number, though I hardly knew it."

"Paula wasn't merely miserable. She was unbalanced, ill in her spirit. All she wanted of me was children, and that preferably if I could arrange for an angel to visit her for purposes of conception rather than my lowly, human self."

Trent cast around for polite phrases, while Heathgate—magistrate, reformed rake, and veteran papa—made no effort to fill the ensuing silence.

"Paula loathed my touch but begged me for more children." Trent longed to breathe the roses through the sparkling glass of Heathgate's mullioned window. "She cried the entire time, every time, but insisted it was what she wanted. At first she sought to give me my heir and spare, and that was enough—more than enough, as Darius will likely wed, particularly did I ask it of him."

He paused, again giving Heathgate a chance to cut him off, but when the silence only stretched, Trent slogged on.

"I relented because Paula must have a daughter, she said, to love and protect, and thank God in his mercy we had Elaine, and then when Elaine was six months old, she rejected the breast. Paula was devastated, and the begging started again."

"For another child?"

"For another child." Trent grabbed on to his composure, hard, hating even a recitation of the drama that had been his married life. "My father suggested I beat my wife, not because she'd learn her place, but because she might enjoy it enough to become biddable. I've never been so revolted by my patrimony."

Which, given his patrimony, was saying a great deal.

"Does this imply your wife might have confided in your father?"

Heathgate's reputation as a rake prior to his marriage had reached even Trent's ears, and his question bore only curiosity—no shock, no revulsion.

"Paula very likely did confide in Wilton, for he can be charming when it suits him." Trent pressed his forehead against the cool panes of glass, while an entire morass of uncomfortable emotions threatened, and the brandy decanter whispered to him from the sideboard. "She importuned my brother to get a child on her, and when Darius told me that, I realized my wife was not sane."

"He told you this?"

"He was concerned she'd take her begging elsewhere, anywhere." Trent had to pause again. Had to slow his breathing by force of will. "That would not have been safe for Paula. From that point, I had her not simply carefully attended, but watched. All was handled respectfully. On her bad days, her outings were curtailed, because the coach horse had thrown a shoe, her maid had a megrim, or one of the children was starting a sniffle, but Paula soon grasped that her wings had been clipped, and her decline was precipitous."

Loud, hysterical, and precipitous.

"Physicians?" Heathgate's quiet voice sounded near Trent's shoulder, but Trent remained where he could see the summer flowers.

"They suggested bleeding, or private estates with trained assistants, but I didn't want Paula to leave my care. She was vulnerable and dangerous, both. I was afraid to leave her alone with her own children and afraid to keep them from her entirely, so I sought to manage her. I undertook a balancing act, between cajolery, a drop of laudanum in her tea, hoping for the good days, and maintaining appearances. Throughout all of this, I came to understand she could not help herself."

Until she'd helped herself in the only fashion left to her.

"And then she died," Heathgate said, gently, kindly even, but the words still had the power to constrict Trent's breathing and make the roses waver in his vision.

"I thought we were finding the routine best suited to keeping her safe, and at least not…miserable. She grew to like the pattern of her days, or I thought she did, and while I relied on slipping her a few drops of laudanum on the bad days, Paula seemed to be settling down. Then the baby started cutting teeth, and Paula became worse than ever."

Out on the high seas, laughter graced the morning air, while Trent had lost sight of shore.

"I wanted Lanie weaned," he went on. "Not only because her mother occasionally took laudanum, which made the baby sleep a great deal, but because I didn't want Paula to unduly influence children who might already share her excitable tendencies. So I made the decision to wean the baby when those teeth appeared, and the baby seemed ready."

"The physicians supported this course?"

"They did. I consulted different experts, for both Paula and the baby, and their opinions were unanimous."

"What did you do?"

"I kept Lanie in the nursery and increased Paula's few drops to a few more. At first, it seemed to work, though I never meant it as more than a temporary measure."

"One develops a tolerance for opium, or a dependence, I believe."

Trent hunched in on himself. "One can. Paula must have seen her companion dosing her tea and tried to wean herself. She accused me of taking Lanie away because of the laudanum, and in a sense she was right."

"You took the child away because of the symptoms that required the laudanum. Nobody would quibble with a mother making occasional, limited use of a tonic."

Trent swallowed back the anger and pain knotting in his chest. At that moment, was Ellie napping in her fanciful bed? Digging among the flowers? Taking tea in the nursery with Andy, because a mother, a good mother, occasionally did?

"Somehow, some goddamned how, Paula found the strength to refuse the drug. She wanted her baby back, and I would not allow that unless I was in the room with them. This went on for days and nights, for I don't know how long, until she seemed to accept defeat. She became docile, then vacant, alarmingly so, and then quieter still."

Heathgate said nothing for a long time. "Overdoses can be accidental," he offered at length.

The marquess had hidden reserves of compassion,

but Trent shook his head. "Her death wasn't an accidental overdose—no laudanum was involved directly—but you can see why her family would blame me?"

Heathgate shifted to stand beside him. His scent was a complex, expensive sandalwood blend that made Trent want to open the window so the simpler fragrances of the summer garden could fill the room.

"Her ladyship's family could attribute motive to you for ending her life, I suppose. You married a crazy woman and couldn't make her sane any more than her family could. At least you didn't pawn her off on some soon-to-be-titled, unsuspecting stranger. She's lucky you didn't beat her, have her discreetly confined among strangers, or send her home to her parents."

Whatever else was true, Paula had been in no wise *lucky*.

"You don't understand, Heathgate." Trent turned to face his host. "If Paula's tendencies were inherited, then somebody, her mother, her older brothers, her dear papa, might be as unbalanced as she. When she was motivated, she could appear as blithe and charming as any young lady of good breeding. To appearances, her family is equally normal and likeable. And yet, in what passes for lunatic logic, I am the murderer, and I deserve to die."

Heathgate's lips pursed, as much a display of surprise as anybody likely saw from his lordship.

"If your children, yours and Paula's, are safely off visiting your sister, then the time to strike has come. Interesting theory."

"Particularly when anybody with a spare shilling could have learned from my town house staff I wasn't coping at all well this spring."

"Can you hire a Runner?"

"To make inquiries in Hampshire," Trent surmised. "I can, but do I bring my children home or leave them summering in Kent?"

"Bring them home. In the first place, we might be chasing our tails on this Gothic theory of murderous in-laws, and in the second, the children, and your attachment to them, could well be what will keep you safe. Then too, a man has a need to impersonate a sea monster on occasion."

Trent smiled weakly, grateful for the cool reason, the fillip of humor, and the underlying understanding from a man who might have been appalled.

"Come admire my roses," Heathgate said. "We might stumble across a band of pirates, but even if we're not that fortunate, you could see a specimen Lady Rammel might put to use in your gardens."

Heathgate needed time to think, in other words, which Trent would happily grant him.

"You met with Lady Rammel?" Trent let himself be ushered out onto the terrace.

"Had breakfast with her, and what a treat she is. If my marchioness had known what a treasure Rammel was hiding in our back yard, Felicity and Lady Rammel would be thick as thieves by now—or pirates."

"Lady Greymoor has made a condolence call." Gentlemen must keep one another informed when it came to the ladies' maneuverings, after all.

Heathgate cut a path across the gardens. "Felicity will do the same and likely dragoon my cousin Lady Amery along, and even our mutual neighbor Lady Westhaven."

"August company. Are they kind?" Had Heathgate asked his lady to rally this support for Ellie?

"You are protective of Rammel's widow?"

He would give up his life for her. "Cut line, Heathgate. Of course I'm protective of her. Rammel was a selfish, dog-kissing bore, his lady has no family of her own, and she's in an interesting condition."

His lordship's smile was fleeting. "She's protective of you, too. Told me I'd best catch Philadelphia Soames and tie him to a chair for a week, or she'd know the reason why. These are my hybrid crosses and among them, my favorite is this little peachy-pink wonder here."

The marquess was tall, dark, and he would have been handsome, except his features had a saturnine, condescending cast, and those eyes of his... But when the man referred to anything—especially a rose—as "peachy-pink," and when his gaze kept straying to the corner of the property toward which his children had disappeared, Trent had to revise his opinion.

"So you liked her. Lady Rammel, that is?" Trent asked.

"She reminded me of my dear wife." Heathgate snapped off a rose and handed it to Trent. "I know of no higher compliment."

Peachy-pink, indeed. Trent sniffed the delicate bouquet of the flower and looked into its throat. The color at the center was the exact same luscious shade as an aroused woman's—

"One more question on our earlier topic," Heathgate said as they turned for the stables.

"I won't like it."

"I'll hate asking it," Heathgate agreed, strolling along among his flowers. "On your wedding night, was your wife a virgin?"

"Brutally insightful." Trent cast back, but memories were interrupted by the implications of Heathgate's question. If Paula had had a lover...

"If her affections had been intimately attached elsewhere, it would explain her disgust of you." Heathgate spoke as if discussing a planned arrangement of daisies and irises. "Also her desire for children, to justify her marriage when she loved another, and to cover up her dallying."

"She knew what to expect," Trent said, the words dragged from him. "I recall being relieved, and I encountered no... physical resistance."

Heathgate paused, which meant the conversation remained out of earshot of the grooms in the stables up the path. "Sometimes no resistance is detectable, or a considerate mother will have a midwife see to the matter before the wedding night."

Every one of Heathgate's attempts to provide a normal, reasonable explanation for the state of Trent's married life only made the memories more corrosive.

"Paula had been crying before I joined her on our wedding night, though she tried to hide it. She knew what to expect."

"In a theoretical sense?"

The man was relentless, for which Trent had to both loathe and admire him. "I wish that were so, but in hindsight I'd say her knowledge was of the act."

"So our circle widens," Heathgate concluded. "Best send that Runner, or I've an investigator who might have time to see to the matter. If Paula had a lover, you need to know who he was and what he's doing now."

* * *

Trent headed for home with every intention of shutting himself up in the Crossbridge library and seeing to a growing pile of correspondence. Arthur chose instead to turn up the drive to Deerhaven, and there to deposit his owner at the manor house.

Trent swung himself off his traitorous beast and handed the reins to a stable boy.

"Might as well put him up rather than walk him," Trent said. "My intentions don't seem to be carrying much weight of late, and I don't intend to stay long."

The groom gave him a faintly "Oh-the-Quality" look, saluted, and took the horse off to the stables. Trent found Ellie on her balcony reading a pamphlet about breeding horses.

"Unless Greymoor wrote it," Trent said, "you're better off talking to the man himself."

"Trenton!" She bounced off her swing, wrapped her arms around his neck and hugged him tightly.

He held her more gently, and in the warmth and fragrance

of her embrace, a weight lifted from his spirit.

"I have much to learn." She eased back and brushed his hair away from his forehead. "About raising horses, and babies. Andy was already three when I got her, so I'll be on terra incognita come Yuletide."

"Is that when you're due?" He let her pull him down beside her, because she seemed to think he belonged there.

And so, for now at least, did he.

Ellie kept her hand in his. "Christmas is months away, an eternity, but it will pass, and then I'll be big as a house. I think of poor Mary riding a donkey in such a condition, and the Christmas story loses some of its romance."

"You'll still be beautiful, but in a different way."

She ducked her face against his shoulder. "Can you already see I'm carrying?"

See it, feel it, sense it. *Rejoice in it.* "I can, because I have children and because you were not shy with me yesterday. Are you feeling well?"

Not shy. Had a man ever concocted a greater understatement? She'd been magnificent.

"I am fine." Her smile was a work of joy, beauty and sheer femininity. "You?"

"Disconcerted," he said, looking away from that smile.

Ellie's smile shifted to a grimace. "Heathgate was here for breakfast. He can be surprisingly charming, but that's almost worse than his glowering, because the charm is convincing, and yet, he's like a mastiff—he has all those muscles and claws and teeth, even when he's playing fetch."

"I've just come from his company because Cato, of all people, raised a theory I hadn't considered."

"You are troubled about this theory." Ellie threaded an arm through his and gave the swing a push with her toe. "Should we take a nap?"

He wanted to do the decent thing, for her, in her delicate condition, and for him, all at sixes and sevens. A nap was not the decent thing, though with Ellie, it didn't feel indecent, either.

"Today you should recover from yesterday's napping."

She pinched off a blown pink rose and cast the petals over the balcony. "Tediously prudent of you. Tell me of this disquieting theory of Mr. Spencer's."

No argument, no pouting, no sulking. Truly, such a woman was worth more than rubies.

"Cato reminded me that my wife was not happy with her station as Lady Amherst. She was unrelentingly miserable, in fact."

Ellie pinched off another blossom and let the breeze snatch away the petals. "Then she was a foolish woman, or not quite in command of her faculties."

"Why do you say that?"

"I went to an exclusive boarding school, Trenton." Now she tossed two pink brocade pillows off the swing, landing them neatly in the corner of the balcony. "The aristocracy is more inbred than one wants to admit, and in the young female exponents of certain great houses, the results are hard to conceal."

A third pillow landed on top of the other two. The lady had good aim. "What results?"

"The school boasted many nice girls, of course." Ellie's slippers—also pink—joined the pile of pillows in the corner. "Some were genuinely rebelling against their life circumstances—betrothal to an old man, regardless of his wealth or title, could disconcert any girl."

"But?"

She scooted around and curled up with her head pillowed on his thigh. "Some of the girls were…"—she waved a hand around her temple—"flighty. One insisted on having her doll learn French with her—a sixteen-year-old, affianced to some old duke. Two others were heavy tipplers, to put it politely, and bribed the staff to ensure their tea was always laced with brandy. They abused tisanes and tonics, which their families obligingly supplied them with."

And thus Ellie had gained her first glimpse of Polite Society?

"Leah and Emily were educated at home." Trent's fingers drifted along Ellie's hairline. "At university, I heard stories from some of the lads who had sisters. I wasn't the only youth raised in trying circumstances, but it doesn't seem fair that the young ladies should be miserable so early in life."

Ellie rubbed her cheek against his thigh, like a cat, or a... wife.

"Those girls helped me appreciate my steady old papa, I can tell you that. One tried to take her own life, and that was the last we saw of her. Another left under peculiar circumstances, and it was rumored she was increasing."

"That didn't close the place down?"

Ellie yawned and settled herself more comfortably on Trent's person. Only then did it occur to him that her balcony, though near the home wood tree line, might not be entirely private.

"For the two girls sent down, it wasn't their first boarding school, by any means, and the fees were intimidatingly high. I always thought the same things went on in boys' schools, because boys are always getting sent down."

"Not at Eton." Trent cupped her jaw then trailed his thumb over the silky warmth of her throat. "Some of the wilder fellows made it to university, but one expects that when boys first get a taste of a man's freedoms."

"Wenching, gaming and liquor." Ellie snorted delicately, but her eyes were closed, and she wasn't going to last long.

"Ellie?" Trent's fingers slipped into the top of her bodice. "I wasn't always kind to my wife." And, God help him, on a few occasions he'd wondered whether some of his father's flat-out nastiness toward his countess hadn't had some justification. Even to Ellie, even today, he could not admit that.

"You were kind to her, Trenton. As kind as you could be, though you are stubborn sometimes, and you take too much on yourself."

"About that nap?"

She blinked up at him. "But you can be reasoned with."

Reason had nothing to do with it. What Trent sought was oblivion and comfort.

He made love to Ellie slowly, savoring her generosity and sleepy lack of inhibition. He treasured her soft moans of pleasure and welcome, lapped up her kisses and arched into her caresses like a lonely cat. Her hands on his body were tender and wondering and kind, and her loving warm and comforting.

He'd intended to tell her exactly what he'd told Heathgate, that Paula's family might wish him harm, but instead he whispered to her how lovely she was in her passion, how beautifully she bloomed beneath him, how he savored her touches and sighs and kisses.

When she again fell asleep, her cheek pressed to his chest, he went on telling her his secrets with his hands—how Trent would miss her, how lucky Dane had been to have had years with her, and how Trent should not allow her to become entangled in his life when somebody was trying to kill him.

CHAPTER TWELVE

Ellie awoke to such a sense of safety and rightness, she was sure she must be having one of those deceptive dreams. She'd had them as a girl, and they usually involved bounding from one cloud to another, or pink unicorns, or flowers that tasted like sweets.

She inhaled and caught the clean, savory scent of Trenton Lindsey, the biggest sweet that life had ever dropped into her palm.

"Hullo." She listened to his heart beating beneath her cheek. "You're alive."

"I've recently come to appreciate that."

"I take it your visit with Heathgate was not encouraging?"

"If you are done napping, perhaps we can discuss it?"

"I don't do it apurpose, though napping puts us into proximity with a bed, and when I get you into bed, delightful things happen."

"You're wicked. A sleeping siren."

She wondered whether she'd ever dare tell him that in her entire marriage, she'd never *slept* with her husband. "A siren who wants to know about Mr. Spencer's theory and whatever else plagues you."

Because something bothered him. She'd felt it in his lovemaking, and she could see it in his eyes when she propped herself along his side.

"Mr. Spencer reminded me that my late wife's family might blame me for her death." For all his slow, even breathing, for all the delicacy with which he brushed her hair back, Trent watched her carefully. "My late wife might blame me as well, in a sense."

"You've said you did not suit." She and Dane had not suited, not really. This made her sad, for them both, but particularly for him, whose short life should have included at least a few years of marital *bliss*. "I can hardly imagine you not suiting any lady, for at heart you're an agreeable man."

"Ever willing to nap, it seems." Trent's smile was rueful. "At least with you. Paula and I argued bitterly over whether to have more children, among other things. She became melancholic, to make a long story very short. It might be said she died of a heart I broke when I would not give her more children."

He clearly anticipated censure for this tale. "Your Paula wasn't very grown-up, was she?"

"No," Trent said, apparently relieved somebody would say it for him, finally. "She did not tolerate disappointment easily, and she was very disappointed in me."

"And you in her?"

"Well, yes."

Perishing Halifax, *yes*. "For God's sake, you gave her three children. I was married for as long as you were, and I was lucky to get a by-blow to raise. Your lady wife was not sensible of her blessings."

While Ellie spared the woman a pang of posthumous sympathy, her protective instincts were all for the man in her bed. On that thought, she shifted up to straddle him, lest he attempt an escape before the issue of his marital shortcomings had been put to rout.

Trent took the end of Ellie's braid and drew it down her brow, nose and chin.

"My wife was not sensible of much beyond her own moods, though her family might hold me responsible for her unhappiness, and that means they could be my enemies."

"This makes no sense." Ellie saw the preoccupation and introspection in his gaze, so she took both his hands and cupped them over her breasts. "I like it when you touch me here, but don't feel you must do anything more. I wouldn't want to be greedy, and you still look tired to me."

"I am tired."

"You are also blessed with warm hands."

Even her compliment didn't banish the worry from his gaze.

"Ellie, if Paula came by her lack of sensibility by inheritance, then her family will not be reasonable in their enmity toward me. They will be cunning, and determined, but not rational."

"I'm not rational. I can't decide whether your touch is more soothing or arousing, but I do know I love it."

"Perhaps my touch has been merely comforting."

The dratted man was in the grip of another pang of noble sentiment, when Ellie wanted to ravish him repeatedly.

"Trenton Lindsey, you think you will preserve me from being shot at again by waltzing off on your destrier and leaving me to get fat as a water buffalo in your absence."

"I think to keep you safe," Trent said softly, his hands going still. "You and your little water buffalo calf."

Ellie dragged her sex slowly over his cock, then did it again. "What if the bullet was meant for me, Lord My-Crazy-In-Laws-Hate-Me? What if Drew is a good actor, and he secretly covets the title endlessly? Dane was a bruising rider on a good horse over a familiar fixture."

"You don't believe that." He disconcerted her from further argument by slipping slowly into her body. A delightful tactic, though not entirely effective.

"You don't know your in-laws have developed a penchant for murder long after your wife has departed." Ellie began to move with him, braced up on her hands so he could still get to her breasts.

"Heathgate doesn't think you're at risk," Trent said, his thrusts gathering force.

"Heathgate,"—Ellie thrust back quite as stoutly—"isn't in this bed."

He rolled her, and drove into her in a deep, steady rhythm. "Say you'll let me keep you safe, Ellie."

She bucked up into his thrusts, marveling at how frustration could serve as an aphrodisiac. "Not if it means you'll become a stranger."

"Please." He shifted the angle and hit the spot deep in her body that unchained her reason and rained pleasure down on her in torrents.

"To Halifax with your theorems." Ellie scraped her fingernails over his nipple and sank her fingers into his muscular backside. "You are afraid I'll sour on you, as she did, and worried you can't keep me safe, and even more worried I'll get too attached."

The confounded, noble, impossible man went still.

"I'm afraid you'll leave me, and afraid you won't?"

Her lover was a quick study. "I'm scared, too, Trent." She urged him down, so she could hold him close.

"Tell me."

"I'm scared your horse will toss you into a ditch, and you'll never draw breath again." She locked ankles at the small of his back, though he was apparently inclined to hear her out. "I'm scared you'll laugh at my inexperience, at my broodmare body, at my napping and crying and odd sounds. I'm scared you'll tire of the novelty and convenience of swiving the widow next door, and I'm very scared you will get up from my bed and convince yourself you must keep your distance in the interests of my safety."

He buried his face against her shoulder and set up a slow, maddeningly controlled rhythm.

"I want to, I want to have the resolve to keep my hands to myself, to keep you safe, to respect your well-being enough not to embroil you in the mess my life has become."

"Please, don't." She clung to him and drew him tightly into her body. "Please don't have the resolve, Trenton Lindsey. I need you to not have it, not now, and not in the foreseeable future."

He didn't reply, not with words, but he loved her, slowly, generously, thoroughly, and then he left her sleeping peacefully in her fairy-tale bed, while he rode away on his destrier.

* * *

Ellie didn't find the note Trenton had left her until she'd dressed the next morning. It helped, but not much.

> *Dear Lady,*
> *We'll talk further. Please remain safe.*
> *Amherst*

Not exactly pink clouds and unicorns but some promise of further dealings.

He was a terror between the sheets, Trenton Lindsey was. He could read her body like a book, giving her exactly what she needed before she'd even formed awareness of her own longings. How on earth, how on God's green and growing earth, had his wife not been happy with him?

"Callers, my lady," Mr. Wright intoned.

"Plural?" Ellie's hand strayed to her hair, which was in need of a thorough trim and unruly as a result.

"Ladies Heathgate, Greymoor, and Amery."

The local equivalent of royalty. "Gracious. Will the family

parlor do, Wright, or shall we put on airs?"

"The family parlor has the freshest flowers, milady. I'll have Missus send up a tray."

She greeted her guests after shoving a few more pins in her hair, but really, nobody warned a lady that pregnancy changed even her *hair*.

"Ellie." Lady Greymoor—*Astrid*, and that after only one visit—held out gloved hands. "I've brought reinforcements." She rattled off introductions to Lady Heathgate and Lady Amery. "Because Felicity is my sister and Gwen my cousin-by-marriage, I can lend them to you on a family-at-large basis."

Whatever that meant. "You can?"

Lady Heathgate, a redhead with a flawless complexion, sent her younger sister an indulgent look. "She can, and I will offer you our official condolences on the loss of your husband. A young man's death is a tragedy on general principles, but you look to be bearing up."

Ellie met eyes of an unusual topaz color and thought of the lady's mastiff of a husband. "I'm faring well, thank you. Probably better than I should be."

"That's because you're to have a child," Lady Amery said, her smile charitable. She too sported red hair, as well as a statuesque build. "I understand from my cousins you also have the raising of your husband's daughter, Miss Coriander."

"Andy," Ellie said, slightly taken aback to have Dane's bastard brought into the conversation so blatantly.

Lady Heathgate's smile remained in place. "Perhaps we can take our tea in the nursery, then. Gwen has a daughter of about seven years, and Rose is always amenable to new acquaintances, provided they're horse mad, if not horses."

"Andy qualifies as pony mad," Ellie said. Lady Greymoor had already taken her arm and was leading her to the door.

"We've much to discuss," the petite blonde said. "Have you chosen names yet, and where is Dane's cousin when you're in a delicate condition and in need of cosseting, and do you need help with the baby's clothes? We've all piles and scads of them, and the little dears outgrow everything they don't stain into oblivion…"

The ladies stayed far longer than courtesy required, and when they left, Ellie and Andy had an invitation to tea the next day with Lady Amery and her daughter, Rose.

Andy aimed a puzzled look at her step-mama when they'd waved their guests good-bye.

"I thought we were in mourning. Minty says that's like when bad weather keeps everybody indoors but you have to wear the right colors."

"It's been more than four months. Your papa would not have wanted you confined to the house, and this Rose is in need of friends."

"Why do you say that?"

"No sisters," Ellie said as they ascended the steps to the front terrace. "I know how that feels, and so do you."

"Maybe I'll have a sister at Christmas."

A beat of silence went by as Ellie took a seat on the top step, and Andy sat beside her. "I should have told you sooner. How did you know?"

"I heard Lord Amherst talking to Mrs. Wright before he left yesterday. He went on and on about peppermint tea and putting your feet up, and chocolates, and pillows for your knees and back, and keeping the windows open so your delicate digestion isn't upset by stale air. He made it sound like you're a princess, Mama. Do you feel like a princess?"

"A little." A lot, when Trenton Lindsey was on hand.

"He said you're not to leave the house alone, not even to garden, and we must take the best care of you."

"I'm to have a baby, but you're to become a big sister, so we should be taking care of you as well."

In a way that Ellie hadn't appreciated before, she saw that children created vulnerability. Andy was precious, and anybody intending harm to Ellie could attain that goal by hurting Andy.

While Trenton had three small children.

Andy dashed for the door while Ellie made more decorous use of the steps. "Does this mean I can have a pony?"

"You had a chance to visit a pony at Crossbridge. You hardly paid Zephyr any attention at all, Coriander."

"Papa hardly paid me any attention, but you're always telling me he loved me."

"He did." To the extent Dane had loved any human female. "You don't like Mr. Spencer, do you?"

"He's… I thought he was Papa's friend," Andy said, pulling a droopy bloom from the daisies in a crystal bowl on the sideboard. "But they weren't truly friends. Papa killed his horse."

The child wandered the front hall, her unwillingness to meet Ellie's gaze suggesting Dane's death still did not entirely make sense to his daughter.

"Mr. Spencer had to put his own horse down, but it was because of your papa's fall and the bad footing, not because your father wished the horse ill."

"He might have wished Mr. Spencer ill," Andy said, frowning at the flowers. "This arrangement doesn't smell very good."

Daisies typically didn't. "The water needs to be changed. It's not too terribly hot yet today. Would you like to do some baking with me in the summer kitchen?"

Andy's expression brightened. "Baking biscuits?"

"Lady Heathgate left me a recipe for muffins. She says they make the whole house smell good."

"The summer kitchen isn't the house. Let's bake anyway, for it's Minty's day for preparations. We'll bring her some muffins, and she'll be in a good mood."

Either the prospect of baking cheered Andy inordinately, or the topic of Dane's death and Mr. Spencer's role in it was so troubling, Andy would look forward even to a sweltering morning spent in Ellie's company.

* * *

"I don't know when I've seen you looking so happy and at peace." Trent observed to his sister as they strolled around the sprawling beauty of Belle Maison's gardens.

Leah was tall and had the same dark coloring as her brothers, but her smile had grown brilliant since her marriage to Nicholas Haddonfield, Earl of Bellefonte. "My husband dotes on me, and Emily's letters are giddy with the pleasure of being Lady Warne's fashionable project. I worry about my brothers, though."

The three siblings were as bonded by worry as by affection, the hallmark of Wilton's patrimony.

"Suppose it's only fair you worry about us. We've spent some time worrying about you. But this... You chose well, Leah. Bellefonte's estate clearly prospers, and he doesn't take his blessings for granted."

"You're comparing my marriage to your own," Leah guessed. "When will you bury that woman, Trent? You're still grieving."

And here, he'd thought Bellefonte's and Heathgate's inquisitions had been uncomfortable.

"Not grieving, exactly." Thirty yards away, the Earl of Greymoor grinned up at Nick, his smile conspiratorial. Greymoor had invited himself along on the journey, ostensibly to talk horses with Nick. In reality, Trent suspected the man's brother had put him up to some informal bodyguarding.

Or governessing a bereaved viscount.

Or snooping.

Trent ambled along with his sister, though Nick caught sight of them and had to blow Leah a kiss Trent pretended not to see. "How bad was Paula?"

"She loved her children." Leah spoke with assurance, and hadn't given the answer Trent had anticipated.

"Did she? When Ford came along, I had to wonder if she loved him or simply enjoyed showing him off." The way she'd initially enjoyed showing off her new husband—on her good days.

"Paula adored Ford. Not many titled women will put their children to their own breast, sew all their clothes, or spend hours reading to them when they're too little to even recognize the words. Ford and Michael still love to be read to."

"I'd forgotten that. She sang to them, too." A low contralto with an inborn strain of melancholy that nonetheless soothed a child to sleep.

"She also painted the pictures for the nursery wing," Leah added. "She loved her children."

"But?"

Trent had the odd wish that Ellie had known Paula, for Ellie's assessment would be even more insightful than Leah's.

"But Paula's candle was short, in important regards," Leah said, gently. "She should have been in a convent somewhere, raising orphans, maybe. She became particularly... eccentric after Lanie was born. She did not understand you, that much was obvious."

Nor had Trent understood her, which probably summarized half the petty marital tragedies on the planet. "Did she have a lover?"

"I beg your pardon?"

Sea monsters and dragons lurked at the edge of the discussion, or thorny roses.

"When one's wife was unreceptive to marital advances but desperately desired children, one wondered if there might have been someone else, such that the lady needed her husband's occasional visits to her bed to obscure the truth."

"She never alluded to another," Leah said slowly. "Never asked me to lie for her, never showed up somewhere I wasn't expecting her, or came later than we'd planned. She once said something odd, though."

Paula had said many odd things, made wild plans, then murmured despairingly, as if the fall of a leaf could presage a French invasion, or a blooming flower ensure the royal succession.

"What did she say?" Nicholas and Greymoor were arguing, loudly, good-naturedly. The horses in the adjoining fields took note, then went back to the grazing.

"Paula said she would never feel good enough to be your wife." Leah fell silent as Nick paused in his debate to wave to her from across the lawns. "The look on her face when she said it was so…sad, so hopeless. Heartbroken."

"Heartbroken. That summarized my late wife, but I can't for the life of me comprehend why."

Leah waved back at her spouse. "Sometimes there isn't a why, not even when you need one most."

Trent bade his sister farewell on that inconclusive note and joined the company of the fools at the stables.

"A word with you, Nicholas?" Trent asked as Greymoor led both Ford and Michael off to make their farewells to Nick's mare, Buttercup.

Nick patted the rump of a passing plough horse. "You may have more than a word. Greymoor will tarry in the stables until Yuletide if we allow him to."

Yuletide, when Ellie would be delivered of her burden.

"You received my letter regarding the gunshot?"

Nick looped an arm across Trent's shoulders, and walked with him out along the paddock fencing. "You'd yet to bring it up, so I wasn't comfortable quizzing you."

Such delicacy fooled Trent not at all.

"I've had some time to think," Trent said, wondering what made a man as affectionate as Nick Haddonfield, and as likeable. "I told you I was with my neighbor, Lady Rammel, at the time of the incident."

"About whom you've also been mightily reticent."

"I questioned whether the bullet might have been meant for her," Trent went on, ignoring Nick's baiting.

"But?"

"But you stock a very fine cellar, and your nightcaps are particularly excellent."

Nick dropped his arm. "You consumed those nightcaps in excellent company is all. I'm convivial and charming, according to your sister."

Nick was much more than that, and Trent didn't need Leah to provide the details. "The company was well enough. I'm reminded that I used to be very particular about my libation." He had prided himself on a discriminating palate, because Wilton wouldn't know aged whiskey from gin, or a Riesling from champagne.

"You're not discriminating now?"

How to explain? "Now I'm trying to limit myself to wine or the occasional tankard of summer ale, but when I was in Town this spring, I was not limiting myself in any fashion."

Nick took to studying a herd of yearlings playing stallion games in a grassy pasture beside the stables. "I never saw you drunk."

"You probably never saw me sober, either," Trent said wearily. "I vaguely recall at some point wondering when I'd started buying the cheaper selections."

"Somebody was skimming your accounts. This can happen when the help gets to taking liberties."

Little boy horses played at being courting swains, while Trent considered further evidence of a life gone badly awry— his life. "I don't think the problem was skimming. I think somebody laced my drinks with laudanum or some other soporific."

Nick paced off a few feet, then glared at him. "Bloody buggering hell, Trenton."

"Hear me out." Trent settled against a stile, because it appeared Greymoor would, indeed, entertain the children until Yuletide if need be.

Yuletide, the season of little water buffaloes.

"I'm not sure myself what I'm suggesting," Trent said.

"When Paula became particularly unreasonable, we'd spike her tea or posset or what have you with a little of the poppy. The household was in the habit, we kept a goodly supply on hand, and yet among my domestics, turnover was high."

Nick paced in front of the stile. If he'd had a mane, tail and hooves, he would have been pawing and snorting. "Your business was probably known to other households in the area then, if your staff took other positions in the same neighborhood."

"I can only assume so. I am ashamed to say I lost a firm grip of who was responsible for what among my staff." Provided his glass had been kept full. No wonder Darius had become alarmed.

Nick scuffed a worn riding boot against the grass, the equivalent of equine pawing. "Dare told us you had no butler. It worried him, because you'd had the same one since you set up your town house."

"Another graduate of Wilton's school of impossible standards. I pensioned the butler not long ago."

"Did your drinks start tasting better?"

Around him, Trent was aware of the summer morning—the building heat of the sun, the light riffle of the breeze over the grass, the swish of a horse tail in the paddock behind them, the scent of the stables upwind.

"You're implying my staff was bribed to poison me."

"Suggesting it." Nick's gaze went past Trent's shoulder to the stables. "You were trying to reach the same conclusion yourself, but you hadn't put your finger on the butler."

Butlers figured prominently in Gothic novels, and never on the side of good.

"I still haven't." Trent pushed away from the stile and marched back toward the stable yard. "Neither can I rule him out. God above, if Dare hadn't shanghaied me, I could have ended up with a pillow to my face, or gone up in blazes because I supposedly tripped with an oil lamp in my hand."

"You're speculating. What of your staff at Crossbridge? Are they loyal?"

"Yes. I came into that place when I was eighteen, and I've owned it for almost half my life. I hired most of the current staff, and when it came down to it, they were the ones who set Dare on me. Paula hired most of the town house staff, and fired them, and hired their replacements and so on."

"She was difficult?"

Nick loved women, all women, and was being gallant, as usual. "You know she was. My sister's entire life is an open book between you two, and that would include Leah's crazy sister-by-marriage."

"Not crazy. Troubled. Leah says she was troubled."

"Mortally, and I thought I was the cause, but I'm beginning to wonder."

"You're also beginning to put off mourning, and that's for the best. Your children were growing fretful."

Nick swiped a sprig of meadow mint and tucked it between his teeth, the most bucolic rendition of a peer of the realm Trent had beheld—except for Glasclare adopting the same mannerism.

"I missed them," Trent admitted as they approached the mounting block. "I didn't even realize how much I missed them, and now I may be bringing them home to danger."

Nick's arm came down across his shoulders again. "It's entirely possible your staff was lacing your drinks, but maybe it started as a way to get you to sleep when you were newly bereaved, and then it became a way to facilitate pinching your pennies. You can't leap from suspecting they spiked your brandy to seeing murder most foul."

Leah had married a spectacularly kind man. Trent resisted the urge to tell him so, for Nick was shy, too.

"I can't make that leap yet, but somebody shot at me at close range, and somebody else cut my stirrup leathers on a particularly sloppy night. I can't ignore those factors either,

Nick."

Nick's gaze strayed to the house, and Trent could hear him thinking: *Leah will be upset if…* "Maybe you should stay with us for a time."

Oh, of course. Far from Ellie, who might also be a target for mischief.

"And bring the problem here? Not for all the brandy in France. I've a few ideas regarding the source of my troubles, and at Heathgate's prompting, I'll enlist the assistance of your friend Hazlit."

"You met him at our wedding. The secret hasn't been hatched that Benjamin can't ferret out, but he's expensive."

"What is the price," Trent said softly, "of living to see Lanie make her bow, or knowing my boys are safely launched? They've already lost one parent and never had grandparents to speak of. I think that's quite enough loss for such tender hearts."

"You sound determined."

"I am determined," Trent replied as Arthur was brought out. "More than that, Nick, I'm angry, and I wonder whether Paula's death wasn't more complicated than it seemed."

These emotions were not pale, passing fancies, as they might have been earlier in the summer. They were heartfelt, tenacious, and proof nobody was spiking Trent's drinks any longer.

Nick watched the horse, rather than Trent's face, and Trent appreciated the courtesy. "Leah told me what she knew of your wife's passing. I'm most sorry, Trenton."

"We all were," Trent replied. "All excepting possibly Paula herself."

CHAPTER THIRTEEN

"I've sent for this Hazlit fellow," Trent said as he and Heathgate waited for a groom to tighten Arthur's girth. Stopping here on the way home from Belle Maison had made sense, particularly when Trent wanted to update the magistrate regarding his latest suspicions.

"Hazlit will acquit himself well in any endeavor." Heathgate didn't pry beyond that, and Trent had the sense the marquess didn't have to pry. Heathgate was born knowing more than a mortal man should be able to divine without celestial assistance.

Trent tugged on a pair of riding gloves that had seen considerable use in the course of the day. "My thanks for sending the women to Lady Rammel. That was a much-appreciated kindness."

"If so, it was overdue. The lady is grieving, and we all know what a fraught journey that can be. Her daughter has become immediate friends with my cousin Rose, though, and we are relieved to see it."

"A younger cousin?"

"Young." Heathgate held his hand out at about hip height. "Though every inch her mother's child, and granddaughter to a duke, but a lonely child. Rose is older than all of mine or Andrew's, so Miss Coriander is filling a felt need splendidly."

"For?"

Heathgate's lips twitched, possibly with impatience. "A friend, Amherst. Friendship is a quaint concept, though for a time I disdained it myself. We all need friends."

Trent swung up onto Arthur's back, saluted with his crop, and sent the beast trotting down the drive.

While Trent considered Heathgate's parting shot.

Trenton Lindsey, Viscount Amherst, was a man without friends. Or he'd let himself *become* a man without friends.

He and Dare had been friends, and Leah as well. As children, Wilton had taken a focused interest in his heir's upbringing, and Lady Wilton had retaliated by making Dare her favorite. Both parents had tried to pit the boys against each other, but each child had been canny enough to see the parental manipulation. Trent and Dare had been each other's only friends, often, and had grown even closer as the need to protect Leah from Wilton had become more apparent.

That had changed when Trent had gone off to school, while Dare had been considered worthy of only second-rate tutors at home.

Arthur, tired as he had to have been, had decided the Deerhaven stables were closer than those at Crossbridge, and once again took himself up the wrong drive.

"Blast you, beast. We weren't going to do this."

"Afternoon, my lord." The groom took Arthur's reins. "Himself looks a little road weary."

Trent patted his horse, who now stood as if exhausted, his head hanging.

"Himself is a scheming tyrant. Some hay and water for

him, and I'll likely just walk him home in hand."

The groom gave him a puzzled look but disappeared with the horse, leaving Trent to wonder how exactly he should convey his intended message to Ellie.

Lady Rammel. The widowed Lady Rammel, who was acquiring friends and who did *not* need her neighbor complicating her life with death threats and dalliances.

"Trenton?" Ellie's voice came from the pergola, followed by her beaming smile. She was barefoot, her hair loosely braided over one shoulder. "Oh, it *is* you. I am so glad you are home."

Home.

She hugged him, despite the curious eyes in the house and the stables, despite his dust and sweat, despite his failure to warn her he'd be calling. She just…she hugged him.

He tried to pull back. "I stink, and you're tidy, and we are not private, and you really shouldn't…damnation…you smell good. I'm glad to be back, too."

He hugged her in return, breathed in the flowery scent of her and knew a hunger beyond food, and a fatigue sleep wouldn't address.

Though napping might help.

"Come up to the house. I want to hear all about your journey." She linked arms with him, while Trent wanted to stand there, breathing in, holding her, being *home* in her embrace.

"Where are your footmen, Ellie? You're not supposed to be out of doors alone."

"One is lounging against the grape arbor. Another is in the pergola straightening up my picnic basket, but now I'm with you so they can leave me in peace. Is your daughter ensconced in her nursery?"

"She is, or she soon will be." The coach having turned up the correct driveway. "So are the boys."

"A wealth of children. No wonder you missed them."

He'd missed them even before he'd sent them to Belle Maison, he simply hadn't known it. "I missed you, too."

She walked beside him, looking pleased, while Trent's rehearsed speech about safety, and business relationships, and fond memories wandered out of his mental grasp.

Off to Halifax, no doubt.

"I understand Miss Andy has been setting the neighborhood on its ear."

"She truly needs a pony now. Her new best friend in the entire world, one Rose Windham, is horse mad and rides a splendid fellow named Sir George. That worthy was taught how to kneel expressly so his owner could knight him."

"If a fellow has only one trick, bending his knee to the ladies is a good one to have. Andy can have Zephyr, because I'll be getting something larger for the boys, and Lanie won't need her own mount for a few years yet."

Sitting on Ellie's pretty balcony, they chatted like that, about children, ponies, and Greymoor's countess and Heathgate's marchioness, about Belle Maison, and Leah's earl, until they'd demolished a plate of sandwiches and biscuits and consumed a pitcher of lemonade. All the while, Trent feasted his eyes on his late neighbor's wife.

Before she could suggest a postprandial nap, he rose.

"I've eaten your pantry shelves clean and left my dust all over your swing, but now I must take my leave of you. You'll continue to take precautions, though, Ellie, promise me."

She nodded and…yawned. "I promise."

"That"—Trent ran his finger down her braid—"is my cue to depart. I am too much in need of a bath to let you start inviting me to nap."

Her brows furrowed with female disgruntlement. "This matters to you? You aren't unpleasant to be near, Trenton, just the opposite." She brushed the flat of her hand over his chest, much as Nicholas had pet the quarters of that plough horse—soundly, affectionately. "Your sister didn't see to your victualing. You dropped some weight on this sortie to Kent."

Her hand on his chest sent spikes of warmth into low places, and Trent forced himself to move from balcony to sitting room.

"I will call on you tomorrow." He brushed a kiss to her cheek. "I spent a great deal of time in discussion with Greymoor regarding the successful management of a horse farm, and I'd like to share some of his ideas with you."

She accepted that pronouncement with some puzzlement, but he forced himself to draw back before he hauled her against his chest and let lust once more talk good sense into a short nap.

"Get some sleep, Trent. Traveling is always wearying, particularly so with children."

She wouldn't fuss him, wouldn't wheedle him into her fantastical bed, wouldn't pout, sulk, or resort to hysterics. He was vastly relieved it was so.

Also disappointed.

* * *

"I wish somebody had told me earlier that friends make little girls sleep more soundly and attend their lessons more easily." Ellie poured a cup of tea, passed it over to Minty, and then poured one for herself.

Minty took a delicate sniff of her tea. "Since when are we having peppermint tea?"

With blond hair and blue eyes, she was the picture of a genteel English lady. Ellie had often assured Minty that spectacles made her look distinguished, not simply bookish.

"We're drinking peppermint tea since Lord Amherst had a word with Mrs. Wright." Ellie took a sip, though she'd never fancied peppermint tea—before. "He says it aids the digestion of women in a delicate condition."

"He's considerate." Minty addressed this comment to her own tea cup. "Andy likes him, and that says a lot."

"I like him." Ellie put down her drink, appealing though it

was. "I like him rather too much, and I fear the sentiment is not reciprocated."

"Which is why he's lecturing your housekeeper, your stable help, your butler, and probably your broodmares, too. He's a good man, Ellie, and you're due for one of those."

"Hush, Araminthea Drawbaugh." Ellie wished the subject would change itself, because all she wanted to talk about, all she could think about, was Trenton Lindsey. "Lord Amherst is kind, and he thought to repair my spirits. He's certainly a responsible man, but I believe his late wife holds his heart."

Minty wrinkled her patrician nose. "Perhaps she does, but you're here and she's not, and his lordship is a flesh and blood man who apparently exercised his conjugal rights with a fair amount of enthusiasm, if the spacing of his children is any indication."

"You are indelicate, Minty. I despair of you." Though Ellie had come to the same conclusion.

"The first child showed up within a year of the marriage, right on schedule where there's a title to deal with." Minty abruptly looked abashed. "Forgive me."

Forgive her, because for five years, Ellie had been unable to present Dane with his heir.

"No offense taken. I can count on my fingers the number of times Dane exercised his rights with me in the first year of our marriage. He said we were in no rush."

Minty delivered a scowl refined in many a schoolroom. "And you blamed yourself. Your husband bore responsibility for the title, too, Ellie. More than you did. He might have exerted himself more consistently in the direction of his own wife."

The longer Dane plied his celestial harp, the more Ellie was drawn to similar conclusions.

"I should have been more like those young ladies I encountered at boarding school," she said. "They fainted and faded and cried without getting their eyes all puffy, and the entire world hopped to do their bidding."

"A woman of that nature could not have survived Dane Hampton's neglect."

Neglect. Minty was ever one for direct speech. Ellie treasured that about her, usually.

Well, Ellie could be direct, too. "A more clever woman would have had such tantrums, shopping sprees, and flirtations that Dane wouldn't have dared take his eyes off her."

"Is that what they're teaching at fancy finishing schools these days?" Minty set her cup down, having drained the contents. "That explains a lot about the decline of our ruling class, doesn't it?"

"My papa attributed it to inbreeding. To me, all that vaporish carrying-on began to make a certain kind of sense."

"You're tired," Minty said kindly. "You're expecting and you're grieving, and this Lord Amherst has inspired you to brooding. Why not marry him, Ellie? He needs a mother for his children, and you need a papa for yours."

Perhaps because he hadn't asked? Because he'd spoken only disparagingly and despairingly of marriage?

In a backhanded way, Dane had given Ellie the gift of clear thinking in at least one regard.

"Why not marry Lord Amherst, Minty? I'll tell you why. He's charming and conscientious and has many fine qualities, but I will never again be a man's convenient comfort again, nor will I compete with a dead woman for top honors in his heart. Bad enough I competed with Dane's horses, dogs, demi-reps, card games, and cronies."

Of those, the cronies had taken up nearly all of his attention, suggesting his casual regard for women hadn't been limited to his wife.

Worse yet, Ellie had chosen Dane from among a horde of eligible suitors. What that said about her and her judgment flattered nobody.

On that lowering thought, she took herself to her pretty,

cozy bed, and thought about names for her unborn child.

* * *

"A caller for you, my lord." Upton stood inside the door to Trent's library, interrupting the third attempt at a letter to Darius.

"Show him in." Trent rolled his cuffs down, not exactly relieved to be spared his epistolary chores. Heathgate had come calling, or perhaps Hazlit, but that would be fast work for a man who'd left for Hampshire only three days ago.

"Her," Upton corrected him. "I put Lady Rammel in the family parlor, and there's a tea tray on the way."

"I see."

Trent finished with his cuffs, weighing his options. He was overdue to call on her, but he'd spent the past three days digging out of the paperwork that had built up while he'd retrieved his children from Kent.

And from before that, while he'd misbehaved with one Elegy Hampton, Lady Rammel. And from before that, when he'd plain misbehaved...

He made his way through the house with a sense of foreboding.

Female hysterics were the last thing he sought from life, but Ellie had every reason to treat him to a royal tantrum. He'd meant to call, meant to send her a note, meant to ride over and explain to her how it had to be, and now she was bearding him in his den. Fairness demanded she tear a strip off him.

Upon entering the family parlor, Trent bowed over her hand formally. "A pleasure to see you, Lady Rammel."

She wasn't supposed to return his call until the second half of full mourning, which was still weeks away, making her visit a breach of strict protocol.

Not that protocol had in any way informed their dealings thus far.

"You're not sleeping well." Ellie rose, and loosened the end of his cravat from beneath his lapel. "Oh, I've been so worried about you and apparently with reason. Are your children having difficulty settling in? Or is it this other business that troubles you?"

Her blue eyes were luminous with concern, her touch welcome.

The urge to kiss her was not welcome. "The heat has made sleep elusive. You're looking well, my lady."

Heat, indeed. She was the source of the heat plaguing his nights, and she looked not merely well, but *luscious*.

"I've been fretting on your behalf." She gave him an oddly dear, peevish look. "While I swill peppermint tea and keep my feet up, you're wearing yourself to a frazzle. Do I need to have a word with your cook?"

"Heaven forfend," Trent muttered, relieved when a maid came in with a tea tray.

Ellie looked over the offerings and frowned. "Do you suppose," she asked the maid, "we could prevail on the kitchen for a little of this and that? Some fruit and cheese, perhaps, or a muffin with preserves and butter?"

"Surely, milady." The maid curtsied and retreated.

"Trenton Lindsey, you are peaked and you were not in the best form when you returned from Kent. Mr. Spencer said he's been keeping an eye on you, but he's only a man." She gave Trent's chest a brisk pat, part scold, part caress, all Ellie.

Kiss her, kiss her, kiss—for God's sake.

"When did you have occasion to interrogate my stable master?" Heaven help him, Trent was waiting for her to repeat that caress to his chest.

"I sent around for him to ride over with me. I was sure you wouldn't want me paying a visit with only a groom as my escort. We took the lanes and a groom, and here I am, except I'm not at all sure I should be."

"Why is that?"

Ellie wandered off to inspect some bit of cutwork that had been gathering dust since Old George's day, while Trent resisted to compulsion to tackle her and drag her upstairs.

"I doubt my welcome, my lord, because, while you might have read that manual on dalliances and flirtations, I certainly have not. Are we done?"

"Done?"

"With our...flirting, and so forth." Ellie waved a hand in the air. "Sporting or whatever the polite but obvious term is. If we are, then you must tell me what rules apply. Perhaps when a man says he'll call but doesn't, one is supposed to divine his intentions?"

He *had* said he'd call, and she was handing him the perfect opening for that speech about prudence, appearances, and fond memories.

"I've missed you." An understatement, albeit not a very helpful one. "I've let things here slip, and the children need me at hand if they're to feel secure, and I've been meaning to talk to you, about..."

About kissing, about how many bedrooms Crossbridge had, about putting his mouth on her—

She sat and patted the place beside her on the sofa. "Go on."

Between lectures to his unruly imagination, Trent perceived that his caller was not having a tantrum. Perhaps this was the calm before the tantrum. Trent did not take the indicated seat. "I don't know where to start."

"You start wherever you can, Trent. And take your time."

"This trouble you alluded to," he said slowly, forcing his reasoning powers into their mental traces, "I've concluded it started long before I came out to Crossbridge this summer. Or I'm afraid it did. I have a man making inquiries, but it's serious, Ellie, and dangerous."

"A bullet whizzing by our heads felt dangerous. Tell me the rest of it."

He sat beside her, soothed by the scent of summer flowers and by Ellie's patient listening. When the maid returned pushing a tea cart, he munched and talked, and fed Ellie nibbles of fruit and cheese, and talked some more.

When the food was gone, he went on talking, about his children, and about Michael having a nightmare the first night but none since, and about Lanie having learned to speak in complete sentences and at a volume Trent hadn't know a two-year-old female capable of.

While he talked, he took Ellie's hand and laced his fingers through hers, feeling as though all the tension and misery in him were draining right out of his body and drifting away on the summer breezes. The lust remained present, but... napping.

"So, you see," he concluded, "I can't in good conscience allow any appearance of a liaison between us. Not now."

Ellie brushed crumbs from her lap while Trent tried not to focus on her hands. A lady's hands were improved by a few freckles. "I thought your investigator said to carry on without yielding to these threats."

"He did, but I will not put you at risk, Ellie. I cannot."

Her lips flattened, which did nothing to reduce the temptation to kiss them.

"I can't exactly climb your castle walls, take you hostage, and hold you for ransom, Trenton."

"That's it?" He kissed the freckles on her knuckles "Bloodless surrender?" Had he *wanted* her to display her pique and argue with him? Even a little?

"Papa!" Ford barreled into the library, committing a social transgression for which Trent would have been stoutly caned at the same age.

"Papa, you have to come! Michael got my kite stuck in the oaks, and Nurse says I'm not to climb up and get it because I'll break my head, and it's soon to storm, and then my kite will run off *into the sky* because a storm will snatch it away, and Uncle Nick made me that kite *for my own*, and Michael's kite is smaller. I don't *want* his kite I want... Oh. Beg pardon, sir."

How Trent loved this dear, earnest, voluble, energetic little dark-haired boy who'd preserved him at least temporarily from a last farewell to Ellie.

"Make your bow, Fordham."

"Fordham Lindsey, ma'am, at your service."

"Hello, Master Fordham. Pleased to make your acquaintance. I'm sorry to hear your kite has gone adventuring in the oak."

"Uncle Nick built it for me," Ford started up again, only to catch his father's eye.

"Let's have a look, shall we? Lady Rammel, will you join us on this outing? The rain isn't quite upon us yet."

While the wind picked up in earnest and Ellie held his coat, Trent climbed a venerable oak in the hedgerow adjoining a yearling paddock. He rescued the errant kite to the delight of Michael and Ford—and, to appearances at least, Ellie—and they all gained the back hallway as the heavens opened up with a true summer thunderstorm.

"Come with me." Trent tugged Ellie past the kitchen and up the first flight of steps, while the boys galloped off for the nursery with their kites. "I have a favorite place here for watching storms."

Though he hadn't taken the time to enjoy a summer storm at Crossbridge in years.

They were on the third floor before he slowed and opened a door into a guest room that boasted a balcony and overlooked the paddocks, the drive, the woods, and—through the tress—the western façade of Deerhaven.

"If you look out there to the east," Trent said, pointing over Ellie's shoulder, "that green rising of the land is the North Downs."

She followed the line of his finger, her back to his chest, then shifted slightly and nuzzled his biceps with her cheek.

"I see it. This is a wonderful view for a guest room."

"Ellie…" He lowered his arm slowly. "We never finished

our discussion."

"We did not." She turned to face him in the tight confines of the doorway. "Perhaps we should finish it now. We have privacy, and until this storm blows through, I can't go anywhere."

* * *

Ellie tried to fathom Trenton's mood as she took in both the clean, spicy scent of him and the heavier, more pungent scent of the storm bearing down on them. She went up on her toes and kissed his cheek, an impulse that had plagued her since the last time she'd done it.

When he said nothing and made no move to reciprocate her affections, she leaned into his chest. "It's all right. I understand you never intended anything serious in our…dealings. You don't have to say anything, just… Hold me, please? I've grown gluttonous when it comes to your embrace, and I'll miss it."

More than she missed her husband, which was old news, but still troubling.

Trent's arms came around her snugly, though carefully, for her pregnancy had become a tidy little fact where she pressed against him. Everything in her leapt toward the warm, vital strength and goodness of the man holding her.

She nuzzled his throat—naughty of her. At the first touch of his fingers on her jaw, she thought he attempted to delicately dissuade her.

Then he cupped her chin and angled her face, his lips descending to gently plunder her mouth.

"I thought…" She panted against his neck, as his arousal firmed against her belly.

"We'll think later," he growled, scooping her up against his chest and depositing her on the high tester bed in the gloom of the bedroom. "We have to talk, but…later."

He positioned her at the edge of the mattress then leaned in and kissed her onto her back, her legs over the side of the bed, her arms around his neck. He got her slippers off, mostly while he was still kissing her, and then in sheer desperation Ellie scissored her legs around his flanks, drawing him to her.

"Ellie, wait." He dropped his forehead to her chest. "There's no rush. Let me…"

She *had* waited. Waited years for her husband to notice her, and now she waited months for her child to be born, then she'd wait more months for mourning to end.

"Enough waiting." She arched against him, communicating a need for immediate, pressing haste.

Trent got his falls undone and her skirts rucked up, and then he swore softly. "You're not…" He was staring between her legs. Right, straight between her legs. "You put me in mind of roses and hot, perfect summer days."

Ellie opened her eyes to prop herself on her elbows and glare at him. "If I wore drawers, they wouldn't stay up, and I'm too…" She waved a hand around her middle and flopped back onto the mattress. "Trenton…*please.*"

She had apparently inspired him to new feats of teasing, because all he gave her, slowly, slowly, was a single finger.

"Damn you, Trenton Lindsey." And bless him, too. Ellie rolled into that finger, some of the urgency leaving her. "Damn you to Halifax, and…oh my."

With his free hand, he'd ruffled her curls then brushed his thumb over a certain spot. She clenched around his finger in retaliation, and he pressed a kiss to the inside of her knee.

"You're looking at me," Ellie said, a little forlorn, for over the small mound of her belly, she could not see him.

Though she could *feel* him.

"I'm looking at you," Trent said, kneeling between her legs. "Inhaling you, tasting you." He swiped her thigh with his tongue. "Feeling you." He moved his finger inside her. "And wanting you."

"You left one to wonder." Ellie got the words out, the last one misshapen by pleasure.

"I'm sorry. Do you want to discuss this now?" He added a

second finger.

"Yes." She closed even more tightly around him. "I thought you'd sampled my wares, restored my spirits, and jaunted off along your way. Oh...God..." His enterprising free hand had abandoned her mons and gone *jaunting off* up to her breasts, where he carefully, carefully toyed with her nipples though the fabric of her dress and chemise.

"I want to keep you safe," Trent said, his hands slowing. "I mean that, Ellie."

"I feel very safe." She thrust up against his hand, emphasizing her point. "Also very frustrated."

He took both hands away and peeled her dress up and off of her, dealing with her jumps and then her loose, summer-length chemise.

"Blessed saints..." Trent bent over her when she sprawled on her back, stark naked but for boots and stockings. "You are mine for the pleasuring. One cannot grasp the extent of such bounty."

"For God's sake, Trenton." She wrapped her legs around him tightly. "Come here and grasp my bounty soon or I'll expire for wanting you."

"I'm still dressed." He sounded surprised.

"I know." She reached between them and searched through his undone falls to wrap her fingers around his cock. "It's naughty this way, and I like it."

He held still, balanced over her, while she traced the length and shape of him, his balls, his belly, and then, when she'd positioned him snugly against her sex, her hands burrowed under his shirt, her fingertips fanning over his nipples.

And he, dear man, withstood her attentions uncomplainingly. Emboldened by the hitch in his breathing, Ellie got his shirt unbuttoned and tried to push it up so she could use her mouth on the skin she'd exposed, but Trent's patience apparently was at its end. He thrust forward slowly, two small inches with his hips, and Ellie went still.

"I love this part." Loved him. "It's all too much with you, but this…"

"It's precious." Trent caged her beneath him, withdrew to the tip, then pushed forward again. "Sweet. Special."

He kissed her, though Ellie would not have minded a few more of his soft admissions. She craved pleasuring *and* poetry, and with his body, his hands and his kisses, Trent gave her both.

"Go easy," he whispered when Ellie began to importune him with her hips. "No more thunder and lightning, just go easy, like ripples on the pond."

He kept his tempo slow, his penetrations lazy but deep, and gradually, Ellie relaxed into the contemplative, cherishing tenor of his loving. Her hands in his hair moved slowly, her sighs against his neck took on a sleepy quality, and her pleasure arrived as a long, powerful, nearly silent submersion into bliss.

The moment when he again went still inside her, and Ellie could simply hold him was both dear and somehow worrying.

"How could you hold back?" And *why* had he held back?

"My back and arms ache. That helps if I can focus on it."

While Ellie's heart ached.

When she'd recovered somewhat, he started again, but more briskly, likely to deter her from falling asleep, and before long, she was again clinging and keening softly against his neck. Then he followed her to that place of sweetest pleasure, until Ellie was so deluged with shared satisfaction, she nearly wept with its slow, inexorable power.

Then he shifted away, and her tears became real.

CHAPTER FOURTEEN

Ellie's tears were different from Paula's, nothing of despair in them, only sentiment and sweetness. Trent would have moved further, but Ellie's hand in his hair stopped him.

"Don't do yourself up," she whispered. "Not yet."

He should never have *un*done himself.

He moved away to stand, panting, by the bed. He used his handkerchief first to blot her tears, then on himself, then tucked it against her and sat beside her where she sprawled on the bed.

The bald intimacy of that shared scrap of linen smacked at his conscience.

"Storm's passing," he noted, pulling off his boots. Sweet, everlasting God, he'd actually swived her with his boots on. He hadn't had sex like that since university, and this had been so much better than any of his harried, boyish escapades. He ran a hand down the midline of her slightly convex belly, and she shivered.

Reaching around her, he pushed her dress to the foot of the bed, extricated pillows from under the counterpane and grabbed a quilt from the bottom of the mattress.

"Scoot up," he urged, climbing onto the bed to prop himself against the headboard. "Let me hold you. I've missed holding you."

He honestly had, which was worse than swiving her with his boots on as a testament to sincere regard.

"How can you speak coherently?" Ellie pillowed her head in his lap. She gathered his softening erection in her hand, swiped her tongue over the head of his cock and settled back for her nap.

Trent endured the resulting shiver of pleasure and arranged the blanket over her, then rested his hand on the swell of her belly. While Ellie dozed, her fingers still wrapped loosely around him, he tried to rehearse what he must now find a way to tell her.

"What was that?" Ellie put her hand over Trent's where it lay against her belly. "Did you feel it?"

He waited while Ellie did the same.

She shifted to stare at her own belly, as if she could see through the blanket. "That. It doesn't hurt, but it's…different."

She tried to push up, but Trent stopped her.

"It's the baby, Ellie." He kissed her temple, a gesture too small for the sense of privilege overwhelming him. "Your child has quickened."

"My child…?" She pressed his hand more tightly to her, and the fluttery sensation came under his palm again. "That's the *baby*? Are you sure?"

"I'm sure. Three children, if you'll recall." Though only with Ford, through several layers of nightclothes and with much blushing all around, but he had felt a child quicken beneath his hand before.

"Did we wake him up?" Ellie's voice held concern. "That wasn't very considerate of us, but there it is… Do you suppose he's playing? Or she. It might be a girl."

"I think it's easier for the child to move about when you're recumbent, or maybe the change in position registers somehow, but you'll feel it off and on until you deliver."

"Oh…my…gracious." She laid her cheek against his thigh and curled against him, keeping his one hand on her belly.

She dozed off again, and Trent let her, treasuring the moment, treasuring the woman who'd shared it with him. When she awoke the second time, Trent marshaled his waning self-discipline and tried to find a balance between affection and pragmatism.

To hell with that. Between love and honor.

"Time to stir, Elegy. The rain has all but stopped."

She pushed up and scrubbed her cheek against his belly. "I realize we must have a trying discussion of difficult matters, Trenton, but someday…" She nuzzled his genitals.

"You are naughty." He sighed with the thought of how naughty, and how dear. "But, yes, someday, if you really want to, it would be my pleasure, though there are consequences, IOUs, for somedays like that."

"Are we still dallying?" She sat up and knelt beside him, arranging him back into his clothing and doing up his buttons.

"We should not be."

She gave him a pat when he was properly covered. "Oh, should. That word needs to be deleted from all manuals. I'll help you tend to the revisions."

"I am, to use your word, gluttonous when it comes to you, Ellie Hampton. You flutter your eyelashes, and my clothes end up on the floor."

She fluttered her eyelashes, then glowered in the direction of his buttoned falls. "The mechanism is faulty, then, for you're still clothed. One hopes it can improve with practice."

Trent traced his finger down her jaw. How he would miss her.

"I'm being stalked, essentially, by my in-laws or somebody

in their employ. If they perceive I've replaced Paula in my affections, then you could become a target, too, if you aren't already."

This time when she touched him through his clothes, the caress held something of regret. "So, caution is in order. Great caution, but I am more concerned for you than for myself."

"You would be. Consider the child you carry, though, and rearrange your priorities, Ellie."

As he would have to rearrange his priorities, so the clamoring of his lonely heart—or his cock—did not further imperil his honor and her safety. For an instant, as he regarded the soft, elegant curve of Ellie Hampton's bare breast, Trent wished he could have one iota more of his father's selfishness.

"Speaking of children." Ellie rummaged around and found her dress, which Trent plucked from her hand. "You have a daughter I've yet to meet."

"My Lanie." Trent sorted the chemise from the dress. "Here." He settled first the chemise over Ellie's head, and while she sorted out the mysteries of properly donning and doing up her jumps, he bent to find her boots.

"Elaine is two, and it's as if she was only dabbling at talking until now, and by God, the world will hear what she has to say, her brothers especially. She has such a combination of sweetness and determination, and she's so dear, and precious, and intrepid—she reminds me of you. Where in the hell did your other boot get to? I can't have you…what?"

Ellie sat cross-legged on the bed, her skirts and the blankets frothed around her.

"You say the sweetest things. You make me want you all over again, and I keep trying for perspective. Some maturity, but it eludes me. I don't think any manual will be of much aid, either."

"The manual is out of date, I fear." Trent peered under the bed. "Found it." He took her foot in his hand to put the boot on her. Instead of rising, though, and getting Ellie the hell back downstairs before the servants sent out a searching party, he rested his forehead against her thigh.

"If it's any comfort," he murmured, "I desire you until I'm cross-eyed and panting with it, and I can't see the attraction abating any time soon." He shifted to pillow his cheek on her belly. "Such an admission is selfish of me, and greedy, and downright ungentlemanly."

When she made no reply but instead stroked a gentle hand over his shoulder, he realized what he'd said. The attraction might not abate soon, but that only implied it would abate later, which wasn't at all what he'd intended to convey.

His attraction to Elegy Hampton, his affection for her—hell, his love for her—was unlikely to abate in his lifetime, however long or short that turned out to be.

* * *

"What has you frowning so thunderously?" Cato moved a pawn and eyed the brandy decanter. The trouble with helping oneself to the good stuff was that the thirst for the good stuff was only reawakened, not slaked.

Just as an appreciation for being warm at night, thoroughly scrubbed at the end of the day, and clad in clean clothes could become an itch under a man's skin.

Even the books in Amherst's library—

"I've had a letter from my brother, Darius." Amherst moved a pawn as well. "He's heading back to Town soon but has had a rollicking good time with Lord Valentine Windham in Oxfordshire. My brother is happy to count out board feet of lumber when he should be contemplating marriage, for pity's sake."

"Marriage is a fine old institution." Cato considered bishop, knight, rook and queen in turn, though volumes of Pope beckoned from behind Amherst's shoulder. "A married man gets to swive his darling without limit, babies appear, life is good."

"Sometimes," Amherst said, but clearly the man knew

Cato wasn't above distracting an opponent with chatter. "Sometimes not."

"Mr. Lindsey struck me as a particularly canny fellow." Cato moved another pawn. "Though skirts make fools of us all."

"Which reminds me,"—Amherst countered by getting his queen's bishop out—"what are you about, fetching Lady Rammel on command? You know she's been shot at once in my company, and squiring her around the countryside hardly keeps her safe."

As if Amherst could have refused Elegy Hampton's summons?

"So why don't you give her ladyship the little speech about your paths parting ways, though it's been lovely, and you'll always treasure the memories, and who knows, your paths might always conjoin in the future?"

"There really is a manual," Amherst murmured.

"Beg pardon?"

"I should give her that speech," Amherst said more clearly. "I've rehearsed it, as well as the lecture about the safety of a woman living virtually alone, and the one about my having no intention of remarrying, but the rehearsals never quite make it out onto the stage before a paying audience."

"Not marry?" Cato sprang his king's bishop. "You'll let one woman's megrims make a dowager of you?"

"Apparently not quite a dowager," he replied, touching his queen. "My enthusiasm for the institution of marriage wasn't much to begin with. My parents were intimate enemies, and my wife was not happy with me."

"I daresay Lady Rammel is not like your first wife." And Amherst was not *at all* like the late Lord Rammel.

"She's not. I, however, am a lot like my first wife's husband."

When he'd sorted out Amherst's verbiage, Cato sat back and folded his arms, his concentration on the game shot to hell by this nonsense.

"No, my lord, you are not. You're older, wiser, a papa three times over. You have the reins of the earldom, your brother and sister are getting tidily situated, and you are not the same man."

Amherst moved another pawn, though Cato couldn't fathom what his strategy might be. "The Irish are supposed to be charming."

"When it suits us." Cato's first decent game of chess in months, and his focus would not stay on the board. Peak would laugh heartily. "You should marry Lady Rammel. You can keep her safe that way and also swive her silly."

"Check." His lordship sat back. "But you can get out of it."

Cato stared at the board, seeing a metaphor for his life. "You'll just chase me around. My mind is not on the game."

"Nor mine." Amherst got up and poured his guest a drink, but none for himself. "You are reputed to have experience with females, Catullus." He passed over the drink. "What makes a woman hate marital intimacies?"

Cato eyed his drink, then his host.

"I was raised among Papists, so I lay some of the blame at the feet of Mother Church, who preaches that bodily urges are sinful, until the wedding night, and then, lo, for the purpose of getting children, those same urges are part of God's plan. This confuses a poor lusty lass, I'm sure, as it would have played hell with me when I was a lad."

"The Church of England hoes the same row." Amherst looked disgruntled at the thought. "We do let our priests marry, so some of the edge comes off the confusion. I don't think my wife's loathing was religious in nature."

"Loathing. One wonders how you managed three children."

"She was fertile." Amherst started putting chess pieces in their velvet-lined box. "Thank God."

"You weren't…" Cato watched the black knight land on a pile of pawns. How in God's name had they strayed onto this topic?

"Bumbling?" Amherst eyed the black queen. "Inept? Virginally inconsiderate? Hardly. I waited almost a month after the wedding to consummate our union, and I assure you I learned as much at university as any other randy young man does outside the lecture halls. Had she not wanted children, though, I'd probably still be waiting to consummate the union."

"This has put you off marriage," Cato concluded. "One can see where it would, but my guess is Lady Rammel wouldn't be that sort of wife."

"One can't know such a thing." He held up the white queen, a right, scowling little wench. "Before I married her, Paula was charming, cheerful, coy, and willing to be kissed a time or two."

"On the cheek?"

"What is it with you and kisses on the cheek, Catullus?"

"I'm asking if she led you on. Teased you down the garden path."

Amherst pitched her royal highness toward the box but missed, so she bounced onto the carpet at Cato's feet. "Maybe."

In courtship, Amherst's late wife had likely led her swain around by his lordly...nose.

Cato set the fallen queen on the table. "Sometimes, the coy ones send a signal they don't intend to, and mischief befalls them."

Amherst tossed the queen in with her court and speared Cato with a look. "You mean someone forced her?"

"This happened to a young lady I know," Cato said slowly. "She was sweet and dear and charming, and did not see when her demure looks were being taken as a sign of willingness. Her innocence got her accosted in the stables, which, when witnesses came upon the scene, resulted in her ruin. Her only option was to marry the fellow who'd tried to rape her, and even if she could swallow that bitter pill, she'd never be quite received."

"You give me something to think about." Amherst closed

the lid of the chess set. "Though I beg your pardon for harping on an unhappy topic. How has the fare been in the servant's hall of a morning?"

"Decent." Cato knocked back the last of his drink. "Fluffy eggs, crispy bacon, plenty of white flour in the toasted bread, hot fresh buns, sliced fruit, and the tea almost strong enough."

"Glad to hear it. What about at mid-day?"

"Meat, most days, plenty of cheese, and fare from the gardens, a definite improvement."

"Progress." Amherst slid the chess set onto a high shelf. "I'm traveling into Town tomorrow, and I might bide a night or two. I'd take it as a favor if you'd sleep up here in my absence."

Oh, yes, now that the warring armies were up on their shelf, Amherst got out his big guns. Even in the servant's quarters, the beds would have clean linen and soft pillows. Likely, sachets hung from the posts, and hot water brought around with the last bucket of coal.

"If I bide at the house, talk will ensue." Cato rose and set his empty glass on the sideboard. Not the least of the talk would be a blistering lecture from Peak.

"My children are here." Amherst's voice took on an edge. "If I want you sleeping here, nobody should question it as a means of ensuring their safety."

"You have footmen, a butler, and myriad other fellows on hand to see to that," Cato pointed out. "I'm your Irish stable master, and I haven't slept on clean cotton sheets for two years."

"Catullus." Amherst's tone was very mild. "One doesn't lose the knack of sleeping on clean sheets, or bathing in a tub. You'll sleep across the hall from the nursery and give the nannies and nurses the vapors. It will be good for them."

"Louise will have apoplexies."

"Good. She's a miserable woman who fortunately knows her way around a kitchen. You'll watch my babies while I'm gone?"

"If you insist." Cato tried to sound put upon, but God in heaven, a soaking bath *and* clean sheets... "You tell Lady Rammel where you're off to, or she'll come toddling about, indiscriminately kissing cheeks in your absence, and there will be no explaining that, my lord."

He'd nearly said, "my friend," for dipping in the creek even in high summer grew tedious.

"Lady Rammel excels at kissing cheeks," Amherst said, with the air of a well-informed man. "I delight to see you discommoded by a mere female."

"If you only knew. If you only knew."

* * *

"You said we'd go to Scotland for the shooting." Imogenie dipped her lashes and pouted her lips, though Wilton purposely turned his back on her best attempt at coyness.

"We might." The earl tossed back a finger of brandy. "Trevisham extended the invitation last night to use his box because he intends to bide in the south this year with his family."

"You said you'd introduce me." The pout in her voice became genuine, as if Wilton might truly have meant to introduce her to Baron Trevisham as more than a passing fancy.

"You've been standing up with Trevisham's get since you let your hems down, my girl." Wilton poured another finger. "Believe me, you would have been bored to tears by the conversation. I'll tell you a secret."

Imogenie patted the bed and tucked the sheets under her arms, eagerness written on her features.

"Lady Trevisham doesn't even come down to table these days. Trevisham is consigned to Tidewell and Thomas's dubious company." He sat beside her on the bed and held the drink up to her mouth.

She obediently drank, though he knew she didn't care for brandy—which was exactly why he offered it to her.

"More," he murmured, putting the glass to her lips again. Half-tipsy, she was ever so much more amenable to his games. "Now turn over."

She looked reluctant but intrigued. "Must I?"

"You'll like it," he assured her.

Imogenie did like it. Whether he laid his hands on her in anger, lust, or a combination of the two, she did like it, and he liked it, too. Slowly, she twisted down and onto her stomach.

"Why doesn't Lady Trevisham come to table?" Imogenie shivered, despite the heat, as Wilton pushed the sheets aside, leaving her naked and exposed.

"Prostrate with shame." Wilton almost chortled regarding the young woman *prostrate* on the bed. "Her sons had to be collected from Town by their papa, again. Seems the older one was dueling and the younger acting as his second."

"I thought that's what young bucks did when they were loose on the Town." Imogenie's voice betrayed a hint of a quaver as Wilton used one of the silk stockings he'd given her to tie her right hand to the bedpost.

"They're hardly young. The oldest is several years Amherst's senior, and it's long past time he set up his nursery. Be a good girl, no squirming."

"I never liked him." Imogenie watched docilely as Wilton secured her other wrist, her expression uncertain. "When I was little, Tidewell always wanted me to sit on his lap."

"He did?" No, that was not exactly what Tye Benning had wanted. "Just think, Genie, if you'd given him what he sought, you might be a baroness by now and we might be related by marriage." He secured her first ankle, giving the binding a little yank to make it snug. "Or the next thing to it."

"Wilton?"

He tied her second ankle to the remaining bedpost, a novelty in their dealings thus far.

"You'll like it," he assured her again, though it was better when he could see the trepidation building in her eyes.

"You'll take me north with you?"

He delivered the first blow almost affectionately, using the flat of his hand smartly on her exposed buttocks. Sexual pleasure blossomed at the sound of his flesh impacting hers, and at the sight of Imogenie hunching in on herself against her bindings.

"That depends,"—he paused to untie his dressing gown—"on how naughty you've been and how naughty you're willing to be. Not a sound, Genie. You're not to make a single sound."

She didn't. Imogenie was the best, most biddable kind of fool. He'd taught her how to keep quiet through their games—he never hit her all that hard, never left many welts or bruises—and then he held her after he'd found his pleasure. That's when he'd comfort her with the lies she liked to hear the most, about what a fine countess she would make, and how he wished he'd met her earlier, and how he'd marry her, once she proved she could bear his heirs.

* * *

"Why the scowl?" Cato settled into one of the library's upholstered armchairs, crossing an ankle over one knee. "And why do you look like you haven't slept since you left here for Town a week ago?"

Trent shifted back in his own chair and stifled a yawn. The clock over the library mantel had taken to whirling away the minutes of late, and yet the hours and days...dragged.

"I damned near haven't slept. Benton writes that Wilton is growing rambunctious, testing the limits of his freedom, and calling upon all and sundry in the district."

"If the highest-ranking title in the parish made no calls, it would look odd."

Trent rose and rubbed the back of his neck, knowing he'd summoned Cato in part because the man was the closest thing he had to a friend on the property—though Cato outranked him—and would be honest with him, regardless of their respective titles, or appearances, or anything.

"Wilton never neighbored very well, unless it was to show up in his finery at the hunt meets, or to shop for my bride. His is the only earldom in the district, and the two barons in the surrounds are in awe of him."

"So he's come late to the pleasures of country life." Cato kept to his seat, tracing one finger along a seam on the chair arm. "You can't refuse him that much without causing a lot of talk."

Cato would know exactly how tedious and corrosive talk could be in a rural earldom.

"I might not begrudge him some socializing with his neighbors," Trent said, "but he's swiving a local girl silly, and she was decent before he got his paws on her."

"She'll dine out on her wicked youth for decades. Moreover, he'll let her go with a parting gift that should keep her in style until her dotage."

"I pay quarterly pensions to two women who were given parting gifts by his lordship." Trent pinched the bridge of his nose. "Half-siblings make one hell of a parting gift. My mother claimed there were others whom she dispatched with lump sums."

Cato shifted, making the chair creak. "Not uncommon for an English peer, particularly with men who ascribe to the old-fashioned *droit de seigneur* school of aristocracy."

Diplomacy was not what Trent sought from the discussion. "Wilton is conscienceless. I will have another very frank talk with the young lady's father."

Cato rose. "Must be awkward as hell, having to warn the locals off your own father."

"Even more awkward having to warn my father to cease his games," Trent said. "He's up to something, planning some grand coup. I can feel it."

"You can feel it?"

"When I was young, he would humiliate me periodically. His tantrums grew predictable. He'd find some fault with my studies and thrash the hell out of me, then leave me in peace for a time until his ire built again. He'd find another pretext, then get out his cane and have at me over a trifle. It became a dilemma."

"In what sense?" Cato poured a drink and offered it to Trent.

A whiff of roses wafted by on the evening air. Trent shook his head, and Cato sipped at the drink himself.

"When I was small, and trying to endure my father's discipline, I'd reach the point where I cried, or screamed, or tried to run off. Then Wilton would beat me for not accepting my punishment. I eventually learned to keep my peace, lest the footmen be required to hold me for my canings."

Cato downed the rest of the drink in one swallow. "If my papa were alive, I'd kiss him on both cheeks for never doing more than swatting my arrogant little backside with his hand, or worse, giving me his disappointed look."

"Thank him anyway. I could not stand the pity of the footmen, so I learned to take my medicine without a word. That only challenged Wilton to see how much I could take."

"Your father is an evil man. You probably don't need me to tell you that, but to go after your own son that way… It doesn't build character, or instill respect, or whatever else he tried to tell you. It hurts an innocent child, plain and simple."

Cato was certain of his point, and that was…reassuring.

"What?" Cato tried to take another sip of his drink, then glared at the empty glass. "You'd argue with me? The man is a monster, Amherst. If he were a horse, he'd be shot for his vile temper lest the trait breed true in his progeny."

"I suppose that's what I'm afraid of." The realization made Trent abruptly queasy. "*I am his son*, and while I don't beat my children…"

"For God's sake. Your boys love you, and that little sprite of a sister of theirs…"

"Yes?"

"When I look at that child, I don't know how much longer I can stand to stay away from my sisters and my home."

Other people had problems, too, even people who outranked Trenton and owned thousands of acres of beautiful Irish countryside.

"You could go back for a visit. Just take a peek."

Though the idea of Cato deserting the stables just now did not…sit well.

Cato's smile was tired as he set his empty glass on the sideboard. "Irish gossip has a quality that the English variety lacks. The grooms and tenants and such didn't just see me up before my papa when I was a lad, they cuffed my ear from time to time, sat me down to milk and buttered soda bread, chased me from their haylofts when I was up to mischief with the dairymaids."

"No privacy." Though Wilton had left his children no privacy either, Cato's experience was not based in a parent's need to manipulate and control.

"No privacy, but worlds of safety," Cato rejoined. "I couldn't slip home for a little spying on my sisters. Clancy's swineherd's mother's cousin would see me fifty miles from home, and the fatted calf would be dead, dressed and cooked before I trotted up the lane."

"But those people,"—Trent made a circling motion with his hand—"the swineherd's cousin's whatever who kept an eye on you, they're how you know for sure Wilton is evil and you are not."

Cato regarded his employer with what Trent feared was pity. "This troubles you. You believe you're your father's son, exclusively?"

Trent sank back into his chair, when he wanted to lay himself down in a bed of fragrant pink flowers. "By the time she died, my mother wasn't much better than my father. She hated Wilton and attributed to him every nasty motive possible. I grew extremely resentful of my own spouse before she too went to her reward."

Resentful and desperate, which his mother had been as well.

"Which only makes my point. You and Wilton are different. He embittered his wife and beat his sons. You cared for your wife and cherish your children. You are not your father."

A silence built, while Trent pointedly ignored the decanter and let weariness make him pathetic.

"I'm avoiding Ellie. I tarried in Town when I could have written to my man of business to sell the house I'll never use there again. I dithered over a visit to my younger sister, Emily, when she's having a grand time breaking in her dancing slippers at various assemblies. I put off coming back here, though I missed my children terribly."

Missed them—and Ellie, and worried about the lot of them.

Cato refreshed his drink with the air of a man resigned to an awkward discussion. "*This* makes you like Wilton, because you don't want to see the woman shot, disfigured, or poisoned?"

"I won't stop taking precautions until I've held my in-laws accountable."

"You think because Ellie has your attention, they might spread their resentment to her?"

"I don't know what to think." Trent rose again and turned away from Cato to survey the back gardens. In the evening light they were for the most part orderly, blooming, peaceful and pretty—also fragrant—thanks to Ellie. "Part of me resents the burden of complication that comes from dealing with a female again. I was growing content in my isolation after Paula's death. Another part of me is scheming how I can climb in Ellie's windows of a night and enjoy every favor she so generously offers me."

"That's easy. On the west side of the house, there's an oak whose branches were never pruned sufficiently. You can climb from it to the porch outside the family parlor. Rammel used to do it when he wanted to escape Ellie's notice after hours, or arrive without benefit of censure from the servants."

Easy indeed, when a man's own sons recognized him as proficient at climbing trees. "How do you know this about him?"

"Rammel had the occasional use for a pint in low places, and the man would talk horses and hounds with anyone."

"The west side, you say?"

Cato's smile grew into a grin. "I would never say such a thing."

"Gentleman stable master that you are, you would never contribute to my moral dilemma."

Cato snorted, sounding curiously like Darius when disgusted with Polite Society. "That wee fellow in your breeches wouldn't know a moral if it swived him silly. I'm merely taking away an excuse."

"An excuse?"

"You say you want to keep the lady safe, and to do that, you don't want to foster an appearance of anything untoward between you. Instead of addressing the appearances—the source of the problem—you're thinking of withdrawing from the field entirely. If you're simply wrestling with second thoughts, you should withdraw and allow Ellie the freedom to choose others, and not tell yourself you're protecting with your neglect."

"Ellie? She's not Lady Rammel to you anymore?"

"She's Lady Rammel to me, *and* Dane's widow, *and* breeding, *and* I can't offer her as much as you can, so no, you needn't bristle at me like a stray dog, Amherst."

"I am bristling, aren't I? Well, hell." He'd doubtless referred to the lady as Ellie in Cato's astute hearing.

"That about sums up the condition of a man in love, particularly one who won't admit his circumstances to himself." Cato tossed back the last of his refill. "I'm off to the stables. You're too tired to be worth a decent game of chess tonight and should seek your bed. Things will make more sense in the morning."

"Yes, Mother." Trent let him go without another word.

The west side of Ellie's house faced the paddocks, not the stables or the outbuildings where prying eyes might see a few shadows moving in the depths of the oak by moonlight.

Trent called for his bath, tried to think of a brief story to read his children before he tucked them in, and wondered how early Ellie might retire on a pleasant summer night.

CHAPTER FIFTEEN

Trent was naked in Ellie's fairy-tale bed, naked in her *arms*, before she woke up.

"Trenton." She wrapped herself around him in welcome, and within the minute, he was inside her willing heat.

When he'd been up in London, making his calls, closing up his town house, he'd been frantic to get back to her. His mind had been set in one direction, like a young man's, completely at the mercy of his desire.

Then he'd returned to Crossbridge, and he'd felt the same reluctance overtake him he'd experienced when coming back from Belle Maison. An anxious, hollow, ache under his cross-eyed hunger.

But now, hilted in Ellie Hampton's delectable feminine sweetness, all he felt was a towering relief.

She levered up and got her mouth on one of his nipples, and he wished she'd consume him, devour him, and take him inside her in every way imaginable.

"I worried for you." She tightened her hold of him as she whispered the words against his chest, while Trent's urgency abated fractionally.

She deserved better than this from him, better than a quick, desperate swiving in the dark. He slowed the undulations of his hips and eased his grip on her backside.

"I've missed you, too," he whispered, finding her mouth with his own.

He mentally started over, though his cock stayed buried in her while he reacquainted his mouth with the taste of her. When her tongue was lazily stroking against his in response, he cruised his nose over the fragrance of her hair, then the delicate scent at the juncture of her neck, so warm and sweet. He took her earlobe between his teeth as her sigh fanned past his temple and her hands winnowed through his hair.

Ellie shifted under him to lock her ankles at the small of his back. "Trenton, please…"

He cupped her breast, giving her the slightest pressure on her nipple, and that was all it took.

She unraveled with a soft, surrendering groan, her body clutching him hard, repeatedly, until she sighed and relaxed beneath him. He gave her a minute to catch her breath while he kept his movements easy and slow, then sent her right back up again in a short burst of more purposeful thrusts.

The next time he heard her whisper, "Trenton, please," it was a plea for clemency, but he'd found his stride, and his sense of purpose—his sense of *home*. She became so sensitized he could send her over the edge with a few powerful thrusts and some well-placed caresses.

He felt when she stopped fighting her pleasure, stopped thinking about how much was too much and how many was enough. And still he wasn't ready to let go, or to give up the banquet that their lovemaking had become. Trent could not have said how long they loved, but he took her from peak to peak, sometimes lazily, sometimes more forcefully, until his own completion ceased to matter, so thoroughly was he attuned to hers.

He'd become relaxed almost to the point of sleep, moving easily, when Ellie's legs wrapped around his flanks again. She slid a hand over his backside, anchoring herself to him as she turned her face into his shoulder.

"You," she said. "This time, you, too."

She used her inner muscles on him, and that sensation was so keenly pleasurable Trent forced himself to keep his tempo slow enough that she could synchronize with his thrusting. He let the tension build, and build, and build, and still, Ellie kept up with him. Vertigo stole over him, and pleasure welled, an inexorable, ecstatic drenching that obliterated his control and shook him from the inside.

"Jesus God, Ellie…" The pull of her mouth, her fingers, her body went on and on, drawing sensation into a tight coil of intimacy and desire. Longing was tangled up in the physical sensations—longing for relief from worries, for oblivion from sorrow, for a life free from duty, appearances, and familial tensions.

Longing for uncomplicated pleasures, and for a future with Elegy Hampton.

She did not relent. She harried and hounded him with her kisses and caresses, she wrapped herself—her body, her scent, her dearness—around him and would not let go.

Trent surrendered to long moments of wrenching satisfaction, after which his pleasure didn't so much end as it dissipated, like the last notes of a beautiful composition, lingering delightfully in memory.

He levered up on his forearms and gathered her close, laying his cheek over hers, only to pull back. "Ellie?" Trent nuzzled her cheek with his nose and confirmed she had indeed been crying. "Love?"

Between them, the baby moved, provoking such a depth of tender feeling Trent's throat constricted with sentiments he dared not voice.

"Elegy," he whispered when she'd quieted. "Talk to me. Don't slip off to sleep and leave me here alone."

She gave a shuddery little laugh that broke his heart.

"Like you left me alone?" She pushed his hair back off his forehead, a sweet caress that didn't hide the pain in her words. "I told myself I wasn't going to do this."

"Do this?" Trent levered up on his elbows, sensing that whatever was on Ellie's mind he wouldn't be able to cuddle and pet her past it.

"Will you please get off me?"

She closed her eyes on a wincing sigh as he withdrew, suggesting he'd made her sore. He had to have—*he* was sore, a novel experience for him. He made use of the washing water and sat by Ellie's hip, passing her a cool, damp cloth.

She tidied herself while he watched, an intimacy he could not recall any other woman permitting him.

"Are we to argue, Ellie?" he asked as he climbed in beside her.

"I hope not." She turned on her side to regard him. "But I find…"

"You find?" He settled an arm around her shoulders and drew her against him.

"I have been unable to govern my emotions adequately where you're concerned, Trenton Lindsey. This past week, while you've been gone, I could not stop fretting for you."

"I'm not used to anybody fretting for me. It's good of you."

They were the wrong words, and yet they were honest words. She was a good woman, plain and simply good. He stopped himself from elaborating in the direction of dear, precious, and other indications of folly.

"Good of me." Ellie repeated the phrase as if finding it underdressed at a formal dinner. "Perhaps it might be, if I felt I had a choice, but I cannot say I do. Nor do I like it, feeling this fretfulness. I did not allow fretting where my husband was concerned, and he at least had the courtesy to drop me the occasional note, to let me know where he was and how long he intended to bide there."

"A note." Trent's post-coital beatitude curled in on itself. He was about to get what he'd told Cato he wanted: leave to take himself off, leave to disentangle himself from a woman who deserved safety, at least.

And other things he couldn't yet promise her.

"A note Trenton, a simple courtesy. You owe me nothing, I know. We are merely dallying, satisfying our animal urges with each other."

"You are not an animal urge to me. Good God, after what went on in this bed, how can you think—?"

Ellie put two fingers to his lips. "After what went on in this bed, how can you deny our animal urges are involved?"

"Well, of course they are, and God be thanked for it."

"Don't do this." Ellie drew her fingers over his lips gently. "Don't try to find soothing platitudes and pretty courtesies, Trent. You are prodigiously talented in bed—I'm not so inexperienced I don't know what I'm giving up—but when it comes to dallying, that manual we've joked about is written in a language I can't comprehend, and my ignorance leaves me discommoded."

"What are you saying, Elegy?" But he knew what she was saying: He had Botched It with her, Badly. He'd wanted her safe, not heartbroken, not sad and angry. He knew that much, even with his brain sizzling from lust and his body chronically exhausted.

"I can't do this," Ellie said softly. "I can't make passionate love with you then go on about my life for a week or so, then welcome you back into my bed, Trenton. Not when your life is arguably in danger and you won't let me come to you. You hold all the cards in this dalliance. I spent five years letting my husband hold all the cards. I thought I could be a merry widow, but I find I cannot. I'm sorry."

He got out of bed, and she watched him in the moonlight, her expression solemn, her gaze sad. He came around the bed, climbed in behind her, and threaded an arm under her neck.

"I'm sorry, too." He kissed her temple, all manner of difficult feelings rioting through him—relief *not* among them. "I did not mean to hurt you, but if this is what you want, I'll leave you in peace."

She kissed his wrist and offered him not a shred of argument.

Or hope.

He was doing the right thing, acceding to her wishes, letting her break it off to keep her safe—and to stop the runaway freight wagon of their mutual feelings for each other while they still could.

Even having given her what she wanted, and what was doubtless best for her, and—his self-disgust was running high enough to fuel brutal honesty—what was least uncomfortable for him—he knew he'd still made her cry again.

* * *

"I'm off for the rest of the week." Thomas Benning tossed his last pair of clean stockings into a haversack, grateful for the excuse not to meet his older brother's eyes.

"Take French leave if you must." Tidewell Benning's voice held supreme indifference, which Thomas knew to be false. "It's what you do best."

"Not fair, Tye." Thomas glanced around the room, anywhere but at the brother who lounged on his bed, boots and all. "I'm damned sick and tired of the nonsense you get up to. That girl was thirteen and you knew it."

Tidewell folded his hands behind his head, not a care in the world. "She was a tart. Girls marry at thirteen, have babies at thirteen."

"You'd know more than I would about that. And there's thirteen, and then there's thirteen." The poor thing had been simple, and the blood…

"You think a house party will assuage your overactive conscience?"

A house party would let him drink himself to oblivion without having to pay for it, and without having to see the disappointment in Papa's eyes.

"Somebody in this family needs to marry money," Thomas shot back. "The house parties are the consolation offered to those who failed to snag a husband during the Season. I'm tired of hearing Papa strut and rant and admonish you once again to choose a bride."

Except the local women wouldn't have Tye, that much had been plain for years. Like Thomas, Tye was tall with wavy, dark hair, but middle age was stealing a march on Tye's waist and his hairline.

Tidewell grinned, showing a glimmer of the charm that had got him into so much trouble. "I have time yet for choosing a bride. You act like we really do need the blunt."

"I'm nearly certain we do, Tye." They were alone, and Thomas was nagged by an obligation to be honest with his brother. "Papa isn't looking quite so sanguine these days, and the past few harvests have been bad. You're his heir. What does he tell you?"

"To keep my breeches up when I'm in the vicinity of little girls whose brothers know their way around a dueling ground."

"Always sound advice." Thomas couldn't muster a smile, because Papa hadn't been joking, though Tye had. "Papa sent Paula into Amherst's arms with a damned generous settlement, but since then…"

Tye's expression became mean. "She needed a damned generous settlement. Stupid twit was barmy."

"She was our sister."

"And she cost this family a pretty penny," Tye retorted, "which you're suggesting we now can't afford." He crossed his boots at the ankles, leaving a smear of dirt on Thomas's counterpane.

"I'm suggesting you talk to Papa. And Tye? You really do need a wife, some tolerant, easy-breeding country girl who thinks being your baroness would make up for your shortcomings."

Which were legion.

"You are turning into an old woman, Thomas." Tye sat up, boots hitting the floor. "If you're so set on the proprieties, you take a wife."

"I'm planning on it." Because if nothing else, a married man could establish his own household.

"As if you could," Tye snorted, eyeing his brother's crotch meaningfully.

"You need to be more careful, Tye." Thomas ignored his brother's insult, which was old and—much to Thomas's relief—groundless. "Papa won't stand for more of your carrying-on, and I'm done with it, too. We've become a perennial joke, with bets laid as to how long we're allowed out of Hampshire before Papa has to drag us by the ears back to the family seat. Pretty soon, we'll be like old Wilton, virtual prisoners of our family's outrage."

"Wilton's no prisoner." A sly look came into Tye's eyes as he crossed to the wardrobe. "He's a canny old thing, and if you had the amusements to hand he did, you might not be off to dance and small talk your way through endless evenings of bad music and low stakes."

Thomas was weary, and not only because he faced a journey of several hours on horseback in the summer sun come morning.

Tye handled the clothing in the wardrobe as if already choosing which of Thomas's belongings to pilfer for his own use.

"Now you envy the Earl of Wilton, whose own family won't have him. Consider what that says about you, Tye, and consider that I mean it: I'm done with your nonsense."

"Safe journey." Tye stepped back and closed the doors of the wardrobe. "I'll be thinking you of, swilling orgeat and showing the debutantes around the archery butts, while I find better sport with an entirely different variety of female."

He gave an airy court bow in parting, and Thomas closed the door with a sense of relief. Old secrets, secrets that went back to childhood, bound them, and so, too, did a reluctant protectiveness on Thomas's part. Tye had been the oldest, the one their mother doted on, and Thomas knew what that had cost his brother.

* * *

"Why are you still awake?" Peak's voice held a note of censure, but Cato knew that voice and heard the hint of concern in it as well.

"Missing me, Peak?"

"Hush your trash." Peak took the seat beside Cato on the bench outside the stables. Right beside him. "Pretty half-moon tonight."

"The moon always seems bigger in the summer. And to answer your question, I am waiting for our errant lord and master to come home."

"Paying a call on the widow, is he?"

"He is." Cato shifted, so his thigh was aligned with Peak's. "Like an idiot, he walked through the self-same woods where somebody took a shot at him."

"Hard to shoot straight in the dark. Even with half a summer moon."

But easy to lurk in the shadows, as Cato had been lurking. "He wants to get shut of the lady, but the poor bastard's so hard up he can't give up his toy." Cato glanced at his companion. "She lets him get away with this."

"Women are fools. Some women."

"Women have their pride. All women."

"Men, too." Peak's teeth gleamed briefly in the shadows. "Lady Rammel is no fool, and once she gets her bearings, she'll send him packing."

"You care to wager on that?"

"How are we to prove our wager if Amherst and the widow come to a parting of the ways? He's not about to blame her for sending him elsewhere to scratch his itch. The woman has a baby on the way."

Peak's insights were interesting, and often deadly accurate.

"You have a point, except Amherst talks to me more and more as if he trusts me. He might admit to being cashiered from her bed."

"You'll abuse his trust, too, won't you?"

Cato blew out a breath and switched to Gaelic. "Do you know how close you push me to the edge, sitting out here with me like this on a soft summer night? How you abuse my trust?"

"I know." Peak rose easily, too easily. "Believe me, Catullus, I know."

Maybe it was Cato's imagination, or his wishful heart, but he could have sworn he felt deft fingers brush softly over his hair before Peak ducked into the safety of the stables.

* * *

"Your mother is asking for you." Robert Benning, Baron Trevisham, tried to keep his expression impassive as he surveyed his older son.

"This is supposed to be news?" Tye took a casual sip of brandy. The quantity of liquor Tye could hold had become… appalling, even for a hounds and horses man who was never far from his flask.

"She's your mother," Trevisham snapped. "She asks little enough in this life. You will attend her before you seek your bed."

"Yes, my lord." The note of mockery in Tye's voice was underscored by a small salute with his drink. "Before I do, Tom suggested I ask you about the family finances. Are we pockets to let, Papa?"

Trevisham winced inwardly, for the familiar address grated coming from Tye. When had his strapping, smiling firstborn turned into such a selfish, useless man? "What has put such notions in your brother's head?"

"Who knows where young Thomas gets his fool ideas?" Tye sipped again. "We both know he's fanciful, but he's also occasionally right."

"The last girl you trifled with," Trevisham said, "her family required a settlement."

"A settlement?" Tye rose, his tone incredulous. "For that little baggage?"

"The little baggage required a surgeon when you were done with her, Tidewell." A mercy she hadn't required the priest as well. "I gather what few wits she had were still out begging a week after your tryst."

"Right. You were taken in by a Drury Lane farce, Papa."

"Perhaps, but I've bought off your last scandal, my boy. Until you get your hands on my title, you're as common as dirt, and you can be held to account for your criminal behaviors. The worry and heartache you cause your mother should be reason enough to clap you in irons."

"You see me." Tye waggled the decanter. "Clapped, as it were." He smiled at his own salacious humor. "If you're so concerned about Mother, why aren't you the one patting her hand and passing her tisanes?"

"She's asking for *you*," Trevisham retorted, but that was as much as he'd say and they both knew it.

Lady Trevisham had been asking for her older son pretty much since the day he had been born, and if the baron had been puzzled at first, he'd soon acceded to his wife's preferences. She loved all three children, of course, but in her eyes, Tye would always be special.

More's the pity all around.

"You've evaded my question, my lord." Tye set the decanter down, though it was almost empty. "Are we approaching dun territory?"

Trevisham considered his son, saw the gray making inroads on Tye's dark hair, the lines fanning out from his eyes. Maybe a serving of reality was in order.

"We're not rolled up. Yet."

"Yet? Do you plan to leave me a bankrupted title?"

That would, of course, be the priority around which Tye's world organized itself. "Of course not. You know as well as I do that harvests have been off lately, the winters long and hard. I've made investments, but they haven't done well this year, and then too, you and Thomas go sporting up to Town as if I were a nabob. Have you any idea what it costs for the two of you to while away a Season in London?"

Even one free of expensive scandals, though Trevisham could not recall when the last one of those had been.

"I'm sure you'll tell me." Tye ran a thick finger around the rim of his glass. When his father named a surprisingly large sum, that finger paused.

"And when I have to drag you home early," the baron went on, "we get no refunds on the houses you rent, no forgiveness for the clothing you leave at the tailor's, or the stalls you reserve in the mews. I am a simple country squire, Tye, and I am competent to manage that lifestyle. You, with your Town tastes and expensive misadventures with the fairer sex, *you* and you alone are what has put us in dun territory, make no mistake."

Tye resumed his seat, not visibly affected by his father's accusations. When Trevisham saw his son would offer no apology—no comment, in fact—he stomped toward the door.

"Don't fret, though," the baron said, turning his back on his son. "I've some things in train that will yield a return sufficient to keep me and mine in adequate style. Not that I'd expect you to care. Don't forget your mother," the baron admonished, and then he was gone, leaving Tye to wonder if he'd ever, at any point in his misbegotten life, been able to forget his mother.

* * *

Ellie rolled over, which became more of a maneuver each week. Outside her window, night was fading and song birds cheerfully noted the approach of day.

Dratted birds.

A new day, one she should start with a sense of relief. She'd concluded her dealings with Lord Amherst, lover and dallier at large. Except she hadn't planned on parting with him, it had just…happened, in an inconvenient and poorly timed display of the good sense she was supposedly known for.

Good sense, and… love. Trenton Lindsey had doubtless strolled through the wood to come calling in the dark of night. Anybody seeking to harm him need only wait for him to take the same risk again, and Ellie would have another grief to deal with.

She had been honest, up to a point. A week of silence from him, followed by passionate tenderness, and no explanation for his absence, that had been difficult. The idea that he might have been followed through the shadows of the wood, that the next time he came to her by moonlight, harm might befall him…

Ellie could not have that on her conscience.

Tears threatened again, the same tears that had assailed her the previous night—part sorrow, to be parting from a man she held dear, and part anger, because regard for Trenton had left her no choice.

"Blast all men to Halifax," Ellie muttered as she swung her legs over the side of the bed and sat for the now obligatory minute to get her bearings. Then she spied the bouquet on her nightstand.

Ellie brought the flowers to her nose, smiling despite the lump in her throat.

"How did he scamper up and down my balcony with flowers?" Rosemary, for remembrance; vervain, for enchantment; wood sorrel, for joy; and campanula, for gratitude.

No roses, for love—that would have provoked at least two handkerchiefs worth of tears—but what lovely sentiments. Trenton had been a busy fellow last night, for he had to have gathered the flowers after Ellie had sent him packing.

After Ellie had cried and held on to him so tightly and cried some more. After she'd fallen asleep still clinging to him in the darkness.

The odd little bouquet wasn't a note, wasn't anything, but she took another whiff, and considered Trenton's farewell gesture. She should dash off a thank you note. A thank you note sent between neighbors for a kindness rendered was the least courtesy required.

CHAPTER SIXTEEN

"You've a very pretty estate over in Hampshire." Benjamin Hazlit, Heathgate's preferred investigator for hire, offered the compliment to Trent and accepted a drink from Heathgate.

"My father has a pretty estate," Trent replied. "But thank you. My memories of the place are not exactly fond, but Benton does a good job with it."

"It's thriving, in case you're interested." Hazlit was turned out in conservative country attire, but his complexion, dark to begin with, had apparently been subjected to the Hampshire sun.

"I make regular visits. I have to pay the trades, and I also want to keep an eye on my father."

"Wilton himself wasn't the object of my inquiry."

"Nonetheless, he's the ranking title in the parish," Trent finished the thought, "and you heard gossip. I doubt we need to be delicate for Lord Heathgate's ears."

"You do not." Heathgate sat on his desk, a raptor in

country-gentleman's clothing. "Try the whiskey, Amherst."

Trent dutifully sipped his drink, then sipped again. "Where on earth did you get this?"

Heathgate's smile was smug. "It's my private label. I think it makes the best argument against abstaining ever there was, is, or shall be."

"To your health." Trent lifted his glass a few inches. "What did you hear, Hazlit?"

"Your father is trifling with one of the local girls. She isn't well liked, puts on airs, but she's from decent people."

To have *this* conversation while sipping *this* whiskey was profane.

"Imogenie Henly. I've talked to her father. I'll do so again, sooner rather than later. What else?"

"Your father is becoming great good friends with your former father-in-law," Hazlit went on. "They rode to hounds together through the years, and now Trevisham has offered Wilton the use of his box in the north."

"Which Wilton will not get around to using."

"One hopes not, though Trevisham can't very well leave Hampshire for an extended frolic on the grouse moors when he's nigh pockets to let."

Well, damn. "How did you learn this?"

"The usual means." Hazlit sniffed at his whiskey, the gesture somehow elegant. "You have a pint or two or twenty in the local watering holes, ask if any of the Quality are hiring, and you hear the baron has started letting his older staff go, he's slow paying the younger ones, hasn't had any work done on the manor in ages, that sort of thing."

What was said at the local watering hole about Lord Amherst, and had Hazlit troubled himself to hear that, too?

"What else?"

"The baroness is not enjoying a social life," Hazlit reported. "She's supposedly prostrate with nerves over her sons' latest debacle in Town, but I was told it's an annual malady. Sooner or later, the older son, Tidewell, must be brought home in disgrace, year in and year out."

"Yet the entire five years I was married to his sister, he couldn't be bothered to call on us, and we generally tarried in London for at least the start of the Season."

"As to that…" Hazlit exchanged a look with Heathgate. "How well did you know your wife before your married her?"

"I knew *of* her," Trent said, knowing as well that his business had been discussed between the other two men in his absence, the way physicians would consult on a vexing case. "She was six or seven years my junior, so we never moved in the same social circles, even in Hampshire. She was Tom and Tye's pretty younger sister; I saw her at services, or assemblies, eventually, but I wouldn't say we were even acquainted."

Another glance between the marquess and his snoop, which even good whiskey could not smooth over.

Hazlit set his drink aside. "I suspected as much. I spoke with a lady who had been your wife's undergoverness some twenty years ago."

"And?"

"She describes a child who went from being sweet but shy to nervous in the extreme, and she attributed the shift to the ceaseless teasing and tormenting of her older brothers."

"Tidewell was fifteen years Paula's senior. You'd think he'd be beyond teasing a sibling so much his junior."

"But Tom would have been less than five years her senior," Hazlit pointed out. "Perhaps he was the more reprehensible of the two. Tidewell is still bothering young girls, though. His latest Season ended when he trifled with a young lady whose brothers took exception to her ill usage."

Every family had its burdens. "Trifled with?"

"The details were not available in Hampshire. They will be in London. He might have called her an indecent name. Duels have been fought over less."

"He might have raped her," Trent countered, thinking of

his late, unhappy, nervous wife. "As a baron's son, Tidewell probably considers himself above the law."

"He likely is, in a sense. His papa paid off the girl's family."

With money the baron apparently could not afford to part with.

"Where does this leave our investigation of the shooting?" Heathgate posed the question from his perch on the desk.

"A little wanting for motive," Hazlit admitted. "I could find nothing to indicate the Bennings are still grieving Paula's passing, but I did hear mention that Lady Trevisham had also buried a sister at a young age."

"Paula told me that. Said she had an aunt who'd died at the age of sixteen at boarding school. Said it made her reluctant to go off to finishing school herself, but she enjoyed it, for all her misgivings."

"Do you know where she attended?"

"Same place her aunt did." Trent closed his eyes in concentration. "Miss Somebody's Academy for Distinguished Young Ladies… Peachem, Pantry…"

"Palliser?" Hazlit suggested.

"Yes." Trent opened his eyes. "In the Midlands on the site of some priory old Henry confiscated. I saw it once on my way to Melton to meet Darius. Pretty place."

"One of my sisters considered teaching there before she took to governessing," Hazlit said. "She's a frightfully intelligent woman, my sister."

Ellie was frightfully intelligent, too. Also shrewd, kind, brave.

Passionate.

And done with him, as she should be.

"Paula was bright enough," Trent said. "She lacked confidence, until her temper was goaded."

"Did she ever talk about her family?"

Trent searched his memory, feeling like a witness in the box before hostile counsel, though neither of the other men could be enjoying this interview.

"She spoke of her father, sometimes. She'd say she missed him, but never asked that we take the children to see him. She left Trevisham Grange to join my household and never once went back."

"Which isn't so unusual," Hazlit said. "What about correspondence? With her mother, her friends from school, anybody?"

Not a detail, and yet Trent hadn't noticed this at the time.

"Nobody. I think the baron's sister had sponsored Paula's Seasons, but the old dame has since died. Even she couldn't spare Paula a note once we wed. It's sad, now that I think on it. At the time, we had other concerns, and the children started showing up."

"What of her mother?" Heathgate asked.

"Why do you ask?"

"In a family of three men, you'd think the mother and lone daughter would become close. Forgive my bluntness, your wife was retiring, Amherst, another trait that would make a girl closer to her mother. Then too, you have the mother's rather eccentric behavior, not socializing when she could be one of the queen bees of the parish. If her sons come up to Town, year after year, why doesn't she? Why didn't she present her own daughter? Something doesn't smell right."

"You have a point." An uncomfortable point Trent resented the man for seeing so easily. "I can't say I know my mother-in-law much better than I knew my wife when I married her. The baroness was quiet, pretty, and legendarily devoted to her children. She didn't strike me as the murdering kind."

"So that leaves us with Tom, Tye and the baron," Hazlit said. "Tom is off at some house party for now; Tye is serving out his sentence before hunting begins in the Midlands in the fall; and the baron is tending his acres in Hampshire and socializing with your father."

The decision became simple. "We focus on the baron,

then."

Heathgate shoved away from the desk. "You two focus on the baron. Whom do we know in the Midlands who can investigate a death that occurred at least forty years ago?"

"Why does it matter?" Hazlit asked.

Something outside the window apparently caught the marquess's attention. "Because," he said, back to his guests, "when a child is sick at boarding school, if it's more than a sniffle, the family is typically notified, primarily so the patient can be transported into their loving care prior to death or protracted illness. Schools are not set up as hospitals, and the risk of contagion if the illness is serious could close the school down. For a child to die at boarding school is unusual."

Hazlit heaved up a sigh that suggested he also chafed at Heathgate's insightfulness. "I'll see if my sister can dig up any connections around the school."

Trent took the last sip of his drink. "I will prepare for another sortie into the wilds of Hampshire. I don't suppose either of you needs a housekeeper who's both empty-headed and possibly carrying my next half-sibling?"

Hazlit snorted. "You might consider making the old boy marry the girl."

No, he would not inflict Wilton on even a willing woman.

"How would I compel Wilton to behave honorably?" Trent placed his glass on the sideboard, though he would have been welcome to more. "I've threatened to deny my sister Emily her come out next year, which hasn't had the intended effect of subduing Wilton's behaviors."

"So send Lady Emily from Town for a bit," Heathgate suggested. "Deny her the Little Season, which is the dress rehearsal for all that nonsense in the spring. She might enjoy it, being the belle of the shire, an earl's daughter, and such. Felicity says the girl was raised primarily in Town but never went about much."

"Never went about at all," Trent corrected him. "Not

unless Dare, Leah or I took her. I hate to think of consigning Emily to Wilton's company again."

"Let him see that his hold on her has slipped," Hazlit said. "That might take the wind from his sails more effectively than anything else."

Heathgate pushed his insightful, helpful self away from the window. "Then too, having his young daughter underfoot might make him less inclined to tryst with his latest inamorata. Having your sister visit Wilton Acres might serve several needs."

"I'll ask Emily and Lady Warne about it," Trent said. "I wouldn't make such a decision lightly, and Mr. Benton will weigh in as well."

"When do you leave?" Heathgate collected Hazlit's glass and set it with his own on the sideboard.

"A few days. I have correspondence to deal with, and I'm closing up my town house prior to selling it. If the two of you would look in on Ellie Hampton in my absence, I'd appreciate it."

Another look passed between the two men, but this one Trent deciphered easily enough.

"It isn't like that." It had *never* been like that. "We're disentangled, and I don't want to hover, but she's…"

Heathgate smiled. "We'll look in on her. Won't we, Benjamin?"

"We will. My sister is serving as governess to Mr. Grey's boys, and I'm out this way periodically to keep an eye on her as well."

Trent left them to their excellent sipping whiskey, but the upshot of Hazlit's entire trip to Hampshire had been to confirm Trent's suspicions: Baron Trevisham was strengthening his association with Wilton, Paula's mother was of an increasingly nervous disposition, and her brothers were a pair of ne'er-do-well scapegraces. Not a one of them had seemed to care a whit for Paula once she'd wed, but they were exactly the type of people who might see merit in putting a period to Trent's life for their own reasons.

* * *

"A caller, my lady."

Drat and damn. Ellie mustered a smile for her butler. "The veranda will do, and we could use some sustenance."

Lady Greymoor—for who else could it be?—was not shy about enjoying her victuals, though for herself, Ellie found the prospect of the lady's company daunting. This was understandable, when Ellie had missed considerable sleep the previous night and had her heart broken in the bargain.

No, you did not, she lectured herself as she took a seat among the roses on the veranda only to be pulled to her feet by none other than the heartbreaker himself.

"Trenton?"

"Good afternoon." He accompanied his greeting with a slight, searching curve of his lips. "I hope I'm not intruding?"

"No, of course not." Ellie gave up trying to hide her answering smile, though worry soon crowded her joy. "Please assure me you did not ride through the wood."

"I did not. Cato rode with me to the foot of your lane. I'm to have one of your grooms accompany me back to Crossbridge, or I'll suffer a scold worthy of Mrs. Drawbaugh in a taking. I know I'm imposing, Ellie, but I'm trying to be sensible about it."

He wasn't imposing, he was taking a risk, racketing about the countryside for the sake of sentiment, and yet, Ellie could not muster a scold, not for one last visit.

"Will you have seat?"

"Unless you'd rather walk?"

Walking meant she could slip her arm through his and have more privacy with him than if they sat in the shade, the obligatory footmen hovering. She shouldn't want privacy with Trenton, but she'd only hours ago given the man his papers. She could hoard up a moment of proximity with him now, for surely there'd be little enough of it in the future.

"You look tired," Trent said quietly as they started off in the direction of the garden. "I'm sorry for that."

"You're not quite in the pink yourself. I can't say I feel a great deal of remorse."

His eyebrows twitched, but then he caught her smile. "One shouldn't. Feel remorse, that is. You shouldn't."

"So is this how it's done?" Ellie asked. He'd taken off his riding gloves, and his bare hand rested over hers on his arm. "You make a final visit to ensure the civilities will be observed?"

"I wouldn't know. I've brought Zephyr over so Miss Andy might have the use of her until she outgrows the beast. My boys will want ponies with more pluck, and Zephyr's pride will be offended when she sees she's been replaced."

Zephyr's pride? "That is… kind of you."

"Not kind. Devious. I needed to see you're managing well enough and that you don't hate me." He looked so uncertain—bashful, dear, tired, sincere—that Ellie fell in love with him all over.

Perishing damned Halifax, she would never attempt to dally again.

"I could never hate you," Ellie said in low, fierce tones. "I only wish…"

Regret joined the sincerity in his gaze. "I wish, too, Ellie."

Well. Wishes changed nothing. Ellie cast around for a remark about the roses, the pansies, anything safe.

"I found your flowers." Not a brilliant gambit, though it marginally changed the topic.

"I couldn't be very creative. I had to climb that blasted tree with them in my teeth—hence, nothing with thorns."

Ellie looked down to admire a bed of daisies, also to keep her smile from showing. "No thorns."

"Then too,"—he surveyed her gardens, which he had seen many times before—"before I denuded your bushes of every red rose, I'd want to have the property owner's permission."

Red roses, for love. They ought to stand for arrant folly, and for widows who had no talent for casual dallying. Lord Amherst didn't appear to have the knack for it, either.

"Gardeners can be a fussy lot," Ellie said. "Permission is a good idea, generally."

"So we're not to be enemies?" Trent's eyes told her nothing, and maybe that was telling in itself.

This time, Ellie let him see her smile. "Never enemies. I will stand up with you at the assemblies when my mourning is over. I will expect you to come admire the new baby some fine winter day. I will want to see your boys up on their trusty steeds in the near future, and if I ever fly my kite into a tree, I'll send for you."

"Tricky things, kites." Trent smiled back at her, a true smile that lifted a weight from Ellie's heart. "I'll be happy to assist."

They whiled away another half-hour on the veranda, with Trent telling her about his decision to sell the town house and let his Town staff go. She approved that choice and was pleased to hear Mr. Darius Lindsey might visit Crossbridge in the near future. Ellie relayed the contents of a recent letter she'd had from Drew, who was at the Hampton family seat, trying to sort out tenants Dane has all but ignored. Then Andy interrupted, for she'd spied the pony trotting along beside Arthur when Trent had come up the drive.

"She's to be mine?" Andy asked.

"That's up to your mother," Trent replied. "I know Zephyr would appreciate having a job and somebody to care about her."

"I'll groom her every day and comb her mane. Does she like carrots?"

"Loves them. Shall I take you for a visit now?"

"Mama? Please, may I?"

Smiling at her daughter was so miserably, awfully hard when Ellie wanted to linger over yet another glass of lemonade with her lov—with her former lover. That way lay more tears, more damp, wrinkled handkerchiefs. She'd be flying kites into oak trees, next—by moonlight.

"I'm ready for my afternoon nap," Ellie said, "and the day grows warm. Mind you don't get your pinafore dirty, Miss Coriander Brown, and change into your boots while I walk his lordship to the door."

Andy scampered off at dead run while Ellie called for Trent's hat and gloves.

"No hat," Trent confessed. "A top hat gets caught on branches or tumbles off when Arthur takes a notion to go dancing."

"Which is why you're growing as brown as a Tahitian native. You do look tired. Promise you won't tarry long in the stables?" She resisted the urge to touch him—to pat his lapel, kiss his cheek, to take his hand.

When Ellie had first learned that Dane had died, when she'd made his final arrangements, met with the solicitors, and explained the situation to Andy, she'd done so in a haze of sorrow—anger and bewilderment had befogged her, lending her days and nights a sense of unreality.

The hurt she endured standing two feet away from Trenton Lindsey now, the sense of frustration and loss, was real. So was her fear for his safety.

"You'll manage?" Trent asked.

What did he need from her, that he'd put such a question to her?

"I'd have been indisposed if I hadn't wanted to see you, Trenton Lindsey, or told you to keep your pony. Drew could find the child a suitable mount if I asked him to."

"You're learning." Trent leaned in and brushed a kiss to her cheek. "You may not have read that manual, but you're picking up the rules."

Damn the manual to Halifax.

"My regard for you it isn't a game, Trenton." Ellie went up

on her toes and kissed *his* cheek in retaliation—also to catch one last whiff of his scent. "Thank you for coming and for the pony, but you needn't feel obligated to come again."

The words came out wrong. What should have been worry for his safety ended up sounding like a dismissal, though maybe that was for the best if it kept him tucked up at Crossbridge.

Fortunately for the remains of Ellie's pride, Andy came tearing down the steps to grab Trent's hand and literally drag him off to the stables. Ellie let them go, because she was—honestly—feeling tired. As she undressed and climbed into bed, she decided that Trent's visit had helped, or helped more than it hurt.

Yes, it hurt to know they weren't lovers, hurt a lot. But it helped to know he cared how she was faring, cared for her goodwill, cared for their continued cordial regard for one another. As she drifted off to sleep, it occurred to Ellie that Trent could have sent the pony over with a note, but he'd come in person and taken the trouble to introduce Andy to the beast himself.

That realization did *not* hurt.

* * *

"I always felt like Paula's mind was somewhere else," Darius observed when the footman had withdrawn from the dining parlor. "Rather like yours is right now."

Trent poured the last of a fine merlot into Darius's wineglass, having limited himself to two glasses. "Sorry. I'm dreading a confrontation with Louise."

"Turn the cranky baggage off. The meal was good, but not worth dreading your own kitchen."

Darius, a mere younger son, had not merited Louise's most impressive exertions though no man was dearer to Trent in the entire world than his younger brother.

"Louise does a fine job for me, but she skimps and cheats on the staff, who need their victuals more than I do. Then I have to take her to task, and she complies for a bit, until my back is turned. Don't suppose you need a cook?"

"I have a cook. I do not need an insurrectionist taking my coin in any guise, and neither do you. Shall I turn her off for you?"

The offer was sincere. Darius had an enviable ruthless streak, witness the way he'd hauled Trent bodily to Crossbridge weeks earlier.

Trent considered another half a glass of wine and decided against it. "I'll give Louise one more chance, and then she gets the same severance and character the Town staff will receive."

"I'm glad you're selling. The house wasn't exactly commodious."

Neither were Trent's memories of the place. "Put three young children in most houses and they aren't commodious for very long. You've seen Belle Maison?"

"Commodious, even for the Haddonfields. Leah's happy there."

Very likely, Darius had made sure of that himself.

"I could send Emily out there for the winter. I'm thinking of sending her down to Wilton Acres for a while first."

Darius pushed a last bite of buttered peas around on his plate. "Wilton will hate having her know he's confined there, but he'll love having his pretty little girl to show off before she's launched. I'd make it a short visit, though."

Because nobody, least of all his sons, trusted anything of value for long in Wilton's ambit.

"I want him to see it as punishing Emily for his misdeeds. I must find some way to haul him up short, Dare, and I'll tell him I've denied Emily the Little Season."

Darius poured them each an additional finger of wine, which was... encouraging. "What's Wilton up to now?"

To have somebody to discuss this with, somebody who knew Wilton in all his wily arrogance, was a relief. Ellie would have some useful insights, of course, but Ellie—

Trent pushed his wine glass closer to the middle of the

table. "Wilton is promising Imogenie Henly she'll be his countess while he no doubt spanks her pretty bum and dares her to cry to Mama over it."

Darius rearranged his cutlery, knife and fork crossed over his plate. "Tiresome but predictable. She must not be carrying yet."

"One hopes not. One prays not." Trent pushed back from the table, his wine untouched, for Darius's show of faith should be rewarded. "I'm bound to deliver the requisite stern lectures all around in the next week or so. I had hoped you could stay here in my absence."

"I can. I can also go over those diaries of yours. I'm likely to see things you can't."

Darius had suggested by letter that Trent read over the journals he'd kept since marrying Paula, a sad, fruitless exercise.

"What sort of things?" Trent led his brother through the house, darkness having fallen while they'd eaten.

Ellie would be abed, her French doors open to the cool night air.

"You said you'd found nothing of note the first year of your marriage. I recall borrowing your carriage shortly after I returned from Italy and the axle broke."

"I'd forgotten that."

"The axle didn't snap. It came unbolted from the chassis," Darius reminded him. "If we hadn't hit a deep rut at a stately walk, there's no telling who would have been hurt by such a mishap."

Trent paused at the foot of the stairs, memory assailing him. "Paula loved to take Ford out and show him off. I often went with them because Ford did not enjoy coach travel for the first three years of his life."

Darius started moving up the stairs. "I will not review those journals with the eye of the man who wrote them, confirming his own recollections with whatever's on the page. I'll see them with a fresh eye and add my own recollections as well."

Trent hesitated at the landing where the stairs turned at a right angle. "Read them if you must."

"What?"

"I appreciate the help, Dare, don't think otherwise, but the journals are personal."

Darius's gaze gave away nothing. "I am your brother, and if you are killed, I will take that very personally as well. You may trust my discretion, Trenton."

A scold, not a reassurance. How Trenton loved his one and only brother. "I do trust you, utterly. Another thing?"

"Ask."

"If you could call on Elegy Hampton, Lady Rammel, in my absence, I'd appreciate it." Simply saying her pretty, feminine name was a guilty pleasure.

Darius's expression became unreadable in an entirely different manner. "Lady Rammel, the widow?"

"We were briefly entangled, though now we're not. She's a dear lady, and her circumstances are trying." Thanks in no little part to one Trenton Lindsey.

Darius smirked as only a handsome younger sibling could. "If you insist I'll do the pretty and let you know how she's getting over you, but perhaps you ought to look in on her yourself."

Trent's very own thought—a useless, mostly selfish, but also sincere thought.

"Brat." When Trent had shown his brother to a guest room, he prepared to do battle with his cook, though he was fortified knowing Darius—notably soft-hearted where Wilton's rejects were concerned—would turn the woman off without a character. Trent found his cook in the kitchen preparing ingredients for the next day's meals.

"Greetings, Louise." They were alone, which suited Trent's purposes. "I've come to scold you."

"That's Cook to you." She went right on chopping walnuts. "And you've no business below-stairs, my lord. You want to scold the help, you ring for us and dress us down above stairs. The earl does his scolding before the footmen for good measure."

Which bit of heinousness Trent knew only too well.

"Be glad, then, that I am not my father," Trent rejoined, only to hear something muttered along the lines of "that's for damned sure."

"Louise," Trent said pleasantly, "I can sack you."

She came up scowling, hands planted on her hips. "You don't mean that. You aren't nasty enough to sack me." She made this a base insult.

"I am not nasty, but this is to my credit, not yours. I am out of patience with you, and if you countermand one more of my orders, misinterpret, ignore, or otherwise subvert my authority, you are gone."

"You wouldn't."

"Have I threatened this before?"

Her hard blue eyes grew thoughtful. "You have not."

"Nor will I threaten again," Trent assured her. "You may feed simpler fare to the help but of no less quality than what you put before me and my guests, or you will soon need concern yourself with how to feed only my former cook. I'm weary of this constant battle in my own kitchen, and it's beneath you as well."

"Beneath me?" She opened her mouth to launch a tirade, but Trent popped half a walnut into her maw.

Had all her teeth, did Louise.

"Chew. You're less likely to choke if you do. Now, having settled matters between us for the last time, I'm off to Wilton again the day after tomorrow and will gladly bear your letters when I go. I'm sure Nancy enjoys your correspondence. My brother and Mr. Spencer will tend the manor in my absence, and you are to show them better courtesy than you do me."

"That worthless *Irish*..."

Trent tossed another walnut at her, which bounced off her

chin. "Catullus Spencer is the most trusted member of my senior staff. You will show him every respect, Louise."

"Your papa wouldn't have let such a one as that presuming Paddy hold his horse."

Trent headed for the steps. "And now my father is banished to Wilton Acres, while Cato Spencer has the run of my house. Think how far you'll get without a character, Louise. All around here know how badly you've treated my help, because the help gossip, as you well know. Until tomorrow."

He left her slamming things onto the counter and muttering, but their skirmish had been brief, and he counted it a victory, because Dare was right: Trent really did not need a rebellion in his own kitchen, and enough was enough.

He climbed the steps to the nursery, there to find Darius usurping the story hour for an uncle's nefarious purposes. Trent repaired to his rooms, soaked away as much of the day's frustrations and fatigue as he could, then sought his balcony.

He hadn't seen Ellie for some days, and her absence left an ache. Not a purely sexual ache, but Trent opened his dressing gown and stroked himself lightly anyway. When he eventually found his pleasure, he found some comfort as well, an echo of the pleasure he'd shared so easily with Ellie.

He found a load of longing and sheer, bodily loneliness, too.

As an experiment, it was ten minutes successfully spent. He'd learned that self-gratification didn't fix the part of him that missed Ellie most, though it made climbing into bed and dreaming about what he'd lost with her that much easier.

CHAPTER SEVENTEEN

"You needn't announce me," Trent told the butler. "I'll just go on up."

Mr. Wright gave him a slight smile. "Very good, my lord. Her ladyship is likely on her balcony at this time of morning."

The balcony that adjoined her bedroom and private sitting room. For the love of God, when would Trent learn to simply send a bloody note?

He went up and knocked on the sitting-room door and got no answer, which made sense if Ellie was out on her balcony. He pushed open the door, calling her name softly, and still heard no response.

If there were a merciful God, Ellie would not be asleep in her bed. His faith was modestly rewarded when he found her dozing on her swing. She had curled down on her side, her slipper dangling from her foot, her lips slightly parted, a pair of wire-rimmed spectacles askew on her nose.

The sight of her hit him low in the gut and had him

hunkered beside the swing without knowing how he got there.

"Ellie?" He carefully unhooked the spectacles from her ears. "Love? You've company." She batted at her nose but subsided back into sleep, so he kissed her cheek.

She batted at her cheek, which had him smiling like an idiot when she opened her eyes.

"Oh, blighted Halifax…" she muttered and tried to push up, but her hair got trapped between the slats of the swing's back.

"Hold still." He freed her hair but brought down the precarious anchorings of her bun in the process.

"I must look a fright." Ellie sat up and stretched. "But you are a welcome sight. Sit and let me apologize for not even waking up to greet you. Who escorted you over this time?"

"Peak. He's visiting in your stables. You look well rested." She looked…delectable, dear and desirable. Trent accepted the place beside her. She passed him some hair pins and set about fixing her hair. "I've intruded on your nap, for which I apologize."

"It's easy to do—the intruding part," she assured him, twisting her braid back up and taking pins from his palm one by one. "I'm still dozing off here and there the live long day. You might take up the sport yourself. You still look a little…"

"Like I ran the Derby and lost?"

"Tired," Ellie said softly. "You look tired, Trenton, so tell me what has you so fatigued."

Missing you.

"I'm off to Hampshire again," he said, glad for the pins in his hand. They prevented him from taking her hand in his, but also had her touching him, however fleetingly, as she put her hair to rights. "I must threaten my father into submission before his bad behavior results in another half-sibling."

Ellie grimaced as she shoved a pin into a coiled braid. "One hears of older men siring children. I've never understood the appeal of having offspring who would see one toothless, confused, and laid low with the rheumatism before the child was breeched."

"That is rational adult thinking, something my father has never held in great regard. Though it is the fate of most mortal men to either die young, or slip into senescence, my father no doubt believes himself every bit as attractive, fit and sound of wit as he was at university. Then too, he's every bit as amoral."

"Having a parent you cannot respect"—Ellie took the last of the pins—"must be a trial."

How easily this troubling conversation came to them, and how much Trent had missed her.

"I wouldn't mind not respecting him." Ellie's fingers laced with Trent's, and his relief at her touch was pathetic. "I mind very much that I can find nothing, not one thing, to like or trust about the man."

"Nothing? Tell me about him."

"He's arrogant, stubborn, and without the redeeming sense of a greater order that rescues so many of his peers from insufferableness. God might make mistakes, but not Wilton."

"He was like this even when you were a boy?" Ellie put his hand on her thigh and traced his knuckles with her free hand. She wasn't wearing any rings and she still sported an abundant crop of freckles. "Or has Wilton become set in his ways as age has overtaken his sense?"

"I'm still adding to my list of nevers, if that's what you're asking." Trent should withdraw his hand, but given the topic, he let himself have the contact—needed it, in fact.

"What is your list of nevers?" Ellie leaned forward, or into him. In any case, the soft weight of her breast pressed against his biceps, and he knew—*knew*—she hadn't meant it as anything sexual. More significantly, he wasn't responding sexually. Her closeness was simply…comforting.

"I started my list when I was about five. I had to print the first entries," he explained. "I intended it to illuminate my efforts to be Wilton, when that fateful day arrived, or so I told myself. Mostly, I kept a record of needless suffering by a lonely and very confused little boy."

He told her about the bones he'd broken trying to learn to ride the first nasty pony his father had put him on, about the lung fever resulting from his efforts to skate, about the tearing shame of seeing his sister Leah try not to cry while she was forced to watch him being caned as an adolescent.

"The worst was when he took me out to the kennels—I would have been about seven—and led me to believe I was to be given a puppy. In a sense, I was."

Ellie remained quiet beside him, and before he could turn the words back, they were running past his lips.

"Wilton told me I either drowned the runt or watched while he shot the bitch and her entire litter. I had to learn to make difficult decisions and see them through. He insisted on that lesson on many occasions."

The feeling of the puppy struggling as Trent held it in the depths of the horse trough threatened to choke him.

"Trenton." Ellie's arm slid around his waist. "I am so sorry. You did not deserve to be treated that way. No child does. Damn your father to… to… *Hades*."

Trent's throat was too constricted to agree with Ellie's sentiments, but he kept his fingers laced with hers, taking care not to hold too tightly.

"It's well your father is off in Hampshire," Ellie went on. "Lest I arrange an accident for him when next he's in the hunt field. To think Dane, who was basically harmless, didn't even see thirty years and such a one as Wilton is given nigh twice that…it tries one's faith."

While Ellie's reaction restored a man's faith. "I must deal with him nonetheless, and possibly my in-laws as well."

Ellie frowned at their joined hands. "Is that wise? You suspect those people of wishing you harm."

"Like most bullies, they're sneaking around to do it. If I confront them, likely they'll desist. Then too, I'm thinking of sending Emily down to Wilton Acres for a time, and I need to solicit Mr. Benton's opinion of this scheme."

"He's your steward?"

"And Wilton's warden."

"Your errands are hardly cheering. You will be relieved to have them behind you, and then you can turn your attention to the harvest at Crossbridge."

"I'll look forward to it. I wanted to let you know that while I'm gone, my brother, Darius, will mind Crossbridge for me, and he's been instructed to keep an eye on you."

"An eye on me?" Ellie retrieved a pillow from the rug and stuffed it behind her back. "Am I in need of supervision?"

"Hardly." Trent let her slip her fingers from his, though it was difficult. "You might be in need of the occasional friendly face or casual caller. Heathgate and Hazlit might drop over as well."

She considered him while the breeze brought him the scent of her gardens in high summer, and of her. "Is this guilt? Do you think I'm pining away here without your shoulder to fall asleep on?"

He rose, smiling at the consternation on her face, though both the rising and the smiling managed to wedge themselves into that growing category of things that were difficult.

"You are indiscriminate in your napping, my dear, as this morning's visit proves. This isn't guilt, but it is concern. I can be concerned for a friend, can't I?"

She regarded him owlishly, and Trent had the notion she might nod off while considering her answer, but then she smiled, a soft, pleased smile.

"You may be concerned, but only concerned—I have certainly been concerned for you. Come along, we can tour my rose garden while I escort you back to Arthur's side. Tell me how your children are settling in at Crossbridge, and you may inform Mr. Spencer he will never see little Zephyr outside of Andy's keeping again."

"He'll keep an eye on you, too, though from a discreet and friendly distance."

"Have you left anybody in the neighborhood who won't be keeping an eye on me?" Ellie asked as they wound their way through the house. "Any able-bodied men, that is?"

Trent thought for a minute. "Peak, possibly, but Peak is rather attached to Cato, so maybe even Peak will ride over this way in my absence."

"Peak? He's the slender lad with the dark eyes. Cato's shadow?"

"The very one, or his conscience." Or something.

Trent led her on a shady path out toward the gardens. "You're not to be running loose without footmen while I'm gone, Ellie. Don't relax your vigilance. I haven't found my culprit, and Mr. Soames remains at large."

Though even if he had found his culprit, Ellie might still have decided that a life of independence suited her better than a headlong rush back up the church aisle.

"So even Mr. Soames may be keeping an eye on me from the safety of the woods," Ellie marveled. "I can only think of one person who won't be dedicating himself to surveillance of me in the coming days."

"Who would that be?"

"You."

* * *

"Just you," Ellie repeated, because Trent seemed surprised by her answer.

She'd felt his kiss on her cheek as she struggled up from sleep, had known he was there by his scent, and some other sense honed by having been more intimate with him than with her own late husband.

She'd been glad to see him, for it confirmed he was safe and whole. She'd been gladder still to touch him, and most glad of all that he still seemed to like her touch as well.

Though she was angry with him, too, and that bore study.

She'd been angry with Dane for their entire marriage and remained angry with the poor man even in death.

They ambled along in silence, until Trent bent to sniff a pretty red rose. "I'd pick it for you, but we're barehanded, and there are those thorns."

"There are, though tell me, Trenton, is it supposed to be like this?"

"Is what supposed to be like this?" He was stalling, as men will, when they're quite certain what was asked but not certain at all how to answer without getting in Trouble.

"We've ended our liaison," Ellie said softly. "I still rejoice to see you, I still enjoy the scent of you, the sound of your voice, the knowledge that you're well and your children are thriving in your care." She should tell him about the anger, though, too.

She'd never once taken Dane to task for his negligence, never demanded he attend her, afraid he'd neglect her yet further if she became *that sort of wife*.

"You *rejoice* to see me?" His tone said he suspected Ellie of a qualified sort of rejoicing, which was perceptive of him.

"Of course I do." Ellie smiled, sadly, because he was still stalling and seemed unaware of it. "I suspect we've gone beyond what's in that manual, though."

"There's no manual, Ellie," he said, his gaze traveling over the lovely gardens in the summer sunshine. "There's only you and me, and how we want to go on, and I can understand why more intimate attentions from me aren't appropriate right now, but that doesn't mean… What?"

"Hush." She shook her head, unwilling to hear from him how much folly he might tolerate from her today, when tomorrow his answer might be different.

"I miss you, too, and that's all that need be said." Because he might tell himself it was her safety he wanted to preserve, but in his hesitance, and his silences, she heard his unwillingness— his inability—to admit other reasons for them to be apart.

His attachment to his first wife, his unspoken resentment of his entire marriage, his right to enjoy a few years unencumbered by any spouse before again seeking a prospective countess.

Whatever his reasons, Ellie had no wish to face them.

He peered down at her. "I miss you isn't adequate," he said quietly. "It's in the right direction, but it isn't nearly adequate."

"If you try to say more, we'll just end up kissing, and then where will we be?"

"Perishing damned Halifax."

She walked him to the stables, and when he bowed over her hand in parting, his lips touched her knuckles.

"Thank you for calling," Ellie said, taking a step back. "I will pray for your safe return from Hampshire, but you really need not keep checking on me."

"Until my journey is accomplished then." He kissed her cheek, hesitating before he straightened, as if making sure his boldness registered. He might have breathed in through his nose in that single moment of gratuitous nearness.

He mounted his trusty steed and cantered off, while Ellie wondered what it meant when a woman told a man, twice, that he need no longer call on her, yet in some shameless, lonely corner of her heart, that woman still treasured him and the kisses he insisted on giving her, and couldn't wait until he called again.

* * *

"Missed you at breakfast." Trent greeted the Wilton Acres steward as they both dismounted at the end of an afternoon that for Trent had been long, hot, and frustrating. "My thanks for the tray last night and the bath."

Arthur groaned as Trent loosened his girth. As a groom led the beast away, Arthur flicked his tail so it whipped against Trent's fundament.

Cheeky blighter.

"You like your comforts," Benton said, "same as I do, but I'll be ordering myself another bath tonight. How did your interview with Henly go?"

"A complete waste of an hour. I'd have been better off clearing ditches with you all afternoon." Manual exertion might also have exorcised a certain quiet, pretty widow from Trent's imagination—or not.

Benton patted his horse—who apparently did not offer his master unsolicited reprimands—and passed the reins to a groom. "As if we'd get anything done with my whole crew gawping at you, the first Wilton heir to dirty his hands on his own land."

"Is that our reputation hereabouts?"

"A collective sigh of hope went up when word got around you had the reins of the earldom," Benton said as they ambled in the direction of the house. "Now Wilton is stuck here, preying on Imogenie, and that hope is waning. He has, though, started to call on his neighbors, and while nobody particularly likes him, they all want him nibbling on their crumpets."

"But not their daughters. He might someday remarry, though God help the woman who'd take him on."

"Imogenie considers herself a countess-in-waiting. Pathetic, but she's a very young woman in love."

"Surely not with Wilton. Maybe with the title and the wealth?"

Benton looked thoughtful, and fortunately, no footmen lurked in the front hall to overhear this exchange.

"Our Imogenie holds some genuine regard for the man, or who she thinks the man is. She's innocent, and viewed from below, Wilton has a certain allure, if not charm."

If allure were another word for manipulative skill, deceit, and arrogance. "Pathetic, as you say." Like the main foyer, which boasted not a single bouquet of roses, despite the estate's army of gardeners. "He'll devastate her, but we can't stop it. Have your bath before the maids faint from the smell of you. I've business below-stairs, and I'll see you at dinner."

"Until dinner." Benton had his neckcloth loosened before

he'd hit the third stair, but he paused. "What is this you wrote about sending your younger sister here for a visit?"

"Emily. We can talk about that over dinner." Trent left his steward yanking at a limp, dusty cravat and went in search of Nancy Brookes.

"Master Trent." Nancy's smile was as quiet as it was rare, but she opened her arms to hug him, and Trent reciprocated.

Nancy had been the one to sneak him a fresh biscuit when he'd been sent to bed without supper, to wink at him when he was on his way to a dreaded interview with his father, and to explain to him that boys at school were beaten only for cause. She'd also taken care of Trent's mother in her final illness.

But when had Nancy become so small and frail?

Trent led her to the oak work table, into which footmen had carved their initials probably from the days of the Wilton barony. "How's the prettiest lady in the shire?"

"So old she can barely see," Nancy retorted, creaking to the bench across from him. "I can tell you're tired, Master Trent, and you've too much to do haring all around the realm and trying to keep up with his lordship's mischief."

"Somebody has to do it. Bake me any biscuits?"

"In the crockery jar. Kettle's on the hob, and we've a store of gunpowder tea above the stove, in case you order a tray."

"I'll share a cup with you. You smell much better than Mr. Benton."

"Don't be criticizing young Aaron." She let Trent fuss around in the kitchen, suggesting she might truly be troubled by her vision.

Or her knees.

Or her hips.

Nobody's lot was easy in service to Wilton.

"You're sweet on our steward?" Trent asked. Benton was likely a third Nancy's age.

"He works mighty hard, and never a word of thanks from Wilton."

"Because he doesn't work for Wilton," Trent reminded her. "He works for me, and for Wilton Acres. Where has the sugar got off to?"

"Second drawer, left of the sink. Spoons are in the drawer above that."

He brought the tea tray to the table along with some cinnamon biscuits and sat beside her. "We shall spoil our dinner."

When she didn't reach for the biscuits, he pushed the plate toward her, then poured their tea and patted her knuckles, but gently for they were swollen. "Mrs. Haines has something she puts on her joints for the aches."

Nancy sipped her tea. "She sends me along some now and then, and always includes a helping of gossip."

"I thought Imogenie Henly was keeping you supplied with gossip." Trent added cream and sugar to his tea. "Have a biscuit. Cook hasn't started dinner, and I'll be less self-conscious if you join me in my gluttony."

"Cook has dinner done. Cold collations, because the heat is miserable and Mr. Benton doesn't like her having to use the summer kitchen or heat up the house."

"Thoughtful of him." Trent started on a biscuit, savoring the combination of fragrant tea and delicate spice, and glad for the cool of the kitchen.

"Is Imogenie telling her ma she's calling on me?"

"She's told her father, in any case. I gather that's a Banbury tale?"

"It's a lie. Her parents ought to know I wouldn't be passing the time of day with Wilton's light-skirt."

"She's a girl, Nancy. A foolish young girl who needs whatever kindly advice you can give her, and she isn't the first to believe the earl's blather."

"Nor the last, God help us. I'll say something to her, does the chance arise. How is Master Darius?"

Trent regaled her with nonsense about his siblings, until

the tea and biscuits were nearly gone and Cook had poked her head out of the servants' parlor, like a squirrel assessing the sky.

"I'm about to be shooed off." Trent filched a final cinnamon biscuit and wondered whether Ellie might like the recipe.

But…no.

"I have letters from my staff at Crossbridge to their confreres here. Shall I give them to Cook?"

"Best do." Nancy rose slowly. "I've work to do, and I've tarried long enough. You give my love to the children, Master Trent, and watch Wilton. That man is up to something, mark me."

"We are watching him." Cook stood in the door, rolling her eyes at Nancy's dire tone, and Trent recalled that Wilton had spies most everywhere. "But who's watching you, Nancy Brookes?"

"We all keep an eye on Miss Nancy," Cook chimed in as she disappeared into the pantry.

"Nancy?" Trent posed his question, knowing Cook might be overhearing. "Why didn't Wilton ever send you packing? You kept his house for years, but he had to know your loyalties were with my mother."

"They were with you children. Your mother left me a competence should I ever leave Wilton's employ."

"A sum?"

"Interest income for life. Wilton has no doubt pilfered the principal, meaning it's easier for him to keep me in the traces while he spends my money. Where would I go anyway?"

"Crossbridge." Trent battled a spike of weary loathing for his father. "Depend upon it, or to Darius's estate, or Leah's. I'm without a housekeeper at present, so say the word, and we'll hitch up the traveling coach."

Nancy's gnarled hand went to her throat. "And me never once leaving the shire in all my born years."

"Baggage." Trent hugged her again, carefully, winked at

Cook and tucked the last biscuit into his pocket. "I mean it, Nancy. You want to shake the dust of Wilton from your feet, you have Aaron Benton send a pigeon."

He was gone, leaving Nancy to exchange a smile with Cook.

"That boy." Nancy swept crumbs from the table. "As if I could ever write more than my name on a good day, much less see what I'd put on the page."

CHAPTER EIGHTEEN

"Louise isn't working out very well?" Benton passed Trent a glass holding two fingers of brandy.

"She cooks competently, but she wants me to be the kind of petty tyrant my father enjoys being and uses her position to push me in that direction. I am amenable to persuasion regarding many things, but not when it comes to following in my father's footsteps."

Benton poured himself a more generous serving, which Trent did not begrudge him. "A cook has more power than one thinks. What will you do?"

"She's on her last chance, and then she'll get what she wants. I'll summarily turn her off." Not as summarily as Wilton had.

"High-handed, indeed." Benton settled his long frame onto the library's sofa. "Now what is this hare-brained scheme to bring your sister down here next month?"

"I'm beginning to think it isn't hare-brained," Trent mused, peering at his drink. He would rather have had lemonade garnished with mint. "Emily hasn't spent time here for years, and she's soon to be fired off, so this will be her last opportunity to sashay around the shire as Lady Emily."

Benton's expression was not cheerful, though he was himself a viscount's nephew and looked utterly at home in the elegant comfort of the Wilton library. "She's an earl's daughter. She'll always be Lady Emily."

"She's not such an earl's daughter as all that. She's seventeen, but looks younger, because she has these great blue eyes and... What?"

"I've met her." From his tone, the occasion had not been happy. "When I first came to your town house in London with Bellefonte. Lady Leah and Lady Emily were outside in Bellefonte's vis-à-vis on their way to the park. She blushed when I bowed over her hand."

Months later, Benton recalled this chance meeting?

"She would blush at true gentlemanliness, though when Nick aims all his flummery at her, she knows it's purest flummery."

Benton left the couch and went off on a progress around the library—a room he could visit twelve times a day if he so chose. "Would Lady Warne accompany her, or would you reside here with her for the nonce?"

The idea of being far from Crossbridge, and Trent's children—and Ellie—sat poorly. "Her own father is here. She hardly needs a chaperone beyond that."

Benton paused before the shelf that held a collection of earthy Scottish poets whose works Wilton kept on hand for vanity rather than verse.

"I'd rather someone besides Lady Emily's father see to her welfare. He cannot be trusted."

Which phrase should be the earl's middle name.

"The one exception to that rule is Emily. If Wilton loves anybody or anything besides his own consequence, it's Emily."

Benton abandoned the poets for medical treatises, also on

display for vanity. "If you say so. When shall I expect her?"

"The middle of next month, assuming she's willing. Wilton can claim he's passing up the hunting this fall to prepare for Emily's arrival, and Emily and Lady Warne can finish up with the house parties."

The steward's expression went from not cheerful to resigned, and he gave up inventorying the shelves. "Where shall we put her?"

Somebody had consumed Trent's drink in its entirety. "She was a little girl the last time she was here. I'll poke around in the family wing and let you know."

"Fair enough."

Such enthusiasm. "You yourself said Wilton is testing his boundaries, and nothing will bring him to heel like the threat of consequences to Emily."

Or so Trenton dearly hoped.

Benton put his half-full glass on the sideboard. "I see two flaws in your reasoning: First, you love the girl and would never truly impose undeserved consequences on her. Wilton isn't stupid, and he'll sense you're bluffing should you threaten to send your sister off to a convent."

Fair enough. Around Emily, Trent would simply have to act more like his father, and hope to survive the impersonation. "The second flaw?"

"He can hurt you through her, as he was wont to hurt you through Lady Leah, and I suspect, through your wife, children and brother."

"That was a long time ago, Aaron." And as close as Trent's most recent nightmare. "Emily is too canny to be used that way, though I'll be mindful of your warning."

"See that you are. By then, harvest will be upon us, and serving as nursemaid to your baby sister is not on my list of things to look forward to."

Trent appropriated the remains of Aaron's drink, puzzled, because Aaron was seldom hard to read, and yet the steward hadn't been entirely forthcoming.

As Trent had not been forthcoming with Ellie, *or with himself* for that matter.

If this visit to Wilton Acres had proved anything, it was that Trent was ashamed of his patrimony—too ashamed to expect a second wife to cope with it, for eventually the Wilton heir would be expected to dwell at Wilton Acres.

Yes, he was concerned for Ellie's safety, but the notion of Wilton's snide comments, philandering, and cruelty in the same household with Ellie...not even for love, money *and* a title would Trent expect a woman to put up with Wilton.

On that daunting realization, Trent set Aaron's empty glass aside and took himself up to his quarters, not at all satisfied with the day's accomplishments. He made short work of his bath, then belted on his dressing gown and headed back to the library in search of a book.

As if a hard day must end on the worst possible note, Wilton was already in the library helping himself to a drink.

"Wilton." Trent offered the slightest sketch of a bow.

"Amherst." The earl didn't even incline his head. "What has you skulking about past your bedtime?" The earl was flushed and smug, and his heavy-handed attempts at insult were tiresome.

"I'll find a book and leave you to your solitude, sir."

"Thought to stage a sneak attack this time, did you?"

"I beg your pardon?" Trent perused the poetry simply for an excuse to turn his back on his father while he endured further aggravation from his father.

"The quarterly bills aren't due yet. You must be down here thinking to catch me out in some violation of the terms of my parole, but here I am. So, alas, your trip was for nothing."

Trent took down a copy William Blake's *The Marriage of Heaven and Hell.* "In truth, I care less and less what you get up to, my lord, as long as you leave me and mine alone and keep your fingers out the family coffers."

"What would I find in those coffers to trifle with?"

"Nancy Brookes' pension, for one thing. You've doubtless pilfered the principal, just as you stole from my siblings. I'll bid you good night, sir, and pleasant dreams."

Trent tucked the book under his arm and headed for the door, though sleep was likely a lost cause after this exchange.

"Heard you'd stopped by to pester old Henly," the earl said mildly. "A waste of time, Amherst, and beneath you. The peasantry will spread their thighs and be grateful for the attention shown them by their betters."

How could a man be a member of the Lords and not understand the difference between peasantry—of which England had none—and yeomanry?

"Imogenie was a decent woman until you turned her into less than a camp follower, Wilton." Trent knew, even as the words left his lips, that much of a retort was more than Wilton was owed.

"A slut." Wilton smiled slightly. "She's entertaining for the nonce and not without her endearing qualities. I might make her my next countess."

"Do as you please on that score." No time like the present to fire a few counter-volleys against the wall of Wilton's arrogance. "I'm sending Emily down here for part of the autumn. You will not entertain your doxy at Wilton Acres while my sister is under this roof."

"Emily?" Wilton set his drink down, his expression abruptly alert. "You're sending her to me?"

"Hardly." Trent made a show of perusing his book as he mentally improvised. "Lady Warne felt Emily wasn't ready for the Little Season and couldn't think of another place to stash the girl where she wouldn't further embarrass herself."

"Emily Lindsey couldn't embarrass herself if she spilled punch on her own bodice."

And yet, for the first time in Trent's memory, Wilton's bluster held a gratifying hint of uncertainty.

"Emily hardly knows how to dance. Her French is atrocious; she can't sit a horse even to show off her riding habit; she can barely thump out a tune on the pianoforte; can't draw to save herself; she has no address, no connections, and all because her dear papa couldn't be bothered to spare her some decent tutors or a finishing governess. It's no matter to me, except that if I'm to start looking for my next viscountess, I can't have Emily a laughing stock because of your parsimony."

Trent snapped the book shut and prayed his sister would forgive him his mendacity.

Wilton put his fists on his hips as he advanced on his son. "If my Emily can't give a good account of herself, it's because that worthless Leah was no kind of pattern card. You will not make Emily suffer for the education Leah begrudged her."

"Leah was, and is, her sister," Trent said mildly. "Not her governess, not her tutor, not her father. You, and you alone, are responsible for the rough go Emily's having in Society, so she can lick her wounds here and perhaps apply herself to dancing and French while there's still time, but heed me, Wilton: If you don't stop trying to find ways over, under, or through the fences set around you, Emily's come out will be indefinitely delayed."

Which Emily would positively delight to hear, though Wilton mustn't catch wind of the girl's sentiments.

"You wouldn't dare," Wilton sputtered. "Emily dotes on those brats of yours and they on her. You wouldn't use your own sister so unchivalrously."

"Darius and I nearly bankrupted ourselves trying to keep Leah from your filthy machinations," Trent said with a coldness that required no dissembling. "I will be damned if I'll let your pet spoil the waters for me should I decide to take another bride next year. If Emily blames you for her reduced circumstances, then so much the better for me. Good night, *my lord*."

He closed the door behind him, quietly, because even in so

small a gesture as a slammed door, he did not want to emulate his father.

He'd spouted pure, rotten tripe and sounded so like his father in his condescension, pique, and egotism, his belly rebelled. He wanted to hurl the volume of verse against the wall, wanted to run howling into the night for the lies he'd invented about his little sister and his feelings for her.

When he arrived to his room, he didn't open the book, but took out writing materials and settled at the escritoire by the window. To soothe his conscience, he composed an explanatory letter to Lady Warne, then a more apologetic explanation to Emily, finishing with assurances that Emily needn't show her face in Hampshire if she wasn't completely comfortable doing so.

Then his pen started on a letter to one Lady Rammel, Deerhaven, East Havers, Surrey. His pride in how Wilton Acres was thriving came through on the page, as did his frustration over Imogenie's situation and his distaste for dealing with his father. He told Ellie he couldn't ever see living at Wilton Acres, nor raising his children here, but Ford at least needed to learn the place and how it worked.

He told her he missed her, and worried for her and her continued comfort as her confinement approached, and bid her to ask Andy to give Zephyr a scratch under the chin for him.

The letter was silly, one a brother might write to a sister, or, more like, a husband to a wife of long years. He probably wouldn't send it, but signed it and sealed it anyway, because that put a sense of closure on his thoughts.

With a settled mind, he turned for his bed, there to toss for a few hours before he once again dreamed of Ellie Hampton and what he could not have with her.

* * *

"What are you doing here?" Peak pushed dark hair back off tired eyes and glared at Cato as he took up a perch on the end of Peak's cot.

"Missing you." Cato offered a smile by way of apology. "Again."

Peak yanked the covers up higher. "You are to be at the manor, protecting the children, Mr. Spencer."

How he loved to hear his name in those tones. Not his title, but "*Mister* Spencer" as only Peak could render it.

"Nonsense." Cato eased back, propping his shoulders against the wall. "I'm doing penance up there—separated from you but reminded each minute of the comforts I've left at home in Ireland. Amherst knows what he's doing."

"He's tempting you into leaving?"

Amherst wasn't applying temptation so much as guilt. "He knows what it means to carry a title and to shirk those responsibilities. Knows it isn't something lightly done."

"You won't give up on this, will you?"

Cato's gaze held Peak's in the wavering light of the lantern. "We can go back, though not as long as you insist on being stubborn."

"You're stubborn, too."

More stubborn than Peak, Cato hoped. Stubborn enough to best somebody who would never know the meaning of surrender. "But I'm stubborn because I'm right, Peak. You know you're wrong."

"I don't want to go back there." Peak rubbed strong, slender arms, though the night was mild.

"You miss home as much as I do. You simply don't want to face anybody, but it wouldn't be like that."

Peak thumped the pillow a few times with a callused fist. "If you need to go, I'll tag along to make sure you don't get up to foolishness, but as for the rest of it, you won't wear me down."

Cato rose, before the sadness in Peak's eyes inspired him to foolishness. "I will wear you down."

"You're not staying?" Peak resumed slamming the pillow as

soon as the words were out, but Cato heard the consternation and silently rejoiced.

"I've been reminded of my duties." Cato stretched to his full height. "I'm off to protect innocents from mischief, while you dream of me and home. But think on this, Peak: If you came home with me, on my terms, you'd seldom sleep alone again."

He sauntered out, knowing it was cruel, but his mind was made up. He and Peak had drifted along, content to mind Amherst's stables, and put off facing the inevitable. Amherst had been the one to suggest a solution, and Cato had had enough of hiding with a muck fork in one hand and a knife in the other—more than enough. If he took away Peak's pleasures, they'd come to an understanding eventually.

Provided Cato could deny himself those same pleasures as long as it took to overcome Peak's stubbornness.

* * *

In five years of marriage, Ellie hadn't received a single letter from Dane. She'd had notes. "I'll be down end of next week. Hope you're keeping well. Rammel." Or, "Blasted stinking rain won't let up. Might stop by for the weekend. Rammel." Or, one she'd particularly treasured at the time: "Need a short repairing lease. Will hope to see you end of this week. Missing the comforts of home. Rammel."

But Trenton Lindsey had sent her a letter, both sides of an uncrossed page, recounting his frustrations, his joys, and his plans, as well as his list of admonitions to her:

"Be sure to put your feet up at every opportunity and rest often."

"Keep your flowers near to hand, for they seem to cheer you."

"Don't skimp on the peppermint tea, it soothes the digestion."

Worst of all, the man had had the temerity to address the letter to "My Dearest Friend."

This letter wasn't romantic, boasted neither a line of verse nor a florid analogy in the whole thing. The prose wasn't the work of a callow swain or a lovesick boy. The words were from the pen of a lonely man and a caring man.

"What has put that expression on your face, Elegy?"

"Good morning, Minty." Minty, whom Ellie hadn't heard approaching in the corridor beyond her sitting room. "I've a letter from Trenton Lindsey."

Minty settled in to her customary rocker all too comfortably. "A letter from a gentleman. Not quite the done thing, even if you are a widow. What does it say, or shall I read it myself and assess his penmanship while I'm about it?"

Ellie passed the letter over.

"Lovely hand. Not at all like a man's."

"I think he likes to sketch." Ellie sipped her peppermint tea. "His father wouldn't let him have a drawing master, though. Said it was a female waste of time, sketching and the like."

"When Andy does it, it's a waste of time. This reminds me of the letters my papa would send my mama. Very…comfy."

"Comfy?"

"As if he were cuddled up beside her at the end of the day or maybe brushing out her hair."

"Araminthea!"

Minty handed back the letter, expression as serene as ever. "My parents were not fancy people. My mother's father was a miller; Papa was the local school teacher, a vicar's son. We barely scraped by, but they loved each other. I would fall asleep on my little truckle-bed, listening to them visit at the end of the day. I've never heard sweeter music than the two of them, chuckling over some student's prank when they thought I'd drifted off."

Ellie folded the letter carefully and set it aside. Were Minty not present, she might have held it to her nose before she re-read it. "Minty, you are a closet romantic."

"You're breeding. You think everything is romantic, but I

will say this: Lord Amherst has been paying attention."

While Ellie's tea grew cold in its cup. "What does that mean?"

"He knows you like the simple flowers—the daisies and jonquils, not the fancy roses and orchids and lilies."

"I like all flowers."

Minty glanced around the room at the daises displayed in profusion.

"They're in season," Ellie protested.

"He knows you'll leave your footmen in the house unless he reminds you otherwise," Minty went on, "and he knows you'll mention his greeting to Andy. He pays attention."

"He's a gentleman. He's merely being polite."

"Right." Minty stared for a moment at the daisies. "Now that you've told him he's persona non grata, he takes to writing you comfy letters. This is a requirement of good breeding between unattached adults I've yet to hear of."

Angry with the man and unwelcoming were not the same at all, particularly when a goodly dose of missing him figured into the emotional mix.

And worrying for him.

"He's not persona non grata. I wasn't dealing very well, and this way is—"

"Better?"

"Wiser," Ellie said, but to her own ears she didn't sound convinced. When Minty merely sipped her tea in silence, Ellie re-read the letter. Again.

* * *

"My lord, a pleasure." Trent offered his former father-in-law his hand while trying to hide his shock. In the several years since Trent had last seen him, Baron Trevisham had aged. He had the kind of blond-going-silver good looks that shouldn't have changed much between midlife and old age, particularly on a man who enjoyed his land and his horses and had no reputation for over-imbibing.

"Amherst! Jolly good to see you." Trevisham's greeting from the door of his saddle room seemed genuine. "Favor a spot of tea, or would you like something stronger? Don't tell m'wife, but there's fine summer ale to be had here at the Grange and not only for the gardeners and maids."

"Ale sounds good." The ride over had been hot and dusty, and what Trent had to discuss wasn't a tea-and-crumpets sort of topic. "How fares the baroness, and how fares your land?"

"Doing better." Trevisham haled a groom without clarifying whether his comment related to his land or his wife. "The past few winters were beastly, but this year's harvest should help us recover. And Wilton?"

"Thriving. I might assume my father passed along that much at least."

"You might." Trevisham slapped his crop against his boot, which prompted a half-grown tabby cat to pounce on the lash. "Except he and Tye get to chatting each other up, and they all know the Town set, while I know little save which mares I have in foal from year to year. How are those grandsons of mine?"

Trevisham scooped the cat up and gently scratched its chin.

"Your grandsons thrive as well," Trent said, relieved the man would think to ask. "They are plagued increasingly by their younger sister, who is now talking at a great rate and tearing around Crossbridge at a flat gallop."

"Is she now?" Trevisham's smile was mellow. "Paula was like that, quiet as a mouse, until she took it into her head to hold forth, and then, my goodness, the girl had a set of lungs. And stubborn! The baroness claims the children get that from me, but I've my doubts. Will you be off hunting with Wilton this year?"

"I beg your pardon?"

"I could have sworn he said he was going up to Melton come November." Trevisham's longing gaze fixed on a bay hunter across the barn aisle. "I should love to go as well, but at some point, a man must admit that field hunting for weeks on end is a young fellow's sport, though I'll not miss a local meet, of course."

He prosed on about his mounts for the coming hunt season and some younger hounds who were promising on the cubbing runs, and Trent recalled that Trevisham was one of the reasons he'd even considered marrying Paula. Her father was one of those unassuming minor titles who was content to mind his acres and had no need of Town life to entertain him. He was salt of the earth in the best English sense.

Or he seemed to be.

"Amherst?" Tidewell Benning came strutting down the barn aisle. His dress was fancy enough for a Mayfair dandy but snug at the seams, particularly around his middle. "Good heavens, it is you."

He stuck out a hand in the manner of the jovial man about town, and Trent saw in Tye's face more evidence of years passing. In the case of the son, rich food and long hours at smoky gaming tables were likely taking a toll. The toll of time on the baron was... different.

"I'm in the area more frequently," Trent said, "and thought to drop in. I've been remiss in this regard."

"Heard your papa had turned Wilton Acres over to you," Tye said. "Don't be giving Trevisham any ideas. I've a good deal more gadding about to do before I'm chained to the ledger books and the steward's lectures."

"Tidewell..." The baron's expression was vaguely exasperated.

"Not now, Papa." Tye's smile might have been charming on a boy. "I'm away to return some of Mama's books from the subscription library. I'll pick up the post while I'm about it. Amherst, a pleasure, and let me know if you're up for a friendly hand of cards sometime. Papa is no challenge whatsoever anymore."

He was off, calling out to the lads, leaving Trent to wonder why on earth Tidewell would take a curricle over the farm lanes, when a riding horse would make the same journey more easily.

Trevisham might have been wondering much the same thing as he set the cat down, and gave it a final pat on the head.

"Would that I could pass Tye the duties of the barony. Tom's better suited to it but won't poach on his brother's fixture."

"Couldn't Tidewell take on something? The hounds or the home farm?"

"I've tried," Trevisham said tiredly. "Here comes our ale." He lifted a tankard from the tray held by the groom. "To your health, Amherst."

"And yours."

"Come, lad. There's shade to be had." He led Trent to a bench and table outside the barn, waving off a pair of grooms cleaning and mending harness.

Trevisham turned to blow the foam off his ale. "How are you?"

"Sir?"

"You're widowed, and that business with Paula had to be hard on you."

"It will soon be two years." Trent hadn't anticipated this, or the keen concern in the baron's eyes. "The situation is improving, slowly."

"Not what I heard." Trevisham took a considering sip of his drink. "When I was up to Town retrieving my miscreant offspring, I asked around and nobody had seen hide nor hair of you, other than to say your sister had bagged herself an earl. Good show, that."

She had accomplished this feat without benefit of a fowling piece, too.

"Leah is happy. I've been more concerned with raising the children than socializing."

"As if you expect me to believe that. The womenfolk don't

let us within ten feet of our own offspring, not until the little dears are swearing and smoking and ready to be shipped off to university, which explains a few things, if you ask me. But without Paula on hand, maybe you can have it otherwise."

"Even when Paula was alive," Trent said, wondering if this was how an old man expressed old regrets, "I had the running of the nursery, sir. Paula was not often up to it."

"You're likely being diplomatic." The baron dipped his head, as if taking a blow rather than expressing assent. "One doesn't like to hear ill of one's offspring, but you'd think I'd be used to it by now."

"I'm sorry." Trent found a name for what he saw in the baron's eyes: grief, and not only for Paula.

"Not your fault," Trevisham said, as the cat hopped onto the table and sniffed at Trent's sleeve. "Maybe not even mine, but Paula's at peace now, and you're still young enough to enjoy life and the children she gave you."

"I can, but do you imply that Paula's delicacy comes as no surprise to you?"

The baron considered his mug of ale, already half-empty. "Her mother's the delicate sort. She's doing better in her later years. Not a particularly lusty woman, if you take my meaning, but she dotes on those boys of ours."

"Was Paula close to her mother?"

"Not especially. Only room for one lady of the house. And Paula was such a surprise, coming along after her brothers. She was my consolation, Paula was, but I think that made the boys jealous, particularly Tye."

He fell silent, lost in his reminiscing, while Trent noted that the baron did, indeed, brew a lovely summer ale.

"I have miniatures of Ford and Michael," Trent said, reaching into his pockets. "Lanie won't sit still long enough yet, and Michael's is very recent." He passed the little portraits to the baron.

"Oh, my. Young Fordham is very much your son, but I

think Michael is more of a Benning about the eyes and chin. Handsome lads, and they look full of the devil."

"They're ready for their own ponies, and they can be handfuls, particularly when they're tired or hungry. They're friends, though, already, and they've spent much of this summer at Bellefonte's seat in Kent."

The baron's brows knit. "Bellefonte? Your sister's earl— great huge fellow who knows his horses? I knew the old earl; pity he's gone."

"The new earl is managing well." Blissfully well, damn him. "If you've a few more minutes, I'd like to discuss a personal matter."

The baron passed the miniatures over, his gaze following them into Trent's pocket. "Your personal matter must be serious."

"Not serious, tedious. You may not have heard the rumors regarding my father's decision to rusticate this summer."

"I'm not much where rumors would circulate. I never did understand why the man would spend summers in London when he could be at Wilton. Town is rife with disease most years."

"I'm enjoying a summer in the country myself, though my father is at Wilton under duress."

"One gathered this," the baron said dryly. "He won't come out and say it, has to dance around it, as if he's making some great sacrifice. Then he and Tye get to rolling their eyes at each other. Makes me wonder why the land is in the hands of those who don't appreciate it, if Wilton is indicative of my betters and Tye of our future."

"Wilton has bungled the finances. He's left my sisters nigh penniless. He's at Wilton on parole liberty, sent down for bad behavior, more or less."

To have this little piece of the truth aired before another felt good, and Trevisham was likely to keep it to himself, too.

"No wonder he and Tye are getting on so famously. Oh,

Wilton makes a pretense of calling on me, but it's Tye with whom he spends his time."

"You know Imogenie Henly is keeping company with the earl?"

Trevisham's bushy brows rose. "Little Imogenie? I suppose she isn't so little anymore. Poor Henly."

"And poor Imogenie. Wilton's intentions aren't honorable."

"Not one to mince words, are you, Amherst?"

"Not about this. I want to warn you that Wilton has agreed to stay at Wilton Acres, and I do mean stay, for the next five years at least. He's not to go off shooting in the North, or hunting in the Midlands, or walking in the Lake District. He's grounded, so to speak."

"Godfrey." The tabby cat bopped the baron's chin with the top of its head. The baron obligingly pet the beast, which created a steady rumble greater than its half-grown size should have produced. "I gather the solicitors are answering to you then?"

"I can show you the power of attorney under Wilton's own seal, witnessed by no less than an earl and a marquess." Trent would *delight* in showing him that document, in fact.

Trevisham pushed his empty tankard to the middle of the table, giving the cat space to strut about. "You aren't merely making a duty call on your old papa-in-law. You're informing the magistrate of a few home truths."

A magistrate sharper than his genial demeanor might suggest, thank God.

"Henly reminded me Wilton might try to take steps to ensure Imogenie's indiscretions aren't thwarted by her parents. I don't mean for you to become embroiled in a family problem." "Such as turning Henly out by decree of the earl?" Trevisham snorted. "Maybe a hundred years ago a man might treat his tenants thus, but no longer. The Englishman knows his rights and will bray about them without ceasing to the king's man. I appreciate the warning, though, as one did wonder. But Amherst?"

Trent set his mug beside the baron's.

"Was my Paula happy with you?"

Trent looked at the two empty mugs and decided to temper his honesty. "Not at the end. You know that much, though I thought she was doing better. She was anxious, mostly about the children. I had the sense we'd reached an understanding about the children, then something upset her and she had a bad spell. For the most part, though, she was as happy as she could have been."

The baron picked up the cat and cradled it to his shoulder.

"She loved those children," Trent added. "On her worst day, I have to give her that—she loved them fiercely."

"Fine quality in a parent." The baron's gaze drifted to the manor house before he set the cat down and rose.

Trent fell in step with him and found himself being introduced to various horses and the occasional hound allowed pet status due to advancing age.

The baron knelt and scratched a floppy-eared brindle hound. "I should have been a hound, going hell-bent across the countryside, my pack along with me, then allowed a place at the hearth when my bones got to aching too much to keep up. It isn't so much to ask, a spot by the fire and some scraps of a night."

He rose easily, then extended a hand to Trent.

"One hasn't wanted to intrude," the baron said. "I'm glad you're faring well, and tell my grandchildren the old baron is glad to hear they're riding."

"I will. Give my regards to your baroness."

Trent was up on Arthur a few minutes later, but he kept the horse to a walk, because he had much to ponder in the miles between the Grange and Wilton Acres.

Trevisham was either a very convincing actor, or Trent's misfortunes could not be laid at the baron's feet.

What of Tidewell, though, and what of Thomas?

CHAPTER NINETEEN

The roads were soft the next day, but not exactly muddy, so Trent made good time. To see his brother and his children, to be home at Crossbridge, those were joyful thoughts. To see Ellie again provoked more complicated emotions, though joy was the predominant sentiment.

And yet, as Trent considered how difficult it had been to remain in the same room with his father, he also had to admit that shame had contaminated his dealings with Ellie. He was not ashamed that they'd been intimate without benefit of matrimony, but he dreaded the day Ellie would see for herself the disgrace whom Trent called Father.

Was giving up on a future with Ellie altogether and allowing Wilton to ruin yet one more aspect of Trent's life the better course?

An answer to that question assumed the entire business of being shot at, poisoned, having his stirrups tampered with—and God knew what else—could be solved while body and soul remained together. At Wilton, no such mischief had befallen him, but both in London and at Crossbridge he'd been a target.

"Welcome." Darius pulled him in for a hug, oblivious to the road dust, sweat, and milling grooms. "One worried for you, having to go into the belly of the whale."

"Benton keeps the place humming," Trent said, "and Wilton and I hardly exchanged two words. Let me have a bath, and I'll join you and Cato in the library for details."

"Fair enough."

Peak, who'd come to take Arthur in hand, tried to hide a scowl.

"Don't fret, Peak," Trent called softly. "We'll send Cato on his way before the moon is up."

The now sheepish groom led Arthur off.

"Does that one ever speak?" Darius asked.

"Apparently gives Cato a regular tongue lashing and does very well with the horses. Rides like a demon, too."

"Come along." Darius hooked his arm through Trent's. "I've your bath water heating and a nice bottle of hock on ice."

"You are my favorite brother."

Darius had him soaking within fifteen minutes, the glass of chilled wine on a stool beside the tub. Within the hour, the bottle was half-gone, and they were dressed for dinner, Cato joining them in the library.

"Good heavens." Darius whistled as he strolled a circle around Cato's person. "Yon stable master cleans up nicely."

Cato grinned and turned slowly that he might be admired in the attire of a country gentleman. "The occasion is special."

"Glad to see me?" Trent hazarded.

"I have plans later this evening," Cato informed them with a smug smile. "Though I am glad to see you safe and sound. I'm also doing you the courtesy of providing you notice in person of my intent to vacate my post."

Well, damn. "Vacate? When?"

"Before winter sets in. I'm not spending another Yuletide freezing my arse off in your stables, Amherst. I'm guessing your plans for a stud operation have come to nothing, and home beckons to me."

"Your situation at Glasclare is resolved?" Trent asked, sipping his wine.

Cato's genial expression slipped, revealing the determination for which the Irish were famed—or notorious. "It will be, one way or another."

"If you need a second…"

Darius's eyebrows rose at that, but he kept his questions to himself and let Trent catch them up on the situation at Wilton.

"What about here?" Trent asked as they sat down to dinner. He waved off the footmen, indicating they'd serve themselves.

Cato spoke first. "All quiet. Louise is cooking and preserving up a storm, the fruit harvests are good and the gardens producing. Your livestock is doing well, we've cleared the ditches and trimmed the hedges. We'll be ready for harvest, as near as I can tell."

"You've been poaching on the steward's jobs," Trent said. "My thanks." Though Cato likely owned twenty times Crossbridge's modest acreage, and the steward's job was well within his ability.

Cato lounged back in his chair, looking handsome, elegant and relaxed. "Peak can handle the stables. Keeping an eye on the land gets me out from under Peak's boots."

"What about you, Dare?" Trent tucked into his beefsteak, the hearty fare welcome after a day both long and grueling. "Did you enjoy rusticating here?"

"I have climbed trees; jumped logs on Skunk with little fellows up before me; gone swimming in the creek; played soldiers, pirates, castaways, and Indians; flown kites, read every story ever written with a monster or troll or witch in it; picnicked for breakfast, lunch, and dinner; and never slept better. I didn't know fatherhood was so exhausting, but my nephews assured me you regularly participated in each of those activities."

"They neglected to mention I do so over a period of weeks."

Darius paused, his wine glass halfway to his lips. "Lying little blighters. They want you to build them a tree house big enough to fit Uncle Nick in it. When I wasn't being run ragged by pirates, highwaymen, or grenadiers, I did read your journals, or much of them."

"And?"

"Somebody is absolutely determined to kill you."

* * *

Scent alone gave him away.

"Trenton?" Ellie struggled up from sleep, knowing he was in her bedroom before the shadows at the foot of her bed shifted to reveal his form. "Is something amiss?"

"Yes." He sat at her hip, making the mattress dip deeply. "Your pillows are all askew."

"Not askew. I have a system, so I can be comfortable as I careen around in my dreams. One for my knee, one for my back. What are you doing here?"

"Looking at the loveliest sight I've beheld in days." He leaned in and kissed her forehead. "I should not be here."

No, he should not, for many reasons. If he was to risk his neck paying a nocturnal call, though, Ellie wanted more from him than mere chaste kisses to her forehead.

Dane had kissed her forehead.

She struggled to sit up, rearranging her pillows behind her back. "You should not be here at this hour. Climbing trees in the dark isn't good for a man of dignified years, particularly when his safety has been jeopardized."

His safety, her heart. Not a fair bargain to either of them.

"Tell that to my brother. How are you?"

"Awake in the middle of the night." Ellie hefted her legs

to the side of the bed and rocked herself upright, then belted a dressing gown around… not her waist, for she hadn't one, but her middle. "How exactly did you ascend to my balcony?"

"Not your balcony. The one down the hall, off the family parlor. Dane used it when he didn't want to rouse the household."

Was this what the gossips meant by the wife being the last to know?

"How you know this about my late spouse, I will not inquire. You pushed yourself on this tour of Hampshire. Not well done of you, Trenton."

Despite her best intentions, she cupped his jaw, because even at the wrong time and in the wrong place, she was still so very, pathetically glad to see him. She dropped her hand and stepped back.

"You might as well get comfortable." Ellie poured herself a glass of water. "Unless you planned to leave another bouquet then be on your way."

"You're not inviting me into your bed." Trent pulled his shirt over his head and removed his boots and stockings.

He did all this while Ellie took a sip of water and stared out at the moonlit gardens like a dog scouring the bushes for game. She searched for balance, for solid footing between a foolish pleasure at Trent's company, and consternation, that he'd once again present himself uninvited, despite her having discouraged him from such behavior.

"I'm trying to exhibit commonsense," Ellie said, passing him the glass of water. "Unlike my neighbor, Lord Amherst."

"I concluded there was less chance of me being seen in your company this way." He stepped out of his breeches. "That you not be seen with me has become imperative."

"Why?" Ellie heard the sharp note in her voice, the tone of a woman approaching exasperation, while Trenton Lindsey approached a state of complete undress.

"My brother went through my journals while I was

traveling, Ellie." Trent banked pillows at the head and foot of the bed, ruining Ellie's system, then climbed onto the mattress. "It's worse than I thought."

"What is worse than you thought?" She climbed in beside him and didn't protest when he wrapped an arm around her shoulders. She'd kept her dressing gown on—some armor that would be—but Trent was here, naked, in her bed, and she doubted she'd be able to resist him did he make advances.

Much less recall why she should.

"Dare read my journals with a fresh eye." Trent tucked his chin over her crown, and Ellie had reason to know that Lord Amherst had not arrived in a state of sexual arousal.

Which deflated her ire at him *considerably*. Had he climbed the garden wall expecting her to *service* him, well, that would have given her some purchase in her attempts to move past their dalliance.

But he was here to warn her, apparently.

"Dare found a pattern of somebody trying to do me harm, and it has to be somebody who knows me and mine well."

"Tell me more," Ellie said, not finding anywhere for her leg to go except across his thighs, where it seemed to fit naturally, as the bump of her belly fit against his side.

"Dare saw a notation that I had planned to admonish him to extinguish his damned cigars when he came calling late at night. He used to do that, stop by between engagements, or come in late and stay with us after Paula died. I concluded he was saving himself coal, but in hindsight, he was also keeping an eye on me."

The drift of Trent's fingers over Ellie's brow was not at all erotic, and yet, it was intimate, cherishing even.

"What did your brother find?"

"On more than one occasion, I'd rouse myself in my study to stumble up to bed, only to find a lit cigar burning on my desk and the doors to the back garden open."

"You assumed it was your brother?"

"Who has never smoked a cigar in his life, though he keeps them on his person as a sort of accessory, like a snuff box. Somebody knew what brand he carried, but not that he'd never smoke them."

Ellie wrapped an arm around his waist, which felt leaner to her than it had earlier in the summer. "Is there more?"

"My town carriage axle came unbolted twice. Once when Darius borrowed it, but I'd forgotten the other time, when Leah and Emily used it for some dress shopping in foul weather. No more carriage mishaps after that, but other things happened."

"So you are justified in establishing distance between us. How I wish you'd been wrong. What else happened?"

"I wish I were mistaken, too, but I'm not. I developed a habit of taking dinner on a tray in the library, though I mostly ordered the food and drank myself into a pleasant haze as the evening progressed."

"You ate little and became peaked." So peaked she'd thought he'd been to war.

"The footmen would have learned of this habit, of course, because they kept my library and personal chambers tidy. The fellow on duty late at night developed a mysterious stomach ailment, one I could say I also had a mild case of from time to time. He was bleeding internally before he sought his brother's home in the country for a repairing lease."

"He was helping himself to your fine meals," Ellie guessed. "A nightly reward for the hours he was working, because nobody with any sense would let good food go to waste night after night."

"So we've guessed, but we'll follow up if we can track the man down."

His fingers traced a pattern on her arm, though how he could be calm, how he could discuss this without ranting and pacing and throwing things eluded her.

"Is there more?"

"I wouldn't have seen it, had Darius not turned his eye on my personal records. I noted a sick footman, Dare put together the rest. I noted the cost of the carriage repairs, Dare saw the consequences of the axle being tampered with."

"He has no idea who'd wish you ill like this—or does he?"

"He's asked if my wife hated me enough to put such things in train." Trent shifted on the bed so his lips trailed across Ellie's cheek, which meant the sense of his words took a moment to emerge from the bodily sigh Ellie felt at his kiss.

"How could he suggest such a thing?"

"His experiences with women haven't been the most sanguine, but the trouble persisted after Paula's death, so I doubt she was responsible."

"And you loved her."

Trent's hand closed gently over Ellie's breast. She had missed that very sensation, missed just that firm, cherishing, knowing pressure in that location.

"I cared for her as best I could." Trent turned and rose carefully over Ellie, then settled his mouth on hers. "I wasn't going to do this."

"I wasn't going to allow you to," Ellie whispered an instant before she kissed him back. "Not ever again."

That sense of not-ever-again imbued Ellie's hands with both reverence and boldness as she caressed Trent's lean back and muscular flanks.

For months, possibly longer, somebody had tried to see him dead. If not his wife, possibly her family, her brother—who knew?

Nothing but good luck had kept Trenton Lindsey alive this long, and Ellie could not bear the thought his luck might run out.

He pleasured her with slow, easy thrusts, and she welcomed him without hesitation, luxuriating in the scent and feel of him making love with her. The tempo eased, became languorous, comforting and arousing at once.

"More?"

"This is lovely."

"Am I too heavy?"

"You're just right."

"The baby?"

"That was him, or her."

Ellie buried her nose against Trent's neck and let him rock her to slow, deep satisfaction.

He could have been poisoned, died in a coaching mishap, been shot, fallen from his horse—so many times, he'd cheated death. Fear, rage, love, bewilderment, all manner of passions gave Ellie's desire a desperate edge.

Trent shifted her so she rode him, then let her relax on her side while he entered her slowly from behind. In that position, he let himself come, a quiet, subtle push-and-hold that Ellie experienced as a small earthquake of pleasure.

He held her for long moments, until Ellie wondered if he'd fallen asleep. When he slipped from her body, his hand trailed over her hip in a staying motion as he left the bed.

"You rest," he murmured. "Let me." He lifted her leg and tucked a cool, damp cloth against her sex, gently lowering her leg to hold it in place.

"You're spoiling me." The feeling was wonderful and much missed, but a nasty rodent of a thought scurried across her awareness: If he'd spoiled his wife thus, why in God's name hadn't the woman appreciated him more?

"The feeling is mutual, Elegy." Trent's hand swept down her back, over her hip, up across her shoulders, as if he painted her with his touch.

Ellie shifted to her back—a position that was becoming less and less comfortable—and tossed the cloth out onto her balcony. Somebody was trying to kill Trenton Lindsey, with a diabolical degree of tenacity and forethought.

Midnight raids on her balcony only presented that much more risk for him, that much more distraction.

"You can't continue to—this has to be the last time."

He turned to lie beside her, facing her, his eyes flat mirrors in the darkness. "I cannot bring the danger stalking me any closer to you than I already have. I understand that, and until I can determine—"

Fear for him made her very determined. She put her palm over his mouth, because "until" was dangerous territory, indeed.

"Understand this, Trenton Lindsey: You can't send along letters, or spying brothers, or ponies. You must end this dalliance in truth and focus on staying alive."

Trent took her hand in his and kissed her fingers. "What are you saying?"

She wanted him alive, of course.

"I'm saying farewell." Ellie's voice broke, so she made another attempt. "I'm saying farewell, Trenton, and meaning it. Part of me wants to wrap myself around you, keep you safe, stand over you with a loaded gun and destroy those who mean you harm, but another part of me…"

"Tell me, Ellie."

She dug past her fear, her terror that she'd be cast back into mourning all over, and for a man who'd never really been hers. Anger lurked in that sentiment, too, much of it at Dane, but some of it for Trenton Lindsey, too.

Somewhere on Trenton Lindsey's list of nevers, he'd decided to never again risk his heart.

He might have assured her that he was hers, and assured her time would sort out their other difficulties. He might have given her promises, as Dane had never done, that she mattered to him. He might have allowed her an understanding, such that mourning would be followed by marriage.

Instead he'd gone to Town, to Hampshire, to Kent… to Halifax. Then he paid Ellie a call, always with some plausible reason that preserved him from revealing uncomfortable feelings. She did not blame him for protecting a heart overburdened with sorrow, but she was entitled to protect her heart, too.

"The other part of me must look to the future, to raising my children and making a home for them." Though children needed a father and a mother. Trenton likely knew that better than most.

"We're not to be partners in raising horses?" Trent posed the question quietly from his side of the bed, and Ellie felt already the chill of a final, genuine good-bye.

Those other partings had hurt, but this one, *she* meant. She wasn't conducting a spontaneous experiment in self-flagellation. This was real.

"We can't. I can't."

"May I hold you?"

Damn him. Bless him, bless him, and damn him.

"I want to say yes." She was crying now, of course. "I want to cuddle up in the warmth and strength and preciousness of you, and drift off to my dreams of you, and wake up with the scent of you on me. I was so lost when you first came to call, Trent, and I owe you so much. I thank you for that, for much, but now, I must thank you to leave."

He gathered her in his arms anyway, pressed a kiss to her shoulder, then rose off the mattress and dressed in silence.

"Ellie, if you ever need anything," he said, folding his cravat into a pocket, "for you, Andy, anything. Promise me you'll let me help."

She nodded, unable to speak, lest she beg him to put this parting behind them.

"I'll be traveling off and on between now and cold weather." He pulled his shirt over his head. "Cato will know how to reach me, and I'll be in correspondence with Heathgate as well. When I get the mystery of my attempted murder solved, Heathgate will apprise you of the details."

She nodded again, tears coursing down her cheeks in miserable silence. How could he think? How could he form words? How could she tell him to leave?

How could she not when he was once again riding away, and possibly into greater danger.

"I never wanted to hurt you, Ellie." He kept his eyes down, buttoning his falls. "Not tonight, not ever."

"Nor I you."

He remained quiet, though she could tell he was suffering nonetheless. He was a gentleman, after all, and if nothing else, he'd hurt a little for her.

"Please stay safe, Trenton. You have to stay safe. I cannot bear another funeral. Not yours."

He offered her a tired, broken smile. "I'll do my best. You'll send for me if you need help?"

"I won't want to, but yes, if ever there's a problem or a danger I can't handle, I'll call on my neighbor."

"Neighbors," he reminded her. "Heathgate and Greymoor are your neighbors, even Mr. Grey is accounted a good shot, though I hardly know the man. Don't disappear again, Ellie. You deserve so much more from life than that."

"I won't." Ellie managed a weak, watery smile. "And thank you—for everything, Trent. I mean that."

She was in his arms again, though she'd intended to keep her distance. His embrace was generous, tender, and comforting, even as it broke her heart.

He let her cling for long, desperate moments, his arms around her secure and patient and so dear, and then he let her be the one to step back. He pressed a handkerchief into her hand, cupped her cheek, and disappeared into the darkness of her sitting room.

When she was sure he was gone from her house, Ellie let herself go, sobbing from low in her gut, from the place where the deepest emotions—terror, exultation, rage, grief—all came.

She cried herself to sleep on the side of the bed Trent had favored, her arms around the pillow that still bore his scent.

* * *

"Cook's lulling me into a false sense of security." For nothing else explained the quantity of food on Trent's dinner plate.

"Who?" Cato posed the question, aiming a look at Darius, who also appeared puzzled.

"Louise. Since I got back from Wilton last month, the fare has been far above reproach both upstairs and in the servants' hall. It's unnerving."

"Is that why you've hardly eaten anything for the past three weeks?" Darius asked, considering a bite of braised mutton. "You think she's trying to poison you?"

Trent picked up his fork. "Others have tried, but no. Louise is likely sending out word to the agencies to gain herself another position. She despairs of me ever learning my place but wants a good character."

"Wretched woman can cook," Darius said, chewing.

"And she didn't run off with the steward," Cato pointed out, following suit. "Are you sure you don't want me to join you on your trip to Wilton?"

"Dare will come, which means you have to stay here and mind the nursery."

"You don't want me to meet your baby sister, and me a belted earl."

"You haven't been invested yet," Dare said.

"Unbelted earl," Trent mused. "That explains why your trousers are so often around your ankles."

"Soon-to-be-belted earl," Cato corrected them. "I'll depart by November first and take Peak with me."

Trent grimaced at the timing. "That's not six weeks away."

"I can send you my cousin Kevin if you'd like a replacement. He's better looking than I am, but I swear he talks to horses and they listen."

"Better looking than you, Catullus? This I must see. Have we heard anything about Ellie Hampton's mares?"

Cato looked uncomfortable and took a prodigious interest

in his buttered carrots.

"Catullus, have you been comforting the widow?"

"Not in the sense you mean."

"In what sense?" The question came from Dare, whose expression boded ill for the man with the wrong answer.

"I sought her out to see if she'd consider selling her mares to the Earl of Glasclare, and she's considering the offer."

"When did you do this?" Trent asked.

"A few weeks ago, when you last departed for Wilton. The matter has required discussion at regular intervals since then."

"What manner of discussion?" Dare's expression was only slightly less pugnacious.

Cato took a leisurely sip of his wine. "Is Amherst eating? Is he sleeping well? Does he play with his children and read them their stories? Does he take a groom when he goes out and about on Arthur? That sort of discussion."

"She's spying on you," Dare said. "You said you were quits with her. What kind of quits is this? Where she must spy on you and know how you go on?"

Trent took a turn studying his carrots. "When you care for a lady, you don't question her motives. If Ellie wants to know if I'm finishing my pudding, then I expect Catullus to give her truthful answers."

"You do?" Catullus marveled. "You want me to tell her you've dropped a stone of weight, you pace the grounds all night, spy on her from the woods, and haven't climbed a tree in weeks?"

"How do you know I spy?"

"Peak and I are often up at all hours." Both brothers stared at him. "With the horses, that is."

Dare spoke up, exercising a brother's prerogative. "You love her."

Cato looked momentarily panicked, while Trent smiled, and not at his carrots. "With all my heart."

"Then why in blazes aren't you storming the castle walls,

304 | GRACE BURROWES

declaring your suit, and setting a date?" That from Cato, who looked genuinely bewildered.

"I am drawing breath only by virtue of a series of coincidences and good luck, Catullus. I cannot ask Ellie to yoke herself to another dead man. Even were I not the object of somebody's hatred, I'm used goods. I come with a lot of unfortunate history, and if Ellie's half as sharp as I think she is, she's heard enough gossip to know I'm a bad bargain over the long haul."

Then there was dear Papa, the Earl of Wilton, spreading ill will and anxiety wherever he bided. How could Trent bear to inflict such a papa-in-law on any woman ever again?

"I don't know," Darius mused. "I've been your brother my whole life. I think you're a fine bargain."

"Here, here." Cato saluted with his wine glass. "You find Delphey Soames and shake a confession out of him, then woo the lady once and for all. I will buy those mares, though, if Lady Rammel can tear her thoughts from you long enough to execute a contract."

Delphey Soames hadn't tampered with the town coach axle or poisoned Trent's dinner, but he might know who had.

"You'd best be concluding your negotiations with Lady Rammel soon, Catullus," Darius said. "You don't want those mares making a winter crossing."

"That can wait a few weeks. I'm more concerned about Amherst and his impending departure—or his impending demise."

"I'll be fine." Trent pushed to his feet. "A walk is in order, lest the rich fare deprive me of another night's sleep."

Darius frowned at Trent's retreating back, but made no move to stop him.

Cato switched his empty plate for Trent's mostly full one. "What? You might as well just say it."

"He's off to make sheep's eyes at the fair Elegy's balcony again. I'm tempted to talk to the lady, because this business of one of us trailing Amherst through the undergrowth of a night has become tedious."

"Don't say a word," Cato said around a mouthful of potatoes. "If you value your brother's dignity and his kind regard, you don't dare interfere. If you do, though, may I have your trifle?"

CHAPTER TWENTY

"Is that baby putting you out of sorts?" Minty posed the question calmly while she embroidered daisies on the border of a receiving blanket.

Ellie laid a hand on her growing tummy. "The baby seems fine."

"Then what troubles you? You look out the window like the second coming was imminent among your rose bushes."

"Just the opposite." Ellie took a sip of cool peppermint tea. "Trent Lindsey is off to Wilton again tomorrow." Mr. Spencer had let that slip out, just he'd let slip most of Trent's comings and goings without Ellie having to ask awkward questions.

Had Trenton put him up to that?

Minty poked her needle up through the fabric and wrapped the thread for a French knot. "Though you haven't had any use for Lord Amherst in weeks, you don't want him leaving his post next door."

"Something like that." Ellie regarded Minty's embroidery

and recalled that daisies were for innocence, but also for the sentiment *I will think on it.* "Somebody is trying to kill him, and I can't help but feel he's safer here where I can keep an eye on him."

Minty jabbed her needle through the fabric again. "And you so spry and such a dead shot. I still say you should never have let him get away."

"I sent him away, Minty." Ellie scooted about on her pillow in an effort to get comfortable. The baby had taken to shifting about too, the sensation no longer a delicate passing flutter.

"You sent him away because you're a chicken," Minty said pleasantly. "Scissors, please."

"I'm a chicken?"

"I can see feathers sprouting as we speak," Minty declared as she accepted the scissors. "Rammel was a rough go, Ellie, I know that. You didn't have even a few years of doting on each other before the clandestine *amours* and house parties and so forth started. He barely paused in his carousing long enough to marry you. Amherst wouldn't be like that."

"But Trenton loved his wife," Ellie wailed softly. "He wanted only a dalliance with a lonely widow."

"Are you daft?" Minty snipped a thread and let the blanket pool in her lap. "I read his letter to you, I've seen him looking at you, I've met you at breakfast on certain mornings when your smile could light up the heavens. He's crazy for you, and because a few specific words haven't been mentioned—and because you chose a dunderhead for your first husband, and because Amherst comes as goes as Dane did, though for far better reasons than Dane had—you think all Amherst's concern and consideration counts for nothing."

Minty enjoyed such conviction about her opinions.

"But Amherst is a widower. He was devoted to his wife."

"Who is *dead.* Did you love Dane?"

"Yes," Ellie answered, confident, because she'd pondered this very question at length.

"But you love Amherst, don't you?"

"It isn't the same thing."

"Don't you?"

Ellie's gardens were past their peak, but still rife with flowers. She'd seen Trent standing on the edge of the home wood in the moonlight, seen him keeping vigil there for hours.

"Of course I love him." Admitting the sorry state of her heart only jeopardized her frequently wobbly composure. "I love him until I'm cross-eyed with it, and I'm so worried for him I feel ill."

"You don't love him any less for also having loved Dane," Minty pointed out. "In some ways, you love him more, because you know life can take from us the people we care about, will we, nil we. So why aren't you grabbing him by his ears, Ellie Hampton, and letting him be a father to your next baby?"

Ellie rose, which now required that she push up with her arms if she wasn't to be completely graceless.

"He hasn't spoken of love and marriage, Minty. He has three children. He doesn't need more. He has a family depending on him—his father is a gold-plated embarrassment, though Amherst keeps finding reasons to spend time with him—and Amherst has troubles I can't help him solve."

The baby moved again, making Ellie's insides ache.

"Amherst sneaks about," she went on, "promising me nothing, when he might be telling me simply to be patient or careful while he promises me…*something*." Then, more softly. "He kept leaving, Minty. He'd make me feel like the most precious woman on earth, and then he'd leave. Dane left too, but he was consistently indifferent. I cannot spend my life waiting for Trenton Lindsey to become indifferent, too."

The baby kicked her in the ribs, a stout jab right under Ellie's heart. She sat, for her ranting to Minty had disclosed a truth Ellie hadn't seen herself: *She had buried her feminine self-confidence with Dane Hampton.* Because her own husband had been benignly indifferent to her company, she'd lost faith that any man could find her worthy of more than passing notice.

"Amherst is in expectation of a title," Minty said gently, "and that weighs on a man, but you love him."

Governesses were the most stubborn creatures on God's earth.

"I love him." Saying the words this time eased something inside Ellie, something profound and not...not *un*happy.

"You're thinking naughty thoughts. That's a good thing, Ellie Hampton. You never had naughty thoughts about Dane."

Governesses were honest and insightful, too. "I don't think he had them about me."

"Funny about that." Minty resumed sewing. "For all his carrying-on, and joking, and winking, I think you might be right, and you're a very attractive lady. Where did I put those scissors?"

* * *

"Trenton!"

Emily wasn't so grown-up she couldn't squeal like a child at the sight of her oldest brother. "And Dare!" She grabbed them each with an arm, forcing a three-way hug that had both brothers smiling sheepishly. "Oh, I wish Leah were here, but she's glued to Nicholas's side when he isn't flitting about the Home Counties. I haven't seen Wilton Acres in so long, but the place looks beautiful, doesn't it, Lady Warne?"

Lady Warne looked as if her last squeal of delight had occurred in the previous century. "A hot bath and some victuals would look lovelier still."

"Your rooms are ready." Trent eased away from Emily, which left Dare's arm around the girl's shoulders. "Supper will be a cold meal on the terrace, so we can hold it until you ladies are settled in."

"I have so much to tell you both," Emily said, whisking off her bonnet. "Trusty sends his love to Skunk and Arthur, though I think he's grown bored with life in a city mews." She chattered on as Trent led the way to the family wing and deposited the ladies in connecting guest rooms.

Trent paused in Emily's doorway, while Lady Warne disappeared with a pair of maids to start unpacking the several trunks brought down with the coach. "You got my letter?"

Emily's demeanor sobered. "I did. You shall be perfectly odious to me when Papa's about, or the servants, and I'm to carry on like a brat and make Papa think my Season is in jeopardy."

"It isn't."

"I don't particularly care." Emily ran her hand over the quilted coverlet on the bed, a pattern of interlocking circles with two doves embroidered in the middle.

"You don't care?" Trent crossed the room and drew her down to sit beside him on the bed. "What kind of talk is this?"

He'd read her bedtime stories a lifetime ago, because somebody should, and Leah had needed the occasional break.

"If you want the truth, this is tired talk," Emily said, leaning into him. "I haven't wanted to say anything to Lady Warne, because she enjoys having me for a pet, but this visiting all over creation, and living out of trunks, and constantly being fitted for clothes, and trying to keep straight everybody's name… I hate it."

Whatever else was true, these were not schoolgirl sentiments. "Hate is a strong word."

"Lady Warne's idea of how to go on is useless," Emily said, her pretty features solemn. "I do not care who sleeps with whom at which house party, or which lady is doctoring her tea or abusing her laudanum. I don't care which gentleman prefers young men, or what gouty old earl just bought his mistress a ruby necklace."

This was—had been—Trent's baby sister. While he was proud of Emily's common sense, Trent felt a pang of loss for the little girl who worried about nothing more than keeping her pinafore clean.

"You have been getting an education."

"Lady Warne wants me forewarned. I'm not to be a lamb to slaughter next year, but an informed purchaser of the wares on the market."

"That sounds cold." Though he could hear Lady Warne using exactly those terms.

Emily pressed her forehead to his shoulder. "It is cold. I feel old."

"If you're old, what does that make me?" Trent tucked an arm around her, thinking such slight shoulders shouldn't have to bear the weight of the world. "Would you rather wait a year before you make your bow?"

"And do what?" Emily straightened on a dramatic sigh. "More house parties? More spotty boys with straying hands and slobbery kisses? No, thank you. I'd rather find a decent man, get the whole business behind me, and be about starting a family."

"Don't settle for decent, Em. You want more than decent. You want fireworks over the royal barge, a hundred-piece orchestra, white doves, galloping horses, pounding hearts." *You want what I have with Ellie.* What he'd had with her and backed away from.

"I do?"

"You deserve them." Trent kissed her temple. "We all do."

"You didn't have that."

Even from her schoolroom, Emily had grasped the truth of her brother's marriage.

"I haven't had it yet, or not in a wife, but that's no reason for you to be so jaded when you haven't even danced your first waltz."

Emily grinned, looking once again like a very young lady. "I have so waltzed. Lady Warne hired me a silly French dancing master, and he made it a game."

"As far as Wilton is concerned, your dancing is atrocious, your French worse, you can't stay on a horse to save yourself, and you've no conversation."

Emily rose. "All of that was true last spring. I've Lady Warne to thank for bringing me along."

"And your own hard work." Trent rose as well. "You're sure you can manage this charade, Em?"

"Of course." She turned abruptly adult eyes on him. "If I've learned nothing else in the past months, Amherst, it's to dissemble on command."

"I believe you." Her intentionally brittle tone and the cool smile she served up with his title took him aback. "Unpack, and be warned, Wilton will likely join us for dinner."

"I shall be insufferable," Emily assured him. "But tell me, is that Mr. Benton joining us as well?"

"He typically does. Wilton won't address him at table, because he's only the nephew of a viscount."

Emily's mask slipped enough to reveal sadness at that observation. "Papa is a fool if he can't tell Mr. Benton is a gentleman and an asset to Wilton Acres."

"We can agree on that much." Trent took his leave, closing her door quietly behind him.

He headed for his own rooms, thinking only to garner some solitude before the performance that would be dinner. He dreaded dealing with his father, much less putting on a charade intended to throw the older man off his arrogant stride. When Trent arrived to his rooms, he didn't reach for a drink, though. He reached for his pen and paper.

He wouldn't send this letter. He'd use it as an exercise, to gather his thoughts, and calm himself before the dinner gong sounded. He began by explaining to Ellie what his situation with Emily entailed and why he was stooping to such a farce. He went on to say that impersonating his father even temporarily made him deeply uncomfortable—being judgmental, snappish, arrogant, and mean-spirited tore at his soul.

He told her he missed her with a physical ache in his chest, missed the feel of her body against his, missed the little flutters and shifts of the child growing safely inside her.

Were he to send the letter, he'd never have included such nonsense. Because he would not send it, Trent told Ellie how worried he was for his brother and sister, that protecting his siblings was so ingrained in him, he wasn't sure he could stand to walk Emily down the aisle at St. George's next spring, not even to marry the most worthy man in the realm.

His worst fear wasn't that he'd lose his life, but that he'd lose his ability to protect those he loved from Wilton and his infernal machinations.

The dinner bell interrupted his reflections, signaling thirty minutes until the meal was served. Trent sanded the pages he'd filled with sentimental tripe, though they'd likely end up in the fire. While the ink dried, he changed for dinner, not into formal attire—they were all but picnicking—but into a clean shirt, and waistcoat, a fresh cravat, and matching pin and cuff-links.

Darius sauntered in after a perfunctory knock. "You ready to let the play begin?"

"Hardly." Trent dragged a brush through his hair. "Who cuts your hair?"

"I do, which saves on coin. Nick trimmed it up for me. Val Windham did a time or two. I can do you up, if you like."

"Ellie likes it long."

"Ellie, whom you will never see again. That Ellie?" Dare lounged in the chair behind the escritoire, looking elegant, careless, and bent on tormenting his only brother.

"The very one. We haven't time to cut it today, but soon."

"Right." Dare fiddled with the penknife. "Soon. You aren't going down to dinner without a jacket, are you?"

"Of course not." Trent kept talking as he went into his dressing room. "Though I feel like I ought to wear a hair shirt. I dread having to speak sharply to Emily."

"Hmm?" Dare glanced up as Trent emerged carrying two different coats. "I'll draw your fire, don't worry. Wear the green. It goes with your eyes."

"But I've used a silver cravat pin."

"So switch it to gold." Cautiously, as if trying not to get sand on his cuffs, Darius moved the finished letter off to the side while Trent changed the silver pin securing his cravat for gold.

"Get this for me, will you?" Trent stuck out his wrist, and Darius obligingly changed silver cuff-links for gold.

"You'll do," Darius pronounced. "I'd best change out of my boots if we're putting on our country manners."

"Wilton will comment on our shabby attire, no matter what we wear." Trent took a final look at himself in the mirror. "I'll see you on the back terrace."

"Let the play begin," Darius said, saluting smartly.

Trent left for the library, there to fortify himself with a drink, while Darius remained by the escritoire, looking handsome, dear, and ready for mischief.

* * *

"This is terrible." Ellie folded Trenton's letter and stared unseeing at the rain pattering down outside the parlor window.

"What is?" Minty worked on a gown for the baby, again embroidering daisies along the hem.

"I'm almost certain Amherst understood he wasn't to be writing."

"You were peevish when he didn't write. Now you're peevish when he does. That child is making you fretful."

"This child is making me fat."

"You're six months along. You aren't fat. In fact, your face looks thinner to me, as do your hands."

"My ankles don't," Ellie muttered. "What's this?" She peered at the back of the letter where a sentence had been added in a less elegant hand. She mumbled the words aloud as she read. "Lady R: Found this epistle on my brother's desk, but I doubt he intended you to see it. Hon. D.L."

"Who is Hon. D.L.?"

"Darius, his lordship's brother. Darius must have gone behind Trent's back to send this."

"Typical brother." Minty bit off a thread. "Is it drivel?"

Trenton Lindsey wouldn't be capable of drivel if he lived to be ninety. "It's comfy, in parts." In other parts, the letter was from a man whose heart was breaking in three directions at once.

"Not that comfy business again. I have it on the best authority Amherst is a frivolous earl-in-waiting, one who merely dallies with every widow who waddles along."

"I'm not waddling. Yet."

"Pardon my oversight."

"Minty, he's having to act toward his sister as if he's his rotten father, and it's tearing him up."

Minty grimaced, pausing in her sewing. "What else does he say?"

"He says that to carry off his charade with Emily, he and she must both act as if each resents the other for merely drawing breath. All he has to do is recall his list of nevers and modify them slightly to suit the situation."

"What is his list of nevers?"

"Never insult your child before company," Ellie said. "Never ridicule your child for the entertainment of others. Never joke about putting your child at risk of serious bodily harm. That sort of thing. Things no decent person should ever—"

"What?"

The child moved, not a kick, but a shift, as if settling in. "Oh… Minty…"

"Ellie? Are you well?"

"I know, Minty." Ellie rose, and all the peppermint tea in the world could not have soothed the upset inside her. "I know who it is."

"What do you know? And sit down." Minty led her to a chair. "Make sense, Elegy, and make it now."

"Trenton's list of nevers. He broke bones trying to please his father, suffered beatings, contracted lung fever that took weeks to recover from. I know where all this vile, nasty, deadly mischief is coming from." Ellie's hand curved into a fist. "God in heaven, Wilton isn't merely old-fashioned or hard-hearted. He's evil."

"Sit down, Ellie, and explain yourself?"

"Wilton is the one," Ellie said, half to herself. "He wants his own son dead. He resents Trent for drawing breath and has since Trent was born. He's put him on dangerous mounts, left him in the cold until lung fever was inevitable, beaten him within an inch of his life, subjected him to trials and torments, tried to turn his own brother against him."

The litany was enough to make Ellie positively ill.

"Ellie? What are you going on about?" For once, Minty didn't sound calm, competent, and in charge.

"The attempts on Trent's life! His father is behind them, I'm sure of it. We need to go to Hampshire, Minty. Right now."

"We aren't going anywhere in this downpour, my girl," Minty said sternly. "Think of the baby."

Ellie shot out of her chair. "I will not sit here stitching receiving blankets while Trent falls neatly into any trap Wilton sets for him."

"You can't be sure of any of this. The weather is beastly foul and getting colder by the hour."

"That wouldn't matter to Trent if I were in danger," Ellie bellowed back. "Send a groom for Mr. Spencer."

"This will be considered a wild start from a breeding, grieving woman."

"Heathgate won't take it as such," Ellie retorted. "Or he'd better not."

Within an hour, Mr. Spencer had brought the magistrate, as well as Benjamin Hazlit, who'd put off his return to Town until the next morning in deference to the state of the roads.

"Lady Rammel." Heathgate bowed, looking not the least

put out to have been summoned from his cozy house into the damp, chilly night. "Mr. Spencer said it was urgent."

"I know who's trying to kill Lord Amherst," Ellie said, not waiting even for the tea to be served. "His own father."

Heathgate glanced at Mr. Hazlit, who'd come calling with the marquess nearly a month past. That Heathgate didn't tut-tut and there-there suggested the marquess's reputation for shrewdness was well earned.

"Plausible," Hazlit pronounced. "On what do you base this theory?"

"Wilton has been trying to kill Lord Amherst since he was a boy," Ellie said. "When it was time to teach Trenton to ride, Wilton put him on a wild pony, took away his stirrups, then sat back until Trent had broken both his collar-bone and his wrist and Lady Wilton got wind of it. Trent had a severe bout of lung fever when he was five as a result of his father refusing him entry into the house until he could skate across a frozen pond without falling."

She had to pause for breath and waved away Heathgate's handkerchief. Over the door, Mr. Spencer was looking damp and concerned.

"Wilton taught Trenton to fence without tipping the foils—when Trenton was barely eleven. Trenton has scars." Her hand waved up and down her right side, and then her voice faded, as she swallowed back a shiver.

"When he reached his majority," Ellie went on, "Darius was likely watching out for him, but when Trenton married and had his own household, Wilton could start up again. Trenton's coach was tampered with twice, his meals poisoned, and you know about the laudanum in his drinks, the shooting. Cigars were left burning…"

"I believe you." Heathgate's voice was all the more arresting for its quiet.

"I wouldn't go to the magistrate with it," Hazlit said slowly, "but intuitively, the facts hang together. The length of the campaign, the cleverness of it, the patience, they all point to a sick mind with a sick motive."

"Amherst is Wilton's replacement," Ellie said. "Trenton has already taken over the finances of the earldom, and he's making Wilton repay what he stole from the trusts for Darius and Leah. With Trent gone, Wilton can petition for guardianship of Ford and Michael and have his earldom back on a platter, as well as control of the funds Trenton has set aside for the children."

"It makes sense," Hazlit said. "Twisted sense, but sense."

"Then we're off to Hampshire." Heathgate said. "Mr. Spencer, does Crossbridge have pigeons to fly from here to Wilton Acres?"

"Lord Amherst took a few of ours to Wilton, but we have none of Wilton's to fly the other direction," Mr. Spencer said. "For what it's worth, I think Lady Rammel's theory is sound, but somebody had better stay here to look after Amherst's children."

"He's right," Hazlit said. "At least one attempt was made on Amherst's life here in Surrey. If that was Wilton's doing, then his factor is still at large, and with Amherst absent, those children are vulnerable."

Heathgate picked up the receiving blanket Ellie had been stitching and fingered the incomplete border of daisies.

"Spencer, tell the children they're going on an adventure and will be spending some time at my house. James and Pen have lately been socializing with Grey's two boys, who are already acquainted with Amherst's offspring. We shall have an assembly of pirates in my nursery."

"When can we leave," Ellie asked, though thank goodness the marquess had a plan for keeping the children safe.

"My traveling coach has ample lanterns, and the rain, while steady, isn't particularly hard," Heathgate replied. "Or would you prefer to ride, Benjamin?"

"We're off to Hampshire?" Hazlit sounded resigned.

"Not without me." Ellie advanced on Heathgate. "I should have seen this earlier. You can't expect me to sit here on my backside and wait for you fellows to drag Trenton home to me, assuming you reach him before Wilton can put a period to his existence, much less that of his brother, who has walked into this trap with him, both of them completely unsuspecting because you men... Oh, please, you have to let me come... You just...*please*."

Heathgate wrapped his arms around her and drew her against his solid frame.

Ellie accepted the embrace gratefully. He wasn't the right man, but he was a good man, and he could get her safely to Trenton's side.

"I'll drive the damned coach myself," Ellie threatened. "I'll walk, I'll crawl, I'll waddle—"

"How soon can you be packed?"

"F-five minutes. We have to get there in time. We have to."

"Wilton thinks he has all the time in the world," Heathgate reminded her. "He's getting a sick pleasure out of toying with Amherst, thinking he can time this murder whenever he pleases. Isn't Lady Warne underfoot and the youngest daughter, what's her name?"

Ellie stepped back, equally resenting and appreciating Heathgate's ability to think so calmly. "Lady Emily. Wilton dotes on her."

"Wilton won't commit murder most foul with his darling daughter on hand," Heathgate assured her.

"We hope," Hazlit added. "I have to agree with Lady Rammel, though. We're not dealing with a rational criminal."

"We're not sure our theory is correct," Heathgate said, sending Hazlit a repressive version of the You-Dolt-There's-a-Breeding-Woman-Present glower. "We'll set out when the Lindsey children are safely ensconced in my nursery. If I might borrow pen and paper, Lady Rammel, I'll send word to my brother of my impending absence, and he'll keep an eye on matters while I'm on the king's business."

A groom was dispatched with the note to Lord Greymoor, Mr. Spencer took off to alert the nursery maids, and Ellie bustled away to toss some clothes into a satchel.

"Shall I come with you?" Minty asked, as they stood under the porte-cochère waiting for Heathgate's coach twenty minutes later.

"I want you here with Andy," Ellie said. "She'll worry for me, disappearing like this. I left her a note, but no details."

"Shall I tell her the truth?"

"Tell her I was very worried for Lord Amherst's safety and had to see for myself that he was well."

"In the middle of a pouring-down rain at well past dark and you expecting the Rammel heir."

"It's misting. I'm carrying a girl, and I can see a few stars."

"In your eyes."

Ellie turned on her. "None of that *matters*. What matters is that Trent isn't safe, and he doesn't know where the danger comes from."

"You don't know he isn't safe. You are going off half-cocked, my girl, and I say—"

"Not *now*, Minty," Ellie hissed.

"I say,"—Minty drew her into a hug—"it's about damned time."

CHAPTER TWENTY-ONE

Trent rose to a disgustingly pretty day. The previous evening had been wet, a soft, pattering rain that refreshed rather than muddied. His decision would have been the same if the heavens had opened up and the roads were quagmires.

He'd had as much sniping and posturing as he could take. He dreaded each meal, and the hurt in Emily's eyes was becoming all too real. He would make his good-byes at breakfast and leave for Crossbridge that day.

And somehow—some damned, benighted how—he would find a way to work things out with Elegy Hampton. A gentleman left the field when he was excused, and Ellie had very clearly excused him.

Then cried her heart out.

The memory of her sobbing as he'd lingered in her darkened corridor weeks before tore at him the way Paula's death had, the way this miserable farce with Emily did. Thank heavens, the latter showed some signs of affecting Wilton.

Trent's father regarded him with a flat, reptilian stare that at least bore a hint of trepidation.

Previously, Wilton's sole sentiment toward his heir had been disgust.

Not wanting to wait for a cup of hot tea, Trent pulled on breeches, shirt, and waistcoat and made his way to the kitchen.

"Master Trent, good day." Nancy puttered at the sink, though not a single lamp was lit.

"How can you tell? It's dark as the pit here."

"I can tell it's you by your scent and the way you move."

Trent lit a taper from the hearth coals, only to find Nancy was already making tea—in pitch darkness. He used the taper to light a branch of candles, and still the cavernous kitchen was mostly shadows. "How well do you see?"

"I can tell you've lit us some candles, or perhaps a lamp." Nancy took a slow breath through her nose. "But no, it's candles. I smell the wax.

"That's the extent of your vision?" Something niggled at the back of his mind, something important.

"Most days I can still see light if it's bright enough, but I spent too many nights doing the mending in poor light or making do with tallow."

"Have you seen a physician?" Though nobody should be this incapacitated in the Wilton household.

"Couldn't see him if I did," Nancy said gently. "Tea?"

"Please. Have some yourself, too."

"Already had my first cup." Nancy poured him a mug as easily as if she had the eyes of a woman half her age. "I do miss my Bible, but Mr. Benton has the vicar come visit and he reads to me on Wednesdays."

"Who reads you Louise's letters? Who writes your letters to her?"

"Louise?" Nancy snorted. "Louise Compton? That besom you took pity on a few years back? Why would I correspond with the likes of her? The entire household breathed a sigh of relief when Wilton tossed her over the transom. Mostly, you feel sorry for a body when the earl takes 'em into dislike, but not that one. She lorded it over all of us when he summoned her to his chambers, and her reckoning didn't come soon enough."

Trent took the hot tea from her hand, dread trickling down his spine.

"Then you don't correspond with Louise."

"I don't correspond with anybody. Wilton was never one for seeing to it his staff could read and write, and he begrudges paper to the few who do. I can make out most verses, because I know my Bible, but what would I write in a letter?"

"That you're retiring to lighter duty at Crossbridge?" Trent suggested.

Nancy poured herself a cup, the scent of gunpowder teasing at Trent's sense.

"Wilton's a canny old thing," Nancy said. "I'm like those mill horses. You show me around, show me my job, then take my sight away, and all I'm good for is working in my own mill. I know where things are here. I can put names to voices and get myself through the day right enough."

"You will always have a home here," Trent said. "But we'll have to find somebody to read you the news, Nancy, not only your Bible."

"Don't go to any trouble. Take your tea and be off with you. Cook will soon be stirring about. We've people to cook for, for a change."

"I'm heading back to Surrey right after breakfast, but keep that to yourself."

She passed him a handful of cinnamon biscuits. "To tide you over until breakfast."

He stepped in and hugged her, no doubt taking her by surprise. She was old, and frail, and *blind*, for pity's sake, but her blindness had given him the clue he needed to unravel the mystery of his impending death.

Trent made his way by the servants' stairs up to Darius's room, pushing the door open without knocking.

"Dare?"

"Sleep."

"I've brought biscuits," Trent sing-songed. "And a nice big cup of hot tea."

"Biscuits?" Darius lifted his head from his pillows, his dark hair sticking out in all directions in the pre-dawn gloom.

Trent perched at the foot of the bed and held out a biscuit to his brother.

"What is this about?" Darius sat up, apparently naked beneath his sheets, and scrubbed his fingers through his hair, then pressed the heels of his hands against his eyes. He munched a proffered biscuit, then took the mug Trent passed him.

"I'm heading back to Crossbridge today. Right after breakfast."

"This is a bit sudden." Darius accepted another biscuit and passed the tea back. "What's the urgency?"

"I've a murdering cook to see to."

Darius cracked his jaw. "More biscuits, please. Don't think I heard you aright."

"Louise." Trent kept his voice down. "She was corresponding with Wilton the entire time she was at Crossbridge."

"Do you know this?"

"I know Nancy hasn't seen well enough to write, much less read, a letter for some time and has no love for Louise."

"That doesn't prove anything. Louise might have been writing her girlish fantasies to Wilton. He trysted with her once upon a time. That's common knowledge."

"He did; then he turned her into his spy. You and I both populated our households with his cast-offs."

"I employ the halt and indigent. I doubt they're spying for him."

"While my town house got the maids, footmen, a butler, my gardener." Trent leaned back against the bedpost. "Louise at Crossbridge and practically my entire staff in Town was composed of people he described as solid Hampshire lads and lasses eager to see a little Town life but not quite appropriate for an earl's household."

Darius glowered at his tea cup. "After he'd fucked all the pretty ones silly. This isn't good, Trent. Who at Crossbridge came from Wilton?"

The question of the hour. "Louise now. Maybe the occasional footman, but they've been with me since I came into the place."

"Can they shoot?"

"I'm sure they can, but I wouldn't put it past Louise, or past Louise to hire somebody for the job. You coming with me? I'd rather you stayed here and kept an eye on Em and Lady Warne."

"I don't like leaving you to deal with Louise and God knows who else alone. Your children are there."

"They've been safe so far, and Cato's sharp. He'll keep them from harm."

"You pray." Darius took another swallow of tea. "This is good."

"Gunpowder." Trent went to Darius's wardrobe, which held a small selection of very well-made attire. "I can send Lady Warne back to Town, but that will take a day or two. When did you turn into such a dandy?"

"The ladies put stock in one's finery. That's a nice ensemble."

"Get your handsome arse into it, and I'll meet you in the breakfast parlor."

Trent left Darius to dress, returned to his room, and packed up the few belongings he'd brought down from Crossbridge. Fear for his children figured prominently in his thoughts, but so did fear for Ellie, who was living next door to a woman who'd kill for coin—or for whatever version of love Wilton tossed at his paramours of late.

And Trent felt a towering anger that his own father would wreak havoc on the people he was supposed to love and protect. Wilton's wife, his children—and God help them, likely even his grandchildren when the time came—were merely so many domestic animals to the earl, their continued existence subject to his whim.

The Earl of Wilton was not sane.

Trent knew this, and the wiser parts of him—the boy who had drowned the puppies, the boy who'd bested the crazy ponies, the man who'd realized his wife wasn't in sound emotional health—they screamed for him to use extreme caution, to avoid Wilton at all costs until further evidence could be gathered.

To hell with breakfast. Darius could make his good-byes for him. Trent shouldered his traveling bag and left not a trace of his habitation in the room.

Exactly how he wanted it.

As quietly as he could, Trent made his way down the corridor of the family wing, thinking to use a servants' stair to slip out unnoticed. He'd put his hand on the latch to the door at the top of the stairs, when the door flew open and an enraged Imogenie Henly emerged.

"Move aside, your lordship." She barged past him, heading straight for Wilton's suite. "That lying, thieving, no-good dog had better have some answers."

"Imogenie," Trent hissed, setting his bag down. "No. Stop now." He grabbed her arm, and she tried to shake out of his grasp. "What do you think you're doing?"

"He gave me paste!" she cried, wriggling furiously. "He gave me jewels, but they're all paste. Not even *good* paste, according to the jeweler in Anvil."

Trent tried for reason, having neither the time nor the patience for melodrama.

"Wilton's not even awake. Maybe there's an explanation. You'll accomplish nothing if you go barging in there now and confront him."

"Oh, really, Amherst," the earl drawled from his doorway. "She'll entertain me, which is the whole point. Good morning, my dear. It seems you've been naughty again."

"I've been naughty?!" She twisted out of Trent's hold. "What about you? You said that once he was taken care of,"— she jerked her thumb at Trent—"I'd be your countess. You promised, but you don't give your countess paste! I'm dumb, Wilton, but I'm not a complete fool."

"So I gave you paste." Wilton looked supremely bored. "Does your farm boast a safe, that you could securely store real gems? I think not. This grows tedious, and you will watch your mouth, my girl."

Something had flickered in Wilton's eyes, though, something Trent felt in low, miserable places.

"Watch my mouth!" Imogenie screeched. "Tye Benning was drunk at the Pig and Pen by noon yesterday, claiming his friend the earl had asked him to have a fast horse at the Wilton postern gate at first light. And he laughed at me. *Laughed* at me! You asked for one horse, Wilton—only one! You weren't thinking to take me with you, were you?"

"Imogenie, what did you expect?" Trent asked. "That he'd keep his word to you after all the people he's betrayed and disappointed?"

Imogenie rounded on Trent. "And you! You're supposed to be dead!"

"Papa?" Emily appeared in the doorway across the hall, looking sleepy and confused in her robe and slippers. "What is all this commotion?"

"Nothing you need bother your head about, Emily." The earl's tone was clipped. "Miss Henly is overwrought and in need of a sound beating."

"Overwrought!" Imogenie lunged for the earl the same

instant Trent dove for her. He bent his strength to subduing her without hurting her, but behind him, a scuffle had ensued.

"Papa!" Emily's voice, raised in alarm.

Trent clamped a hand over Imogenie's mouth, hauled her up against his chest, and turned to see that Wilton had Emily in a similar grip, Wilton's shaving razor pressed against Emily's throat.

"Oh, dear Jesus." Imogenie went still and silent. Trent gently pushed her toward the servants' stair, then took a step toward his father.

"Wilton, let Emily go."

"You let me go," Wilton said, "then I'll let Emily go. I've had enough of your terms, Amherst, enough of you. Now the terms are mine."

"I comprehend this, and I won't argue. You can do what you want with me, but let Emily go. You love her. She's the only good, right and dear thing in your life."

"She is." Wilton drew the blade lightly across Emily's throat. "She's also my only bargaining chip, now that your crazy wife is no longer available for that purpose."

Somebody drew in a sharp breath behind Trent. Imogenie, maybe, too stupid to protect herself when she could.

"My wife wasn't crazy, but she was miserable, and you'll be miserable, too, if you hurt Emily. You can still leave and take me with you, or kill me and leave, but you don't have to hurt your own daughter to get what you want."

Wilton casually nicked Emily's throat. "Do you honestly think I'll believe a word you say? You hate me, you always have, exactly as your mother always did. She took you from me and turned you against me. Emily will turn, too, soon enough. Maybe Tye has the right idea—get 'em while they're too young to think for themselves."

A bright red line welled on Emily's neck, while she closed her eyes and sagged back against her father.

"Please, Papa. Don't hurt me. I love you."

Wilton rolled his eyes, but then his expression shifted as heavy footsteps came down the hall. In the split second his father's attention wavered, Trent launched himself across the hallway and wrested Emily from Wilton's grasp. At the same moment, he pushed his father's hand straight up, smashing it hard enough against the door frame that the razor fell to the carpet.

"Wilton." Heathgate's voice sounded with cold calculation.

Trent had never been so surprised—or pleased—to see his growling neighbor.

"Desist, or I'll happily—*delightedly*—shoot you where you stand for resisting arrest."

Trent stepped back, beyond the range of his father's fists. Like a benediction, he caught a whiff of roses, as if Elegy Hampton were with him in spirit.

"The local magistrate is on his way," Heathgate continued. "One Tidewell Benning will be arrested as accessory after the fact to attempted murder, assault, and as many other charges as I can encourage these witnesses to think of before we put pen to paper."

Wilton drew himself up. "I do not know you, sir. You are under my roof, and you will do me the courtesy of introducing yourself."

Though Wilton had, in fact, crossed paths with the marquess previously, Trent rose to the challenge of observing the civilities in a situation beyond bizarre, and all the while, Ellie's sweet, soft scent gradually steadied him.

"Wilton, may I make known to you Gareth Alexander, Marquess of Heathgate, whom I have never been happier to see. I will cheerfully swear out charges against you, Wilton, for the attempted murder of my sister Emily. Imogenie will likely sue you for breach of promise. I can toss in assault and many, many counts of attempted murder of your own son."

Wilton examined his fingernails. "Why would I bother to kill you?"

"Sheer malevolence, I suspect. But you didn't quite see the matter done, did you? You didn't get your hands on all that lovely money Paula had me set aside for the children; you didn't get your hands on our beautiful children; and you didn't get your power of attorney back, either."

"Paula—another example of your inability to do a single thing right," Wilton scoffed. "After what her brother put her through, you were never likely to bed her, much less get three brats on her."

"Be silent, you!" Ellie Hampton advanced from behind Trent, who was too stunned to grab her.

"Shut your filthy, deranged, criminal mouth, you vile old lecher. Whatever else was true, Trenton Lindsey loved his wife, and she loved him to the best of her ability. You will not defile her memory with your evil slander."

Wilton arched a silver eyebrow at Ellie's girth. "Who have we here? Been a busy widower, haven't you, Amherst?"

"I have to agree with the lady." Trent slipped an arm around Ellie's waist, tugging her back against his side. "Shut up, Wilton. If you value your life, not another word."

He sounded every bit as arrogant as his father, every bit as autocratic, and for the first time in his life, *he cared not one whit about the resemblance.*

Wilton scanned the small crowd in the hallway with exquisite disdain. "Look at the lot of you, consumed with righteousness and all over a stupid family drama. You're idiots, and you," he sneered at Trent, "you won't press a single charge, just as Leah's hulking earl didn't, because if I'm convicted of a felony, the personal holdings will be stripped. Your son will inherit a beggared earldom because of what you did to your father. Think on that, why don't you?"

"You think I care about the *title?*" Trent felt only weary when indignation should have lent him rage. "To hell with the title and the lands and the wealth. We'll manage, provided the Crown finally puts you down like the sick beast you are."

The earl flinched, minutely, but Trent had the satisfaction of knowing he'd surprised his father.

"You don't mean that," Wilton hissed. "You wouldn't do that to your sister. You wouldn't visit that scandal on your children."

"If you ask me,"—Darius's voice was laden with scorn—"the fact that you continue to draw breath is the scandal. Emily, what say you?"

She leaned heavily on Aaron Benton, his handkerchief stained crimson at her throat. "That man is not my father. I don't know who he is, and I don't care what becomes of him, provided no one else comes to harm at his hands."

Benton turned her into his embrace, shielding her from the rage on Wilton's face.

"You don't mean it," Wilton blustered. "The Lords will never convict me."

"Don't be so sure about that." Baron Trevisham made his way through the growing crowd in the corridor. "You were dimwitted enough to take my oldest son into your confidence, Wilton, and your plans and schemes are being taken down in his statement as I stand here."

"You'd take the word of a deviant *boy* over that of a peer of the realm?"

"I'd take the word of a rabid hedgehog over yours, meaning no disrespect to the hedgehog," Trevisham muttered. "Now, you lot." He gestured to the maids and footmen clustered at the end of the hall. "Be about your duties or we'll know the reason why. Heathgate, I haven't manacles with me, but perhaps we can find a stout length of rope."

"Trenton." Ellie gestured at the door, where Wilton had slipped quietly back into his rooms.

"He won't go anywhere," Trent said. "This is the only entrance to his suite, and it's a thirty-foot drop to the ground. Let's fetch some rope, and paper and pen, and Emily, we'll send for the surgeon, if you want us to."

"She'll be sound enough," Benton replied. "The bleeding has all but stopped." His arms stayed around her.

"A cup of tea, then." Trent met Benton's eyes and got a nod. Emily would be taken care of, come fire, flood or famine. "And the rest of you." Trent gestured to the servants. "You heard the baron, be off with you."

They shuffled away, parting to let Benton lead Emily through their numbers. Darius turned to go as well, when a single, sharp report sounded from within Wilton's chambers.

"Trenton, no!" Ellie tried to stop him from opening the door to Wilton's suite.

Darius sprang forward to add his weight to Ellie's. "Listen to Lady Rammel. It could be a trap, and by God, I do not want to explain to your children that Wilton made orphans of them."

When Trenton would have argued, Heathgate shouldered around them, a heavy horse pistol in his hand. "Baron, you'll maintain order here," the marquess directed. "Benjamin?"

Hazlit made his way forward, then stood aside while Heathgate kicked the door open with a single stout blow. Both men darted into the sitting room beyond, then stopped short, blocking the scene within from the view of those in the hallway.

"Jesus Christ, our Lord and Savior." Heathgate's muttered prayer told the tale.

"That's it then," Trent said wearily. "Suicide opens the door to forfeiting much of the family's wealth."

Silence followed, broken only by Darius's soft, continuous cursing.

"Darius." Trent slipped away from Ellie. "Hush." He wrapped his arms around his brother. "It's over. It's finally over, and inside, he was already dead. He was."

Darius said nothing, but buried his face against Trent's shoulder, as he had so many times when they were boys.

The hallway cleared, leaving Trent and Darius curiously

alone. Hazlit tugged Ellie away on his arm, while Heathgate and Trevisham tarried in the earl's sitting room.

"I hate him," Darius said. "I will always, always hate him. He was evil. He hurt even Emily, and he tried to kill you. He tried to cast Leah into the gutter. He wanted to see me ruined. What did we do, Trent? What did we ever do?"

Darius wept silently in his brother's arms, while Trent had no answers. None at all.

* * *

"You will let me find you a bed." Hazlit's voice was stern, the voice of an older brother with a nigh hysterical younger sister. "You will put yourself in it, and you will go to sleep."

"Mr. Hazlit, Benjamin," Ellie retorted, "who's with Trenton? He shouldn't be alone now, and if you can't bestir yourself to see to him, then I will."

Hazlit meant well, but he was out of his depth, and Ellie did not intend to indulge his manly displays.

"I'll see to him, my lady, I promise, but you've been traveling all night and need to get off your feet. Think of the baby."

"The baby is fine!" Ellie bit out, dropping his arm. "Somebody needs to look after Trenton, Darius, and Emily." She marched up to a young footman who was trying to look inconspicuous, though his face was wet with tears. "You. Have the kitchen send morning tea trays up to the family parlor."

The man shot Hazlit a panicked look. "Which family parlor, milady? We have three."

"Which one is most comfortable?"

"The green one."

"Tea, to the green family parlor. And scones with clotted cream, nothing heavy, no bacon or kedgeree, but…comfort food, and make sure there's a pot of peppermint tea as well."

"Peppermint tea, milady?"

As if an earl's household would never indulge in such a plebeian concoction.

"To soothe the digestion, and gunpowder for Lord

Amherst." By commandeering staff, giving orders, and ignoring Hazlit's exasperated looks, Ellie organized the green parlor as a center of operations.

Imogenie's statement was taken, but, thank a merciful Deity, she'd slipped down the back stairs before Wilton had spewed the worst of his bile.

Word came that Tye Benning had been secured in the local jail.

Emily's statement was taken, while Aaron Benton hovered at her side, holding her hand, and making her sip peppermint tea.

When Ellie saw matters were going smoothly, she slipped away and asked directions to Trent's room. He wasn't there—he wasn't anywhere she could find him—so she climbed into his bed and—once again—waited for the man she loved to come back to her.

* * *

Trent pushed open the door to his bedroom, his heart weighed with a weariness so great as to eclipse even his sorrow. He'd given his statement and accepted the stern lecture Heathgate had delivered, but mostly, he'd kept track of Dare and Emily, both of whom were shaken. He'd seen Ellie ordering servants about, hugging Emily, and conferring with Lady Warne, but he'd made no effort to approach her.

She had come. After sending him away, after showing great good sense on numerous occasions, she had charged headlong to his side.

How did a man thank a woman for giving him back his life? For seeing his situation more clearly than he'd seen it himself? For putting herself and her unborn child at risk on his behalf?

He stopped short before his bed.

His personal avenging angel was the picture of exhausted, if somewhat gravid, innocence.

She'd taken the time to get out of her dress, which was consistent with the servants having no clue as to her whereabouts. He peeled out of his own clothes and climbed in beside her.

"Trenton?" She spooned herself around his back, her belly snug between them.

"Hold me, Ellie, please?"

"Hush." She kissed his nape, wrapped her arms and one leg around him, and held him until he slept.

When he woke she was still there, holding him.

"You awake?" He laced his fingers through hers and squeezed gently.

"I am. My arm is going to sleep."

"I'll trade you," Trent suggested, prepared to hold her for a while. A long while.

Ellie shifted to straddle him. "How about this?"

"Fair enough." Trent's arms came around her. "How did you know, Ellie?"

She had come haring down to Hampshire with her reinforcements for no less purpose than to save Trent's life. Heathgate and Hazlit had both made sure he knew that.

"He hated you," Ellie said. "The truth was in all your nevers and in the way he treated your sister Leah. He was a man capable of hating his own children. I cannot comprehend this, but nobody else bore you such enmity."

"In the end, all I can say is he spared me having to put him down by my own hand."

Ellie kissed him, a condolence of a sort that only intimates could share. "He took his life in a desperate effort to bring shame on you and yours. Some parting gesture."

"He'll be denied his victory." Trent filled his hands with her hair and brought her braid to his nose. "I have taken a leaf from my departed father's book and altered the facts to suit my convenience. Heathgate will report the gun went off by accident while an old man with failing vision cleaned it. As for the rest, Wilton will never be tried."

"So he's not a suicide? No burial at the crossroads?"

God bless her, she sounded disappointed that Wilton would not be held accountable even to that extent.

"No disgrace. Not for me, or my children, though I'll make sure they know the truth."

"Hazlit said your wife's maternal aunt took her own life at boarding school. I cannot fathom such a sad end."

Trent's hands went still. "I didn't know that. Paula took her own life, too."

Ellie rose over him and cradled him to her. Her warmth and fragrance, the generosity of her comfort and her curves brought the only consolation Trent could have asked for.

"Trenton, I am so sorry."

"Thomas Benning explained some of the why of it to me just today," Trent said, gathering her close and needing to say the words, to her, if not to anyone else. "Tye Benning preyed intimately on his younger siblings. Paula escaped by going to boarding school, then marrying me. She feared her brother might someday visit his attentions on our children, but she couldn't confide her past in me."

"You don't have to tell me this. She's at peace now, Trent."

"Maybe now she is," Trent said softly. "Thomas has a letter from her, sent immediately before her death. She charged Thomas to give the letter to me if Tye ever attempted to have contact with the children, and that letter details Tye's perversion."

"Thomas kept this letter?"

"I told him to burn it. Thomas is a wreck. He suspected Tye had turned his attentions to their younger sister, but Thomas went to his mother about it, who told him he mustn't get his brother in trouble over silly schoolboy peccadilloes, and that was the end of it. I've my suspicions about the mother, as, I think, does Trevisham."

"So much sadness," Ellie murmured. "Your father knew Paula was fragile, didn't he?"

"He knew exactly what she'd been through. Tye would

snicker to him about it when in his cups. Wilton bet I'd never get children on her, but Paula was stronger than Wilton guessed. Just not strong enough."

"You blame yourself," Ellie concluded, levering up to hug him close. Her belly came between them, a soft, wondrous swelling of new life incongruous with the events of the morning.

Trent nuzzled her neck, loving the scent of her. "Paula needed to escape a life at the Grange, where sooner or later, her brother could have got her with child. She did what she could, and she protected her children as best she could. In a sense, it's a relief to know much of what plagued her wasn't personal to me."

Ellie subsided against him, no doubt hearing what he wasn't saying: Much was not personal to him, leaving some that was.

"We will talk more about this," she said. "How's Darius?"

"He disappeared on his horse for most of the morning, which is probably for the best. Hazlit's keeping an eye on him. In his own way, Dare is as innocent as Emily. He still thinks in terms of right and wrong, black and white, and in his world, parents shouldn't try to kill their children."

"In any world," Ellie said sternly. "Could you put Ford on a dangerous pony?" "God, no. Never."

"It's a new list of nevers, Trenton, and you are not your father. One wonders if Wilton was your father in truth."

What a merciful, cheering thought. "One does, though I've his height and his coloring."

"England boasts many tall, dark-haired men."

"It's something to think about," Trent agreed, though his mind was turning to a sluggish mixture of fatigue, shock, and regret. "Ellie, I've a favor to ask."

"Name it." She cuddled against him, her weight and proportions an even greater consolation than her voice in his ear.

"Never call me by the title," Trent said, his voice low

and fierce. "No matter how you might want to, for whatever reason, I don't ever want to be Wilton to you."

"Of course not." Without hesitation, as if she'd anticipated his request. "Is that the only favor you'd ask?"

"No."

He arched up, got his mouth on hers, his one hand on her breast, the other planted over her derrière, and held on. "Let me love you."

She did not *let* him love her, she went on a campaign of tenderness, arousal, and intimate caring that enveloped Trent and held him captive. She took him prisoner and sheltered him from the grief, worry, regret, and despair trying to drag him into darkness. Ellie was light and love to him, his safe harbor, his friend, the guardian of any pretensions he yet held to decency and honor.

Before she was done with him, he was silently crying, and coming, and holding on, while Ellie clung, and loved him, and crooned meaningless comforts as the love and the relief—the profound, soul-deep relief—took him under.

CHAPTER TWENTY-TWO

The funeral was small enough to confirm that Wilton was not at all well regarded, but large enough that the Lindsey family knew their neighbors felt for them. From the family parlor at Wilton Acres, Lady Warne presided over the whole business with the unsentimental competence of the hale elderly. Imogenie Henly had the good sense not to show her face, but was seen later putting flowers on the grave, a quiet Hiram Haines lending her escort.

Thomas Benning did not attend either, but took his father up to Melton for a few weeks of hunting over some of the best fixtures known to man, hound, or fox, while Lady Trevisham kept to her quarters, attended by three shifts of nurse companions.

Tye Benning was found guilty as an accessory after the fact to attempted murder and assault. He was given transportation and seven years. If he survived the close quarters of the outbound voyage, a life of decent nutrition and basic good health suggested he might survive the sentence as well.

Darius Lindsey took himself off to London, where, he told Trent, he had a christening to attend.

Emily Lindsey had a few quiet, subdued days, but responded well to Mr. Benton's continued insistence that she ride out with him and enjoy the last of the temperate fall weather.

Lady Warne agreed to stay as chaperone for as long as needed, though Trent considered it might be in everybody's best interests if Emily spent some of the requisite period of mourning with him and the children at Crossbridge.

In the midst of all the comings and goings, Ellie Hampton quietly departed with Hazlit for Surrey, and Trent had no choice but to let her go.

"I will one day marry your sister." Benton passed Trent a glass holding two fingers of brandy, bringing to mind other occasions when they'd shared a drink in the library. "I know her come out will be delayed because of Wilton's mourning."

"Does Emily consent to this?" For Wilton's passing should not interfere with the happiness of the vilest rat in the vilest sewer of the lowliest slum.

"She would," Benton said carefully. "Were I free to ask it of her."

"You've spoken to her?"

"I have." Benton looked a little abashed, and a lot determined. "The timing is wrong, my prospects are modest, particularly if my uncle's new wife should bear children. Emily's above my touch. I know that."

True love made loquacious, honorable fools of all men. "If she's determined to have you, then there's little enough I can say to it. Emily wasn't looking forward to a Season, anyway. Em wants children and a man she can depend on. If you can give her that, you have my blessing. Leah can present her in a couple of years if need be."

"So she wasn't making that up?" Benton said, some of the fight leaving him. "About being disenchanted with all the spotty boys?"

"She's honest," Trent said, feeling more than a little sympathy for his steward. "Be warned. I think she'd like it here. She hasn't the memories of the place her older siblings do."

Benton tugged at his cravat. "She has enough bad memories here."

"So get her over them. Put your suite in the east wing, build a dower house to live in. Set it up however you need to for Em to be happy. You've turned Wilton Acres into a profitable enterprise. You should enjoy the fruits of your labors."

"You'd let us stay here?"

"She's my *sister*." His baby sister, and Wilton had held a blade to her throat. Trent knocked back a slug of brandy. "I want her happy, plain and simple. God knows I don't want to live here, but you'll have to put up with Ford from time to time. He's the heir, God help him."

"I love children. Especially boys."

"You are doomed. Utterly doomed."

"When can we marry?" The question was painfully full of hope.

"That's up to you and Emily. If you become engaged, you might consider having the nuptials at Belle Maison. Your family needs to know you're marrying well, and I'm sure Nick and Leah will want to put their imprimatur on the match."

"Bellefonte will claim he knew we'd suit."

"He will probably be telling the truth. Lady Warne can stay here for the nonce, and she can help Emily plan the details."

That Emily's life, at least, was falling into place was some satisfaction. Not enough, but some.

"What about you?"

Benton was a canny soul. He hadn't used Trenton's title, but he couldn't exactly address his employer by name, either, could he?

Trent endured a pang of longing for Ellie, like the first

sharp shaft of autumn light slants through a forest still lush with summer greenery. Piercingly sweet, but tinged with loss.

"What about me?"

"You'll toddle off to Crossbridge and let the widow slip through your fingers?"

Trent held up his empty hands. "She has slipped. Lady Rammel is a good friend. She brought the reinforcements that arguably saved my life and Emily's, but she's gone, Aaron. When all is said and done, Ellie's gone, and I'm not sure what that means."

Because Ellie had provided such generous, intimate comfort before she'd left, Trent would always be in her debt. Could a woman love like that and simply walk away?

"Did you invite her to stay?"

"For a suicide's farce of a funeral?" Trent took another tot of his drink. "I did not."

"What else was she to do?"

Trent sighed mightily, wishing canny Aaron would go make calf eyes at Emily. "My father killed himself; my wife killed herself; and for most of my tenure in Lady Rammel's life, my father had people trying to kill me as well. Ellie is entitled to reconsider our situation."

To put distance between them, God help him. Was this what he'd left her to feel? Anxious, hopeful, helpless? Though Trent wasn't giving up. Falling back to regroup, taking a repairing lease from his repairing lease, but not giving up.

"Elegy Hampton would have you," Aaron said, expression serious. "She made me promise I'd see that you ate. I was to note when you went to bed and what you had for breakfast. I was to make sure you kept your nightly tryst with Arthur and not for the sake of the beast, because he hardly notices who tosses him his hay. I was to write to her if you seemed to be going into a decline. For God's sake, man, she's at least six months pregnant and can't be tarrying wherever she pleases."

She had been the embodiment of feminine abundance

in his arms. Lush, warm, generous…though more than a bit *round*. Trent mentally started counting months.

"She didn't want to leave?"

"I heard Heathgate lecture her. His marchioness has had some difficulty in her confinements, and he grew very stern with Lady Rammel about her duty to the title and her own life, and what an unpleasant death a complicated childbed can engender. He out-gunned her, though it took some heavy artillery."

"I would have liked to have heard this discussion."

Though Heathgate had the right of it. A woman heavy with child should be propping her feet up before her own hearth.

"Lady Rammel did not want to leave your side," Benton said emphatically. "Heathgate put the fear of miscarriage in her, and God knows what else he said."

Trent set his drink down, feeling the first rekindling of forward momentum since his father's death.

"I'll find my sister and wish her well, then take myself off at first light. Mind my first niece or nephew isn't a six-months child, Benton."

"A six-months…? Oh, right." Benton's ears colored nicely. "No chance of that. Yet."

Trent left at first light, as intended, but he took his time, seeing the countryside clothed in the pleasant attire of early autumn. The temperature remained comfortable for traveling, the roads dry. The journey had become familiar enough that he hardly had to remind Arthur which lanes and turnpikes led where.

When Arthur turned up the lane to Deerhaven, darkness had already fallen. Trent caught the horse in his unsanctioned suggestion, though, and kneed him right along until they reached the Crossbridge turn-off. At the foot of his own drive, Trent dismounted and walked Arthur into the trees, letting the gelding pick his way by moonlight to the bridle path leading to the back of Ellie's property.

"You were right, old son." Trent patted Arthur's neck. "My apologies."

They stood for a long time, Arthur likely glad to rest, Trent glad to see the light burning in Ellie's window. He wasn't about to intrude again uninvited, but he could wish in the dark, and hope the woman who'd told him good-bye so convincingly, then braved distance, darkness, and worse to save his life might still entertain a fondness for him.

A passionate fondness, though what woman facing impending motherhood should have to fend off a randy widower?

"I'm tired, Arthur." Trent's horse flicked an ear in agreement. "I want my own bed, and I want to see my children asleep in theirs. Cato's leaving us, you know? But we're to have his cousin Kevin."

Rather than wake his help, Trent intended to put Arthur up himself. He didn't light a lantern, the moonlight in the stable yard illumination enough for loosening a girth.

"Trenton Lindsey?"

From a bench under a tree in the stable yard, Ellie's voice rang out, full of curiosity, and something else—relief?

"Elegy Hampton, what are you doing abroad at this hour?"

"Mr. Benton sent a pigeon to Crossbridge," she said, emerging from the shadows. "I set my grooms to watching in the village. Are you well?"

"I am." With the saddle over one arm, he led Arthur into the barn. "Let me get a lantern from the saddle room, and you can explain to me why you're lurking in barn yards when you should be in bed, sipping peppermint tea and swaddled in quilts."

"It's only coolish," Ellie rejoined, following him into the barn. "Not exactly cold. You're sure you're well? You look tired to me, and one worries."

Trent slipped Arthur's bridle off and let the horse find his stall. "Of course I'm tired. While it's good of you to be

concerned, it's hardly worth lying in wait for me. Come along."
He took her hand and pulled her toward the saddle room,
where a soft glow beamed from under the door. "The night
is chilly, not just coolish, and I'm sure we've some blankets in
here, and a—holy Halifaxing saints, Catullus!"

Trent wasn't fast enough to pull Ellie back with him, so she
got an eyeful of Cato Spencer's muscular form, naked from
the waist up, his falls undone, his hips working a slow thrust
and retreat while Peak, perched on the edge of a table, used
both arms and legs to clutch Cato close.

"Cato?" Peak's voice was dreamy, but before Trent could
haul Ellie from the door of the saddle room, Peak's face came
into view over Cato's shoulder, and the curve of one soft,
naked, female breast caught Trent's eye.

"Oh, gracious." Ellie dissolved into giggles, though Trent
had wits enough to tug her away and close the door behind
them. "Gracious Halifax." Ellie's eyebrows rose, and fell, and
rose again in the moonlight. "That was certainly unexpected."

"Holy perishing… Unexpected?" Trent glared at the closed
door and took a half-step toward it when Ellie's hand on his
arm stopped him.

"She's wearing a ring, Trenton."

"What? Who?"

"Peak. Or whatever her name is. On her left hand." Ellie
pointed to her own left hand, though no rings graced her
fingers. "Mine no longer fits."

"That was all she had on!" Except for a smile Trent would
never, ever forget.

"You're upset?"

"Bad enough I'm harboring an Irish peer in my stables,"
Trent retorted, "but he's harboring a blasted…*female.*"

"Mr. Spencer is a peer?" Ellie's brows went traveling again.
"Our Cato?"

"That would be Glasclare," Cato rumbled, coming out of
the saddle room decently clad and closing the door behind

him. "My apologies for abusing your hospitality Amherst—or it's Wilton, now, isn't it."

"Not if you value your life."

"What does one call you?"

"What does one call *you*?" Trent shot back. "Keeping some sort of personal harem in my stables, for God's sake, Catullus. That woman groomed for me, groomed at the local meets. What were you thinking?"

"I can answer that." Peak emerged, dark hair tucked up into her cap, dark eyes fixed on Cato. "He was thinking to keep me safe."

"You're a female." Trent's tone was such as a gentleman ought not to use on a female, much less on a possible countess. He'd apologize for that later, when he'd settled his nerves with a drink or three.

Peak exchanged a smirk with Ellie, who looked again on the verge of giggles. "Trenton, may we finish these explanations up at the house?"

Rather than succumb to the merriment tugging at him, Trent took Ellie by the hand.

"A fine idea. The house, where it is nice and *warm*, and certain viscountesses can put their feet *up*, while they swill peppermint *tea*, and behave themselves in a manner befitting their *delicate condition*."

"You could toss me over your shoulder," Ellie suggested. "Though I might overbalance you, mightn't I?"

Yes, she could overbalance him, preferably right into a shared bed.

Cato kept his peace and kept Peak's hand in his the whole way up to the house. Trent waved his butler off but ordered a pot of tea for the ladies.

When the party assembled in the library, a cheery fire taking the chill off the evening, Trent aimed a look at his *best lad*.

"Tea's on the way, unless Peak would like something stronger? Her feminine sensibilities have no doubt been sorely tried, living in my stables with the likes of you, Catullus, particularly given the liberties you were taking, for the love of God and all His creatures."

"Careful," Cato said, smiling besottedly at Peak, "lest you give insult to my countess."

"Congratulations." Ellie patted Peak's hand. "You must be very pleased."

"She is," Cato answered, and clearly, so very clearly, the Earl of Glasclare was even more pleased than his lady.

Ellie beamed up at Trent, her smile sweet but also pleading. A wife sent her husband such a smile, a silent request for understanding, for forbearance and tolerance when exasperation threatened.

Nick and Leah exchanged such smiles, Benton and Emily, Heathgate and his marchioness.

A fearful weight of dread and determination eased in Trent's chest, and he took a place beside Ellie, helpless not to return her smile.

"Peak is the lady caught in a compromising position," Trenton guessed. "The one facing marriage to a scoundrel."

Cato kissed his wife's knuckles. "Chesapeake Whitley Spencer. I could not be her alibi, because I was with another lady at the time, behaving myself for once, and my Peak was pressured to take another for her own, as was I. I might have married for duty, but I could not allow Peak to be shackled to a varlet. To the undiscerning eye, Peak makes a passable boy. She's been horse mad since birth, and she refused my honorable offers—until recently."

"I don't want to hear about your other offers," Trent interjected. "Do I take it you're well and truly married?"

Another kiss to the lady's knuckles. "Special license. I'm Church of England when the Regent is looking. Peak understands because her papa is cut from the same cloth."

"Congratulations, then," Trent said, saluting with his glass.

"Catullus," Peak said, "you wanted to explain about

Rammel to his lordship."

Amazing how lovely Peak's voice sounded now that it belonged to a female.

"After the shock we encountered in that saddle room," Trent said, "explain carefully and only if you must."

Because anything affecting Rammel affected his widow, too, and as much upheaval as Ellie had endured, Trent wanted nothing so much as to get her to bed.

To sleep.

Mostly.

"First," Catullus began, "you need to know Louise has been taken into custody and bound over for the assizes on charges of attempted murder. Mr. Soames saw her tramping about in the woods with a fowling piece, and then heard about the attempt on your life. He fled the area out of fear of Louise coming after him, but his missus got word to him at his brother's place in Sussex."

"I am losing staff from this estate at an alarming rate," Trent said, though the expression on Cato's face suggested his explanations weren't complete.

"I hesitate to embarrass a lady," Cato went on.

"How could you embarrass a lady more than you already have?" Ellie gently asked.

Cato colored up, to the very tops of his ears. "As to that... Lord Rammel, may he please rest in peace, came upon me pressing my attentions on Peak the morning of the hunt meet."

Ellie's grip on Trent's hand tightened. "The day Dane died? You and Peak weren't..." She waved her hand.

"We were only kissing," Peak said. "Or Cato was kissing, and I was trying to warn him it wasn't safe."

"Hush, love. This will be difficult enough." Cato patted her hand, the gesture indicative of a man doomed to decades of marital bliss. "Peak and I were kissing, but his lordship came upon us, and Peak scampered off, leaving me to face a grinning and amused Dane Hampton."

"Dane was a tolerant sort," Ellie said, "and it was just a kiss."

Cato looked anywhere but at Dane's widow. "It was."

"His lordship misconstrued what he saw," Peak offered softly. "He did not know my gender, so he assumed Catullus was importuning another man."

"I see." Ellie's tone said she saw nothing.

"Not yet you don't," Cato said. "Forgive me, my lady, because I mean the man no disrespect. When Dane saw me with Peak, he drew erroneous conclusions about Peak, but also about me."

"He thought you preferred men," Trent supplied, lest Cato trot out some less delicate term.

Cato studied the ring on his countess's finger. "He attempted to take the same liberty with me."

Ellie's free hand went to her rounded middle. "He kissed you? Dane kissed you?"

Cato nodded again, looking miserable.

"A kiss-kiss?" Still, she did not comprehend.

"A carnal, forbidden kiss between men," Cato said. "I'm sorry. I tell you this only because when it became apparent he wasn't going to desist despite my lack of, shall we say, welcome, I backhanded the blighter and told him to keep his sodding paws off me."

That was probably the short version.

"You struck my Dane?"

"Only the once. Miss Coriander saw him kiss me and saw me belt him. His lordship laughed heartily, cantered off on my horse and died."

"Sweet Saints." Trent left Ellie's side long enough to pour Cato another finger of brandy. "So you went through the inquest, wondering what else Andy saw, to whom she talked, and if you would swing for murder. Why didn't you leave?"

"Peak hadn't yet married me. I could not leave without

implicating myself in murder, and if she came with me, she might have fallen under suspicion, too. Thank God, Heathgate is a sensible sort, even if he does take life too seriously. I have worried about the child, though. She might have seen her father going at me like a sailor on leave."

"My lady, are you well?" Peak asked.

"You outrank me," Ellie said distractedly. "Trenton?"

"Right here, love."

"I need to put my feet up."

"Of course you do." Trent resumed his place beside her. "Catullus, you and your bride may consider yourselves my guests for the duration, but right now, Lady Rammel needs some peace and quiet."

"Come along, *mavourneen*." Cato tugged Peak to her feet. "You can scold me for my lack of tact all night long, for once in the comfort of a nice, clean, fluffy bed, may God be thanked."

Trent poured Ellie another cup of tea, added sugar, and then a dollop of spirits.

"Drink." He passed her the cup. "This will warm your innards."

"My innards are a busy place," Ellie murmured, but she took a sip, then another. "Interesting drink."

"Talk to me, Ellie. It has been a night for surprises."

"Why would Dane have kissed Catullus?"

He could think of no delicate phrasing, no deft allusions. "Dane kissed Cato because he desired him. He desired him the way most men desire women." *As I desire you.*

Ellie looked adorably perplexed, also a trifle unnerved. "But Dane was my husband. I'm having his baby."

"For some individuals, the two are not mutually exclusive. He loved you, Ellie."

"But he kissed Catullus," Ellie said, setting her drink down very carefully. "On the mouth."

"He did."

Ellie pushed herself forward and rocked herself to her feet. "Me, he did not kiss on the mouth."

"I rarely kissed my wife on the mouth. She didn't enjoy it."

"I am not Paula."

"For which I thank God." Trent paced along with her as she began a slow orbit of the library.

"I beg your pardon?"

"You are not Paula," Trent said slowly, "and I'm damned glad of it."

"You loved her. She's the mother of your children." Ellie gathered speed, until Trent's hand on her arm stopped her.

"Ellie. Elegy, I love *you*. May we please sit down?"

"No." Ellie stared at his hand on her arm, and her breath caught. "I'm cold." She pitched herself against him, planting her face against his throat as his arms closed around her.

"Don't say those words, Trenton Lindsey, to comfort the grieving, increasingly pregnant, increasingly distraught widow. My husband tossed them at me before he disappeared for weeks at a time to ride through the mud with a bunch of smelly dogs and drunken peers, to kiss the lads—perishing Halifax—and to gamble the night away. I'm in no condition, to be humored."

"I love you," Trent said again, stroking his hand over her hair. "I desire you, I love you, and I want you in my life on any terms you'll allow."

"My husband didn't love me," Ellie got out. "Now I find he didn't even want me. God. *God in Halifax*. No wonder he was least in sight for most of our marriage."

Trent gave up on words and instead walked her over to the sofa, sat, and pulled her into his lap. She cuddled up like she was cold, but temper and hurt rolled off her in red, steaming waves.

"Dane hardly ever summoned me," Ellie said, nose against Trent's throat. "And he'd always been drinking. Minty said that was why he wasn't eager. Not like you get. Not like you at all."

"Ellie, hush."

"He'd blow out the candles, Trent," Ellie went on, "and apologize, and pat my shoulder, and heave about. Sometimes"—her voice dropped to a whisper—"he'd just give up. I felt so *lonely*. With my husband inside me, I felt so lonely. Other times, Dane would be all pleased with himself when he was done, and still I'd feel empty, and it was awful, for both of us, and now I see…"

Trent gathered her close. "You see you were both doing the best you could, and even if he was torn in his desires, Dane cared for you. He wouldn't have got a child on you, Ellie, did he not have some fondness for you. He wouldn't have tried—he had an heir in Drew, but Dane probably knew you wanted a child."

Ellie sighed a mightily put-upon sigh. "I will comfort myself with that conjecture, though I also know this: I had a list of nevers, too, Trenton, and a foolish list at that. I would never again be a man's convenience. I would never again be the dutiful, sweet, biddable wife, content with the odd notes and lonely bed. So I sent you packing and blamed you for my cowardice, when what you wanted was to keep me safe. Blast Dane anyway."

Trent searched for words, for a truth she couldn't reach toward herself. "Dane didn't kill himself to get away from you."

Ellie peered up at him, putting him in mind of his first call on her, when she'd been bewildered and bereaved. "Oh, Trenton. Is that what *you* thought? That Paula hated being your wife so much she took her life?"

"I didn't know. I had no other explanation, but she was so unhappy generally, except for the children, and I denied her any more of those. I took from her the one thing that made her life meaningful."

Ellie scooted up in his lap. "That is utter nonsense. She had three beautiful children—heir, spare and a daughter—to dote on. Many women aren't so blessed, much less within five years of marriage. She was simply tired, Trent."

Ellie sounded very certain, reassuringly certain.

"Tired?"

"I was tired," Ellie said, very softly. "Dane and I couldn't talk about what plagued us, and he was staying away longer and longer, and still we'd produced no heir. Maybe Paula realized her children would be safe with you, and she simply put down her tools and went home."

"She switched her tea with her companion's," Trent said. "And when the woman nodded off, Paula took a knife to her own wrists. She was gone before I found her, and there was no note."

"But she wasn't buried at a crossroads with a stake through her heart?"

Trent closed his eyes and held Ellie as a tightly as he dared. "Of course not. I wrapped up her wrists, cleaned up the blood, and summoned one of her well-paid physicians who pronounced her dead of premature coronary arrest."

Ellie hugged him back every bit as tightly. "That is ghastly."

"I realized this summer that I was carrying the manner of her death around in my head, held at such close range that I'd forgotten other people didn't know, not even Dare. The manner of Paula's death was a large part of what made the oblivion of drink so appealing."

"Do you think that's why Dane drank?" Ellie sank back in his arms. "Because he was so unhappy?"

"You were unhappy. You didn't drink."

"I had Andy. I had made my list of nevers and withdrawn to Deerhaven, even before Dane died."

"You are very much here now," Trent said, kissing her temple. "More of you is here by the week, in fact."

"Awful man. I was fading into oblivion, Trent, as surely as you were fading into your drugged brandy. If it weren't for Minty, and Andy, I would have soon become one of those reclusive females who sleeps all day and reads Gothic novels all night."

"No, you would not. You're strong, Ellie. I love your strength. The first time I saw you, I thought you were a dairymaid."

"A dairymaid?" This provoked a naughty smile. "I was in mourning and a near stranger to you. How could you have thought me a dairymaid?"

"You were damned near naked, singing, and enjoying my pond thoroughly. I loved you a little bit then, too, for being so pleased with life and yourself and a hot summer morning."

"You awful man. You spied on me."

"I spied on a vision of paradise in my own back yard," Trent corrected her. "Marry me, Ellie."

She turned her face into his shoulder, remaining silent until Trent felt her tears seeping under his collar.

"Then argue with me, my lady. I deserve a chance to wear you down. You run around heedless with strange men in traveling coaches through the rainy night; you take on lunatic, murdering earls; you lie in wait for my errant self only to find my help misbehaving by moonlight. Somebody should take you in hand."

"I'm not that sort of female," Ellie said quietly, miserably. "I'm good old Ellie. My shoulder is pattable, my forehead kissable. I can be forgotten for the entire hunt season. I know this, and I couldn't bear for you to marry me only to—"

That maudlin and patently ridiculous tripe wasn't worth considering as an argument, so Trent didn't fashion words in response. He wrapped one hand around the back of her head and anchored his fingers in her hair, the better to steady her for his kiss. She trailed off on a groan when he brushed his mouth over hers.

"I'm not kissing your forehead," Trent said against her mouth. "Or patting your shoulder." He cupped her breast. "I love you, you love me. Marry me."

He kissed her again, harder, longer, deeper, until he felt her surrender to the truth of his words, then go straight on past to other truths: She desired him, he desired her, and the door wasn't locked.

"Say yes, Elegy, while I still allow you the breath to spare."

"Yes, yes, yes."

She said yes frequently as the evening wore into night, and as they awaited the birth of her child. She said yes many more times as the rest of the children came along, and as the years turned into decades.

And Trenton said his share of yeses to Ellie, too.

They named Ellie's first child Hallifax Chesepeake Hampton. She rode like a demon, could not sew a straight seam, and had a habit of flying her brothers' kites into trees.

ABOUT THE AUTHOR

New York Times and *USA Today* bestselling author Grace Burrowes hit the bestseller lists with her debut, *The Heir*, followed by *The Soldier*, *Lady Maggie's Secret Scandal*, and *Lady Eve's Indiscretion*. *The Heir* was a *Publishers Weekly* Best Book of 2010, *The Soldier* was a *Publishers Weekly* Best Spring Romance of 2011, *Lady Sophie's Christmas Wish* won Best Historical Romance of the Year from RT Reviewers' Choice Awards, *Lady Louisa's Christmas Knight* was a *Library Journal* Best Book of 2012, and *The Bridegroom Wore Plaid*, the first in her trilogy of Scotland-set Victorian romances, was a *Publishers Weekly* Best Book of 2012. All of her historical romances have received extensive praise, including several starred reviews from *Publishers Weekly* and *Booklist*. *Darius*, the first in her groundbreaking Regency series The Lonely Lords, was named one of iBookstore's Best Romances of 2013.

Grace is a practicing family law attorney and lives in rural Maryland. She loves to hear from her readers and can be reached through her website at graceburrowes.com.

CPSIA information can be obtained
at www.ICGtesting.com
Printed in the USA
BVOW04s1741041216
469751BV00002B/147/P